MW00582703

EPOCH

A NOVEL

JAMES ADDOMS

Michele —
Thank you for
the Guidance &
Support —
Jim

PHILOMATH
PRESS

This is a work of fiction. Names, characters, places and incidents are the products of the author's imagination or are used fictitiously. Any resemblance to actual events, locations, organizations or persons, living or dead, is entirely coincidental.

E P O C H. Copyright © 2014 by James William Wentworth Addoms. All rights reserved under International and Pan-American Copyright Conventions. Printed in the United States of America by Philomath Press, LLC. No part of this book may be used or reproduced in any manner whatsoever without written permission except in the case of brief quotations embodied in critical articles and reviews. For more information address Philomath Press, 323 North Salina Street, Suite 36, Syracuse, NY 13203.

Text on pages 151-153 taken from *Die Fragmente der griechischen Historiker,* by Felix Jacoby after Karl Wilhelm Ludwig Müller's *Fragmenta Historicorum Graecorum,* (1841–1870). Text on pages 250-251, and 293-298 taken from 'The Histories of Polybius, Vol. I,' trans. from F. Hultsch by Evelyn S. Shuckburgh, Macmillan & Co., London, 1889.

Philomath ISBN: 978-0-692-24691-7

THIS IS AN ADVANCE READING COPY.

Library of Congress Control Number: 2014912335

www.epochnovel.com

Printed in the United States of America

For Ann and Bill

❖

There are too many mentors to be thanked for the influence they had on the shaping of this project. I must first thank those friends who have guided, sustained, endured and challenged me at every turn. They are, in alphabetical order: Megan DiCarlo, Kathy & Steve Eachus, Rick & Shannon Eachus, Adam Gaffney, Jayme Halpin, Garrett Heater, William C. Kashatus, Theresa Kintz, Sean Lantry, James McCarthy, John McClure, Anthony McEachern, Phillip McMullen, Jack McGrath, Bill Pendziwiatr, David Pimentel, Adam Snide, Mark Rozelle Tietjen and Justin Wynn.

I must also thank my mother, Miriam Addoms, and my aunt, Marcia Thomas, for their unfailing support. This work would have been impossible without them. I must also thank my grandparents, Bill and Ann Thomas, true philomaths of the first order. This novel is dedicated to them.

I must also acknowledge the influence of the great dreamers of antiquity, celebrated and unknown, to whom our civilization owes a great debt. In the doggedness of their perseverance and the grace of their curiosity I have found this lesson: Of all the puzzles yet unanswered none are as important as those in the pursuit of which we realize the edge of our own reason and in the striving to overcome it, glimpse the face of truth in a single grain of sand.

❖

A NOTE ABOUT THE TEXT

The major historical figures mentioned in the text are real. Every attempt has been made to faithfully reproduce their world and their interactions with their contemporaries. To the best of my ability I have endowed them with as much and no more knowledge than a creative mind of their age could have possessed. The mathematics, both ancient and modern, is represented as faithfully as possible. The societies and allegiances are accurately represented except where detailed information has been lost.

The modern inheritance of the mathematical journey begun in antiquity is, perhaps, not stressed enough. The recent discoveries contained within the Archimedes Palimpsest, for example, have illuminated a greater extent of conquered land on the intellectual landscape of antiquity than was previously understood. A direct empirical comparison with our own epoch is difficult and, arguably, undesirable, but if we are to take generally agreed upon divisions between intellectual ages, we may, without much imagination, at least equate antiquity's achievements with the first stirrings of industrial Britain and Germany in the nineteenth century CE. Archimedes and his contemporaries were possessed of the creativity if not the impetus of labor shortages which helped spur our recent industrial revolution. The power of steam was well understood and magnetism was the subject of great debate. It is too hard to resist imagining an alternative history in which the legacy of Archimedes has been taken up by the later inventor Hero of Alexandria and in which the mechanization of pneumatics and the harnessing of electromagnetism from a spinning steam turbine has been put to wider use. Though antiquity suffers in comparison from a much smaller (and ambitiously industrious) middle class than her chronologically separated descendant epoch, the intellectual capacity of its leading lights is not to be seen, with important exceptions, until the development of the medieval university and the much more modern 'think tanks' such as the Institute of Advanced Study at Princeton, of which the likes of Einstein and Kurt Gödel were fellows.

Still, these are primarily technological distinctions. Many observers credit the ancients with *at least* a comparable literary tradition, made the more prescient and influential by the unidirectional flow of time, that present works necessarily cannot stand wholly alone without the presence of antiquity's poets and playwrights, and antiquity's foundational presence in our world of ideas. Shakespeare cannot exist without Homer; the transistor owes a debt to Greek natural philosophy as much as it does its predecessor scientists of the Arab civilization of the first millennium CE who inherited and synthesized the concepts of the atom of Democritus upon which the modern world is built and with whose aid this novel is written and distributed.

This is a story of the bankruptcy of 'epochism,' which Vallicella has called "the arbitrary denigration of entire historical epochs." A stronger definition might be the systematic sublimation of the past in favor of the present, across all disciplines, within all records, in almost every mind. I leave it to the reader to gauge their own similarities with their distant kinsmen as they walk along the common ground between themselves and the omnipresent past.

The history of Ptolemaic Egypt is very well documented. Its capital, Alexandria, was a centerpiece of learning for seven centuries. The court chroniclers of the pharaonic government were so organized as to have left detailed records not only in the capital region, which was referred to in antiquity as Alexandria *near* Egypt, (a place apart and not "of" or "in" Egypt) but among the many nomes and outposts in the Egyptian interior. The entire history of Hellenism is beyond the scope of this novel. Many important advances and achievements had to be omitted, and it was necessary for the flow of the narrative to condense the forty anni mirabilis of Eratosthenes' librarianship in Alexandria. Technology, even of the advanced nature discussed in the novel, evolved less rapidly than modern equivalents. While a sense of the creative energy of ancient discoveries should not be diminished, I have condensed some historical events to fit the pacing of a modern story.

The cults depicted of the Hellenistic world were critical to public life. The syncretic Greco-Egyptian cult of Serapis (a blending of the Egyptian cults of Osiris, god of the afterlife, and Apis the bull-deity with the anthropomorphism familiar to ruling Greeks) flourished until it was outlawed by Christian edict in the fourth century CE. The Eleusinian Mysteries have origins in agrarian cults from Greek Mycenaean prehistory and were practiced covertly well into the second millennium CE. It is believed that some small pockets of adherents still practice these ancient rites to this day.

The problem of distinguishing prime numbers from composite numbers and of resolving the latter into their prime factors is known to be one of the most important and useful in arithmetic. It has engaged the industry and wisdom of ancient and modern geometers to such an extent that it would be superfluous to discuss the problem at length. Further, the dignity of the science itself seems to require that every possible means be explored for the solution of a problem so elegant and so celebrated.

—CARL FRIEDRICH GAUSS

Mathematicians have tried in vain to this day to discover some order in the sequence of prime numbers, and we have reason to believe that it is a mystery into which the human mind will never penetrate.

—LEONHARD EULER

The definitive clarification of the nature of the infinite has become necessary for the honor of human understanding itself.

—DAVID HILBERT

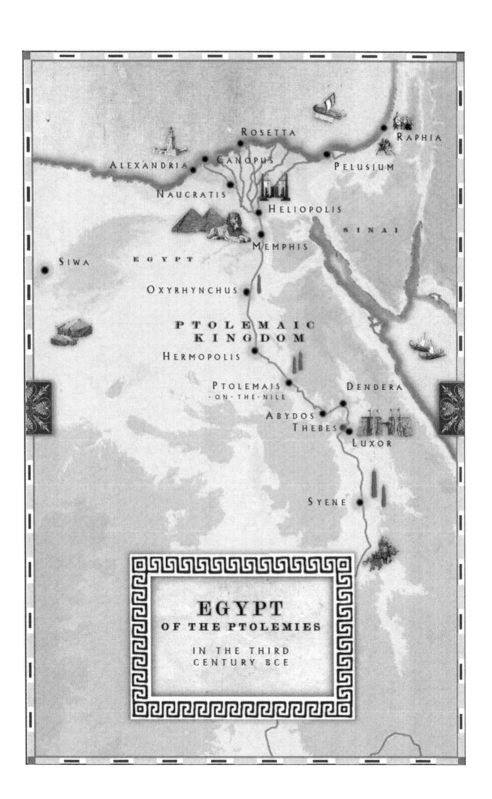

ROSETTA

RAPHIA

ALEXANDRIA

CANOPUS

PELUSIUM

NAUCRATIS

HELIOPOLIS

SINAI

MEMPHIS

SIWA

EGYPT

OXYRHYNCHUS

PTOLEMAIC
KINGDOM

HERMOPOLIS

PTOLEMAIS
·ON·THE·NILE

DENDERA

ABYDOS
THEBES

LUXOR

SYENE

EGYPT
OF THE PTOLEMIES

IN THE THIRD
CENTURY BCE

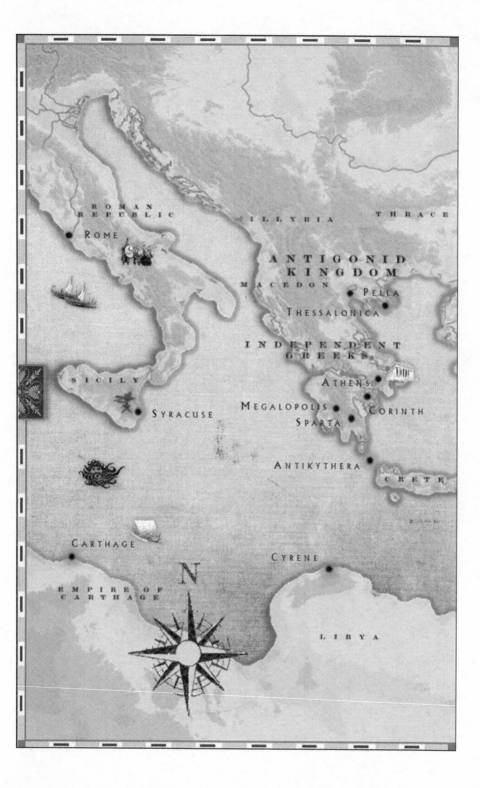

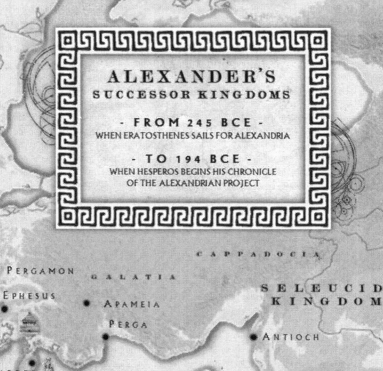

ALEXANDER'S
SUCCESSOR KINGDOMS

- FROM 245 BCE -
WHEN ERATOSTHENES SAILS FOR ALEXANDRIA

- TO 194 BCE -
WHEN HESPEROS BEGINS HIS CHRONICLE
OF THE ALEXANDRIAN PROJECT

CAPPADOCIA

PERGAMON   GALATIA

EPHESUS   APAMEIA   SELEUCID
             PERGA   KINGDOM

RHODES   ANTIOCH

        CYPRUS

                    COELE
                    SYRIA

              TYRE   DAMASCUS

           JERUSALEM

           RAPHIA

ALEXANDRIA
         PELUSIUM   TO BABYLON,
                          PERSEPOLIS &
                          THE MAURYAN EMPIRE

SIWA   MEMPHIS
                         NABATAEA
  PTOLEMAIC
  KINGDOM

    EGYPT

THE ACADEMICIAN'S
CRUSADE OF
PTOLEMY III

AND THE EASTERN
JOURNEY OF
ERATOSTHENES &
ARCHIMEDES
- 239 BCE -

ARM

CAPPADOCIA

NINEVEH
GAUGAMELA
SELEUCID

PERGA
ANTIOCH
DURA EUROPOS
MESO

CYPRUS

TYRE
DAMASCUS
COELE
SYRIA

JERUSALEM

N

RAPHIA

PELUSIUM
ALEXANDRIA
PTOLEMAIC
KINGDOM
MEMPHIS
EGYPT
NABATAEA

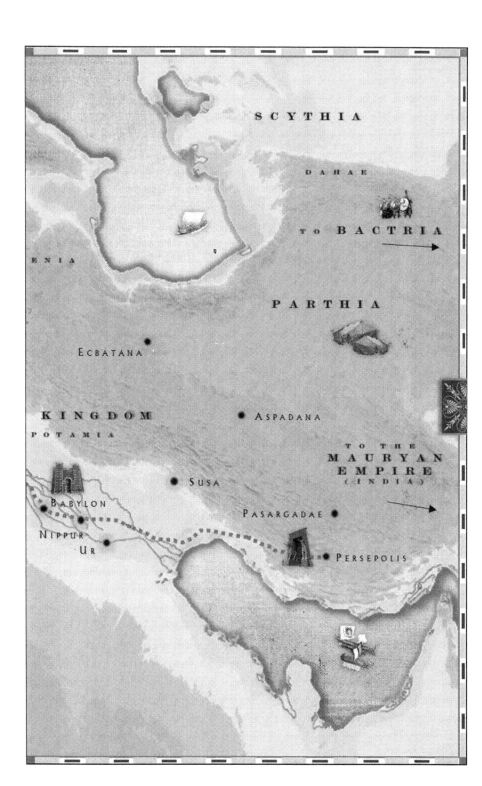

SCYTHIA

DAHAE

TO BACTRIA

PARTHIA

ENIA

ECBATANA

KINGDOM

POTAMIA

ASPADANA

TO THE
MAURYAN
EMPIRE
(INDIA)

SUSA

BABYLON

PASARGADAE

NIPPUR

UR

PERSEPOLIS

PROLOGUE
THE VERY NEAR FUTURE

BLIND. Darkness is fluid in his lungs, gravity suspended, adrift, unmoored. Cavernous expanses swept away from him as close as the atmosphere against his skin. *Theresa, in your ecstasy did you ever feel such exquisite anticipation; Galileo have you truly heard the music of the spheres?* Elemental rough-smooth cold of motionless atoms longing across great chasms of nothingness; fiery vibrations - *harmonics* of imperceptible perfection. The cavern. *It has to be here.* His footfalls proved him right. *Just as I knew it would be.* The floor of the cavern was an immense grid of squares roughly one natural human stride in length and width. The dim light from the natural oculus in the ceiling of the cavern through which he'd rappelled illuminated a small circle around him. His eye fell on an irregular form several paces away, directly beneath the oculus.

He crouched near enough to run his smooth academician's hands across the worn carving. He recognized instantly the familiar seal: the triune sheaves of wheat, representing the bounty of the Earth, and the torch, searching below for what had been taken from above. *As above, so below.* He smiled; the overworked phrase had been so distorted by generation after generation of fortune seekers, false prophets and uninitiates that the Order's intent was both obscured and in the obscuring, fulfilled. *When the Mysteries become all things to all people, they become nothing.* He reached in his pack and brought out a plain vessel and a thermos. He entered the contents of the thermos into the vessel, a *kylix* of ancient design. He raised this sacred *kykeon* up, toward the oculus and spoke in low tones first an ancient praise of the Muses and then, the solemn words of the initiate:

"I have fasted, I have drunk the kykeon, I have taken from the *kiste* and after working it have put it back in the *kalathos*."

He had devoted his life to finding this place. His childhood in the orphanage, where Father had given him mathematics books to read; Father had said then that mathematics was the language of God. The earthly books were but simulacra, human digests of the Universal Mind. The Universal Mind was not nuanced, there was no room for nuance or subtlety in Truth – the truth *from* the One, the Perfect, the True Mind of the Universe. Like all phrases obscured and secunded to metaphysics, he also sought the One, and, finishing his kykeon and setting it down next to the seal, *from* the One, he exhaled, slowly, and began:

A single step, turn. Another step turn. Two steps, turn. Two steps turn. Three and then turn then one. Two steps, turn. Four steps, turn. Two steps, turn. Two and then turn and then two more. *There must be an easier way,* he thought. Three steps, turn, three more. Two more steps. Turn. Six steps, turn. *A more direct way. Yes, that is what I have come here to find,* ἐποπτεία, *contemplation.*

Father had sponsored him, had nurtured him through the Society. His service was service of the secular intellect through which he would search for the True and the One. Father had shared this passion against the sway and press of the order he had joined. He would now vindicate Father's passion by discovering the True and the One for himself *derived from the six sources.* The truth is out of the false light. The One is one with the darkness.

Father called it The Map. Just as he recognized the office of the Holy Scripture as a simulacrum, he invoked the ordinary to describe the exquisite. *I am in the footsteps of the Greats, the initiates of the Mysteries, the Illuminators, the authors of the six sources.* He carried with him the notebook in which he had recorded every scrap of information from all the minds who took up The Problem and who had been as likely to be elevated as driven to madness in its pursuit. The notebook's first page, inscribed in a child-like hand – his first entry, a boy in Father's small library in the orphanage, the works of Euclid in Father's collection:

Theorem.
There are more primes than found in any finite list of primes.

Proof.

1. Call the primes in our finite list p_1, p_2, ..., p_r. Let P be any common multiple of these primes plus one (for example, P = $p_1p_2...p_r+1$). Now P is either prime or it is not. If it is prime, then P is a prime that was not in our list. If P is not prime, then it is divisible by some prime, call it p. Notice p cannot be any of p_1, p_2... p_r, otherwise p would divide 1, which is impossible. So this prime p is some prime that was not in our original list. Either way, the original list was incomplete.

He also carried with him the ancient document, known only to a few select members of the Order who had been compelled by its own fine polyglot hand to prove its authenticity. Others had only fragments of it. He had found it in its entirety. It was the miraculous answer to the Universal Mind's greatest challenge: *The Lord said, Know ye not that ye are gods?*

» BOOK I «
THE PROBLEM OF THE PRIMES

"Land and Sea alike
And sounding rivers hail King Ptolemy.
Many are his horsemen, many are his targeteers,
Whose burdened breast is bright with clashing steel;
Light are all royal treasuries, weighed with his;
For wealth from all climes travels day by day
To his rich realm – a hive of prosperous peace.
No foeman's tramp scares monster-peopled Nile,
Walking to war her far-off villages:
No armed robber from his warship leaps
To spoil the herds of Egypt.   Such a prince
Sits throned in her broad plains, in whose right arm
Quivers the spear – the bright-haired Ptolemy.
Like a true king, he guards with might and main
The wealth his sires' arms have won him and his own.
Nor strown all idly o'er his sumptuous halls
Lie piles that seem the work of laboring ants....
None entered e'er the sacred lists of song,
Whose lips could breathe sweet music, but he gained
Fair guerdon at the hand of Ptolemy.
And Ptolemy do Muses votaries hymn
For his good gifts – hath man a fairer lot
Than to have earned such fame among mankind?...
Ptolemy, he only, treads a path whose dust
Burns with the footprints of his ancestors,
And overlays those footprints with his own.

　　　—THEOCRITUS, The Praise of Ptolemy

When the god proclaimed to the Delians through the oracle that, in order to get rid of a plague, they should construct an altar double that of the existing one, their craftsmen fell into great perplexity in their efforts to discover how a solid could be made the double of a similar solid; they therefore went to ask Plato about it, and he replied that the oracle meant, not that the god wanted an altar of double the size, but he wished, in setting them to the task, to shame the Greeks for their neglect of mathematics and their contempt of geometry.

—THEON OF SMYRNA, Platonicus

1

The world is filled with the dead. I have come from the agora with Onesimus. He travels everywhere with me. His are my eyes in this city of Alexander, rough-hewn from all the senses, in which I must assuage my diminished eyesight with the not inconsiderable pleasures of smell, sound and touch. My palate is less perfect than it used to be when the Master taught his Egyptian slave how to discern the varietals of Mareotian Wine – none are excellent, but some are better than others and all are fit for the dilettante Greeks who must drink them and the laborers who produce them.

Among myrrh and putrefaction and the cantankerous industry of stonemason's mauls we have walked back to the Academy from the funerary preparations of Eratosthenes, who in public pronouncements has of late been granted the epithet, *of Cyrene*. As we passed the Soma, where the young body of Alexander *Megas*, the great helper of mankind, has lain in uneasy sleep since the dissolution of his empire, I am reminded that no one but Alexander is a true Alexandrian. Onesimus is a true Greek, by which I mean that he is a true Macedonian. He privately claims kinship with the family of Lagus, father of Alexander's most cunning general and successor Ptolemy, and therefore claims kinship with the current pharaoh Ptolemy V Epiphanes himself. To say so openly is treason, as Lagus is no more the official father of this foreign dynasty of the Ptolemies as Phillip of Macedon is the official father of Alexander. It is treason if one cannot raise an army. Alexander is in death as he was in life, descended from Achilles, Serapis, Helios, Zeus Ammon and Ptah, who called the world into being.

Our struggle in Judea and Coele-Syria and the imprint of the Jews will confer upon successive regents lineage also from either Baal or Yahweh, when such supremacies have been sorted out. Small as their sect is in Alexandria they are not yet to be afforded a forebear among the pantheon. I suspect Onesimus' father was immortal also, but he has neither the nerve of a Macedonian, the invention of a Greek, the litigious cast of a Jew nor the persistence of an Egyptian to indemnify his assertion. Such claims may rise unbidden only in the darkness of drink at the symposium or among the boys of the Academy; those who prefer young girls know that they are already women and are trained early to please lavishly and trust sparingly.

As for me, I am descended from Prometheus, who gave man fire and was punished for his impunity. Perhaps it is from this lineage of men who stare at fire that the world now folds in on me, and perhaps it is because I have traveled the stone streets and gazed upon the glistening granite and marble monuments of this city for fifty years that I now begin to lose my sight. It is no matter. I have seen everything worth seeing.

Like Eratosthenes, I was a transplant to the Academy. My boyhood presence at the Musaeum was as an unusual representative of the native Egyptian population on my mother's side. I was not a slave in the way the barbarians of Latium mean the word. I am merely descended from the Egyptian soil itself, which is the property of Ptolemy alone. I was and am still no more a free man than a seed fallen from a Lotus blossom is free to grow into a fig tree. My father of vague and possibly Attic background had discovered, during a visit to the interior, a beautiful girl whose lineage was descended from the ancient and timeless farmers along the course of the wide river in Oxyrhynchus. When her father refused his consent to their union on the grounds that my father was an adventurer and a foreigner my Greek father raped my Egyptian mother in a reed thrush. She and her father submitted to him fully when the shame from the failure of the Silphion leaf, the second most famous export from Cyrene after Eratosthenes, could only be assuaged by embracing him as her husband. Alexander conquered by the sword and the War Elephant, lesser men conquered by the intuition of the phallus, as blind in its environs as I am now.

The late Herophilos has done numerous studies with sheep in the zoological gardens and has proven the efficacy of pure Silphion. Most likely my mother was given a placebo and sent into solitary confinement as the family gave offerings at Siwa. They were disowned by their kinsmen for embracing a foreigner and were forced to flee Oxyrhynchus. I do not know my mother's family, but I must have descendants alive still wandering in the desert and harvesting chickpeas. Perhaps it is fitting that I am of a family from a town named for the species of "sharp-nosed" fish known to my native people to have devoured the phallus of Osiris, god of the afterlife.

Onesimus travels with me for another reason. Even with a lifetime of ascendancy within the Academy, I am still, at root, an Egyptian trespasser. This is an inconvenient time to claim kinship with the natives. If Alexander can claim as father god of eternal Egypt, I fear it is not too base now to claim Prometheus, a perpetual outsider chastened for bringing light to the darkness. The darkness descends like a blanket on this city, and the miracle of its founding is borne away on a trundling catafalque which stirs up in its wake manufactured differences between our races. At root, we are all fleeing the night made day by Helios, by Ptah, by Prometheus. We all strive to see in the Light. I speak of Eratosthenes, and write of him now, because he was as much a follower of the Light as any other man. His end punctures a ribbon of consciousness we have all – Greek, Egyptian, Phoenician, Jew and even the rampaging barbarians of Latium – inherited from time itself. When the ancient oracle at Siwa pronounced Alexander a living god almost one hundred fifty years ago, it was only in recognition of the latest of those whose passion for the light was worn like a chlamys about the shoulders did they make their pronouncement. It is my opinion - and this is treason of course - that Alexander was neither the first nor the last Great King of the Light; he has had other brothers since and will have many more still. Perhaps, in our own way, we are all living gods, our essences as immortal as eternal Egypt.

Onesimus has the memory of a bureaucrat and I the memory of a poet. It is said that I am often a notorious enemy of exactitude, but this is true for all men, for what is reality but the mind's perception of the struggle between fact and will? They wade into the Nile from opposing banks until fact falters in the slipstream of perception and will carries it across to the far shore. For myself, I must record the events of the Master's life in full awareness of the influence of these two forces upon me. Dionysus *and* Apollo be praised! The perception of loss is greatest now and the reality of it overcomes me, but as a young man, working beside the Master in his adopted city, it seemed that all things were possible.

Onesimus was not yet born when Ptolemy IV pushed back Antiochus III at Raphia. He was yet a babe at his mother's breast when Archimedes fell at Syracuse and not in his tenth year when Ptolemy IV, the corrupt and profligate son of the great benefactor, Pharaoh Ptolemy III Euergetes, met his end. Thus, living in this turbulence of the regency of the child-king Ptolemy V, dear Onesimus knows only from the stories in the library of the strains upon our northeastern border during the period when the Master first made the journey from Athens to Alexandria, and the gains to be made by men so formed as to aid in its defense.

I digress from the Alexandrian Project, so named by its friends and detractors those many years ago, which is to be my main subject here, but indeed, Onesimus was the harbinger of such recollections at an impromptu symposium several nights ago. Many of us had gathered informally to pay homage to the late Master. Men of the Academy, select students, mathematicians, critics, fellows of the Project and admirers of the late Chief Librarian assembled in the gardens between the library and the Soma, where Alexander still stares on in disbelief at what anarchy of the soul the destruction of his empire has wrought. Eratosthenes *of Cyrene*, the late Master, was of such subtle brilliance and such austere pretension that it was almost a trespass upon his memory that we should begin engaging in drink on the chaises arrayed within the courtyard, fragrant with evening scents and walled up against the stench of the industrious city outside.

I believe it was dear Onesimus, with his child-like imitation of the adult world, who poured me my first kylix of wine. I drank it slowly, listening to the faint chants from the Serapeum and the lumbering of merchant's carts returning from the agora. *Life moves forward, there is no death in the Light.*

He filled the others' cups and returned to mine. Filling it again, he asked, "How is it that the Master was called to Alexandria from Athens? I know so much of his tenure here but very little of its beginnings."

I waited, hoping that another's voice would fill the silence. I have little patience for nostalgia beyond the confines of my own mind. After some time I caught the eyes of loyal Aristophanes, who had supported Eratosthenes even when the Master's influence at court had spent itself entirely. His oldest friends, the men with whom I had labored at the Master's side on the great Project, were all with the Eternal. Callimachus the grammarian is gone. Apollonius the Rhodian, a dear friend to the Project, now chases Callimachus in death as well as literary criticism as in his *Argonautica* Jason chased the Golden Fleece.

The great Archimedes had been here when the Master stepped from the boat which bore him from Athens and he was foremost of those who supported the construction of the device unveiled before the pharaoh forty-five years ago in that infamous lecture. Archimedes the polymath - the engineer – the other *strategoi* of the Project had been nearing a solution to a problem which hindered the progress of the device when his beloved Syracuse fell to the Roman Marcellus. More elegant writers have elegized his death. It is now said of him that he was lost in a haze of drawing his circles in the sand when he was inadvertently set upon by a Roman soldier.

The story is of a doddering old man obsessed with abstraction who met his end by a whisper from a callous Roman General. I know better. For two years, Archimedes' catapults and the accuracy of the differential gearing mechanisms which he and the Master perfected in pursuit of the Project forestalled the capture of the city. Rome was in need elsewhere of the forces besieging Syracuse, and it was all but certain that Marcellus would be recalled and the impenetrable city given a reprieve. I myself arranged for the secret couriers from the Master to Archimedes describing the erosion of Rome's political support for the siege and therefore bolstering Archimedes' conviction that his native city was on the verge of winning the stalemate. In the end, a defector arranged to leave a door unlocked at an appointed hour. The guards were easily overrun and within a short time the entire Roman force controlled the city. The defector was paid well and made preparations to leave with the departing fleet.

A Roman officer, as aware as every soldier of the ingenuity of the famous Archimedes, held him personally responsible for the depravations that had befallen his brother soldiers in the encircling army. The officer, finding Archimedes not in a sandbox of circles but the councils of war, recognized him by his stooped posture and the unkempt grey hair which he had long since lost an interest in dyeing as once he did in Alexandria. Against the orders of Marcellus that Archimedes be captured alive, he was dragged into the street for execution. He was tortured by the pulling of fingernails, his side was punctured with a spear, and he was garroted as he watched in his last seconds in the Light the walls of his workshop consumed by flames. I know this from a countryman of his acquaintance who has settled quietly in the Egyptian Quarter. The soldier and the defector were taken to Marcellus, who had them promptly crucified – a grizzly Roman spectacle – on the walls of Syracuse in front of her citizens and the mustered Roman army. Marcellus could find among Archimedes' destroyed workshop only one small orrery, a model of a much larger device, which it is said he prized more than any other spoils from the sacking of Syracuse. He wore it as a charm around his neck until he died, a constant *momento mori* of the fickleness of revenge.

Again, I am easily diverted here from writing about the Master. Perhaps it is my reticence to discuss the Master in the past tense. I still cannot imagine a world without the mind and will of Eratosthenes. Perhaps it is only my rural Egyptian lineage that pulls me back into flowery destruction epics. After all, mine are a people whose history is born aloft on the extravagant diversions of chanted choruses and valiant odes, like the Greeks before the apotheoses of Alexander and bureaucracy.

Mercifully, Aristophanes, the new Chief Librarian, burst upon the quiet.

"The Master was a Stoic. That was his tradition, a tradition in ascendancy in the Athens of his youth. But he had become an apostate." The other men laughed in agreement.

"He was the only man I've ever known," I said, "to be fully restless when his view of the world was in constant harmony. Most men change facts to fit their worldview. I believe this alone drove him. His *daimon* was forged not from fire or earth, but from the immortal ether of change."

"Yes," said Aristophanes, "he had that rare quality of honoring the ineffable while maintaining the capacity to take one side and take it strongly. Yes he was a Stoic in Athens. As I understand his family life, though he spoke of it precious few times, he had not the means to position himself immediately with a tutor. It was only through contacts made from Lysanius, head of the Cyrenaic School, that he was afforded the opportunity to travel to Athens where, impressing Ariston of Chios by an ingenious solution to the Delian problem, he received his position with the Stoics."

Hearing this, the young Aristarchus from Samothrace, (who smelled of the vain and rather bizarre mixture of eucalyptus and myrrh rubbed upon him in some unspeakable way), arose from a far chaise, filled his kylix, and sat upon an empty chaise nearby.

"I don't believe he solved the Delian problem in Athens," he said.

Aristophanes rose to fill his cup. "Aristarchus, you must be correct. I don't imagine that the Stoics would be interested in a solution of the Delian problem, or any other logic puzzle. Ariston had by then *reformed* the school."

"Eratosthenes of Cyrene was a Stoic," I said, "but he was, as you say Aristophanes, a lapsed Stoic. Many stories flowed from the kylix at the home of Archimedes, and the two of them would concoct lavish histories in that code of theirs, always testing to see if an eavesdropper could discern the truth of them.

He was no more an abjurer of passions than you, Aristophanes – Or Onesimus here, who has stubbornly-"

"Yes! Onesimus," said Aristophanes goading him. "He has wrestled with a longer, more inclusive proof of the Master's solution for the Delian problem."

"Yes, that is true Aristophanes. I've nearly solved it," said dear Onesimus, filling a kylix.

"Well, no matter with the Stoics," said Aristophanes. "They'd never have congregated, much less coalesced in Alexandria."

"Yes and the late Master," said Onesimus, "was always a didact when reflecting on his time in Athens."

"'Oh yes,'" I mocked, 'Oh Athens, the navel of the world! To have been a fly in the throat of Pericles! Or a chisel in the hand of Phidias!' – the Master would offer some such sly paean when rummaging his mind for the solution to a difficult problem."

"Hesperos," said old Diocles, who was just now motioning to a servant to set up a chaise, "you give Eratosthenes too little credit. He was sarcastic, but by his own admission the time he spent there was among the most stimulating of his life. It was indeed a Silver Age."

Diocles' word play was not lost on the assembly. It was well known that the same silver mines, once owned and enjoyed jointly by the citizens of the Athens of Pericles, the same mines whose great wealth stayed the advance of Xerxes, were now in Macedonian hands. The mountains and undulating hills of Attica hung like a plum-bob from the silver mines of Greece.

"Eratosthenes' passion was always for the new science," I said.

Diocles and Apollonius of Perga, two mathematicians who had known the Master – and the Project – well, nodded their gray heads in agreement.

"He had proven himself at criticism," said Diocles with the precision of a man who had just had a stroke, "and his lute was quite fine. I had even heard him sing the old odes of Pella with a deep resonance. But the new, applied science was his Light. And his Light has become our own – all of us."

"As the Master is gone, and, to be so bold," said Aristarchus, nodding to Aristophanes, "I beg the leave of the *new* Master to say this. Eratosthenes' gift was mathematics – the most subtle, the most abstract, the most practicable - the holy of holies."

"You need not my leave to say it, Aristarchus," said Aristophanes. "You are quite correct. It was The Master's – the *late* Master's mathematics which impelled if not sustained his heights at Alexandria."

All in attendance shared glances and, seeing that no one displayed the usual reticence when hinting at state secrets, like all courtiers flamboyantly displaying ink-stained hands from the chancery, Onesimus, the youngest and therefore the most honest said, "I know of the Master's early - felicity - with ciphers."

Aristophanes crookedly offered his kylix to the epicycles churning above. "Yes, The Master was ingenious with ciphers-"

A cry rang out from all, again to the intoxicated epicycles: "Aristophanes is drunk!"

"*You're* always drunk, Hesperos," shouted Aristophanes with a heavy slur. We all laughed because this is true.

I fought half-heartedly for my honor. "I am often to be found with a kylix in one hand, but always the bound-gag in the other. Both make it to my mouth in equal measure and always one accompanies the other."

"If you old men will not tell the story then I will. The Master giving leave, I believe the boy ought to know the heights to which a man may rise in Alexandria by applying his penchants. With honest genuflection to the Muses –" Aristophanes nearly collapsed in his obeisance but was grappled on both sides by Onesimus and Aristarchus and reinstated once again, precariously and near prone upon his chaise, "whom we all serve, I say to you now that Calliope herself is moved by the *application* of wisdom and virtue in Alexandria."

"Perhaps an admixture of water," cautioned Onesimus.

"The wine aids the remembrance, boy. By the gods, boy, you are a Stoic yourself! The remembrance is strong of The Master's early triumphs. But of course, Hesperos, you were there at the beginning."

"I *was* there at the beginning," I said, "or at least I was there in the background, and observed The Master closely."

"You were there. Tell these men of Athens."

"I am no Athenian. I'm not even a Macedonian."

"But The Master told you how it all began, In Athens. A courier, wasn't it, bearing a message from, from –"

"From Calliope!" I smiled.

"Yes, from Calliope! A verse in code."

This prodigious event is still on its way, still wandering; it has not yet reached the ears of men. Lightning and thunder require time, the light of the stars requires time, deeds, though done, still require time to be seen and heard. This deed is still more distant from them than the most distant stars—and yet they have done it themselves.

—NIETZSCHE, *Die fröhliche Wissenschaft*

2

"The whole thing's a mystery. Not so much the plot as how he got an agent to say yes."

"Well," I said, slurping a scotch down to the sand granules from which my tumbler was made, "at least he got a 'yes.' That's more than we've got."

"Another?"

"Yes, actually. That sounds great."

My best friend and fellow collaborator Perry McDonald staggered off to the bar to trouble once more the lone barman. I sat staring out at the swirls of snow dusting the street. Twenty minutes into this week's writers group meeting it appeared as if we would be the only attendees. There isn't much to critique when you've become so familiar with each other's writing style you could pass one another's work off as your own.

Perry returned with two more doubles and a cloth napkin. He sipped his drink through his teeth. "Here's Tim's novel as I read it." He found the center of the napkin and pinched it with his thumb and forefinger, making a steep mountain of it on the table. "Here, we have the insane exposition. It takes, like, five chapters. It's so full of name dropping and character development that by time we get here," he said, indicating the peak of the napkin, "we've forgotten why we care about the characters at all.

"By here," indicating the dénouement with a flick of his fingers that knocked the napkin over, "we've realized that half the exposition wasn't necessary, that two-thirds of the characters are superfluous, and that it all just comes down to a ridiculous McGuffin. So, like the Maltese Falcon or Bogart's Letters of Transit, we're left absolutely dying inside because we've just spent a weekend and $19.95 to learn where the Freemason's secret library is."

"And," I said, "I mean, I jumped forward at points, but it seems Hitler had a secret pact with FDR to hide manuscripts at the Library of Congress to be divided up among some cabal after the war - I can't remember making sense of it, honestly."

"Right."

"So, it seems to me, that we are wasting our time. I'm broke, you're almost broke. Tim's got an agent, probably a book deal, and the world has another secret-chamber-lost-secrets-thriller, Umberto Eco is again grievously betrayed, and we're maxing out credit cards in a bar, in downtown DC, in the winter, getting drunk."

"That's about it."

"Perry, we need to shift genres, because it can't be done."

"What can't?"

"This," I said, indicating the toppled napkin. "In fact, you've picked the perfect thing to demonstrate how ridiculous this genre is. There's nothing in the world that will flesh out a story, to make it really significant." I propped the napkin up once more. "Look, there's nothing inside. Why do we care where a buried treasure is? There's nothing that a serious reader would believe was worth finding, that's really revolutionary. Monetary treasure's been done. Who really cares if someone finds Blackbeard's gold on an island in Nova Scotia? Who would believe that a secret society is protecting the lost secrets of Atlantis? I mean, really. Who cares?

"My argument is this: I don't think that the plot device exists that can make a serious reader believe what they'd have to believe for the payoff at the end. First, we have to create a treasure that's not only historically significant, it has to have been believably concealable for generations - so it can't be a secret island after more than a half century of satellites - and it has to be held as valuable consistently across centuries. It can't just be gold doubloons. A sophisticated reader has to care. Second, it can't be too rarified, because a lost manuscript isn't going to get the world excited. I mean, in the book, it might make the characters wealthy, it might even change what we think about the author of the lost work, but anything other than a mass-market, overly-credulous audience is not going to believe that discovering, I don't know, that Newton actually turned lead to gold and wrote it up in some secret manuscript is plausible. The sophisticated audience knows that alchemy isn't real. They don't believe in magic. I don't, you don't. Aliens are an awful idea, though maybe they're in Tim's book too."

"I've got it," said Perry, stomping his foot mockingly. "Our heroes discover a rare manuscript. Wait, hear me out. They discover this manuscript in a strange hand. It's found at a garage sale. It makes sense. It satisfies the condition that the people well-placed to be intrigued by a string of clues stumble across them. They're – let's make them rare book collectors. There's no conspiracy theory to start, ok. They just love old books. A father and son team or something. So, they know the value of the book when they see it. They'd also have enough knowledge on board to make it credible that they'd be able to recognize something odd about it, something that impels them to an immediate recognition of the potential value of its place in history."

"Ok," I said, "I'm listening."

"Ok, so that satisfies that problem. And because they're rare book collectors, they move in those circles, and it's believable that they have a colleague, perhaps with shadowy intentions." Perry took two more sips of scotch waiting for me to stop him. I quietly sipped on mine, waiting for him to continue.

"Ok," I said finally. "Ok, so there's a figure with unknown motives, who comes in contact with the manuscript through the heroes. He's consulted or something."

"Exactly, he's consulted. For good measure, he lives somewhere exotic. Marrakech or something."

"Christ Perry, Marrakech?"

"Wherever. An Inuit village. Create a crazy backstory. But somewhere out of the way. He gives the heroes just enough to whet their appetite, to make 'em believe they've really got something. Then the reader is intrigued. They don't know whether-" Perry stomped his foot again "It's an unreliable narrator and we hint at it from the beginning. So the reader doesn't quite trust the information they're getting, right along with the heroes. They're equally skeptical."

"Perry," I said, "this has been done, like, dozens of times."

"Well, ok, we'll flesh that out. Because you're the one with the great need to have this all-encompassing treasure that satisfies your anti-bourgeois hatred of things that other people find valuable, why don't you tell me what they're looking for? What's the big hook? What do we use instead of the found shipwreck, the deciphered manuscript, the stolen painting?"

"We've talked about this, which is why I think we should both go back to the stories we were working on before."

"You're doing your boring as hell literary shit."

"Oh ok, boring as hell? And you're going back to the post-apocalyptic '1984' bullshit?"

"Ok, well then, I like the idea of this genre, and I think we've been decent at it, but you're right, we need a hook that's better than gold and manuscripts and Edgar Cayce's Atlantis and Egyptian secret records."

"The trick is," I said, "we have to nail down what really matters to people. I mean, front page of the newspaper, New York Times headline bigger than the moon landing. And if we're sticking with this genre, it has to have some historical meat to it. 'The President's been shot' won't work. No one will protect a secret for millennia about the continuity of government of a relatively new country on a continent that wasn't known before the printing press. What could catastrophically ruin lives, could fundamentally change human relationships? Whatever that is, make it relevant but not so dependent on current technology, culture or economics that people thousands of years ago couldn't have known about it. Remove any nonsense about religion, mythology, mind-body connections, secret priesthoods, alien visitors and free energy, and throw it into as unusual a framework as we can sell.

"That's all you. If you can find something that satisfies those criteria, I'll hear you out. But I don't think you'll find it. The historical-cabal secret-knowledge thing requires a little give here and there. It requires a suspension of disbelief and the audience's willing inflation of the perceived value of some historic revelation. That's the genre."

"Let me think about it. Another round?" Perry nodded as I took out my credit card. As a writer, I'm wary of the moment when everything clicks, when you have a flash of creativity that suspends itself in mid-air, immune to questionable falsifiability and the pants-wetting sensation of selling out. I've had this feeling too many times only to pick it apart from the outside-in. But as I looked down at my Visa card I realized I had found the answer to our problems. I found the hook in a piece of plastic. I found the axial moment in a magnetic strip the size of a finger. It was as ancient as it was timely. It was based on technology as old as the human species and as modern as every desktop computer.

The only problem: it was real. It wasn't fiction at all. And even though Perry didn't know it yet, he was about to become the wise old man. He wasn't in Marrakech, or an Inuit village, and we had no shadowy cabal following our every move. It was simple mathematics, mathematics Perry knew well enough to explain to me in endless tirades about the graduate program in finance his Wall Street father had pushed him into, a graduate program that exposed him to others who would be in a position to help without our having to give the game away. I gave up *fiction* in that moment. I had an instant realization that Perry and I were on the brink of a story so engaging, so conspiratorially satisfying and so true that we had an instant hit on our hands. We had only to write it down from the beginning and follow it through to the end.

Dog, dog! Restrain yourself, my shameless spirit!... Much knowledge is a sore ill for anyone who cannot control his tongue; He is like a child with a knife.

—CALLIMACHUS, Aitia (*On a scholar's interest of practicing humility in the presence of his patron*)

3

The other men gathered round, some strolling over from the conversations they had been pretending to have with one another, some barbarically dragging chaises alongside our circle. They were all by now quite interested in my story. I made sure that all had a full kylix. I motioned to Diocles not to be mean with his pour. I took on the posture of the late Master, reclining on one arm in the Athenian fashion.

"Eratosthenes did indeed receive a courier some few years before sailing to Alexandria. He described the delivery of a small package wrapped in goatskin upon which a papyrus note had been fastened. The note directed him to open the package and, 'in the spirit of the *Mysteries*, take from the kiste and after working it put it back in the kalathos.'" The men smiled. Dear Onesimus, recently initiated, could not tell if the mention of the Mysteries was allowed. He looked around the circle, noting, finally that all were fellow initiates in the *New* Mysteries, one of the Master's most ingenious inventions.

I continued. "Unwrapping the package he found a lead tablet bearing a diagram of a circle and an enciphered text. The Master could not remember its subject exactly, those many years later when he retold this story to me, but it took him only days to reveal its meaning. In other words, the puzzle the courier delivered to the Master asked the recipient to take from the box an enciphered text and return to the sender its contents, revealed by the Master's ingenuity.

"The end of the text provided directions for replying to the note, which he did immediately by the same courier, who had, surprisingly and quite optimistically, remained in Athens. Some days later, another more detailed text arrived by a different courier, but bore the same style of enciphered writing. He easily revealed the message, and repeated the correspondence. He had deduced that his correspondent must be in Athens or just beyond.

"After several volleys of messages his curiosity got the best of him and he undertook to follow the courier on his return journey. Some bits of the story are lost to my memory, but no doubt in his retelling The Master sensationalized the journey through Athens he was compelled to take by the cautious courier. He was unable to trace the source, and began responding to the correspondent in his own cipher. After a slightly longer delay, he was given a response in kind. The messages became more complex in both their mathematics and the codes they employed.

"Unable to repress his curiosity any longer, in the following manner the Master undertook a small diversion to flush his correspondent from the shadows. Eratosthenes ended a particular response by introducing to his correspondent a deliberately erroneous property he claimed to have observed repeated both in the proportions of the Phidian Caryatids of the Erechtheion and the famed temple of Athena Parthenos, both, of course, on the Acropolis. He arranged this 'property' in such a way that a skeptical, naturally curious reader would be compelled to conduct his own measurements of the temple on a particular day of the year in the Metonic cycle some few weeks hence.

"The correspondence, which he admitted had, by then, eclipsed his other studies and engrossed his fascination, ceased immediately. The particular day's sun rose and fell, and the agents he had stationed at the temple could make no report of unusual activity. The Master was horrified that he had weakened his position with the correspondent and tarnished the esteem he had accumulated by the obvious, though intended, error in his last communication. He waited several more weeks. Despairing of ever hearing from the correspondent again, he once again took up his lute and his criticism and pursued his own theorems.

"Then, one day, speaking with colleagues in the agora, he heard reference to that same unusual property he had erroneously embedded in his last message months before. The Master inquired as to the source of the observation and was directed to a young man with whom he was well acquainted, a student of Archimedes. The student, after much coaxing and not too few cups of wine, revealed that his Master, Archimedes himself, had considered the property while strolling through the Acropolis on a particular feast day some weeks ago. The student had not seen the proof, but his Master was so assured of its truthfulness that he had thrown himself into its study and had neglected all other cares and aspirations."

"And that's how the Master befriended Archimedes," said Aristarchus, "or rather, how Archimedes tested Eratosthenes for friendship?" Diocles and Apollonius both smiled at the mention of mathematics as a medium for secure communication.

"The Master saw it as more an initiation rite than a test," I said. "Of course, Archimedes had already become an initiate of the Mysteries at Eleusis, the cult unfortunately already waning in popularity after Alexander. The Master suggested that he, too, had begun his initiation in the Mysteries at Archimedes' urging while then in Athens, and not later in Alexandria, as is generally believed. And yes, that is how their close friendship began. They of course knew each other, but the reforms of Ariston among the Stoics, to whom Eratosthenes was publicly bound, eschewed the practical for the numinous. They even began debating in the agora on the virtues of applied knowledge as a means to embrace ethics, with Eratosthenes playing antagonist to Archimedes' practicality."

I waved to Onesimus, closest to the wine. He spoke while he refilled my kylix. "And then – it couldn't have been much later – Archimedes sailed at the invitation of the prince who was our noble King's grandfather, Ptolemy III Euergetes – to aid in the preparations for the Laodicean War in Syria?"

"Yes, Onesimus, he left Athens for Alexandria, lured by a generous salary. But he had by then fully embraced Eratosthenes, who by this period had all but disavowed the Stoics, in thought if not in display. Eratosthenes was brought into the Light by Archimedes, as I was by The Master many years later – but young Onesimus wants the axial moment. Dear boy, the man was removed of the Stoics but they never fully from him. History rarely spins one spoke upon another, but like a sphere in ether, revolves about itself in numerous epicycles.

"Still, there was a moment when his fortunes changed fully, when he was called into the world from the quaint college town of Athens to Alexandria, the center of the world."

"The troubles in Syria," said Aristarchus, knowingly.

"Yes, Syria, and the perfidy of the usurper Seleucus II."

I pause now in my recollection at Onesimus' urging. The events of the territorial jealousies between Ptolemy II and Antiochus and the events following the near coincident elevation of their successors Ptolemy III Euergetes and Seleucus II Callinicus are widely known even today. But in the spirit of Clio, and for future readers, who will regard with the same curiosity – and ignorance! – as they cast upon Priam and Agamemnon our child-like *diadochoi* bleating at every transgression, I outline it here.

In the years before Eratosthenes sailed for Alexandria, when he was coddled in the staged revival of empire – Oh the riotous stories Eratosthenes could tell of the pretense of midnight walks in the gardens of the Academy, the rehearsed arguments in the Stoa, the half-resurrection of tragedy in the traipsing of mere copyists of Aeschylus, Sophocles and Euripides! let me not be detained too long with these hilarious accounts – the diadochoi , the successors to Alexander and their kin, moved their prey of toy garrisons like pharaohs at the Senat table – how all cultures play the blocking game! Ptolemy II, in his final days before relinquishing his throne to Osiris, was presented with an informant's evidence that his daughter, Berenice Syra, who had been wedded in a dynastic joining to Antiochus II, King of Alexander's great eastern possessions, would be maligned in favor of Antiochus' first wife Laodice. Upon Antiochus' death and the quickly following accession of Ptolemy III Euergetes as Pharaoh of Upper and Lower Egypt, a plot was set in motion to deprive Berenice's son of his rights in favor of Laodice's son, Seleucus II. By the strength of the warnings of more informants, Euergetes sent an advance force under the mercenary general Xanthippus of Sparta to protect Berenice and support the claims of her son, Ptolemy's nephew.

Though I record the history here for later readers, it was in possession of this common knowledge of our day that Aristarchus formed the vanguard of his questioning.

"These informants were carefully placed at Antioch, Aristarchus. In the tensions before the accession in both kingdoms, everyone was observed with suspicion. The supporters of Laodice had employed a cipher of such cunning and invention that it was said only Ares alone could have devised it."

"And The Master, in Athens, perhaps on a midnight amble in the gardens of the Academy, was presented once again with a coded message. It came not from the courier of Archimedes, but from the embassy of Ptolemy himself, bearing his royal cartouche in the Egyptian style. The entire message was enciphered in the hand of Archimedes. That text was easily read, and within the message itself lay another message in an unknown cipher. The Master set to work for several weeks, and only at the point of exhaustion and collapse did he uncover the brief message. This he encrypted in the familiar cipher of Archimedes and delivered it to the Ptolemaic embassy. The message contained details of a plot to restore Laodice and her son as co-regents after the death of Antiochus."

"And that is how The Master was called to Alexandria, to aid in the decryption from these informants?"

"Not exactly, Onesimus."

"Yes, Hesperos," said Aristophanes, "you are correct, The Master was yet another year in Athens."

"Yes," I said, "he was. And he maintained his appearances in the Stoa and attended the piddle at the Odeon. But the work of decoding more and more messages consumed him. The process was laborious, and by Ptolemy's own command his were the only eyes permitted to view the contents of these dispatches. The men of the embassy, unnerved by their sidelining, and perhaps jealous too, were nevertheless unable to participate in the bureaucratic fashion, and were cut out. Eratosthenes received more and more messages with pieces missing or that had been purposely jumbled in transcription and had long since lost the character of Archimedes' own flowing hand. He contended with message within message, compounded with willful, if slight, sabotage."

"It became necessary for Eratosthenes to relocate to Alexandria," said Onesimus, "to view the dispatches at the receiving end?"

"Yes, that too," said Aristophanes. "It certainly provided for a quicker response, but I don't believe it was solely for the purposes of expedition that he was called to Alexandria."

"In those days, intrigue flowed like the Nile itself, in its own good time," I said, with a glance to Aristophanes, who was on his back gazing dreamily at the stars.

Sensing this, he leaned over on one shoulder and with an earnestness a drunken man summons only by long practice said, "Hesperos, tell them the Master did not come to Alexandria to avoid the censors of the pharaoh's embassy."

We all stared, motionless, past each other, suddenly exposed, aware of our own drunkenness.

"The first stage of the Alexandrian Project had begun," said young Aristarchus, "and Archimedes needed the other great strategoi?"

"Like Onesimus here has mentioned," said Diocles ironically, "Eratosthenes was renowned for his mastery of the Delian Problem."

Diocles lashed his kylix about. His only work at the Academy other than his mathematical insights concerning the Project was a purported solution to the Delian Problem using a geometric curve. Diocles is a creative thinker, however singular the fruits of his creativity.

"You have stated," said Diocles, "that the Stoics cared little for the Delian problem. On that score you are quite correct. Zeno perhaps, but not Ariston."

I set my kylix down softly upon my chaise. Apollonius was not content to see the achievements of his friend, and, some say, lover outdone by a casual comment.

"Hesperos, you knew him best. You see it most clearly." Apollonius stood up, bowed slightly and turned toward Diocles. "It is by the graces alone that the late Master's *attempt* of the Delian Problem should have aided him so heroically in his rise at the Academy."

Cryptography is a most unusual science. Most professional scientists aim to be the first to publish their work, because it is through dissemination that the work realizes its value. In contrast, the fullest value of cryptography is realized by minimizing the information available to potential adversaries. Thus professional cryptographers normally work in closed communities to provide sufficient interaction to ensure quality while maintaining secrecy from outsiders. Revelations of these secrets is normally only sanctioned in the interests of historical accuracy after it has been demonstrated that no further benefit can be obtained from continued secrecy.

—J H ELLIS, The History of Non-Secret Encryption, 1999

4

Two weeks earlier Perry and I had found ourselves similarly abandoned at our bi-weekly writers club. Perry enjoys the solitude. I do too, but I also crave the solipsism that accompanies attempting – with varying degrees of success – the most literate stuff within our tiny circle. In the past we had been subjected to stories about nursing and retirement homes, pet birds, summers in Florida – there are only two stories about Florida that ever go well, living in poverty in the shadow of the bourgeois extravagance centered in Miami and Orlando or living in extravagance and knowing how absurd one's life is – fishing trips in the Adirondacks, family members with Alzheimer's that never quite successfully walked the line between measured sympathy and blatant exploitation, etc, etc. Incidentally, I once wrote a short story about the history of English phrases of continuation. Greatly influenced by *The Girl With the Pearl Earring*, the story was set in Mainz, Germany in 1450. The essentials of the story involved Johann Fust, a sort of prototypical loan shark preying upon the famous invention of Johann Gutenberg. Fust loaned Gutenberg 1600 gilders in two years to advance the latter's dream of developing a cheaper way to distribute mostly sacred texts on a previously unrealizable scale. A subplot involved the introduction of Latin phrases of continuance such as *et cetera,* (etc.) *et alii* (et al.) and *et sequentes* (et seq.) into general usage to save the expense of time and ink. The story wasn't a huge success with the group – no house cats, no romps through the Everglades, no heartbreakingly degenerative neurology - and it remains to this day simply another set of electromagnetic indentations on my computer's hard drive.

At this particular meeting a fortnight ago, well into our third round, Perry lamented the surcharges his bank had imposed on an overdraft. Calling the bank, he said, he was told that overdrafts aren't purely punitive, as he had argued to the person on the phone, but imposed to recover costs associated with the extra transactions involved with tallying up electronic credits and debits in a server in cyberspace. Perry, having found limited satisfaction with his complaint, rehashed the argument in favor of little to no fee for these transactions. The general thrust of our conversation:

"Surely the bank does incur a cost?"

"Not at all, or very little. If this were 1960, I'd agree that a physical transfer of information had taken place and probably taken place again during the reversal of funds. But this isn't the 1960s. I'm talking about the physical transfer of actual funds or other bearer instruments, like checks, between branches, back to the local Federal Reserve Bank and, if necessary, bank to the local branch again after an overdraft."

"And it's all electronic now, so it should be cheaper?"

"It should be orders of magnitude cheaper, because while certainly there's a cost for the infrastructure to encode these transactions, it's comparatively cheaper than the systems preceding it while being orders of magnitude more complex – *and secret*."

Secrets, even secrets involve the minutiae of e-check routing, usually make me curl my lip and slightly diminish the pace of my drinking.

Perry, taking my queue, launched into an assertion that the essentials of transferring encoded information had changed very little between the battlefields of Ilion and the First World War. "Essentially, code making and the symbiotic field of code breaking had begun with substitution cyphers. An alphabet would be written across a page in the appropriate language. Directly underneath it another alphabet would be written shifted a specified number of places. So, a message from Agamemnon to the recalcitrant Achilles begging for a proportioned response might be encoded by aligning each Greek letter with another. Achilles need know only the presumably prearranged number of spaces of that day's shift to decode the message and promptly ignore it.

"The substitution cypher was cleverly employed by Julius Caesar in the form of a *scytale*, a stick of known diameter that could be wrapped with animal hide and imprinted with Latin letters. Because the sender and the recipient had rods of identical width, the letters matched up with the appropriate substitute letters and the message was revealed. The substitution cypher has come down to us bearing his name. In an era where the pace of information was glacially slower than today, special agents in antiquity would have their heads shaven, receive a tattoo of a message in the Caesar Cypher and wait until the hair grew back, thus concealing the message in the event of capture.

"As innovative as it was," Perry excitedly waved his hands without spilling his drink, "the message employed by Mary Queen of Scots in the infamous Babington Plot against Elizabeth I was essentially a Caesar Cypher interspersed with logograms representing ideas. This correspondence was easily broken by Elizabeth's spymaster Francis Walsingham, who added to one intercepted message an additional line of text written in the language of the cypher asking for the identities of the conspirators. Walsingham reproduced the cypher so faithfully that a full membership list from the conspirators was received in kind, Babington and his cohort were unmasked and Protestantism in England was secured up to the present day.

"Plausibly known to the Elizabethan Court was an ingenious ninth century CE Arab method born of extensive analysis of the Koran. Al-Kindi, a brilliant Arab polymath, realized that given a large enough sample, the relative frequency of certain Arabic letters stayed consistent across texts. The application of this observation to cryptanalysis was inescapable, and the Caesar Cypher was easily broken. Take, for example, a code written with a substitution of one space. Perry wrote this out on a napkin:

```
A B C D E F G H I J K L M N O P Q R S T U V W X Y Z
z a b c d e f g h i j k l m n o p q r s t u v w x y
```

"An alphabet is written across a page in normal order. A second alphabet is written directly below it and shifted exactly one space. Thus, each 'A' in a text will equal a 'B', each 'B' a 'C' and so on. It is possible, Al Kindi showed, to simply apply frequency analysis to an encoded text. In an English text, it is very likely that the articles 'the' and 'an' will appear more often than 'Xylophone' or 'Zoology.' If a series repeats enough times with "SGD" and ZM" then it is reasonable to attempt a solution of the entire text using a substitution of one place."

"Ok," I said, "I think I was aware of some of this stuff. It's pretty interesting. Where is this going in relation to ATM fees?"

"Well, follow me on this," he said, turning the napkin over. "A way had to be conceived that would obscure this glaring crack in the façade of cryptography. It seems it was left to the French to solve the problem."

Perry was, among his varied minors, an ardent student of the history of the Francophone world. He had a particular interest in French military history and was eager to regale anyone who would listen. Apparently, building on the crumbs of several Renaissance Italian innovations, a certain sixteenth century CE French diplomat, Blaise de Vigenère, ushered in a quantum leap in the application of the Caesar Cypher. Working for the nascent French intelligence community, Vigenère applied not one but twenty-six possible alphabetic shifts in what was the world's first truly polyalphabetic cypher.

"Vigenère's genius," indicated by Perry with a gesticulation like one demonstrating one's bass-catching prowess, "was in encoding a message using some or all possible shifts."

Perry had finished scrawling a rudimentary table on a cocktail napkin:

	a	b	c	d	e	f	g	h	i	j	k	l	m	n	o	p	q	r	s	t	u	v	w	x	y	z
1	Z	A	B	C	D	E	F	G	H	I	J	K	L	M	N	O	P	Q	R	S	T	U	V	W	X	Y
2	Y	Z	A	B	C	D	E	F	G	H	I	J	K	L	M	N	O	P	Q	R	S	T	U	V	W	X
3	X	Y	Z	A	B	C	D	E	F	G	H	I	J	K	L	M	N	O	P	Q	R	S	T	U	V	W
4	W	X	Y	Z	A	B	C	D	E	F	G	H	I	J	K	L	M	N	O	P	Q	R	S	T	U	V
5	V	W	X	Y	Z	A	B	C	D	E	F	G	H	I	J	K	L	M	N	O	P	Q	R	S	T	U
6	U	V	W	X	Y	Z	A	B	C	D	E	F	G	H	I	J	K	L	M	N	O	P	Q	R	S	T
7	T	U	V	W	X	Y	Z	A	B	C	D	E	F	G	H	I	J	K	L	M	N	O	P	Q	R	S
8	S	T	U	V	W	X	Y	Z	A	B	C	D	E	F	G	H	I	J	K	L	M	N	O	P	Q	R
9	R	S	T	U	V	W	X	Y	Z	A	B	C	D	E	F	G	H	I	J	K	L	M	N	O	P	Q
10	Q	R	S	T	U	V	W	X	Y	Z	A	B	C	D	E	F	G	H	I	J	K	L	M	N	O	P
11	P	Q	R	S	T	U	V	W	X	Y	Z	A	B	C	D	E	F	G	H	I	J	K	L	M	N	O
12	O	P	Q	R	S	T	U	V	W	X	Y	Z	A	B	C	D	E	F	G	H	I	J	K	L	M	N
13	N	O	P	Q	R	S	T	U	V	W	X	Y	Z	A	B	C	D	E	F	G	H	I	J	K	L	M
14	M	N	O	P	Q	R	S	T	U	V	W	X	Y	Z	A	B	C	D	E	F	G	H	I	J	K	L
15	L	M	N	O	P	Q	R	S	T	U	V	W	X	Y	Z	A	B	C	D	E	F	G	H	I	J	K
16	K	L	M	N	O	P	Q	R	S	T	U	V	W	X	Y	Z	A	B	C	D	E	F	G	H	I	J
17	J	K	L	M	N	O	P	Q	R	S	T	U	V	W	X	Y	Z	A	B	C	D	E	F	G	H	I
18	I	J	K	L	M	N	O	P	Q	R	S	T	U	V	W	X	Y	Z	A	B	C	D	E	F	G	H
19	H	I	J	K	L	M	N	O	P	Q	R	S	T	U	V	W	X	Y	Z	A	B	C	D	E	F	G
20	G	H	I	J	K	L	M	N	O	P	Q	R	S	T	U	V	W	X	Y	Z	A	B	C	D	E	F
21	F	G	H	I	J	K	L	M	N	O	P	Q	R	S	T	U	V	W	X	Y	Z	A	B	C	D	E
22	E	F	G	H	I	J	K	L	M	N	O	P	Q	R	S	T	U	V	W	X	Y	Z	A	B	C	D
23	D	E	F	G	H	I	J	K	L	M	N	O	P	Q	R	S	T	U	V	W	X	Y	Z	A	B	C
24	C	D	E	F	G	H	I	J	K	L	M	N	O	P	Q	R	S	T	U	V	W	X	Y	Z	A	B
25	B	C	D	E	F	G	H	I	J	K	L	M	N	O	P	Q	R	S	T	U	V	W	X	Y	Z	A
26	A	B	C	D	E	F	G	H	I	J	K	L	M	N	O	P	Q	R	S	T	U	V	W	X	Y	Z

The breakthrough, according to Perry, was the method's resistance to frequency analysis. While 'A' must always equal its paired twin in a Caesar

Cypher, a Vigenère 'A' might equal any other pair inconsistently throughout a text, rendering any attempt at frequency analysis extremely difficult.

Seeing my eyes starting to wander, Perry waved off the rest of the French bit as "fascinating but not essential" and jumped several hundred years to the Victorian era, and the arrival of Charles Babbage, inventor of the Difference Engine, a device near-universally recognized as the world's first mechanical computer. Babbage – inventor also of a delicious mélange of Victorian concepts ranging from the railway cow-catcher, dendrochronology, mortality tables and the speedometer – struggled with the Vigenère for years, some say leading him to the brink of madness.

Babbage, in between his quest to regulate postage prices and rid the crowded London streets of organ grinders, realized that the Vigenère did indeed have a small weakness: the limits of human memory. A key in cryptography is an agreed upon algorithm between sender and receiver. Given an enciphered text, Perry explained, the sender and receiver might select a key as long as the text itself, making decryption impossible. But this was rarely the case. In fact, a key length as long as a message was given a specific name in cryptography, the *one-time-pad*. This, he said, was a concept he would return to in a moment.

For convenience sake, the key was almost always a short phrase or even a single word, which meant that given a long enough text, the Vigenère would cycle back again to the beginning, using only the amount of shifted alphabets as the keyword was long. Using a key like "CODE" for example, would mean that only four lines out of twenty-five would be used, in this case those lines starting with the four letters in the key. Babbage figured this out by noticing repetitions in frequently used words such as articles and prepositions. While the word "the" might be encrypted in different ways relative to the keyword, eventually, Babbage proposed, the key would reset and repetition would occur. Repetition, according to Perry, was the toupée of cryptanalysis, easy to spot if one looked hard enough. Babbage extrapolated with difficulty first the length of the keyword, the keyword itself and eventually the contents of the message in its entirety. Apparently, Babbage didn't publish his work, and the credit is given to a later identical discovery by a retired Prussian Army officer, robbing Babbage the credit due him while simultaneously giving Britain a decade head-start during which it successfully engaged Russia in the Crimea.

All this, according to Perry, took code making and breaking more or less unchanged to the Second World War and the mechanization of a much more complicated Vigenère encoded into the famous Nazi Enigma Machine. The Enigma, and its allied counterparts, used a constantly changing internal configuration of rotating dials, plug boards and scramblers. The real history of computing began in response to the efforts of the top-secret installation at Bletchley Park in Britain to match the mechanization of encryption with the mechanization of decryption. An early luminary there, Alan Turing, established principles that still guide the underlying infrastructure of the world's fastest supercomputers. Indeed, the 'Turing Test' of a problem's computability remains the theoretical standard. The team at Bletchley exploited repetition, mistakes, even intelligence about German signalmen known to use the names of sweethearts as daily keys.

"The key, here, is critical," said Perry. "I don't mind being charged a bit if I make a mistake with my debit card, that's on me. But secure information transfer has become so cheap, I can't see the outrageous charges. If the bank had to send an intermediary between me and its processing facility every time I wanted to make an ATM withdrawal or shop on the internet, I could understand that. If, for example, every time I charged a round of drinks, I had to first use the resources of my bank to arrive at a key for encoding my credit card, I would understand their frustration when they had to reverse a charge or make a negative report on my balance. But we don't have to exchange keys anymore, not physically, not via courier, not by telephone, not by radio. Key exchange is simple, key exchange is reliable, and it's incredibly, incredibly cheap."

I continued nodding. "So what happened after Turing and the Enigma and Bletchley Park?"

"Nothing, nothing immediately happened. Governments, the Federal Reserve, big banks, big corporations, they all still had couriers scurrying around with these one-time-pads, maybe a day's worth, maybe a month' worth. There was a considerable cost here, not to mention the risk of interception, human error and tempted couriers.

"So, in post-war cryptography, the spread of electronic communication called for an even more secure system to be employed in financial transactions, business telephony and government agencies. As I have said, in many cases, the one-time-pad was employed. This method was and remains impossible to break. Unfortunately, it has the misfortune of being the most inconvenient to implement. A one-time-pad is simply a letter-for-letter key. A blank page is covered with random – or pseudo random – letters. One copy is retained by the sender and another is sent to the intended recipient. Generating a truly random sequence is critical, and the technology to simulate randomness was not easy or economical at the time; it was used for none but the most important transmissions.

"The distribution of a key was also of great importance. If a bank in the 1960s wanted to transmit secure financial information, every other branch and business with which it communicated must have a copy of the key – demonstrating the logistical problems of securely distributing keys on a national and international scale. This was the state of the art in the 1960s, when banks might justify the fees they had to assess on unnecessary transactions."

Perry promised that all this was leading to the most interesting application in the evolution of cyphers from Caesar to Vigenère to Enigma. That application consisted of something called a one-way function. While the mathematics involved were, according to Perry, quite beyond both of us, the premise was essentially that of two parties sending a lockbox through the mail. The sender placed a message in a box and locked it with a padlock to which only he had the key. The box would then be sent through the mail. Any interceptor would be unable to retrieve the message without the original key. The recipient would similarly be unable to open the box and would instead place their own padlock – to which only he had the key – alongside the sender's. The box would make its way back to the sender, who would then remove his lock and send the box back. The recipient need only remove his own padlock to which only he had the key to retrieve the hidden message.

"Cryptographers," said Perry, "looked for an analog for the dual padlocks in the world of mathematics and found it in mathematical curiosities called one-way functions – the multiplication of incredibly large prime numbers into even more unimaginably large composite numbers through some operations that were known to all (public keys) and other operations that were known only to sender and recipient, respectively (private keys). This incredibly large number was in fact so incredibly large that the computing time required to try all possible combinations would negate the utility of deciphered information. Thus, in a series of breakthroughs in the 1970s, Public Key cryptography was born and quickly became a cheap standard for instantaneous, secure transactions."

The cheap part is what had infuriated Perry. He was incensed that the 1s and os of his electronic information, having been handled (and re-handled) in a second with trillions of other 1s and os - this data untouched by human hands - should inspire such a punitive $35 fee from a bank which incurred only an infinitesimal cost in processing his overdraft.

I later easily found online the seminal paper on the topic by three MIT professors. Writing in the mid-1970s, they aggregated all the mathematical breakthroughs into a workable system for Public Key Cryptography using one-way functions and built on the relative computational difficulty of the factorization of an immensely large composite number (a one-time pad) into two similarly large constituent prime numbers:

An encryption method is presented with the novel property that publicly revealing an encryption key does not thereby reveal the corresponding decryption key. This has two important consequences:

1.) Couriers or other secure means are not needed to transmit keys, since a message can be enciphered using an encryption key publicly revealed by the intended   recipient. Only he can decipher the message, since only he knows the corresponding decryption key.

2.) A message can be "signed" using a privately held decryption key. Anyone can verify this signature using the corresponding publicly revealed encryption key. Signatures cannot be forged, and a signer cannot later deny the validity of his signature. This has obvious applications in "electronic mail" and "electronic funds transfer" systems.

A message is encrypted by representing it as a number M, raising M to a publicly specified power e, and then taking the remainder when the result is divided by the publicly specified product, n, of *two large secret prime numbers* p and q. Decryption is similar; only a different, secret, power d is used, where $e \cdot d \equiv 1 \pmod{(p - 1) \cdot (q - 1)}$. The security of the system rests in part on the difficulty of factoring the published divisor, n.

—R.L. RIVEST, A. SHAMIR, AND L. ADLEMAN, A Method for Obtaining Digital Signatures and Public-Key Cryptosystems

In other words, the system, Perry insisted, was based on prime numbers, natural numbers divisible only by themselves and 1, and anyone who figured out how to crack the "prime factorization problem" would make a fortune. Perry went on like this for some time. I found it initially interesting, but not as interesting as my short stories on typography. I filed it away with the other pedantry that Perry and I occasionally regurgitated while binge drinking.

Later that week Perry and I convened to share some more frustration about our stagnant writing careers. While slurping our second round at our usual place in Adams Morgan, I noticed a CNN segment on the TV behind the bar. The closed captioning told the story of a small museum in Baltimore that had recently been given a curiosity on loan from an anonymous donor who the project curators were at pains to stress was involved "in the high-tech industry but not Bill Gates." The curiosity was a small prayer book which was, at auction, initially dated by its epigraphy to the time of the Crusades. It was recently discovered in a library near Jerusalem, the team was explaining, and its new owner realized almost immediately that it was a palimpsest, a work written on recycled parchment dating from an earlier time containing an earlier text.

The museum had shown success with a prior palimpsest, the Archimedes Codex, which revealed beneath the writing of a tenth century CE religious work a copy of an original manuscript by antiquity's most famous polymath, Archimedes of Syracuse. Archimedes flourished in the third century BCE in his home town of Syracuse, on the island of Sicily bordering the Ionian Sea. Then an independent city-state, Syracuse's most distinguished citizen became famous for developing siege weapons and a kind of sun-harnessing laser that forestalled the capture of Syracuse by the Romans.

In a noted flowering of posthumous apocrypha, Archimedes is said to have shouted 'Eureka' (I have found it!) naked in the streets of Syracuse after discovering while bathing the principle eponymously attached to him of the testability of differences in density between certain metals when measuring their displacement in water. This so-called Archimedes principle, and his 'method of exhaustion' to calculate the area under the arc of a parabola with the summation of an infinite series to provide a remarkably accurate approximation of pi were well-known accomplishments in his lifetime.

He moved to the intellectual capital of his day, Alexandria, Egypt, and while a fellow at the famous Library of Alexandria, he furthered mathematics by defining the spiral bearing his name, outlining formulae for the volumes of surfaces of irregular solids and developing with his friend Eratosthenes an ingenious system for expressing very large numbers. The Archimedes Codex, subjected by the museum team to digital processing of images produced by ultraviolet, infrared, visible and raking light, and X-rays had revealed even greater engineering and mathematical discoveries that had been rediscovered only in late Renaissance Europe.

The team of resolute archivist-glove and lab-coat wearing technicians proudly displayed a tiny book which was projected via camera onto a large screen in the studio. While the acquisition had only recently begun to be analyzed, they had already discovered some "amusingly puerile" poetry about the physical features of the inbred Greek dynasts who ruled Alexandria in Egypt in the wake of the Conquests of Alexander the Great. Dubbed the "Alexander

Codex," by the museum staff, it contained a long tirade by an unknown author about the crushing imperial taxes imposed at the time on the exportation of papyrus, a commodity more valuable to Alexandria for its absence in rival libraries and the resulting paucity of information distribution among competing cultural centers than as a thing in itself.

All very interesting. I had drawn Perry's attention to the show. We both sipped our scotch as we read the captioning. Somewhere between the third and fourth round one of the curators discussed a curious line by another, possibly distinct voice from within the substrata of the palimpsest. The tiny book was again projected via camera onto a large screen in the studio. Infrared light showed a very solid script in what one of the curators explained was Koine Greek – or 'common' Greek – the dialect of classical Greek that Alexander's conquests had spread from Southern Egypt to Italy and throughout the lands of the disintegrated Persian Empire to the Indus River. The image might have been in a language created by Tolkien for its familiarity with the vast majority of viewers, but the closed captioning gave form to a curator's translation. On the bottom of the screen, below a constant CNN news ticker and the day's financial numbers, a sentence flashed that was, like the rest of the faint text, at least 2300 years old: *"I have discovered a solution to the problem of the primes."*

I am aware that the Sophists have plenty of brave words and fair conceits, but I am afraid that being only wanderers from one city to another, and having never had habitations of their own, they may fail in their conception of philosophers and statesmen, and may not know what they do or say in time of war, when they are fighting or holding parley with their enemies. And thus people of your class are the only ones remaining who are fitted by nature and education to take part at once both in politics and philosophy.

—PLATO, Dialogue of Timaeus

5

Onesimus and I yesterday made offerings to Serapis. We first entertained the thought between us that we should inspect the foundation in advance of the dedication of The Master's funeral pyre. Having disturbed the pharaoh's peace by asserting to his carpenters and their overseer that such would be the crowd assembled on the appointed day that the pyre should be constructed near the broad plaza directly in front of the Soma and not in its planned location in the agora, we hastened to the nearby Serapeum to demonstrate our humility.

On the way, Onesimus and I recollected on The Master's genius in all matters relating to the mystery cults. Indeed, all academicians must be seen to embrace the festivals of the city. The Master had become adept at his sometime role of priest of the Temple of the Muses, as, of course, the Musaeum is known formally. Most academicians understood that the outward displays of the mystery cults - Greek, Egyptian and syncretic – were for the benefit of the masses in the capitals and cult centers throughout the remnants of Alexander's

Empire. Yet, The Master took the best of these traditions and used their secret rites as a palimpsest within which to conceal a necessarily clandestine universal collaboration. It was this dexterity in blending secret content with existing rites that secured as much of a future for the Alexandrian Project as is possible in these days without the Academy's greatest Light.

Several of the youngest students who had been standing about gawking at the preparations followed us into the house of Serapis. We soon realized that they were on an outing with none other than Aristarchus, who had taken over from the new Chief Librarian, Aristophanes, the onerous task of teaching introductory applied Pyrrhonian Skepticism. Noting our presence, Aristarchus smiled across the temple and bid us join the group. He then motioned to the custodians, that they might clear away the remaining supplicants. Having seen this display many times, we took a stance behind the semi-circle of students as Aristarchus delivered his lecture.

I thought back to my first visit to the Serapeum with the Master, when he displayed impish delight at the 'miracle' now about to be performed. Then, the Master had brought me at the height of the Festival, when the Serapeum was awash with the greased mechanical obeisance of Greeks and natives and visitors from throughout the Mediterranean.

Aristarchus, who by now has lent his name, somewhat to his approval I must say, to a person of severe criticism, was nevertheless an adept showman. He was, in a small way, famous, (or infamous) for gutting some passages of Homer and forcing the great poet into a grammatical schema of Aristarchus' design. Today we saw nothing of the *aristarch* about him. These demonstrations of practical philosophy were a welcome distraction, he often said, from his cloistered existence in the halls of literary criticism.

As the last supplicants filed past the colossal bronze doors, Aristarchus took a burning torch and lit a large brazier beneath the feet of Serapis. While the fire billowed, the reformed aristarch asked the students each to explain the purpose of the Serapeum. The usual responses: honor, protection, supplication, prostration, *certainty*. The fire continued to build in strength as the cavernous temple filled with the smell of burning animal fat.

"No," said Aristarchus, "all physical manifestations of the divine are designed to amaze and control."

The smartest (or boldest) students replied that even though a worldly purpose was served by a shared religion, surely a divine order governed the motions of the universe.

"Perhaps, and that is the pursuit of all Philosophy. But as skeptics in the spirit of Pyrrho and Timon of Phlius, whom we have read widely, we must meditate on the nature of things. Now, in this Temple of Serapis, if I tell you that we may offer the correct propitiations to the cult of Serapis and thereby incite a physical reaction or counter-reaction, what say you to this proposition?"

The students agreed that an experiment must be carried out to that effect.

"Indeed," said Aristarchus, "Indeed!" he smiled and turned to Onesimus and me. "Learned men of the Academy, won't you help us in our demonstration?"

"We would be delighted," I said, volunteering both of us.

"Fine. Now, Hesperos, I ask you to take this torch and light the smaller brazier here, to the left of the main fire, and you, young Onesimus, you stand ready to light the brazier to the right."

"Now, gentlemen, while they set about their task of propitiation, I ask you to consider, does Serapis care if one fire is lit or three?"

The students responded that the god should probably not concern himself with a trifle like that, but if pressed, they agreed that three were better than one.

"Indeed," said Aristarchus, "and why?"

The students, after intense deliberations, stated that because the fires were lit in his honor, that three worshipful deeds, though small, were better than one.

"Fine. Now, let us consider the current situation in light of the principles of *epokhe*, or suspension, as we have discussed recently. Let us take as a baseline that this burning fire, here in the center, does not please Serapis enough to cause him to manifest a reaction in the physical world. Now, my searchers, my *zetetikoi*, let us enter into a state of epokhe, in which, like the Stoics, we do not dogmatically assert that nothing can be known, but unlike the *hard* Stoics, we find ourselves observing a moment out of time, an epokhe, in which we suspend all judgments about all action and causes of action in the natural world. Let us assume that all realities are equally probable, that Serapis cares about fires lit in his honor, that he has a preference for how many are lit, and, most importantly, that Serapis exists at all. Can we, then, say that each reality is equally likely?

The students agreed that, in a 'somewhat heretical' state of epokhe, one must assume this.

"Fine, now, let us test these hypotheses. We have had one fire burning for some time, and we have had no reaction from Serapis. What conclusion then? Either Serapis does not concern himself with fire, he does not concern himself with a single fire, or he does not exist."

The students, deep in epokhic suspension, some, to our amusement, even closing their eyes, nodded agreement.

"Now, bold Hesperos, will you light the second fire?"

I placed my torch in the center of the brazier, producing a growing flame. The animal fat curdled and popped before me.

"Now, students, observe. Can you detect a change in the physical world?"

The students, a squadron of zetetikoi, strained to detect the motions of Serapis.

"It appears as if all the possibilities still hold. It is possible that Serapis is not yet concerned with our fires. Can we agree, then, that we have proven only that Serapis, if he exists, is not concerned with the combined effect of these two fires, either because he does not contend with fires or because these particular fires are not a sufficient enticement for him to show himself?"

The students again nodded. I saw Onesimus struggle to contain a yawn.

"Dear Onesimus," said Aristarchus, prodding him on the foot with the bottom of his torch, "shall we see if we can't rouse Serapis?"

"Of course," said Onesimus, plunging the end of his torch into the brazier.

The students stared at the fire with the anticipation most reserve for the Festival of the Ptolemaia.

"Ahh," said Aristarchus with eponymous drollery, "What have we concluded? It appears that we have shown only that –"

A monstrous metallic grinding sound from above echoed throughout the temple. The students stared in disbelief, jarred from the state of epokhe by the great arms of Serapis moving down to point bronze fingers at them. Behind us, the doors of the temple, 80 feet high, swung closed, throwing the chamber into near darkness. The only light came from the three billowing fires at the feet of the moving statue. Several students let out cries. One threw himself on the ground, shouting incantations to a foreign deity he had brought with him from some far corner of civilization.

The students all shouted that the proposition was proved. Indeed, Serapis did concern himself with fire, and indeed, he was moved by the presence of three fires rather than one or two. The question of his existence was no longer open to debate. As the students regained their composure, I motioned to Onesimus to wipe the smirk from his face.

"Now, my zetetikoi, from your posture of skepticism, is that all we can say about Serapis?"

After some time, one student stepped forward. I later learned with pride that he was, in fact, a native Egyptian. Long dispossessed of his own pantheon he stood universally doubtful of the displays of any religion, including the gods of Hellas.

"It is possible, Aristarchus," said my countryman, "that all the propositions stand as untried, because this statue, this temple and its contents are not in communion with Serapis. That is to say, no action taken, at least here, can induce, represent or falsify the proposition."

Aristarchus smiled. "Indeed, sir, indeed. Shall we test this hypothesis? Gentlemen, will you snuff the fires?" Onesimus and I put out all three fires. The arms and fingers of Serapis retracted into their original positions as the midday sun began streaming in once more from the opening doors. "Let us test this new hypothesis."

Aristarchus led the students to the back of the statue. He removed a panel from the calf of Serapis. Inside, the aristarch's torch illuminated bronze pipes running the length of the statue. He then removed a bronze plate from the floor, showing similar bronze pipes running from the statue in the direction of the enormous doors of the temple. The students, all but the Egyptian, stood dumbfounded with wounded pride.

"Now, now," said Aristarchus. "There is no room for hurt feelings in natural Philosophy, especially in this, the ascendancy of the Stoics. But what have we learned? We have learned that we cannot always trust our eyes, and more importantly, we cannot always trust our passions. We must live life as it exists, but we must strive in this class and at particularly suitable moments, to enter into epokhe, a withholding of judgment. In this way, we may continue to see the world free of prejudice and preconception. Without actually claiming that we do not know anything, we must exercise a suspension of judgment or the withholding of assent. None of this implies that we have no rationale to choose one kind of action over another; rather, one kind of life or one kind of action cannot be definitively said to be the 'correct' life or action. Now, who would like to see how Serapis actually comes to life? We have a few moments before the hall fills again with the faithful."

The students pondered the words of the aristarch while he led some into a passage behind the statute that the more mechanically inclined might descend to the lower level of the temple, the second best place in Alexandria to witness the mechanical genius of the late Ctesibius, former master of the public works. It is possible this would be the first time many of these young people had witnessed the power of steam, connected to camshafts and gears, to transform bronze in repose into the living flesh of the divine. More out of nostalgia than interest I bid Onesimus follow me into the machinery below.

It is a reminder to me always how life continues, how young life can flourish unbounded by the weight of the past. Inspired by the pneumatic pumps and corroding gears and crankshafts, Onesimus devilishly suggested in front of the Egyptian student that I recount how a slave of as humble an origin as I became entangled in the study of mechanical devices. He finds the story amusing. Onesimus is of the class of young men who had odes sung to them as children. I came from the lower registers. I was taken with indigestion yesterday, much to the amusement of faithful Onesimus – no doubt due to the excessive show of piety - and only now record the story.

I realize and accept that I have taken on the Master's style, and nothing pleases me more than commanding an audience. I spoke in grand generalities of a close association with The Master. I spoke of mechanics and mathematics. I spoke of my own boyhood as a carpenter's assistant and Eratosthenes' frequent visits to my own master's workshop in the Egyptian quarter. At the height of my story, Aristophanes appeared in the hall with some friends in observance of the feast day, and I suspect, to observe the teaching style of Aristarchus.

Aristophanes joined us eventually and after some pleasant greetings and quite a good laugh about the character of the newest priestess of Aphrodite – she has apparently arranged for a torch-race in which *women* will ride on horseback! – we were drawn by the students once again into myths of creation.

"It is forgotten now," said Aristophanes, "How important to the prestige of the dynasty was the possession of Coele-Syria. Because it is now lost to us – if one cares of such territorial matters – we no longer desire it, but there was indeed a time when that scrap of land the Jews are so fond of and claim as their ancestral homeland stirred every passion, even within the Academy."

"It was a natural border, its possession has been sought since the time of Ramesses," I said, perhaps too proudly invoking a distant past with which, unlike the Greeks, I may justly consider myself linked. "But then again, it is a wasteland. I have been to Jerusalem, the only city worth seeing. The temple of the god of the Jews is a marvel but they make no show of hagiography. How their priests do not starve without the spectacle of the temple, which the supplicants cannot enter but must stand outside, is yet another marvel. And the stench! It's an arid place, like Raphia, but inland without the relieving breeze from the sea."

The crowd thickened around us. A dewy fog was forming through which whispers spread that the priestesses of Aphrodite were assembling near the Soma.

"You were there, were you not Hesperos, in Raphia," asked the Egyptian student blankly, staring past me hoping to glimpse the gyrations of Aphrodite's attendants.

"Yes, Raphia was the watershed, now forgotten, like the desire for Coele-Syria and Judea itself, wiped from memory or transmuted into a symbol of Serapis' love of the Ptolemies."

Another student, slightly more interested than his coreligionist, turned toward me.

"You were actually at the victory at Raphia? You actually saw it?"

"There was a small contingent of us who traveled with the court," I said. "Eratosthenes went as an observer. I followed him."

"Archimedes was there too," said Aristophanes. "Their ingenuity was of immense import in the great victory. The catapults and ballistae which survived are now rotting in the harbor, pushed into the sea and broken as filler for the perennial expansion of the palace complex."

"It is somehow fitting that the devices of such ingenuity support the palaces of our pharaoh, as they once supported his father's maintenance of his kingdom."

In a hushed tone, almost as an afterthought, Aristophanes said, "The application of knowledge by great men now supports our king's decadence. *The Academy has always had this relationship with the state.*"

This remark of Aristophanes struck a chord with me and has returned to me several times since. Perhaps it would be best to include those events that led to the development of the Project, for it was not developed in the ether. It, like the universe, had a prime mover. I am inclined now to recollect a brief correspondence I found among The Master's papers which were left in my keeping. I rediscovered these letters late last night, in the midst of my wakefulness.

The Master had written to his pharaoh about a new project, one that would come to define and shape his tenure at the Academy. Indeed, the Project inaugurated those pursuits for which he is so justly celebrated among initiates in the order he created from the artifice of the rites of the Mysteries of Eleusis. The discussion yesterday of the victory at Raphia as well as Aristophanes' indiscretion – could even he have been drunk in the early afternoon – merits its mention. It is dated shortly after The Master arrived in Alexandria, and I include his own copy here, at Onesimus' urging.

To the Pharaoh Ptolemy III Euergetes, the Lord of Light, the most wise, King of the Upper and Lower Nile, in the second year of his reign, third year of the 133rd Olympiad

By your grace, it is my custom to refer to you all questions whereof I am in doubt. Who can better guide me when I am at a stand, or enlighten me if I am in ignorance? To the recent dispatches written in the new way in which Seleucus II Callinicus has secreted his messages I believe the learned Archimedes and I have discovered an opening. I have brought this matter to the attention of the chamber and to your faithful servants Procopios and Polymius, who serve you loyally and wisely, my Lord, as attachés to the Academy. I am afraid that Polymius, (who is excellent in all respects as a man of expedition and probity on the battlefield), did not understand fully our request, and I believe Procopios, (of whom no man may say is not among the most adept advisors in your service), may find it a threat to his position. I must, therefore, prevail upon your wisdom and detain you once more from the reigns of state held taught so nimbly in your grip. Because your mind turns to these things like a true philosopher, I herein provide a detailed account of the progress.

Like all ciphers, the veil drawn over the recent dispatches uses as its key an arrangement of convenience to the sender and recipient. Your gracious funding of the mechanical shifter, which Polymius so dexterously manipulates and of which he is very fond, still benefits our endeavor. How he delights in cranking the handle until a recognizable word appears! The laborious task of aligning two alphabets and shifting them until order is brought to chaos is much hastened. Let us, for example, shift the alphabet 16 spaces:

A B C D E F G H I J K L M N O P Q R S T U V W X Y Z
k l mn o p q r s t u v w x y z a b c d e f g h i j

Let us assume this enciphered message:

F J E B U C O   Y Y Y   U K U H W U J U I

Using this method, from the gibberish in an almost Canaanite tongue, your own glorious name issues forth:

F J E B U C O   Y Y Y   U K U H W U J U I
p t o l e my   i i i   e u e r g e t e s

Recently Polymius has been deprived of the pleasures of willing words to appear from the cogs and crankshafts of the device. The new cipher, which he labeled *incipit* keys after their first few lines, have begun to employ a phrase denuded of all repeat letters, and the remaining letters of the alphabet are then placed in their proper sequence behind it. For example, let us assume, my lord, that the key agreed upon is the tiny name of the fallow claimant to the north, Seleucus Callinicus. The repeated letters removed, the beginning of the key is as follows:

S E L U C A I N

The resulting word is small, but effective (In code as in the affairs of men, wise lord, your name looms large, we are doubly blessed, both by the awe it engenders and its length itself: **PTOLEMYURGS**, an incipit nearly half again as long as that of the dog of Antioch's). The recipient need only apply the next letters in a known series to arrive at the first instance of the key:

S E L U C A I N B D F G H J K M O P Q R T V W X Y Z

The alphabet is then aligned beneath the key as follows:

S E L U C A I N B D F G H J K M O P Q R T V W X Y Z
a b c d e f g h i j k l m n o p q r s t u v w x y z

Many of these recent dispatches have also shifted the alignment an agreed upon number of spaces to add another layer of complexity. A shift of 16 spaces as before yields the following result:

S E L U C A I N B D F G H J K M O P Q R T V W X Y Z
k l m n o p q r s t u v w x y z a b c d e f g h i j

If you will permit a diversion; It is well known that your wisdom does not stop at the councils of war, and the fond memories I hold of our games of Senat during your coronation festival impel me to couch within a request of the utmost audacity and gravity a slight diversion along the lines in which you so excel:

```
OI CI UI F BYNI YYNBHZXNOHYHNI T
BXABRYDZMJ FITBUZFLHI RLMI OF
KZRKBOYHJ EYOI CI MFI OLYNI YJ B
ORGZRADUI RLBFBF HMFZCZRBKOY
DYZIRZYNBFI RLNI TORGRBTBFNI
LNI J OYI YOZRHZMYNBOFZURYNBD
CI DMI OAORYNBOFKZRKBXYOZRZM
XNOAZHZXNBFHI RLHYI YBHCBRI R
LCI DRZYQRZUUNI YYNBDLZI RLHI
DORYOCBZMUI FUNBRYNBDI FBMOG
NYORGZFNZALORGXI FABDUOYNYN
BOFBRBCOBHI RLYNEHXBZXABZMD
ZEFKAI HHI FBYNBZRADZRBHFBCI
ORORGUNZI FBMOYYBLJ DRI YEFBI
RLBLEKI YOZRYZYI QBXI FYI YZRK
BJ ZYNORXZAOYOKHI RLXNOAZHZX
ND  XAI YZ  LOI AZGEBZMYOCI BEH
```

The Seleucids, who disrespect even their own local gods, have nevertheless refined their practicalities. We may effectively apply the current device to the second stage of the decryption, but we must now laboriously attempt an unthinkable amount of attacks upon the true meaning of the message by placing every conceivable incipit at the head of the alphabet. One of only the few recent ciphers to be broken to any extent used a phrase so vile and putrid that the sender and recipient must be quite imbecilic in their hostility toward us. It was discovered only when young Aristophanes perused a current compendium of Seleucian argot recently seized and copied from a Rhodian cargo vessel.

I, Hesperos, add a comment here that I beg Onesimus to remind me to redact in later drafts of this manuscript, but I must now relate my amusement: The Master has scrawled in the margins exactly what that early decrypted key phrase was, a less than kind appraisal, untrue as far as I know, of the late pharaoh's unnatural interest in beasts of burden. Soldiers' humor may not have the polish of Theocritus but the length and employment of so many uncommon letters is a credit to cryptography. I digress, as is usual:

The text of the latest intercepted dispatch is no doubt already known to you through the usual channels, and I will not repeat it here. Let us use the text above, a text worthy of the imagination employed in the high arts of encryption and decryption which now fly with you across the landscape of Judea. You may desire to pause now, my lord, and attempt the decoding of the message above, a skill easily found in those born to rule, unraveling as they must the hidden thoughts of men. Not only is the process of decoding these messages difficult, but it must take some time to encode them, a fact that may run to the advantage of our vanguard, even now as you march to Anatolia.

The message that was sent to you through Polymius and Procopios took us a full two months to reveal, and that was only after your faithful servants deigned to share with us some of their intelligence gathered at the northern court. A chance remark by Polymius about the low birth of one of Seleucus' commanders gave us the clue. Having at the Musaeum no current biographical information at all about our adversaries, it was a precious insight into the vast stores of that type of information your loyal servants have accumulated from all continents for all time. The local name of that commander's city's patron deity gave us the clue, and it was the delight of Polymius that, the device so adjusted, his turn on the crankshaft should reveal the message that you have already received.

I have made the point of outlining the process here so that you might better appreciate the need for rapid testing of each possible configuration of the incipit and, perhaps even more importantly, the rapid enciphering of our own secure messages with a new code of my own design. The next pages contain a list of supplies and a request for the payment of additional personnel. These persons will not be exposed to the contents of the messages, but will aid only in the fashioning of a specific piece of the new apparatus, brought together under the *protection* of your loyal servants Polymius and Procopios. I ask also that I might redirect the efforts of other men of the Academy to your service, as is prudent.

Your wisdom, which is unbounded and unrivaled only by that patience which I have so sorely tried, is the glory of Serapis.

> -Your *Most* Loyal Servant
> Eratosthenes, Head Librarian
> > *By way of trusted Leontius who resides in the care of Apollo*

Such was the state of affairs when Eratosthenes first arrived here. I laugh aloud when I remember the formality of his writing, but he knew better than I how to traverse the winding mountain road bordered on one side by the abyss of sycophancy and the chasm of jealous suspicions and on the other the villas of aspiration nestled in the slopes of Olympia. Onesimus is now "hooked," as his generation says, on the correspondence, and eagerly awaits the pharaoh's reply. It took me some time to find it this morning. The Master's papers, once so meticulously ordered, bear the stamp of their recent hasty disorganization. The pharaoh's brief reply in full:

To the Head Librarian, Alexandria.

This letter has reached my secretaries at Jerusalem. I am personally overseeing a much-needed renovation of their temple complex (and the construction of a humble edifice to honor my family's connection to divine Alexander) and will be detained some few more weeks here. I have sent bold Xanthippus north to Tyre and Damascus that he might provide further intelligence on the Seleucian force.

You have adopted the proper course, dear Eratosthenes. I share your esteem for my agents gifted to *your service* at the Academy, as your service is service to the state. You will by now have received the bulk of your request from noble and loyal, if suspicious, Polymius and Procopios, who were told by my agent that this was not the fulfillment of that same request which their refusal to grant was circumvented, but that I was in possession of knowledge from the god of the Hebrews that granted me prescience!

As for your choice of personnel, I laud your caution. Let them divide up the labor, as you have suggested, so that no one person may understand into what sort of service they are pressed. I leave it to your judgment how this shall be accomplished and what men of the Academy should be given access to the undertaking.

You will forgive the late arrival of my own written response, but I wished to reply in kind. Without the aid of your – preliminary – device, I was detained in my answer, making an educated guess a quarter way through due to my familiarity with the passage (I appreciate your difficulties; should this have been a note with abbreviated place names and coded battle tactics, I would be utterly lost!):

X F Z K Z X O Z H O H I L Z G I R L X Z A D C O E H
O H I K N O A L J E Y Y N B O F A Z D I A Y D O H E
R S E B H Y O Z R B L

Plato is a fitting choice and his sentiment is proven here. But using a shift so obvious as my position in the dynasty is careless, as careless as a shift representing the number of times our embassies have been shunned and our treaties broken.

The blessings of Serapis and my eternal father, Ammon.
-Ptolemy

Onesimus has just broken the cipher – what imagination he has with the organization of letters, a regular Callimachus! We have found The Master's reply, and I include it here:

To the Pharaoh Ptolemy III Euergetes, the Lord of Light, the most wise, King of the Upper and Lower Nile, in the third year of his reign, fourth year of the 133rd Olympiad.

By your grace, I appeal to your mercy and patience once more. The supplies were thankfully met, and generous beyond all reckoning. We have relocated our workrooms to a larger hall, and we have constructed a new device that is capable of constantly shifting and implementing keys based on phrases and scraps of information your loyal servants Polymius and Procopios have, through your largesse, now begun sharing with us. We have trebled the speed at which we decode most dispatches. Still some remain veiled to our most vigorous attempts. We therefore have constructed two more identical devices, which are dedicated to those dispatches which your loyal agents have identified by the circumstances of their interception as of particular value.

Still, there is one dispatch that eludes all attempts, and confounds the spinning arms of Polymius, who has grown frustrated and no longer delights in his old pastime. Procopios was at first concerned that the informant had copied it incorrectly, or worst that he had been compromised and was now being given gibberish to absorb us in inefficiencies, a dire reality indeed, indicating as it might a breach of the identity of our agents. But through that same informant some weeks later we received a message coded in the familiar way and of usual import, the contents of which you are already well aware. The second letter describes a most recent and confirmed event, and we can therefore, I believe, lay aside our fears of exposure.

We continue to work on the unknown cipher. Due to the gravity of the problem, and for the glory of your kingdom, I have asked for and received the welcome addition of several men of the Academy. In addition to Archimedes, our effort is strengthened by the presence of the renowned engineer Ctesibius, the mathematician Philo of

Byzantium, Abdaraxus and Nicomedes. Conon of Samos, your court Astronomer, due to his affinity for large quantities of data, has been of immense help owing to his methods of creating a special store of information, which have been nimbly adapted to our shared project by the young Diocles and Apollonius of Perga. Even ancient Callimachus, who is glad of a respite from the criticism of Apollonius of Rhodes and still professes to "abhor all common things," has adapted his catalog to the project in an insight we now call frequency analysis.

I believe our clandestine society has lit upon a tentative method of decoding the unknown cipher. I have instructed the disparate workmen in the fashioning of yet another new device which will tabulate the relative frequency with which various letters are used. It is my hope that this will make the incipit of the key as irrelevant as if the encoder had used a meaningless jumble of letters and a shift of an arbitrary number of places. Again, prevailing upon your wisdom and grace, the specific request is contained herein.

>   -Your *Most* Loyal Servant
>   Eratosthenes, Head Librarian
>   *By way of trusted Leontius who resides in the care of Apollo*

In this letter lay the foundations of the real Project, several years before the famous lecture, thus meriting its inclusion. Onesimus, as ever resplendent in the childish quest for axial moments, has at last found one here, in print, in the Master's own hand.

We have just now located the pharaoh's reply, which was inconsequential, save for suggesting support and praise for the enterprise. It is obvious from the brief response that the Pharaoh must have at some time shortly before or shortly after writing indicated through other channels his interest in inspecting the device himself, for he writes with the excited anticipation of the *extraepistolarian*, one who knows or expects soon to know more than that which he sets down in writing. This is a word of my own creation, in the style of Aristophanes and the late Callimachus, whose advice, *mega biblion, mega kakon*, was refulgent in the pharaoh's reply.

These letters were written at the time of my first association with The Master. Onesimus has guessed as much, but his interest is piqued, he is "hooked" upon the specifics of that first meeting. It is of little import to posterity how it came to be that I became well acquainted with The Master and his mechanical inventions, but it is of great meaning to me. The indulgences of an old man and intrepid curiosities of a young man impel me forward, headlong into the abyss of memory.

My history before Alexandria was brutish, but not free of achievement. Generations before my mother had been raped by a Greek in a reed thrush on the banks of the Nile, my ancestors worked for a noble Macedonian family near Oxyrhynchus. After my family's disgrace we fled north to Memphis. When I came of age, I had little chance of doing much more than they had done for generations. At fourteen, when I was old enough to be useful as a laborer, I became expert in working the water pump. For eighteen hours a day save feast days, I would rise with the rays of Ammon and, later, Helios.

I soon realized that the pump could be rendered more efficient by the addition of a counterweight at one end, and worked late into the evening, (and once secretly on a feast day), gathering stones and fastening them with reed-twine into a large bundle which I affixed to one end of a long pole. I then balanced the pole between a pivot and fastened that to two large acacia branches. The overseer discovered my handiwork and took credit, but it wasn't long before I came to the attention of Amasis, the estate manager, who demanded even greater innovations. It is the way of the field that the better one does, the worse off one finds oneself. Perhaps it is no different at the Academy.

I worked alongside an older slave, I can't remember his name now, but his face was as worn as the cliffs of Dendera. He was known as a troublemaker. He became jealous of this special treatment and resolved to sabotage my success. One afternoon, Amasis, as much a native as I, was proudly showing off "his" new invention to our employer. He had promised a new pump that could irrigate the fallow hillsides rolling away from the Nile Valley. I soon realized through some trial and much error that a series of pumps would be required and set to work under the guidance of Amasis knowing the credit would be his alone.

The first pump pulled water directly from the Nile and propelled it along parallel earthen aqueducts. One of these channels branched out at regular junctions into the current fields in the traditional way. The second used the pressure from the weighted pump to force water through mud-brick pipes set down at a gentle gradient and at considerable expense. This pipe emptied into a cistern and was, in turn, propelled upward to another level where the process was repeated. It was unknown to me then, and to our employer, that this technology was widespread in Greece and was received wisdom beneath the streets of Babylon. There is a reason why the pharaohs refer to *eternal* Egypt. We have not in our pantheon a goddess of change.

We headed for the summit of the waterworks, beyond a gentle rise in the flood plain, where the final pump would press the precious waters of the Nile into the palm of the land beyond her reach. We found there only a pile of rocks and sticks, a pyre on which I watched the immolation of my hopes reflected in the fiery Greek features of our employer. I was accused and beaten. The other slaves were beaten too. I could do nothing to protest my treatment. How could I tell them that I had prayed that the waterworks succeed and how, in the face of such failure, how could I explain that I had helped design it and would be the last boy in Egypt to wish its destruction? Then as now the natives are always suspected, and the Greek landowner, who had invested a considerable sum in mud-brick and labor, threw Amasis out, alleging sympathies with the small but fervent native resistance. I heard later that he replaced us all with Greeks and was ruined within a year when they embezzled his small fortune and sailed for Attica.

I had been told by the rumblings of other natives that someone with a mechanical cast of mind might find work in Alexandria. After several weeks begging and eating dirt and licking fish bones in old Rhakotis, the Egyptian quarter, I was once again reunited with Amasis, who somehow recognized me under the filth. He had found employment with a shipwright near Lake Mareotis repairing the shallow draft boats that sold the wealth of Egypt to the Mediterranean. I told him I wanted nothing to do with him. He had deserted me, I said, taking all the credit during the preparations and casting all blame on the insolent slaves who had conspired to embarrass him and ruin his employer. I resisted for a day or two, but consuming the last of the good graces of the refuse piles beyond the city gates I found myself accepting working as Amasis' 'apprentice'. Our invention soon surfaced and *we* once again made improvements, this time to rigging configurations, which brought us some small recognition with the owner of the boat-works, who promptly marketed the concepts to his colleagues. This, Amasis, whose contribution was not miniscule, took in stride, and we soon were pressed to solve a problem that seemed to have no answer.

Seagoing ships and boats, until that time, were more expensive for the Greeks to import than those of only slightly inferior quality built locally. Ship-works on the Mediterranean shore constructed vessels for the merchant trade throughout the scattered points of Alexander's old empire. They carried Egypt to the Aegean, to Spain, even to the Black sea. Boat-works on Lake Mareotis provided smaller craft for the Nile, which can only be entered from the sea at acceptable risk when the Nile is at its lowest. The passage from the sea is impossible during the inundation, when Isis spreads her waters at the command of the Pharaoh. This had kept Egypt nearly secure from invasion by sea for thousands of years. As I later learned, invaders could and did establish successful beachheads in the north or when they hazarded the overland route through the Sinai in the northeast. As a slave of sixteen, I knew only the problem at hand, that such a threat, this time from the Seleucids by a northeasterly overland route, had interrupted all delivery of precious wood from Judea, from Palestine, from Lebanon, from Coele-Syria. Just as our master had begun to profit from our more efficient rigging, the supply of wood for domestic boats and ships disappeared. The greatly reduced supply of lumber had halted production of ship-building in Alexandria.

At the time, and for time immemorial, Egyptian ships were giant hulks of fitted beams which fanned out gracefully parallel with the keel – I will not detain Onesimus, who with rolling eyes has slouched in his chair listening to my reverie of the commodities market and shipbuilding in the time of Euergetes. It was understood then, that a solution had to be found, and that a much more efficient method of manufacture was the only answer. Again, without knowing it, I borrowed from the Greeks. A fair trade: their industry for our wealth, our history for their gods.

Amasis and I set to work on the foolhardy task of engineering a shallow draft boat that was made of a rib-like structure, emanating in the keel, terminating at the deck line and tied together with cross-bracing. It truly was an independent invention. Amasis and I had never seen the interior of a Greek vessel, yet that's exactly what we developed, but for the shallow Nile which few foreign vessels had even known. That invention saved the boat-works. Foreign ships were still imported for commerce on the Sea, but I do believe we single-handedly saved the dockyards on Lake Mareotis.

Onesimus has that impertinent habit of young men of constantly rolling the eyes – perhaps he is epileptic. No matter, he will be old one day and young men will roll eyes at him.

Of course, this invention profited our employer greatly. He was heralded in the taverns, and even a few students from the Academy came to discuss our methods with him. Amasis expected that he would be given some credit, and truly some of it was his due. Expecting a visit from scholars of the Academy, our employer instead sent us on a mission down the Nile to deliver one of these boats to a barley merchant in Memphis. It was the first time that I had seen Memphis since I had been chased out almost four years earlier. It was then that I learned of the true fortunes of our old employer. The story at the tavern went that the absconders were cursed by the gods and had had their ship sunk in the Gulf of Corinth. Our old employer, utterly destroyed, ran off with a native girl to Gaza, where they opened a brothel and he developed a case of madness. Amasis says it must have been a disease of the lower organs but whatever the result, he apparently died of neglect when his young wife left him. For all we knew, the landowner and his loyal Greek staff might still be breaking the backs of young Egyptians, his rebuilt irrigation system nurturing the cargo which our sturdy, light little boat would turn into a fortune for the gentlemen farmers and merchants of Memphis. I chose to believe the story told at the tavern and considered the matter closed.

Upon our return, Amasis and I learned of the academician's visit. Apparently, these men of the Musaeum had been joined by some mid-level court officials, and our employer had negotiated an exclusive contract with the palace. Our names were never mentioned. Our employer chose an early retirement. His son took over the daily management and became even more of a cutthroat than his father. I believe this soured Amasis toward Greeks for all time, and I look back now at the impossibility of his becoming anything other than that which he became. At the time we commiserated as equals, and set to work that we might one day expose the father, outwit the son and own our own boat-works – a dream to which I was still committed when another academician paid a visit to the now-famous boat-works on Lake Mareotis.

Young Onesimus now urges me to return to The Master, which I was almost prepared to do. As his eyes rolled just now they fell upon another of The Master's letters I had rediscovered this morning.

To the Pharaoh Ptolemy III Euergetes, the Lord of Light, the most wise, King of the Upper and Lower Nile, in the third year of his reign, fourth year of the 133rd Olympiad

By your grace, your glories resound throughout the lands of Ammon. For you, whose bountiful kingdom is protected by your father Helios, whose wisdom and might is known beyond the Pillars of Hercules and the tribes of Asia, I humbly supplicate myself at the doors of the Temple of Serapis, who sustains Egypt through you and who is celebrated for his generosity.

Your grace was unmatched in your favorable impressions of our humble project. I have continued working along the outlines sketched some weeks ago. We have gained some purchase in the decryption of the new cipher. The pertinent pieces have been forwarded. Polymius and Procopios are now prepared to assert that the evidence supports your conclusion that the message is from Seleucus himself, intended for a recipient of close association *outside* his own territory.

Due to the delicacy both of the information and the position of the recipient, I must now prevail upon your continued generosity. Procopios believes, as I have come to, that your own government's communications must be safeguarded against interception and decryption by an intelligence sophisticated enough to develop this remarkable code and entrenched enough to embed within this message such details as only your closest courtiers should be aware.

While we work toward the complete unveiling of this *particular* message, I must humbly recommend that you adopt a broader policy of secrecy in government dispatches. It is on this topic that I have again included a detailed accounting of the proposed additional capacities I would like to incorporate into the new device.

As we have discussed, the studies of the frequency of repeated letters in messages have largely made the Seleucid shift-incipit cipher (and by extension our own similar methods) useless, and we had assumed that the advantage was ours. We can, for example, employ the device in placing probable values on letters used in code as frequently as they are used in plain text. We can then use a combination of this method and the device's ability to attempt many solutions to the key much more quickly than a room of scribes – to your valued courtier's continued, if mild, irritation. It is exactly because this new message resists this method that we believe it must employ a *variable* shift cipher.

It is our wish, and I believe I now speak for Polymius and Procopios, that our combination shift-incipit ciphers be supplanted in favor of this variable shift cipher. I believe this is the nature of the message now impenetrable to us. The details I lay out here in such a way as to honor the curiosity in all things displayed by our philosopher-king.

If this is indeed the method adopted, then let us assume that rather than the traditional shift of a singular alphabet, several shifts are used. Let us use as our secret text the name of the usurper and his inevitable fate should he deign to engage the kingdom with Ammon, Serapis and Ptolemy as its protectors:

s e l e u c u s c a l l i ni c us de f ea t ed

Traditionally, wise lord, we and our enemies have chosen a shift, perhaps with an incipit, perhaps not. As we have shown, the incipit now makes little difference, so we may simply use a plain alphabetic shift of a known number of places, 5 in this example:

a b c d e f g h i j k l mn o p q r s t u v w x y z
V ＼Λ X Y Z A B C D E F G HI J K L MN O P QR S T U

The message is then encoded and decoded after only five sequential tries or a maximum of twenty-five, (one configuration is simply one alphabet laid atop another with a shift of no spaces and is therefore useless):

s e l e u c u s c a l l i ni c us de f ea t ed
N Z G Z P X P N X V G G D I D X P N Y Z A Z V OZ Y

This was the genius and the efficiency of the first device, which could try each shift mechanically until Polymius drew words into being. The incipit added great difficulty, as did the changing value of the shift, but your wise largesse gave us the tools to uncover underlying meaning. What I believe we must do now is implement further lines of shifted alphabets. I next underscore the phrase with not one, but two or more alphabetic shifts:

```
a b c d e f g h i j k l mn o p q r s t u v wx y z
V WX Y Z A B C D E F G HI J K L MN O P QR S T U
Q R S T U V WX Y Z A B C D E F G HI J K L MN O P
O P Q R S T U V WX Y Z A B C D E F G HI J K L MN
```

It is both enthralling and maddening when we realized, as you have no doubt already done, that this method need not follow in sequential order. It would be easy enough to have a prearranged sequence employing a primary alphabet in the fifth position and a secondary in the tenth position and a tertiary in the twelfth as above. But it would be only slightly more difficult to remember a key which required changing the shift based on the conditional travels of the constellations in the sky, or the first letter of sequential (or non-sequential) passages of the dialogues of Plato, of which there are thousands. The basis for the keys, if not the keys themselves, wise lord, are quite literally infinite. The message in code so easily broken by the analysis of the repetition of the letters becomes exponentially complex. Instead of tidy repetitions (made obvious in longer passages but suggested here by the repeating l's in Seleucus' epithet), our coded message now appears as:

```
s e l e u c u s c a l l i  ni c us d e f e a t e d
N Z G U P X K I  S V B Z D I  Y QI  GY S A Z QO U T
```

The meaningful repetitions disappear and any emerging repetitions frustrate attempts to analyze their frequency, as we can no longer count on the decipherment of even one word to aid in the decryption of any another. We may well assume the message bears Seleucus' name with his epithet. In the original coding the decryption of these eight letters thus uncovered nearly a third of the message, from which other assumptions could be made. The new code renders each painstaking advance insular and atomic to the elemental whole.

As your superior wisdom no doubt informs you, our humble recognition of the problem suggests that the issue be given the highest priority. The small portion of the message deciphered through arduous trial and error further suggests three necessary and immediate courses of action. First, as I said, we must immediately suspend the use of the shift-incipit cipher as a matter of policy, as your grace pleases. Second, we must develop an even stronger cipher for our own use which is impenetrable to the enemy. I have made some improvements on this score with the help of a curious mathematical property that I will explain in detail in the presence of your royal personage. Third, and most important, we must detect the source of the enemy's knowledge concerning the progress of our decipherment which prompted the change in Seleucus' encryption policy. For my part, I wish to dismiss those contractors currently at work on the project who possess the ability to interpret the intended result of their labors, deduce the techniques built into the device and maintain the breadth of foreign commercial entanglements to relay those techniques to interested parties. As you have trusted in my judgment before, I will ask for that trust again as I remain for all time,

-Your *Most* Loyal Servant
Eratosthenes, Head Librarian, Director of the Musaeum
Delivered in person to his Excellency's chancellery, Alexandria

I therefore continue, at young Onesimus' urging, with the story of my first meeting with The Master; I, a native slave, poor and ignorant of the outside world and he, The Master, who brought forth the Light.

I would in the future make a machine, which would simultaneously print in printer's ink on paper any arbitrary arithmetical progression... and which would halt of its own accord, when the side of the paper was full up. After setting the first figure, all one has to do is to turn a handle.

—JOHANN HELRICH MÜLLER, a German engineer describing his conception of mechanized calculation, 1784.

6

Perry and I followed the progress of the Alexander Palimpsest via a live video feed their website offered of the preservation and recovery efforts. The conservators worked in a cleanroom where, the website explained, air quality, particle density and temperature were closely scrutinized. The manuscript's new home was a far cry from the dusty exposure it had seen for centuries in the old library where it had been found between two deteriorating bookcases. It now rested in a climate-controlled vault where archivists, papyrologists, physicists, paleographers, lexicographers, historians, translators, mathematicians, digital-image experts, representatives of Hewlett-Packard who donated the scanning technology, and museum officials stood watching the images on the screen.

The room was set up in assembly-line fashion. A large table held the palimpsest itself. Conservators skilled in removing ancient binding and adhesives painstakingly severed each page from the next and passed the liberated sheet to another station, which treated each page with a compound intended to stop the growth of the mold covering a significant portion of the text. The next station, on a much larger table, held a bulky machine capable of focusing light at various wavelengths. The majority of the action was a hovering camera making painstaking passes over each page, sometimes taking up to several hours to render a high resolution image in any of several false color spectrums. That image would then be displayed on the large screens in the room and uploaded to the project's website. The images themselves weren't immediately revelatory. They simply showed the prayer book text in bold relief with a tantalizing hint of an underlying script beneath. Every few days, after a page had been scrubbed through spectrographic devices used to lull the ancient text to the surface, a translation would be posted alongside a false-color image of the page.

After only a few days the project had concluded that they were dealing with some sort of personal history interspersed with copies of letters and journal entries of others. The team was, for example, very excited on day five of viewing the feed that they had discovered a hint of a quote of Theocritus, a poet from antiquity. Day six produced two pages that discussed the interior layout of a dormitory and what appeared to be a description of an ancient symposium, or a kind of learned drinking binge. These discoveries made headlines in conservationist publications, but, beside the brief exposure on the news segment that caught our attention, little mention was made of these extraordinary new insights into antiquity.

The very name of the Alexander palimpsest, given it informally, was a misnomer. The Koine Greek did indeed date the text to a specific historical epoch. The project's historians had dated it to between 300 BCE and 300 CE, a span of 600 years in which much political upheaval had occurred from Britain to the Sahara and from Spain to India. The author or authors of the palimpsest, by the very virtue of their literacy, were likely to have been scribes in one of the centers of learning in antiquity. The team bristled with excitement at the most attractive option, that at least one of the writers was resident at the Great Library of Alexandria, and would therefore have been witness to much of the pivotal moments of the age.

Built by Ptolemy II, the son of one of Alexander the Great's most trusted generals, the library was infamous for its acquisition strategy. At the height of its power, Alexandria was the lynchpin of a maritime system of commerce that facilitated trading between the far reaches of Alexander's old empire. Though governed ostensibly by the Greek Ptolemaic Dynasty, Egypt was still very much a land of ancient traditions. One might find in Alexandria native Egyptians with roots stretching back thousands of years into the age of the Pyramids. Carthaginians traded with Romans, Macedonian Greeks with Seleucids from the extinguished Persian Empire. Alexandria stood during this time as a crossroads for the ideas of antiquity, its great lighthouse guiding foreign ships into its gentle harbor. To ensure the ascendancy of his library, Ptolemy II issued an edict that all ships entering the port of Alexandria be searched for books. Scrolls from

Babylon, Syracuse, Crete, Cilicia, Cappadocia, Edessa, Susa and Ecbatana were greedily copied and interred at the library. From Athens, Ptolemy III requested permission to borrow the original scripts of Aeschylus, Sophocles and Euripides, for which the Athenians demanded the enormous amount of fifteen talents as guarantee. Ptolemy III happily paid the deposit, over eight hundred pounds of silver, but kept the original scripts for the library. That Athens could not avail herself of a force to compel their return speaks to the power of Alexandria over Athens and much of the Hellenistic world.

Still, some observers maintained, it was possible that the author was associated with another of the great libraries of antiquity, the Library of Pergamon, which flourished at approximately the same time as its rival library in Alexandria. Formed by the Attalid Kings – others of Alexander's successors ruling in what is now modern-day Turkey – most historians agree as a counterpoint to the Ptolemaic model, the Library of Pergamon contained nearly 200,000 scrolls, almost half as many as its rival. When the Ptolemies stopped exporting papyrus, partly because of competitors and partly because of shortages, the Pergamenes invented a new substance to use in codices, called Pergamon or parchment after the city. This was made of fine calfskin, a predecessor of vellum and paper.

Because the Alexander palimpsest was written on parchment and not papyrus, a Pergamene origin became an attractive theory, but many supporters of an Alexandrian provenance argued that the work was almost certainly a copy of an original, though quite possibly contemporaneous with the life of the author, and whatever the original material, it had later been recorded using the then most economical material available to the copyist. Thus, they argued, the author could have lived and written his account in Alexandria, the copy having been made later at Pergamon. Radio carbon dating, used initially to absolutely confirm its authenticity, could only place the text within the early Hellenistic age (from circa 300 BCE – 100 BCE). Due to the margin of error inherent in carbon dating, the exact century of the text could not be determined.

The eighth day of our subscription was another snowy Saturday during which Perry and I sat braced against the cold Washington weather in a bar, scotches in hand and laptops tuned to the conservatory work. As we sipped and talked of plot angles, one of the conservators, hovering over computer monitors in a corner of the room, could be seen waving to another conservator, who then waved to a small contingent of others standing on the opposite side of the clean room. In the excitement, everyone in the room turned toward and then began approaching the conservator near the computer screen. The feed could be tuned between the work in the room and the specific page currently under examination. Perry switched the image and we, and the perhaps hundreds or so other online subscribers, were now looking at the same image the conservators were viewing.

The page was shown in the usual fashion, bathed in white light. A conservator used a small pointer to draw the others' attention to specific words throughout the page. Of the several the conservator indicated, Perry and I soon realized that they were all the same word. Sensing the importance of such a gathering of the project members at one spot in the conservation room, Perry, possessing a near-eidetic memory, scrawled the word on a cocktail napkin as best as possible given the deterioration of the text and his unfamiliarity with Greek:

We continued watching for some time. Eventually we switched back to the wide-angle feed, continuing to sip our scotch.

"What do you think that means?" Perry rotated the napkin toward me.

"I have no idea. It certainly seemed to get their attention. I don't know much Greek either. If it was just Modern Greek we could probably find a translator online. Let me check."

I tried several times to match Perry's handwritten word to various Greek letters. The online translators kept shooting out gibberish. I explained to Perry that it wasn't surprising. A computer has to have perfect input to provide a translation. A non-native reader of a language written in the Latin alphabet, for example, might see the word 'translate' but they would only be recording images of letters, in essence logograms, not letters meaningful in themselves. A native reader of English would recognize a 'D' whether handwritten or typed in any number of fonts and typefaces. A non-native reader might detect similarities, but lack the certainty to distinguish a handwritten 'D' from a hand-written 'O,' depending on the quality of the penmanship.

Perry and I decided to quit for the night. He shuffled back to his apartment and I to mine. It was several days until we realized the significance of the small cluster of archivists around the computer screen that evening.

Various writing projects consumed our time. Perry had met frustration with his graduate thesis and suggested a few drinks might re-center his mind. We met again at the same bar and, drinks in hand, brought up the live feed of the conservators of the Alexander Codex. Though the project's website was unchanged, the live feed was no longer available. In its place was a message stating an "institutional change" had directed the cessation of the live video service and subscription fees would be refunded. Updates would be posted regularly for the public, it said, and parties with "an academic interest in the palimpsest" might contact the museum for more information.

Our curiosity mounted; conspiracy theories shot between us like the clanking of the ice in our glasses. The word, we decided, must have been very unusual. Perry suspected it was a proper name, identifying the manuscript with a known historical person.

"What if it said 'Archimedes?' Or, it said, 'by my own hand, Archimedes,' I mean, what if they discovered it was in Archimedes' own handwriting?"

I responded that it might indeed have said 'Archimedes,' that it would be an exciting discovery, but would have no consequences other than skyrocketing the popularity of the project and the value of the manuscript. What museum wouldn't want to discover that they were working on a manuscript written by a lion of antiquity; what owner would not beam with pride that he, in recognizing the shrewdness of his purchase, had secured an actual artifact connecting him and his collection with the preeminent scholar of the ancient world?

I was certain it must be a word out-of-place. That would explain the attention given to the repetition of the word itself rather than the content of the page.

Perry, given to extraordinary credulity for a man of his intellectual ability, decided it must then literally be a word-out-of place, an anachronism. Perhaps it said, 'airplane,' or 'nuclear energy.' Eager to tamp unsubstantiated enthusiasm, I argued that it was unlikely there was a ready-made single word in Koine Greek for these concepts.

Perry said that he did know someone, a professor at school, who might be able to help. We were to take the napkin – yes, he said, he still had it – to this *éminence grise*, a semi-retired professor emeritus who might, just might understand the meaning of the word-picture Perry had scrawled days earlier. Perry sent his professor friend an email and received after another round of scotch, a brief reply. He was very interested, he said. He had not followed the live stream, but was very interested in the manuscript, having followed the team's public releases and the few early scholarly articles to have been published. He was available the next day. We were to arrive at 1PM, on a Sunday, when, we were told, he would be happy to shed some light on our cocktail napkin.

Now have we journeyed to a spot of Earth
Remote – the Scythian wild, a waste untrod.
And now, Hephaestus, thou must execute
The task our father laid on thee, and fetter
This malefactor to the jagged rocks
In adamantine bonds infrangible;
For thine own blossom of all forging fire
He stole and gave to mortals; trespass grave
For which the gods have called him to account,
That he may learn to bear Zeus' tyranny
And cease to play the lover of mankind.

—AESCHYLUS, Prometheus Bound

7

I was content to remain silent. The academicians had come and gone, and the palace was well enough pleased with our old employer's son's satisfaction of his contractual responsibilities. The days were long but gave form and purpose to our lives. Amasis and I continued refining our methods, and Amasis had long since stopped treating me as the slave from shores of the Nile he had wronged years before. We gradually became equals in shared purpose.

I spent what little free time I had in the draftsman's office pouring over schematics, enveloping myself in the artistry of hull forms and hydrodynamics. I built small models and tested them on Lake Mareotis. I pulled models at high speeds until they capsized. I loaded models until they sank. I used bellows to fill sails until the canvas tore from the masts. All of these tests I recorded in notebooks in my own disjointed argot Greek – a code, so natural to a boy of self-education and so crude to accomplished writers, I believe only I can decipher to this day! Our new employer watched all this with amusement. Idle and now rich, he had that curious failing of inherited wealth - he was incapable of suspecting a poor man of great ambitions.

I suppose my interest in mathematics and engineering – how limited was I then! – formed an early sort of apotropaic magic to ward off the evils that dissatisfaction and alienation had sired in the interior and in the dark corners of the Egyptian quarter. The newly crowned pharaoh, Ptolemy III Euergetes, had shrewdly devised his own apotropaic celebration designed to ward off the very same evils and announced that, nearly two years into Amasis' and my toiling anonymously near the docks of Lake Mareotis, the season of the Ptolemies' grandest festival, the Ptolemaia, would once again fall upon the great city. All Alexandria assumed this Ptolemaia would be subdued, the diversion of funds from public spectacle recently having been undertaken in support of Ptolemy's campaign against Seleucus. Many were the old men of the docks who remembered where they were when news of the first Ptolemy's death reached them, when their anticipation of the traditional coronation festival which became the quadrennial Ptolemaia boiled in the cauldron of their collective imagination. That first true Ptolemaia of Ptolemy II was a moment immortalized in men's minds – Greek and native alike - the memory a tenth muse to even the meanest of the pharaoh's subjects.

The Egyptian quarter was soon awed when word spread that the palace sent envoys to our employer to arrange for the construction of ten large hulls which would be built with our unique shallow draft and keel design. It was clear to me then how unusual it was that the specifications should call for the shallow drafts which were our specialization but I kept this to myself. The work order, which I was permitted to read, indicated that the hulls would then be ported overland to the great harbor where they would be fitted out in the shipyards and prepared for the festival to be held in six months' time. The order was immense and required the activation of every native workman in the Egyptian quarter who was not already engaged in the pharaoh's service. For sixteen hours a day, men sawed trunks into timber, steamed and bent planking into serpentine lengths joined together and covered with pitch. Women and girls, long valued as craftsmen in their own right in the old dynasties, were once again mobilized in the production of rope and the manufacture of canvas.

The hulls gradually projected like fingers of the gods pressing down upon the banks of Lake Mareotis. Hulls one and two were almost double the size of the others – themselves super-galleys equipped with twenty banks of oars against the usual seven, and Amasis was given an unusually privileged position in their design. They were to be the flagships of the Ptolemaia spectacle. Their superstructures would include a marble temple to Serapis and a bath complex complete with heated floors and several pools for ritual ablution. In the great frenzy of the construction I was given some responsibility with the overseer of a particular stage of hull number six, and instituted some of my observations in its construction. In the third month of construction, visitors from the palace exercised a provision in the contract to change the dimensions of the eight smaller but by no means unimpressive ships to be nearly fifty percent larger than planned and accommodate twelve banks of oars instead of the planned ten. This sent our draftsmen into despair, as the ratio of keel to sidewall would almost certainly exceed the limits of seaworthiness.

I recognized my moment and quickly drew attention to the improvements I had made throughout the construction of my hull that made the adaptation of the adjusted plans possible. I was told that I would explain these improvements to an assembly of my superiors.

On the appointed morning, my heart beating with apprehension and pride, I watched as a crowd of palace officials walked toward me. Though my Greek overseer had demanded that I explain my improvements to him, he stared blankly at the sketches I had prepared, no doubt regretting his decision to incorporate those innovations which now brought him attention he was not sure he could wield to his benefit.

The delegation addressed the overseer and the draftsmen and seemed to be pleased enough with the vagueries I had planted with my superiors. As they began to move away from the hull satisfied with what they heard and in general agreement that these innovations should be extended as best as possible to the entire project, one plainly dressed man stepped forward and addressed me directly. I couched my answers diplomatically in deference to the overseer, the draftsmen and the owner of the boat-works. My heart pounded with frustration that I could not be recognized and fear that I might be discovered and alienated, dismissed or made to disappear as an embarrassment to my Greek employers. The man then turned again and asked a more pointed question to my overseer, which he stumbled through with the obscurantism that I have since realized is the hallmark of mediocrity. I was addressed again directly, and this time I could not hold my tongue. Though I did not ascribe them to myself, I explained in detail the improvements, the interior structure of the ribs, the hydrodynamics of the hull design, and the relative ease with which the existing substructure might absorb the stresses of the new design. The man seemed satisfied with the answer and moved toward the group, which moved as a clattering whole back toward the offices of the boat-works.

That afternoon my overseer tried to beat me, and as I was now a young man of nineteen and stronger than my middle-aged overseer, I was able to repel his attack. He approached me later in the draftsmen's room that night with two Greeks, both of them armed with clubs used to beat out rope. One hit me across the shoulder, sending searing pain down my back. I was flush in a moment with the realization that they meant to kill me. I kicked one Greek in the sternum, knocking him over a drafting table. The other Greek, smelling strongly of Mareotian wine, cursed my native heritage with an oath I still remember whenever I smell the taverns in the docklands. He swung at me, just missing my kneecap. His club crashed into the table, knocking tools to the floor.

Fury seized me, the fury of denied opportunity, the fury of class bias and ignorance. Surprising myself, I took a strong hold of the Greek and drove his face into the tabletop. I must have broken his nose because he started screaming and swearing even more oaths. As he cupped his bloody face in his hands I saw the other Greek pick up a long chisel in one hand and a maul in the other. It was a moment of clarity of decision I will never forget. A draftsman's square was within my reach. I picked it up and squeezed it so tightly that I drew my own blood. The bloody Greek still closest to me drew back his fist. I took the end of the square in both hands and swung at his face, knocking into his left eye with the elbow of the square. The other eye gave me a look of pure hatred. I slashed at his face again, and immobilized him with a kick to his knees.

The remaining Greek looked at me with surprise. I cannot remember what racial oaths I muttered to him as I slashed his face open with the square, but I will never forget the look in his eyes moments before I cut them out of him, a Greek, another human being. The overseer fled, but the rage within me propelled me to catch up with him. Chisel in hand I caught him by his tunic and swung him into a wall. He begged with me to be merciful. I held the chisel to his throat and took the stonemason's position with the maul in my other hand, prepared to sculpt his living flesh. I pressed the chisel into his neck, forcing some blood to trickle down its blade. I was possessed by all of the strength and none of the wisdom of Helios or Ammon, but something made me stop. In the overseer's face I saw the manufactured shame of my family, our exile, my abuse in Memphis, the filth I had to endure here, the constant usurping of my intellect, the derision flung from Greek to native, from conqueror to conquered. I stopped and stared at that face lit by moonlight through the windows in the drafting room. I pulled back the maul and dropped the chisel on the floor. I let him run away. He fled with only a cut on his neck. I fled, crying, into the Egyptian quarter, with a wound so raw that I feared it might never heal.

Onesimus is appalled. So should he be. As a man of the Academy and a Stoic I abhor violence. But I remind young Onesimus that I was not always an academician, and hunger and neglect breed the ignorance which, as the Roman apologists say, is the *casus belli* of the chief mischief of the world. As Onesimus has guessed, the academician who addressed me that day was the late Master, Eratosthenes, Head of the Library of Alexandria. On the same day that I met my mentor and the Light of the World, I drove a draftsman's square through the skulls of two Greeks with the rage of Achilles avenging Patroclus. Onesimus nods with understanding – *this is why I have never heard the story of how Hesperos met Eratosthenes.*

The two Greeks were found the next morning. One had been so drunk that he was unable to wrap his wounds and died only steps outside the draftsman's office. The other, near death, was given treatment but was so severely scarred that he was made an outcast, living in the same filth that had greeted me in Alexandria. I hid with friends. They soon became suspicious and demanded to know why I did not return to the boat-works. The story of the abuse of the Greeks soon permeated the hovels of the Egyptian quarter. It was finally agreed that because the two men had been seen quarreling with other Greeks the day of their attack, they must have set upon each other. Besides, went the folly of reasoning conjured by the magistrate, only a Greek would have the audacity to attack another Greek. The fallacy of this way of thinking, demonstrated by the employer's son and shared by many of his countrymen – that the poor have no ambition – has already been stated here.

I still waited for the overseer or the blind Greek to implicate me, but almost two weeks went by – weeks in which only Amasis would bring me food and news of the boat-works. I was a hero to Amasis, he had said, and rumors among the men that a native had bested two young Greeks with instruments from their own workshop were rallying the workers in a small way to consider a broader insurrection. The notion was absurd and anyway, I had used the implements of my own passion, the chisel and the maul, and most symbolically, the draftsman's desk over which I'd hurled the first Greek and with which I had broken his nose. *My* countrymen were not the men who saw the draftsman's square and the shipwright's chisel as weapons of war, but any man who esteemed these instruments of science, discovery and enlightenment.

I remained uneasy of Greeks, but I abhorred my blood-countrymen's response to what I had done, what I had been forced to do. Amasis soon sent word to me that that the overseer had never returned to work and my presence was needed on the hull. Apparently, inquiries had been made of the young man who spoke intelligently of load and hydrodynamics. Amasis had informed them that I had been taken with a fever and upon recovery I would resume duties, this time as overseer of the entirety of hull number six. The boat-works and men from the palace did contribute some forward thinking to employment decisions, and qualifications of race, if not set down entirely, were set aside in service of the successful completion of the hulls in time for the Ptolemaia.

I returned, heart beating and pulse racing, to the boat-works, and to my surprise I was treated as if nothing had happened. The draftsmen inquired as to my health. I assured them that I had made a full recovery. Nothing was said of the matter, but I often received knowing and admiring glances from laborers as they heaved beams into position at my command.

We soon began day-round shifts, working through nights illuminated by hundreds of huge censors burning with crackling animal fat. A healthy competition developed among the foremen of the hulls. There was no doubt that Amasis' group would win. He was given the most manpower in the boat-works. He often called upon me informally with design questions, which I gladly answered in the spirit of now loyal, if sometimes uneasy friendship. But the competition spurred us on, and for some time I forgot about the bellicose Greeks, and Memphis, and the sabotaged waterworks of years ago and thanked Ammon that I was a respected engineer in the pharaoh's service. Almost a month after my return, my hull finally reached the towering height of nearly five stories, the first team after Amasis' to reach that height. I was supervising the joining of a critical cross-brace when I was summoned to the chief draftsman's office.

I entered to find him talking to the same academician, Eratosthenes, whose interest had inspired me to speak for myself and whose visit had prompted my bittersweet elevation. The Greek head of the center of scholarship of the known world, just paces from where I had gouged the eyes out of a Greek drunkard and wounded another for life, held out his hand to a barbarian and asked him simply: "Have you ever reflected on the mechanics of calculation?"

METALOGUE
THE VERY NEAR FUTURE

8

IMPOSSIBILITY. He stared at the rock-face. He had successfully navigated the maze of tunnels carefully designed to look like natural caves beneath the earth. The only indication of artificiality was their strict adherence to a curious mathematical principle Father had shown him in his youth. He again touched his pack. He knew from their proportions that the passages were created in the style of the Ulam Spiral, named for the man who (re)discovered it while doodling at a mathematics conference. A spiral of integers starting with '1' was written down in the following way:

401	400	399	398	397	396	395	394	393	392	391	390	389	388	387	386	385	384	383	382	381
402	325	324	323	322	321	320	319	318	317	316	315	314	313	312	311	310	309	308	307	380
403	326	257	256	255	254	253	252	251	250	249	248	247	246	245	244	243	242	241	306	379
404	327	258	197	196	195	194	193	192	191	190	189	188	187	186	185	184	183	240	305	378
405	328	259	198	145	144	143	142	141	140	139	138	137	136	135	134	133	182	239	304	377
406	329	260	199	146	101	100	99	98	97	96	95	94	93	92	91	132	181	238	303	376
407	330	261	200	147	102	65	64	63	62	61	60	59	58	57	90	131	180	237	302	375
408	331	262	201	148	103	66	37	36	35	34	33	32	31	56	89	130	179	236	301	374
409	332	263	202	149	104	67	38	17	16	15	14	13	30	55	88	129	178	235	300	373
410	333	264	203	150	105	68	39	18	5	4	3	12	29	54	87	128	177	234	299	372
411	334	265	204	151	106	69	40	19	6	1	2	11	28	53	86	127	176	233	298	371
412	335	266	205	152	107	70	41	20	7	8	9	10	27	52	85	126	175	232	297	370
413	336	267	206	153	108	71	42	21	22	23	24	25	26	51	84	125	174	231	296	369
414	337	268	207	154	109	72	43	44	45	46	47	48	49	50	83	124	173	230	295	368
415	338	269	208	155	110	73	74	75	76	77	78	79	80	81	82	123	172	229	294	367
416	339	270	209	156	111	112	113	114	115	116	117	118	119	120	121	122	171	228	293	366
417	340	271	210	157	158	159	160	161	162	163	164	165	166	167	168	169	170	227	292	365
418	341	272	211	212	213	214	215	216	217	218	219	220	221	222	223	224	225	226	291	364
419	342	273	274	275	276	277	278	279	280	281	282	283	284	285	286	287	288	289	290	363
420	343	344	345	346	347	348	349	350	351	352	353	354	355	356	357	358	359	360	361	362
421	422	423	424	425	426	427	428	429	430	431	432	433	434	435	436	437	438	439	440	441

The builders of the cavern, already in possession of this pattern, created forks in passages at most points at which a prime would be represented, and it was only in appreciation of this fact that a searcher might follow the correct path.

"As represented above," he thought, as the indissoluble numbers are divine, "so too below – the indissoluble numbers mark the axial moments."

He continued retracing this pattern for some time. He knew the end of the path would lay with a number of extraordinary importance. *That is how the builders honored the One and the Light. That is how the initiates of many mysteries, particularly the Mysteries called Eleusinian honored the True.*

He stopped in the middle of the passage. He could see only darkened expanse before and behind him. There was no junction. He raised his lantern up to the cave wall. His spirit soared in the cramped compartment before him. In the dim light he touched his pack again, remembering another of the sources:

Theorem:
If $2k-1$ is a prime number, then $2^{k-1}(2^k-1)$ is a perfect number <u>and</u> every even perfect number has this form.

Proof:
Suppose first that $p = 2^k-1$ is a prime number, and set $n = 2^{k-1}(2^k-1)$. To show n is perfect we need only show $\Sigma(n) = 2n$. Since Σ is multiplicative and $\Sigma(p) = p+1 = 2^k$, we know

$$\Sigma(n) = \Sigma(2k-1) \times \Sigma(p) = (2k-1)2k = 2n.$$

This shows that *n* is a perfect number.

On the other hand, suppose n is any even perfect number and write n as $2^{k-1}m$ where m is an odd integer and $k \geq 2$. Again Σ is multiplicative so

$$\Sigma(2^{k-1}m) = \Sigma(2^{k-1}) \times \Sigma(m) = (2^k-1) \times \Sigma(m).$$

Since n is perfect we also know that

$\Sigma(n) = 2n = 2^k m.$

Together these two criteria give

$2^k m = (2^k-1) \times \Sigma(m),$

so 2^k-1 divides $2^k m$ hence 2^k-1 divides m, say $m = (2^k-1)M$. Now substitute this back into the equation above and divide by 2^k-1 to get $2k_M = \Sigma(m)$. Since m and M are both divisors of m we know that

$2^k M = \Sigma(m) \geq m + M = 2^k M,$

so $\Sigma(m) = m + M$. This means that m is prime and its only two divisors are itself (m) and one (M). Thus $m = 2^k-1$ is a prime and we have proved that the number n has the prescribed form.

 —LEONHARD EULER

  Then he remembered the number again, the miraculous number in the sixth source appearing two millennia before it should have been known to be prime.

$$2^{31} - 1 = 2147483647$$

His journey had just begun.

I have found power in the mysteries of thought,
Exaltation in the changing of the Muses;
I have been versed in the reasonings of men;
But Fate is stronger than anything I have known.

—EURIPIDES, Alcestis

9

I continued working at the boat-works for some months after my introduction to The Master. Eratosthenes urged me to stay until he could secure funding for my full-time study. I believe it was so that my new position would not raise the suspicions of an early departure. So it was to be that I barked orders to my countrymen during the day, but at night made my models and conducted my experiments not with crude toys on the Mareotian shore, but in the workrooms and lecture halls amid the mysteries of the Academy.

The grandest of these mysteries, to me, was the device itself. Some few days after my "recruitment", Eratosthenes led me into a basement storage room that resembled in many details the infamous draftsman's workshop. Diagrams were pinned to every surface not covered with gears and rotors, lathes and drills. Eratosthenes had given a vague outline of the project that day in the chief draftsman's office, and I had expected to find a vast team of academicians and metalworkers stooping over workstations and consulting blueprints. The room was mostly empty save for a few other students I had met at the Academy. I nodded to Diocles and Apollonius of Perga, younger than I and always inseparable. Abdaraxus greeted me with a genial embrace. They had all been kind when I had first been introduced to them. Aristophanes, a youth of nearly the same age as I, was a trusted student of the project. He gave me an understanding but irreverent look as I was shown around the workroom. Archimedes greeted us.

"So this is the young man who solved the Delian problem of the docklands?"

Smiling, Eratosthenes replied, "He did indeed, but not merely by doubling the altar, but by anticipating the needs of the Oracle."

Not understanding what the Delian "problem" was, but wanting to demonstrate my eagerness to attempt its solution, I murmured something about leading me to the altar that I might make measurements of it. Both older men laughed, the young Aristophanes briefly cocked his head to one side and then resumed his study of a schematic.

"We have been aware of your ingenuity for some months, and – what is the boy's name, Eratosthenes?"

"The boy has an Egyptian name –"

I opened my mouth to speak my name but was cut off by Archimedes.

"Yes, that will never do, not if the boy is to work closely with us at the Academy," he said. He turned to me. "It's not me boy, it is expediency. In this environment..."

"I measure a man's talent, not his ancestry," said Eratosthenes, "and you have shown great promise, and great... restraint, great probity among your countrymen *and* in your pharaoh's service."

I froze – did they know about the incident with the Greeks?

"Indeed," said Archimedes, "that is why the boy is here, but he is Greek now. It must be so."

Eratosthenes turned to me and placed his hand on my shoulder. I will never forget it.

"Boy," he said, "You must honor yourself and your traditions. We honor you by bringing you here. To be Greek is a complicated business, and for our purposes, your... your isolation among the inhabitants of this capital is almost as important as your abilities. But you will need a Greek name. You will be known as my kinsman from Cyrene, who has just arrived at my recommendation. You will take one of my deceased kinsman's names, Hesperos, and you will be known by this name here. You must accept this identity, if worn only lightly. I demand no allegiance other than to your own conscience and the pursuit of excellence and creation, which I believe are of the same substance within you. Beyond these rooms, however, even among the other academicians not engaged in this work, you must accept this identity and this name."

Onesimus stares at me now, unable to imagine such a request. I remind Onesimus that his is a tradition of privilege unmarred by considerations of self, and that he might seek humility in the story of Oedipus and his own tortured realization of his true identity. His was hidden from him and mine was given to me. There is much to be learned by young men in the study of their own ability to manifest by brutal will a reality that can either lift them up or cut them down. Onesimus has nodded his agreement and has reached for Sophocles. Besides, he has heard the next part of the story many times, and would tire of its telling again.

It was then that I became Hesperos, but as I know now, even as I cut down the men in the boat-yards, I was never truly only an Egyptian. I had become Greek sometime in the heroic past, beyond a specific moment in my memory, when my mother was taken in the reed thrush, when an Egyptian youth destroyed my waterworks, when I ran from a Greek nobleman who exemplified none of the heroic characteristics of Heracles and Achilles and none of the civic characteristics of Socrates.

I accepted the name as what I thought was a capstone gesture of my initiation. I had not realized that what I would see next would propel me headlong into the complete service not only of Ptolemy III Euergetes or Egypt herself, but all of Hellas for all time.

Eratosthenes greeted me by my new name. Archimedes imitated him. They both took each of my hands and welcomed me to the Academy. Aristophanes greeted me coolly, but with some interest. The three of them then led me down a corridor to a door locked with a mechanism of unique design. With a flair for the theatrical that was Eratosthenes' hallmark and which I later imitated – Onesimus has paused his Sophocles to agree with me – the Master cranked a handle several times which protruded from an immense iron door. He aligned ten dials to an apparently random series of numbers and wound the handle several more times. A series of gears moved in unison until bolts made themselves known through their successive whirring from the top to the bottom of the door. Eratosthenes pulled on another handle and the door pushed away from us gracefully, revealing a cavernous room beyond. We entered into what appeared to have been a storage facility that ran almost the entire length of the Academy. Dusty casks of wine and empty amphorae still lined the walls. The masonry ceiling was supported by vaulting and posts at regular intervals. The interior was brilliantly illuminated by a trough set into the base of the vaulting which contained some flammable liquid. In the center of the room: a hulking tower of glistening bronze and iron shafts and cogs of similar design to the lock on the doorway through which we had passed. The device appeared to be unfinished, but many parts of it were in action, spinning silently. Several men stood at what was obviously the front of the machine.

Eratosthenes led me over to the men. One reached out his hand.

"I am Procopios, the pharaoh's advisor for military intelligence. This is Polymius-'

"I am Polymius – the pharaoh's secretary of war," he said, booming at me.

I hesitated momentarily and only after a reassuring glance from Eratosthenes did I dare to say, "I am Hesperos, the Chief Librarian's – kinsman – from Cyrene."

Both men looked at me with non-expectation and bemusement.

"You may save all that for the tradesmen and the contractors with whom *you'll* be dealing, *Hesperos*," said Procopios.

I was shaken, but I could not stop myself from looking past him at the device in front of me.

I spoke directly to Procopios. "It's magnificent. It's bigger than the statue of Serapis."

"Not exactly," said Procopios, "but it's so far four times as expensive."

As I have said, I remained in service at the boat-works. Though I was not a slave in the traditional sense – I did not have an owner - by tradition I owed a debt to my employer should I wish to leave his service. Eratosthenes arranged this artfully and at some expense. While these arrangements were being made, I continued with my duties on hull six and began recording my experiences at the Academy. Onesimus and I are reviewing my childish notebooks in my peculiar phonetic Greek – I was only properly tutored in Greek by The Master and his circle once I became an active member of the Academy. Such flights of Theocritus, such foolish language! Yet the sentiment is true, and in many places, quite touching:

> *March 18 – The Master lent me his copy of Hesiod, it is my duty to absorb it entire and be its master.*

> *March 23 – My third meeting with Archimedes. The device is sheer brilliance and I have never been in the company of greater minds than the men devoted to its service.*

April 11 – The Master has given me Euclid and though I struggle with it, it seems as if I've come home!

April 19 – First symposium – completely out of place and did not feel welcomed. Misquoted Hesiod. The youth Aristophanes made quite a biting joke at my expense.

The Ptolemaia was just two months away, and the day was arriving where the finished hulls would be ported across the isthmus of Alexandria and slipped into the great harbor. I worked tirelessly to finish my hull, and helped many other teams besides. Rumors began to spread that I had found employment elsewhere. Once I was even followed to the palace quarter and I later learned that I was now known to be maintained in some sort of illicit position with an academician or courtier. I denied the rumors when they were spoken aloud, but mostly I ignored them, adding the convictions of silence to the evidence against me.

Amasis slipped away to just as secretive pursuits. Constantly frustrated by his attempts to rise in the esteem of his employer, he took first to heavy drink and then to mild subversion. I knew that he sabotaged a demonstration for palace officials. I had helped prepare the demonstration and confronted him after its embarrassing failure. He admitted to his complicity only after I pretended to be proud of him for making a fool of our Greek employer. In fact I was enraged and made ever greater demands on myself that I should continue to advance on my own merits beyond the confines of the boat-works and the politics of Amasis. As Amasis distanced himself from his work I tethered myself more tightly to it.

The day arrived for the delivery of the hulls to the palace shipyards. The immense problems of engineering required even Archimedes' attentions. We did not acknowledge each other as he watched the massive pulleys and winches of his design that hauled the hulls one by one through the streets of Alexandria. Their journey was a matter of state ceremony. Ptolemy, still on campaign against Seleucus, was represented in golden effigy poised on a litter carried by forty men. He had sent his consort, Berenice, to supervise the parade from a two-story dais of solid granite. Wine was distributed to the entire city from a fountain mounted on a golden cart drawn by twenty horses. It was the beginning of the season of the Ptolemaia.

Speeches were made by enchanted courtiers. Camels, introduced to Egypt for the first time, carried officials in gilded howdahs shaded by silk canopies died in exotic colors. The sight of fat Polymius balancing precariously on camelback was an occasion for great derision among native and Greek alike. A towering effigy of Alexander and his greatest General Ptolemy I, wearing Egyptian state dress, lead the procession and passed the royal dais at the Soma. All of Greek Egypt was in one place bearing witness to the glory of the marauding, and therefore absent, Ptolemy III Euergetes, a fact not lost on Amasis and his countrymen.

Having completed my work at the boat yards I was now a free man, a Greek youth and a ward of the Chief Librarian of the Library of Alexandria. I continued my chronicle in a small way:

> *May 18-21 – I have spent three days discussing differential gearing with Archimedes. The youths Diocles and Apollonius of Perga, never one to be found without the other, have shown themselves amenable to my presence at the Academy. With Ctesibius I collaborated on a small improvement to the gearing mechanism of the incipit decoder which was met favorably by Philo and Eratosthenes.*

> *May 21 – Second symposium – mostly silent, but contributed a line of Hesiod, which I now know by heart. Aristophanes unimpressed but others gave a generally favorable response.*

> *May 23 – Arranged for production of camshafts from Casanios the Jew and metal screws from Euridates in the Egyptian quarter. To Casanios I am conducting an experiment in spacing road markers. Euridates is happy to think I am developing knives with detachable blades that may be more easily concealed. This is his suggestion of which he could not be disabused.*

In the great harbor the carpenters, the masons, the lead fitters and the mosaic layers worked through the night as we had on the other side of the city. With each day the deck line rose on each of the ten hulls, pushing them lower into the water. The ships had been nearly outfitted with their entire superstructures. As they had seemed the fingers of the gods along Lake Mareotis, fanned out in formation with the great lighthouse beyond they now seemed the festooned and bejeweled reach of Ptolemy himself.

May 27 – Observed "my" hull in the great harbor. Remarkable view from the roof of the library. It has been given an ornamental outrigger of gold plate from which twelve banks of oars project on either side like towlines into the sea. A temple to Calliope built of solid marble rises on its aft deck. The foredeck is a lush garden overflowing with flowers and running fountains! The wonder of Alexandria!

May 28 – Saw Amasis in the agora today. He accused me due to my absence of finding accommodations as a Greek's erômenos. I accused him of jealousy and charged him with slander at such allegations. He repented and embraced me. I have seldom felt as uncomfortable in his presence.

We worked for weeks. New information came in almost daily by agents scattered throughout the Northeast. Some employed the *scytale* to further confound us. In such a practice, a coded belt is wound round a stick - the scytale - of prearranged size to line up a message, usually itself in code. It did not take long to adapt the device to account for diameters of scytales within a range that would be convenient for the recipient. One very ingenious enemy courier himself encoded the already enciphered message in an obscure tongue, which he admitted under torture was a dialect of his Phoenician ancestors.

In the early days I was not privy to the contents of the messages, only the methods by which they were decrypted. Eratosthenes would parcel out parts of a project to me and to Aristophanes, who had a particular gift for languages and an especial affinity for the regional dialects in which many dispatches were written. Other students were employed on particular translation projects which the paranoid Procopios insisted be broken up into passages containing every second or third word and given to as many individual translators. The Jews with their Septuagint were not faced with such a disjointed task of translation.

Eratosthenes and Archimedes became even more obsessed with the device. Eratosthenes' kind attentions to my crash-course in Greek and the humanities slowed and then ceased altogether. I was given increasingly rudimentary tasks for which I was still thankful – I was, after all, studying at the Great Library of Alexandria. I collected camshafts and the metal screws and fasteners of my own design. I often worked on the device itself, learning about its mechanics and recommending refinements and additions as I became better acquainted with it, but I was not given access to the mathematics enshrined within it.

Aristophanes would tauntingly reveal a clue here and there, and often with deep sarcasm in the pronunciation of my Greek name. From these clues, the window Aristophanes provided into his limited understanding of the device was not entirely opaque. I deduced a particular problem The Master was having with the synchronicity between each bank of distinct alphabets which were rotated in turn to attempt the various combinations of alphabetic shifts.

Onesimus reminds me that I have already included in this account The Master's letter detailing the difficulties of a variable shift cipher. I have reminded Onesimus that I, of course, did not have access at the time to the correspondence between the Chief Librarian and his pharaoh. I was only able to work through the problem as best I understood it, and only by my small addition to the solution to this problem was I propelled into the next phase of the device's development.

I desperately wanted to prove my value to Eratosthenes and the project. I somehow became possessed of a self-confidence that I had only demonstrated when I had previously taken matters into my own hands. I had improved the water pump though I had not been asked to do so. I had helped Amasis with the rigging and draft problems years ago, though we were thought by our employer little better than tramps with strong backs taking refuge in Alexandria. I had taken charge of the improvements to the hull, and though nearly killed for my pride that day, I had impressed the head of the Academy of Alexandria. Would not another display propel me to even greater consideration?

I began working on my own with parts I secreted out of the workshops. I knew this was dangerous. At best I might be accused of stealing, at worst of being a spy or saboteur. I found an unused storeroom and again set to work putting ideas into practice. After two weeks filled with the greatest guilt and conflict, I prepared myself to display the small prototype to Eratosthenes. He was returning from a meeting when I surprised him in the workshop. I asked that he spare one moment to examine a project I had been working on. Assuming it was the accumulation of more supplies, he stared blankly and followed me to the storeroom. In imitation of him, I unveiled my machine with great theatricality by quickly uncovering with a wheat sack a motley collection of discarded gears and camshafts greased with putrid chicken fat I had applied days earlier. Before he could speak I spewed my description of the small change

I suggested in this small gearing improvement. A retractable cam attached to a shaft running aside each bank of alphabetic columns, I explained, would allow him to move forward with his calculations. He asked if I had done this myself. I responded that it had been my idea alone.

His expression was odd, part pride but also a hint of relief. He burst out too, saying that he had indeed been busy and had neglected my instruction, but that he began noticing pieces missing from the workshop and that Aristophanes had once seen me pocket several gears that, though discarded from earlier versions of the device, bore recognizable patterns a sophisticated machinist might be able to reproduce.

He had suspected me not of industry but treason! I begged his forgiveness and fell at his feet. He picked me up and asked me calmly to carry on with my duties.

The next day I went through my routine in fear that I had ruined my truly miraculous position at the Academy. The day following I was summoned to the cavern in which the machine was kept. In the presence of Eratosthenes, Archimedes, Polymius, Procopios, the friendly students and the dour Aristophanes I was given a detailed explanation of every aspect of the machine. This orientation included the mathematics, which I was induced to study rigorously, to the gearing of some parts of the machine which were unknown to me. Most surprisingly, Procopios himself, with Polymius' blessing, gave me every detail of the decryption effort so far and the problem now facing them.

For two days I refused to eat, so engrossed in the problem had I become. A boy of nineteen, I was now engaged in the direct service of Ptolemy's intelligence apparatus, a de facto adviser to the pharaoh of Egypt.

Onesimus again glares at me with mischief, his eyes accuse me of the hubris of Oedipus! I have assured Onesimus that in this one instance I refrain from hyperbole, for I was really there, an assistant to the Chief Librarian, head of the Academy, tasked in no small measure with the unraveling of the one code that had yet to be broken by the device.

My prototype had been crude, and because I was acting on partial intelligence gleaned from the impish hints of Aristophanes, had been, therefore, partially incomplete. I refined once more my suggestions and spent many laborious hours grafting the approved design onto the existing framework of the device. Many unsuccessful attempts at decryption later and in constant consultation with The Master, I eventually implemented the plan with many suggestions from Philo and Archimedes, in particular.

The message was once again run through the device and, while forming new strings of characters, precious few real, if out of place, words appeared. The message may have included the word *Ptlmy*, which Aristophanes argued was merely indicative that the sender had added a layer of difficulty by removing the vowels. The name of our pharaoh was an encouraging discovery, as his name was naturally to be found in such a dispatch. In an entirely different configuration it may have included the words *attack, navy,* and *throne*. The nature of the code meant that these were mutually exclusive and the presence of vowels in the second rendering left much confusion. We decided that we were now wishfully observing words which we expected to see and that further configurations should be attempted until an undisputable pattern emerged.

Days passed and the device refused to reveal the secrets of the message. The smaller previous devices continued to decode less important dispatches. We learned that Seleucus had sent for a doctor from Tarsus renowned for his treatment of a distasteful disease of the genitals. We learned that an influential eunuch named Pharaleus had been up to mischief in a garrison in Damascus. We all began to despair learning more important news, and Eratosthenes eventually came to doubt the phrases he had originally decoded and forwarded with haste to Euergetes himself:

a t t _ _ k b y

which he had interpreted as "attack by," a piece of text almost certainly to be followed by a direction, person or place name, and, perhaps more alarmingly:

d _ f e c t _ _ n

which he interpreted as a report or reassurance to potential Seleucian allies of a defection in Ptolemy's own general staff and a favorable and brief conclusion of hostilities should a calculated war be undertaken for Coele-Syria. Though these two "words" had appeared in the same configuration of the device, Eratosthenes now worried that his alarm had been in haste. It was to everyone's astonishment that, weeks after the minor adjustments had been made, the previous words now lined up. In a completely different configuration of the alphabet and with an incipit distinct from that used in the initial decipherment they appeared again. This time, the third word was intact and unimpeachable. In the body of the same message that revealed the words above was written simply:

p t o l e ma i a

A trusted rider was dispatched to Euergetes immediately.

My beautiful proof lies all in ruins.

—GEORG CANTOR, on his proof for the Continuum Hypothesis

10

Perry had taken a course with Professor Martin on Hesiod, a major Greek poet. Professor Martin was, of course, fluent in Koine Greek. We found him in the small office one imagined an emeritus shoved into. The room was stacked floor to chest high with books, some of which were sunken into the carpet and had been vacuumed around so many times they seemed embedded original ornaments to the room's furnishings. Professor Martin greeted Perry warmly, shook my hand and asked us to sit down. He maneuvered around several atolls of books to pull a Koine dictionary from a shelf. Sitting behind his desk, he asked to see the napkin, which Perry provided with apologies that he hadn't made a better showing of the small Greek to which he had been exposed in Professor Martin's class.

"Now gentlemen, this is most exciting – a real mystery. I'm sure a public museum like that is bound to publish the findings soon, probably in installments. But it does seem quite dramatic, Perry, the way you explained their intense interest in this word. It's something out of Roswell."

Perry again brought up his anachronism theory. I said again that it was highly unlikely, for numerous reasons. Conspiracy thrillers were made of this stuff, but not real textual analysis. If the word did represent an impossibly modern concept, it was unlikely that two centuries of professional historical analysis of the Hellenistic epoch had not found other references to an ancient understanding of human flight or atomic power or alien visitations or whatever other anachronisms Perry had allowed himself.

Perry was one of those intellectuals one might accidentally take advantage of. He had very little social ability and even less of an ability to feign interest in other people. One may think the two skillsets are equivalent, but I've found I can will my natural social ineptitude to demure to a strong enough desire to appear as if I'm well-adjusted. I first met Perry as an undergraduate, in Introduction to Archaeological Method. It was in that class, in the third row of five – far enough away to decrease the likelihood of having to speak in class and far enough forward to avoid the appearance of discomfort – that Perry and I began our friendship. As our classmates were busying themselves with thoughts of spring break, I nervously asked him if he was planning to attend a popular music concert being held on the quad that evening. He responded that he had no idea what I was talking about, his face an easy blend of disinterest and kindness.

That same semester, he had gldly worked through a large research hurdle for a classmate because it interested him personally, an insight which the classmate submitted as her own. He had many times helped me brainstorm projects for which, while formal acknowledgment was not expected in undergraduate theses, I gave him credit informally in our small department. We had even coauthored a paper on the effects of the deforestation of Easter Island that we jointly submitted to the appropriate scholarly journals and which remains unpublished. Perry's kindness bordered on blind credulity, a sometimes intolerable failing in an otherwise highly intellectually curious collaborator.

Though I considered myself a model of logical virtue, I suppose I too allowed myself a little romanticism in the moment when Professor Martin set eyes on our napkin. I expected to see an immediate glimmer of recognition, as one might if one had presented an authentic lost Shakespearean play to a Shakespeare scholar. My romanticism was quickly subdued; Professor Martin turned the napkin to the side, pulled it close to his face, pulled it away and then, finally, in an act of complete devastation, turned the napkin upside-down.

"Well, some of these aren't Greek letters at all, boys. Not that I'm familiar with. I can't really make out a word at all. As you've written it it's Greek-ish, but it's just a jumble of letters and doodles." He made a 'tsking sound with his teeth. "This is clearly the Greek letter Beta and this, here is Mu, I'm sure you both knew that. This again is Beta, and this is Sigma, and here again Alpha. This is not a Greek letter, nor is this. This might be Chi, this could be Eta."

"Ok, I said, "but, I mean – if a non-native English speaker brought me the word, say, automobile, and had written, A-CHARACTER-T-CHARACTER-CHARACTER-A-CHARACTER-OBILE, I'd be able to guess its meaning."

"Good for you. Unfortunately," he said, "Koine Greek is compounded by the difficulty of representing large numbers which this must be, if it isn't gibberish. The Greeks of the third century BCE would have used letters to represent numbers, very much like the Roman numerals we're familiar with. It's alphabetical, sure, but without a clear copy of the letters – and as I've said, some of these aren't Greek letters at all – it's impossible to tell for sure what –"

Professor Martin leaned in closer to the napkin, tracing his index finger across the word.

"What," said Perry, "What is it?"

"You said this was repeated several times on the page?"

"Yeah, one of the members of the conservation team was pointing to it several times on the page."

"How many times?"

Perry and I looked at each other.

"I don't know," I said, "maybe two or three times."

"If it's from the Alexander Palimpsest, this is Koine Greek, and I understand your difficulties in writing, as a picture, letters you're unfamiliar with, and I'd have to see the original scanned image to be sure –"

"But?" Perry said expectantly.

"Look here," said Martin, pointing to the first part of the word. "This is obviously part of a proper word, but the rest makes no sense, the way it's written. The rest is either gibberish or it's a string of numbers."

"What numbers?"

"It's a string of digits, one, two, three..." He counted across the napkin. "There are fourteen of them." "Doesn't mean anything to me. Maybe a – I don't know, maybe a calculation. Some aren't Greek numerals per se, but, if *this* is meant to be a type of exponent," he pointed to a spot on the napkin, "and *this* is meant to be a multiplier." He started doodling on a scrap of paper. I can't imagine a Koine Greek text talking about a number in the billions. Certainly Archimedes had discussed large numbers abstractly, notions of infinity for example. He'd tried to calculate grains of sand on a beach and in the universe and so forth, but it was more of a thought experiment, though he did develop a very sophisticated positional numbering system. The Greeks had several different methods for counting, often using base sixty, inherited from the Babylonians, which of course, survives today in angles, coordinate systems and, of course, time. In fact, quite interesting, the Archimedes Palimpsest included a complete copy of some of his proto-equations."

"Proto-equations?" I asked.

"Well, yes," said Perry, nodding at Martin, "The Greeks would have used certain shorthand to represent ideas and conditional relationships, what we would call an algorithm today. The very word, 'algorithm' is an English transliteration of the name of a famous Arab mathematician, Muhammad ibn Musa al-Khwarizmi, who studied the concept in the eighth century CE."

"Indeed," said Martin. "In fact, you have to allow this one digression. If we're actually talking about a true third century BCE manuscript from Alexandria," his voice grew pitched with excitement, "then there are quite a few parallels between that center of scholarship and another a thousand years later, in Baghdad, called the House of Wisdom."

Perry's face formed into the benign contortion I've seen so often at the grad student bar, when a casual conversation about politics, science or philosophy takes a turn down a corridor within which one present has spent their entire academic careers. Their expression shows that they do not know from which of a dozen angles they might accrete to the group's conversation their own specialization and erudition: 'No, actually, that's a common misconception about the influence of x upon y,' and 'the vernacular terminology is scarcely able to capture the nuances of that particular z.'

Perry launched several of these potential approaches at once, to Martin's delight and for my edification, of which I digested only small pieces of a larger whole:

"Current geopolitical situation... blinds us to Arab-Islamic intellectual achievements... Christianity suppressed antiquity's greatest... only through the Arab civilization... numerous scholars... House of Wisdom... translation movement... Islamic Golden Age... eighth and ninth centuries... Alexandria at its height... Al Khwarizmi... quadratic equations... algebra... Banu Musa brothers... The Book of Ingenious Devices... contemporaries... Al Kindi... frequency analysis... manuscript... deciphering cryptographic messages."

"Wait, what," I asked. "What was that?

"Al-Kindi. Eighth century CE," said Martin, delighted. "His work, *A Manuscript on Deciphering Cryptographic Messages*, well – it was pivotal. Al-Kindi developed frequency analysis."

"I told you about this, remember, at the bar?"

"Oh right," I said. "So, where are we going with all this?"

Perry shuffled backward several paces in Martin's congested office. He was actually 'backing up,' for the sake of the only Philistine in the room. "My point is, we're talking about this number and," Perry ran his finger across the napkin, "if the rest of this *is* a number, then maybe this part makes sense as the prefix 'mecha.' What do you think, Professor Martin? My Greek isn't perfect."

"It might," said Martin, "but that's a stretch."

"OK," said Perry, flicking his thumb out in a counting motion. "One, we have this word, maybe representing a number, 'mechanism', or what-have-you, right?"

I nodded, Perry flicked out the next finger. "Two, we know that Greek mathematics was impressive, we know this from Euclid and the surviving writings of Archimedes, but we also know that they didn't have formulas, as we understand the concept. They used diagrams and illustrations as proofs, just as we would use symbols for relationships, or equations, today."

"Ok," I said.

"Ok, so a positional counting system is a kind of algorithm, right? I mean, think about it. We use base ten most of the time. Implicit in that understanding is modular arithmetic, meaning that once we reach ten units of something, we up the 'tens' column by one unit and reset the 'ones' column. We could just as easily use any number of other bases. The Alexandrian Greeks used several bases. Of course, sixty was popular, but it was usually written out in a table format. We use base ten, and we get it from the Arabs. In fact, our numerals are 'Arabic' numerals, also including zero. Actually, we really use an ancient Indus Valley concept–"

"I know all this," I said. "What does Al-Kindi have to do with the Alexander Palimpsest?"

"It doesn't," said Martin. "Not directly."

"No," said Perry. "What we're looking at is something a thousand years older than the type of numerical representations you'd see in The House of Wisdom. It doesn't make sense. And the only reason we know as much about antiquity as we do is because the Arabs copied much of the Greek texts into Arabic, for dissemination throughout the Near East, where they became prized. Much of the Greek texts in the West were discarded, left to rot, intentionally burned as heretical or–"

"Scraped over for re-use?" I said. "Like a palimpsest. Like the Archimedes and Alexander Palimpsests."

"Here," said Martin. He spun the scrap of paper he'd been scribbling on. He had written four similar ten-digit numbers in Arabic numerals. "So, we know the Alexandrian mathematicians were playing around at creating a notation that would work with their broadening understanding of large numbers – very large numbers, much larger than this relatively small number and always abstractly represented before this time. I wonder."

"What?" Perry and I asked at the same time.

"I don't know if I have anything here. Give me a second." Professor Martin began picking through his stacks of books. "No, I don't know. Now if we head over to the library."

I realized he was probably searching for an index of mathematically significant numbers. I pulled out my phone. "Let me see the paper."

"Here," Martin said, pushing it closer to me.

"Ok, let's see." I typed each number into the search engine on my phone. One of the numbers appeared in a large search result box typical of an important piece of information.

<h2 style="text-align:center">2,147,483,647</h2>

"Two billion, one-hundred-forty-seven million, four hundred eighty-three thousand, six hundred and forty-seven." I pressed on the number on my screen. My phone returned an instant Wikipedia result:

TABLE OF THE FIRST NINE MERSENNE PRIMES WITH DISCOVERER AND DATE OF DISCOVERY						
#	p	M_p	M_p digits	Discovered	Discoverer	Method used
1	2	3	1	c. 430 BC	Ancient Greek mathematicians	
2	3	7	1	c. 430 BC	Ancient Greek mathematicians	
3	5	31	2	c. 300 BC	Ancient Greek mathematicians	
4	7	127	3	c. 300 BC	Ancient Greek mathematicians	
5	13	8191	4	1456	Anonymous	Trial division
6	17	131071	6	1588	Pietro Cataldi	Trial division
7	19	524287	6	1588	Pietro Cataldi	Trial division
8	31	2147483647	10	1772	Leonhard Euler	Enhanced trial division
9	61	2305843009213690000	19	1883	I. M. Pervushin	Lucas sequences

I felt goose bumps as I read the search results. "This is a 'Mersenne Prime," I said, reading the screen: "In number theory, a Mersenne Prime is a prime number of the form $M_n = 2^n - 1$."

"Well," Professor Martin said, "there you have it. The Alexander Palimpsest is obviously written by someone familiar with prime numbers. We have Euclid's *Elements*, which deals at length with prime numbers. That seems fitting for the time period. It does speak to the author's living and writing either in Alexandria or perhaps Pergamon. Scholars were fascinated with prime numbers. How very interesting."

"Yeah," I said, "except the article says, 'this form of prime number is named after Marin Mersenne, who studied it in the early seventeenth century CE.' And *this* specific Mersenne Prime wasn't discovered by him."

"Who discovered it?" asked Perry.

"Leonhard Euler, in 1772. It says it took him several months working it out on paper. He used trial division, having to prove that it was both a prime number and a Mersenne Prime using three hundred and seventy-two divisions *and* using methods only developed in Italy in the 1500s. So how did it end up in a third century BCE journal?"

"I knew it," said Perry. "It's an anachronism."

"You, know," said Professor Martin, "Something's odd about the juxtaposition here. While *most* of what you wrote is a number, this prefix is very, very unusual. Part of it sort of connotes an invocation to Nike, goddess of victory, of course, but also reminiscent of 'winged,' 'flying' or 'swift' victory. It's usually used to connote a concept akin to swiftness. It's almost like the author's trying to indicate that this number was arrived at swiftly. I actually know of only one other time when I've seen something like this prefix. Hold on." Professor Martin again dug through stacks, pulling out and opening on his desk a hefty volume, again in Greek. "Have either of you ever heard of something called the Antikythera Mechanism?"

We both had. It was a centerpiece of Perry's ancient anachronism fascination. We had discussed it several times in our pedantry.

"The orrery, found by sponge divers – in 1900 or so, I think – off the island of Antikythera in the Aegean, near mainland Greece," said Perry.

"Yeah," I said. "It's amazing. It can model the phases of the moon, the date of the Olympic Games. They're still trying to reconstruct models of it. The gearing is light-years beyond what archaeologists had previously known Hellenistic science was capable of. People call it the world's first computer."

"Well, that's just it," said Martin, "consensus is that it is that and only that, an orrery, a kind of astrolabe – an exquisitely intricate one – but basically a very advanced mechanized calendar. Except–"

"What?" I asked.

"Well, something always intrigued me about what most people agree is the mechanism's owner's manual. It's true it has instructions on how to use it. It has the requisite homage to the gods, et cetera. But it also has a curious little statement about its "swiftness" of operation. Here."

Martin opened the book to a large high-definition image of the mechanism. The left page had a full-color image of the device. Very pronounced gears were rusted together into a patinated jumble of other gears, cogs and crankshafts. On the right was an x-ray of the interior of the device, showing dozens of tinier gears with finely cut teeth and seemingly flawlessly cut cams.

"Most people assume," he continued," that it's meant as a boast by its designer. Something of an advertisement, like, 'try our Antikythera Mechanism, it's faster than the competitors' Antikythera Mechanisms.' Only, that really doesn't make sense. An object similar to the Antikythera Mechanism has never been found. Most archaeologists believe it was one of a very few like devices to have been made. It would be like DaVinci saying, 'buy my Mona Lisa, it's the best Mona Lisa available.'"

"So what are you saying?" Perry asked.

"I don't know. It seems like this prefix could be a kind of short-hand. Here," he said, straddling an atoll of journals to retrieve a copy of *Nature*, "look at this. This study on the Antikythera inscriptions was done by an international team about six years ago. This is a photograph of the inscription. It's pieced together, and it's obvious that much of the inscription has been lost."

The photograph was of a few dozen tiny scraps of bronze. A false color image enhanced and enlarged some sections so that Greek – Koine Greek, Martin noted – was clearly legible.

"In fact – here," he said squinting at the page, "there it is, the same prefix, and here it is again, twice on as many lines."

"So, where are we with this?"

"Well, if I had to guess, we're looking at a very rarely used Koine Greek prefix. Up to now, because of its similarity to the Koine for 'swift,' or more precisely, 'swiftly accurate,' we've assumed that this was a literal translation of the prefix. But it's possible it conveys a similar but distinct concept."

"Well, what is it?" asked Perry, nearly panting for information.

"Gentlemen, I'm intrigued, and I'll have to get a few other opinions, but I bet I know why the folks in the room at the Alexander Palimpsest project got pretty excited. This doesn't mean 'swift' or even 'swiftly accurate,'" he said, gathering confidence in his assessment as he spoke. "This doesn't mean that at all. This is a marker, a kind of quality control stamp – a validation of both the process used to discover the Mersenne Prime and, at least some of the functions of the Antikythera Mechanism. I'd say it really is – it's a very old notion of a very modern idea. I'd say it's someone's term of art, a word coined for something brand new at the time, something we take for granted today.

"See, the complete phrase you brought to me doesn't make sense as a whole, but it makes sense if the first part is – well here, take a look." Martin wrote on Perry's napkin: μηχανικός.

"Then," he said after a long pause, "this word might be 'επίθμηχανικός.'"

"E-pi-mee-ka-nee-sis?" I mimicked back. "What does E-pi-mee-ka-nee-sis mean?"

"E-pi-mee-ka-nee-sis," he said, mocking my pronunciation, "it means, contrivance, or device, or - mechanism."

"What mechanism?" asked Perry?

"What do you mean, 'mechanism'?" I asked.

"Taken next to the world's first manuscript mentioning what will eventually be termed Mersenne primes, I think someone in the third century BCE, two hundred years before Julius Caesar met Cleopatra, six hundred years before Christianity became the state religion of the Mediterranean, when Greeks ruled Egypt and worshipped Serapis, when the greatest empires of the day were fighting with swords, pikes, elephants and arrows, somebody developed a new term: I think this literally means, 'mechanized thinking.' I think this is meant to indicate a conclusion or result of guaranteed accuracy, 'calculated by machine.' I think this means '*computer*.'"

» BOOK II «
THE SAND RECKONER

The triad is pervasive in the nature of number: for there are three types of odd number—prime and incomposite, secondary and composite, and mixed, which is secondary in itself, but otherwise prime; and again, there are over-perfect, imperfect and perfect numbers; and in short, of relative quantity, some is greater, some less and some equal.

The triad is very well suited to geometry: for the basic element in plane figures is the triangle, and there are three kinds of triangle—acute-angled, obtuse-angled and scalene.

There are three configurations of the moon—waxing, full moon and waning; there are three types of irregular motion of the planets—direct motion, retrogression and, between these, the stationary mode; there are three circles which define the zodiacal plane—that of summer, that of winter, and the one midway between these, which is called the ecliptic; there are three kinds of living creature—land, winged and water; there are three Fates in theology, because the whole life of both divine and mortal beings is governed by emission and receiving and thirdly requital, with the heavenly beings fertilizing in some way, the earthly beings receiving, as it were, and requitals being paid by means of those in the middle, as if they were a generation between male and female.

One could relate to all this the words of Homer, "All was divided into three," given that we also find that the virtues are means between two vicious states which are opposed both to each other and to virtue; and there is no disagreement with the notion that the virtues fall under the monad and are something definite and knowable and are wisdom—for the mean is one—while the vices fall under the dyad and are indefinite, unknowable and senseless.

They call it 'friendship' and 'peace,' and further 'harmony' and 'unanimity': for these are all cohesive and unificatory of opposites and dissimilars. Hence they also call it 'marriage.' And there are also three ages in life.

—IAMBLICHUS, The Theology of Arithmetic: On the Mystical, Mathematical and Cosmological Symbolism of the First Ten Numbers

I know indeed what evil I intend to do,
but stronger than all my afterthoughts is my fury,
fury that brings upon mortals the greatest evils.

—EURIPIDES, Medea

11

Several days have passed since my last dictation. I have spent many happy evenings with colleagues reclined beneath the canopy of the heavens gazing motionless at the constellations that watch over our double port, always beginning by counting light upon light and ending with awe at the beauty of their arrangements. I interrupt the narrative now reminded by dear Onesimus of honoring the Muses. I have reminded him of my prodigious outputs at these symposia and, thinking this a rather rough joke at their expense, make amends by resolving to insert, at Onesimus' suggestion, several short passages at the beginning of appropriate breaks in this narrative. I will select several that work upon me and have instructed Onesimus to include them at regular intervals. Always a student and lover of Theocritus, I make a suggestion that the Idylls be appropriated. It is often impossible for me to imagine how Onesimus will arrange these interpuncts between the transgressions of an old man's dotage.

Onesimus reminds me once again that I have strayed from my story, and redirects my attention back to the intelligence received in the months before the greatest Ptolemaia the city of Alexander had yet seen. But to properly understand the impact of the threats made against the Ptolemaia, I must first describe the history of the Ptolemaia in full form. I become restless with concern that, as eternal is the knowledge contained in the Library, the Musaeum and the Serapeum, of the two vessels of the transmittal of knowledge - memory and papyrus – I lament that the former is ephemeral and the latter is still bound only to the physical constancy of the library itself.

The pharaoh in the times of the Master's triumph, the light of the Nile Ptolemy III Euergetes, was then still a young man, not yet thirty. His father, the lord of the sky, Ptolemy II Philadelphus, son of Ptolemy I Soter the chosen of Alexander, resolved in the Greek way to institute a quadrennial ceremony in honor of his ancestors who were made gods by their relation to Alexander Helios, Conqueror of death and of Asia. It was decided that a vast festival would be held to honor both the traditions of the ancient heritage of Egypt to which I humbly attach myself, as well as the ancient mysteries of the gods of Hellas.

The first of these Ptolemaia was held with great fanfare, universally acclaimed a triumph equal only to the great celebrations of Zeus at Olympus. Ptolemy II invited representatives of the Greek cities and Alexander's successor kingdoms to participate in a grand procession. The cortege was headed by high court functionaries on the upper Nile and made its way by glittering barge past the ancient sites of Elephantine, Syene, Thebes with its ancient temples at Karnak and Luxor, Oxyrhynchus, Memphis, Heliopolis and Naucratis. The entire assembly proceeded through the Canopic mouth of the Nile to Lake Mareotis, where the barges full of treasures beyond compare to any other kingdom were offloaded in the evening while a great festival was held on the first night of the Ptolemaia in Alexandria. Several nights of feasting honored Philadelphus' parents as gods while simultaneously honoring the apotheosis of Alexander at Siwa. I will insert the words of the late Callixenus of Rhodes who was in attendance at the first Ptolemaia and from whose thin volume in the library I know repeat the following brief account.

> The first act of his reign, or rather the last of his father's reign, was the proclamation, or the ceremony, of showing the new king to the troops and people. All that was dazzling, all that was costly or curious, all that the wealth of Egypt could buy or the gratitude of the provinces could give, was brought forth to grace this religious show, which, as we learn from the sculptures in the old tombs, was copied rather from the triumphs of Ramses and Thûtmosis than from anything that had been seen in Greece.

As I read this now I am reminded of the anticipation in the hearts of the citizenry in the time of Ptolemy III Euergetes. It is the goal of kingship to outdo the conquests – cultural and military - of one's predecessors. Ptolemy III, young as he was, was more eager due to the turmoil in his early reign to make his first Ptolemaia a giant to the opulence of his father, and he resolved to double the intended effect of his festival. He too demanded a procession down the Nile to the Canopic mouth, past the ancient sites of the pharaohs. But his was an empire that looked out to the Mediterranean for its prestige as much as it looked inward to the interior for its wealth. Thus were the orders for the great hulls delivered to the boat-works, thus was the timing of his great need of information about the movements of his northern adversary, as I have mentioned, the coward-dictator Seleucus Callinicus.

With such anticipation of an even greater Ptolemaia surrounding the court, and the Master having been secreted in study of the various dispatches coming from the agents of Seleucus, I was quite surprised when the Master asked me to accompany him to an audience with the Pharaoh himself, recently on reprieve from his campaign.

We were ushered in through a secret passage from the waterfront, where Eratosthenes had pretended to be taking astronomical measurements – in clear daylight! A beggar approached us and, showing a pre-arranged signal, bid us follow him behind a privet and into a secret corridor. Past storerooms and workshops, we achieved a staircase and ascending it, found ourselves escorted through a narrow tunnel that ending in an abrupt terminus. The beggar removed his hood to display a carefully coiffured mane and a well-tended beard in the Greek style. It was immediately obvious to me that the Master had begun sending his letters directly to Ptolemy's agents himself through such trusted channels and not, as had been customary for government dispatches, through the normal couriers of the chancery. Indeed, the Master did not seem surprised at the labyrinth of cramped corridors we passed through, giving me the impression that he had travelled this way before.

Our escort tapped a particular pattern on a wall at the end of the corridor and, to my surprise only, the wall slid open with perfect quiet. We were now facing a beautifully appointed octagonal room, beset with light from an oculus above and lined all around with scrolls shelved in encasements set into the thick granite walls from far Aswan, the quarry of the old dynasties.

The escort quickly disappeared. We were left alone in the room. My quizzical look to the Master concerning the method of our entry into the great room was met with amusement.

"Harmonics, Hesperos," said Eratosthenes. "A device of my own design. Hollow pockets of air of various volumes are suspended within a chamber within the false door. When the correct sequence of pitches is applied, they vibrate ever so slightly to move a cam on a crankshaft. When each cam has been triggered in the appropriate sequence, a door latch is triggered on a spring to release the door from its moorings. Closing the door resets the crankshaft for use once again."

"Ingenious," I said, admiringly.

"Nothing, simple harmonics. I have written a small monograph on the matter. I am collecting similar works into a larger treatise on the frequency of sound which I will display to his highness when–"

"Whenever you wish, Master Eratosthenes." A simply-clothed Ptolemy III spoke as he glided into the chamber. The Master bowed slightly. I froze and then feigned the best stoic obeisance I could.

"Great Lord," said Eratosthenes.

Ptolemy lashed a troubled smile toward me.

"Ahh, yes, Wise Lord," said the Master turning toward me. "This is Hesperos, my ward."

I made an effort to genuflect again when Ptolemy reached his hand toward mine. Grasping it, he bid me rise in front of him.

"We have very little need of courtly gestures here, young man. Master Eratosthenes has told me of your loyalty – and your ingenuity – and, may I say, your trustworthiness. You are an Egyptian by birth, yes?"

Hesitant to speak my eyes looked to the Master for permission. Receiving it, I said simply, "Great King of Kings, Your Majesty is correct, in this as in all things, Wise Lord."

"He looks me in the eye, Eratosthenes, he's not a native, not anymore. By the gods he is a Greek, though he has graced me with a Persian title." Ptolemy III poured himself a kylix of wine. "So, tell me of this latest dispatch and the preparations."

"Procopios and Polymius, your humble servants, have informed you, sir, that we have intercepted dispatches from Seleucus of the gravest kind."

"Indeed, that is what they have told me. They tell me that an attempt will be made on the eastern border two weeks before the Ptolemaia, and having overrun my garrison there, Seleucus hopes to raise up the native population, whose loyalty to the state he perceives as tenuous. Given these new numbers, Procopios and Polymius believe Seleucus will attempt a march on Pelusium or Hermopolis, then Naucratis and then Alexandria herself."

"Yes, Lord, that is their appraisal of the intelligence so far."

"And your appraisal, sir?"

"Given the intelligence available to them, I believe their interpretation is sound. It is true that, begging your majesty's permission, while the loyalty of your most magnificent majesty's subjects in Alexandria is beyond doubt, some in the borderlands are easily misled, particularly by the priestly class, who cling to the old ways."

"Indeed, and you believe we should move on Judea and Coele-Syria before Seleucus does?

"My lord, I am not a military strategist, I am a mathematician. But the dispatches mention Raphia specifically. It in itself is nothing. Your general, Xanthippus, by all accounts, has held with little difficulty the line south of Antioch while Seleucus sends recruiters from as far as Pergamon in the West to Babylon and Ecbatana in the East. Raphia, south of Gaza, has no wealth to speak of. It is hardly worth a scribe's attention to mark on a map of your vast territories, yet it has one thing that no other location does, wise Lord. It has a peculiar geography. If I may, sir." Eratosthenes approached a wall into which a mosaic of the Ptolemaic kingdom was inlaid. His hand traced the route from Alexandria to Naucratis to an unmarked spot in the homeland of the Jews. "Raphia, sire, near Gaza. This plain must be won by Seleucus if his intention is to move through the Sinai. And long before that we would have reports, not the least from Xanthippus, of Seleucian movements to the south.

"Indeed, as my strategoi tell me. All my generals are in agreement sir."

"Indeed, wise Lord. But I have brought you one message that I am at pains to reveal to Your Majesty personally and not through the usual channels. I make no accusation of any man," said the Master, "but after decoding the message that has so alerted your councils of war-"

"Yes, it was the message that called me back from Jerusalem, though it was my intention always to have decamped in time for the Ptolemaia."

"Indeed," said Eratosthenes. "Young Hesperos here began deciphering some of those messages we had, by the circumstances of their interception, judged of less importance."

"I see," said Ptolemy, staring out through an archway to the lighthouse beyond, the black smoke of its signal fire trailing off with the eastern winds. "Young Hesperos, you decoded these messages?"

"Yes," I said, at once meek and prideful. "It remains my great honor and privilege to humbly serve the living god in your majesty Ptolemy Euergetes, benefactor of all that is great and wondrous." I had become gradually adept at the type of art of address which flowed so masterfully from the senior courtiers and academicians of Alexandria. "I had but a small role, sir, the glory is the Chief Librarian's alone."

"Yes, yes, but what did it say then, gentlemen? Why all the secrecy?"

"My lord, because these messages were deemed of slight importance, mere side work, it was not customary to involve your loyal servants Polymius and Procopios. Young Hesperos is in the habit of running the intercepted text through our device, and he then delivers the deciphered messages to Aristophanes, among others, for translation before placing them into a digest for later review by your loyal ministers. Only, young Hesperos noticed a curious pattern in several of these dispatches and it was then that he alerted me to their contents."

"And, my dear Chief Librarian, what is contained in these dispatches?

"Wise Lord, your Chief Minister, Sosibius, was mentioned by name."

"Sosibius? It isn't unusual is it, that my chief minister would be mentioned by the enemy? Certainly he himself might be a target of their machinations."

"Indeed, sir. The evil displayed by the usurper of the East is boundless. Yet, I urge you to read the message in its entirety."

"I will if you feel it prudent."

Eratosthenes pulled two scraps of parchment from the inner lining of his cloak. Of the first, which he handed to Ptolemy, he said, "this, sir, is the cypher text. It is written in almost the same style as the other dispatches from the usurper."

Ptolemy held the papyrus up to the sun that beamed through the archway, reflected from the great inner sea beyond. "Almost?" he said.

"Indeed, sir, almost. And here," he said, handing the second scroll to the pharaoh, "is the plaintext of the encoded message."

Ptolemy read it silently to himself and then, pausing to look out over the bay, he shouted for a sentry in the adjoining corridor. Two guards appeared instantly. He demanded that his chief courtier, the great Sosibius, be brought to him at once.

The intervening silence was impossible to bear. I avoided making contact with either the Master or great Ptolemy, whose grandfather had fought with Alexander across the battlefields of Persia so many years before.

After long minutes of silence, large doors of carved Lebanon cedar opened. Sosibius burst forward into the chamber. He bowed so low that he caught his cloak underfoot and, rushing to the center of the room, nearly fell into a bust of Aristotle.

"Lord of Light," he said, recovering the balls of his feet, "what service may I offer?"

I am just now making an imitation to Onesimus of Sosibius' ridiculous entrance. Onesimus will laugh at anything. Just yesterday he was mocking an old woman of nearly forty balancing two baskets of fish on her shoulders as she made her way through the agora. Her movement was reminiscent of a light tender unmoored among ships of war. It is more likely that she was drunk at midday and for that I was the more understanding than Onesimus was derisive.

I am not usually one prone to caricature, as I have often been the object, both in public and in private, of painful jokes about my pedigree, even among the enlightened men of the Academy. To be a permanent outsider is to sustain these occasional insults, and I have never been one to reproduce them idly. But Sosibius was a walking caricature of courtiers: at once a stooped sycophant prepared to follow the pharaonic seat of authority through the dangerous shoals of Plouton as long as it continued to sustain his position.

Though harsh on Sosibius privately, the Master, ever objective, would often remind his circle that all courtiers are scientists in constant study of the nature of power and its attainment, and all academicians, in their own way, are courtiers maintaining a grasp on the wellspring of benefaction with one hand even as they cling to the mysteries of nature with the other. Court intrigue shifts from pole to pole, and even as Sosibius gained immense favor in the carrying on of internal matters, the pharaoh played his foreign ministers Procopios and Polymius against Sosibius by separating both camps into specialties so that no one faction might rise to threaten the autonomy of the pharaoh himself. It was in this light that the Master and I first saw him on that day, busy with the preparations of the Ptolemaia, an interior matter, and ostensibly ignorant of the foreign intrigues pulsing along the roads and sea lanes from Antioch to Alexandria.

As Ptolemy greeted Sosibius, the Master noticed my look of surprise at never having seen the great courtier in my capacity at the library when I had been exposed to other luminaries at court.

He whispered to me, "I believe it is true of most courts that the prince's most esteemed advisors seldom congregate except for the most solemn and mandatory ceremonies. This is partly a calculation meant to limit the potential for the appearance of collusion and impropriety that has undone the most cautious of courtiers. But it is also a concerted effort by court intermediaries, particularly the eunuchs and scribes attendant on these principals, to keep power decentralized and in the decentralization to fashion for themselves a niche from which they may add their own self-interested policy flourishes. By doing so they inflate their own importance at court."

As always, the Master explained in a moment the complexities of human nature. Sosibius continued with compliments and platitudes until waved off by a royal gesture of dismissal.

"Sosibius," said Ptolemy, "how are the preparations for the Ptolemaia, sir?"

"Gracious Lord, they are well underway. The vessels have been portaged, as your Excellency was made aware, and are even now becoming the crowning achievements of the entire Mediterranean. The foreign diplomatic corps has been prepared with the appropriate protocol, and I trust Procopios and Polymius have made great preparations for the appropriate homage of your majesty's loyal forces in Alexandria. And the entertainments, sir! They will rival anything seen since Alexander's entrance into Babylon."

"And, you, Sosibius, friend and loyal servant, you are responsible for the security of the event itself?"

"Wise Lord, if there is some misguided force that would work against your majesty, you may be assured that they will think twice before making their intentions known while I have charge of your majesty's safety."

"Truly, you are a wise man, Sosibius," said Ptolemy, turning to the Master. Sosibius followed his gaze and flashed a resentful smile toward the Chief Librarian.

"And the Academy sir," said Sosibius, "no doubt you have been working diligently on your part of the procession?"

"Sosibius," Eratosthenes said with a slight bow, "We have planned such marvels of learning, literature and automata and I believe several of the finer poets have composed some triumphant odes that will amaze and overwhelm all the senses."

"Well, there now," said Ptolemy. "It sounds as if it has all become quite suitably replete with spectacle."

"Oh, indeed wise lord, indeed."

"Fine then, Sosibius, carry on with your work."

"Sire," he said as he began to back out of the room while maintaining the stoop of a pronounced bow.

"One last thing, sir."

"Majesty?" said Sosibius, rising slightly.

"When, exactly," said Ptolemy, "are the Seleucian-led rebels planning on overrunning the city and the court, and who, exactly, have you planned to take my place when I've been executed in the uprising?" Ptolemy flashed the dispatch in front of Sosibius' face. "The intelligence is unclear."

Sosibius threw himself at Ptolemy's feet, shouting denials and oaths of loyalty. Amid Sosibius' moans of protestation, the pharaoh signaled to a courtier that Sosibius was to be taken into custody. As the courtier moved to call the guard, the two great doors opened and another courtier burst forward out of breath as if he'd run from Marathon.

"Great King," he said prostrating himself, "I beg one thousand mercies."

"Yes, out with it." said Ptolemy.

"Pharaoh, light of the Nile, the great usurper's younger brother, Antiochus Hierax, has declared himself king of Anatolia. General Xanthippus has sent word that Seleucus has withdrawn the bulk of his army from Coele-Syria to march north to Antioch. Word has just spread from the docks. It happened a week ago, wise lord."

I heard the Master breathe uneasily, but he needn't have done so. Intelligence was his trade, comforted Ptolemy, but all information was not intelligence, just as much intelligence contained misleading information.

"Court secrets," said Ptolemy, "are sent through secure channels adeptly; a monarch's deposition is broadcast instantly to the meanest fishmonger at the docks. It is likely you will supply me with more intricate knowledge of the new insurgent king's defenses and disposition, but I am not surprised to first hear of this from the dockyards."

He then turned to Sosibius and said, "I imagine this changes *your* plans, sir.

Sosibius groveled and cried out his innocence at Ptolemy's feet as two of the pharaoh's bodyguards pulled him, prostrate and screaming, from the royal apartments. His unequivocal denials surprised even the Master, who seemed to show a moment of remorse before his pharaoh.

Seeing this, Ptolemy said, "he is a *master* tactician, it seems, as wily in the shadows as melodramatic at the feet of his pharaoh."

My subsequent inquiries have produced several new methods of solving functional equations containing only one variable quantity and much more complicated, and have convinced me of the importance of the Calculus, particularly as an instrument of discovery in the more difficult branches of analysis. Nor is it only in the recesses of this abstract science that its advantages will be felt: it is peculiarly adapted to the discovery of those laws of action by which one particle of matter attracts or repels another of the same or a different species; consequently it may be applied to every branch of natural philosophy, where the object is to discover by calculation from the results of experiment the laws which regulate the action of the ultimate particles of bodies. To the accomplishment of these desirable purposes, it must be confessed that it is in its present state unequal; but should the labours of future inquirers give to it that perfection which other methods of investigation have attained, it is not too much to hope that its maturer age shall unveil the hidden laws which govern the phenomena of magnetic, electric, or even of chemical action.

—CHARLES BABBAGE, Part II of his Essay towards the Calculus of Functions, 1816

12

It was this initial meeting that gave me the first stirrings of the idea that coalesced at a later writers' group meeting. It was this idea that led Perry and me to launch into a fictional story about the intersection of ancient mathematics and modern cryptography. I had no idea how close to the mark our fiction would find itself. To further our story, and more importantly, to sate our growing curiosity, we were eager to meet with Professor Martin again to hear of any insights he might have come up with.

After this first meeting all of our subsequent calls to Professor Martin went unanswered. Perry sent emails, having little hope of being answered by the emeritus professor in that manner in the most ordinary of circumstances. Perry and I contrived a meeting at his office, only to find it in exactly the same managed disorder we had seen days prior. The department receptionist said that Professor Martin had missed his only class the day before, that he had called minutes before the class to say that a relative had died, he was sorry to have missed the class, and that he would be back in time for the following week's session. As an emeritus, it wasn't unusual for him to stay off-campus for several days, and his abnormal office hours were legendary. We waited an agonizing week during which we continued to leave voicemails on his direct line and with the receptionist, to whom we tried to sound casually interested in meeting with him again about a "shared interest." Perry thought we were coming across like stalkers, and as neither of us were current students of his we worried the message might not be given the urgency we'd like.

We finally cornered him as he walked out of his morning class. Slightly disjointed, but seeming unsurprised to see us, he directed us to follow him up to his office. After we all stepped into the small space, still overflowing with texts in dead languages and stacked floor to ceiling with journal articles, he casually locked the door behind us.

"I don't want us to be disturbed," he said. "Now, gentlemen. I've been traveling a bit the last week or so."

"Yes," Perry said, "I'm so sorry for your loss."

Professor Martin gave us a look of coy regret. We all knew there had been no death in the family.

"Now, listen," Martin said, "after you left, I made a few phone calls. I'm not an historian of mathematics. I wanted to discuss this with some specialists I know. One of them was my old thesis advisor at Stanford."

"Dr. Pratt!" said Perry. "I met him once. He guest lectured once for Dr. Martin when," he turned to Martin, "you were attending, I think it was a conference. He was fantastic. He got us truly excited about literature that was written 2400 years ago. He kept going on about 'epochism,' – how it's a terrible human practice to assume one is living at the height of excellence, that entire historical epochs were 'leading up' to the present, as if their only value was a precursor to the integrated circuit, the space age and reality television."

"Exactly," said Martin. "Classical antiquity, for him, is more than a job, it's a passion – his life's work is the understanding, preservation and dissemination of the culture and achievements of mid-antiquity. When I was studying with him at Stanford he was working on an out-building on his property – a faithful reproduction of the Villa of the Mysteries from Pompeii, right down to the plaster and frescoes. He often hosted graduate students at mock symposia, where we'd recline on chaises and discuss philosophy and literature in the Socratic style. He's really one of half a dozen preeminent scholars on late Athenian, early Hellenistic mathematics."

I was aware of the real Villa of the Mysteries. It was one of many surprisingly intact villas on the outskirts of Pompeii that had been well preserved by a heavy coating of ash from the eruption in 79 AD of Mount Vesuvius, south of Rome on the Gulf of Naples. The Villa's owner was unknown, but, Martin was saying, Pratt had advanced the theory that it had been built on instructions from Augustus and given as a gift to his wife Livia. Pratt had spent considerable time as a graduate student strengthening the argument for Livian occupation, tying Augustus, the posthumous heir of Caesar and a relative outsider at his adoption, to the various religious ceremonies depicted on the Villa's walls. Livia, Pratt argued, was heavily involved in the cult of Dionysus or the Eleusinian Mysteries and the rituals – or mysteries – that comprised the initiation rites associated with membership among its ranks, imagery particularly suited to a relatively unpedigreed military ruler wishing to present his family as welcome initiates in ancient rights of privilege and intellectual prestige.

"Well, as you can imagine," said Martin, "before your visit, I had contacted him when I heard of the discovery of the Alexander Palimpsest. We talked about it for hours. Then I called him several days ago. At first our phone conversation went as it usually does. I should call more, I said, diving into a list of student projects and catching up on the usual paucity of new research in classical language and literature. Then, I mentioned you two, the Alexander Palimpsest, the abrupt ending of the web footage and your 'E-pi-mee-ka-nee-sis.' I expected him to launch into his usual enthusiasm, especially for a project so innately connected to our field and so potentially promising to the advancement of our understanding of the period.

"He suddenly became very reserved. Now, gentlemen, you have to understand. Something like the Archimedes Palimpsest did get a little media coverage, and there was a flurry of initial interest surrounding the Alexander Palimpsest, to be sure. That's how you gentlemen came to hear about it. But, in our community, in the classics 'world', the possibility that an unknown masterpiece by one of antiquity's greatest thinkers is a, well, what would it be like for you two – it would be like a week in Vegas, like a free cruise around the world or something, right? I mean, something like this is a once-in-a-generation find if it turns out to reveal unknown work from scholars at the Library of Alexandria. Only marginally more exciting might be a lost play of Sophocles, right? But from my mentor, sitting at home, semi-retired, his enthusiasm heightened at the hint of the slightest new discovery – nothing. He said calmly, 'I have to see you in person,' told me he'd be expecting me the next day and hung up the phone."

Perry and I waited for Martin to continue the story. All three of us stared at each other for what seemed like minutes until Dr. Martin finally interrupted the quiet. He leaned slightly forward in his chair and, at almost a whisper said, "He *was* following the project. One of his former students is a consultant on the project. Apparently this student's specialty is the history of mathematics. He was contacted early on when the team discovered diagrams that were similar to those drawn by Euclid and Archimedes. They needed an expert to help give context to all the graphic representations throughout the Palimpsest.

"I spoke to Pratt on Sunday evening, after your visit. I was on a plane Monday morning. By Monday afternoon I was sitting in the Villa of the Mysteries, having a glass of wine and joking about the cloak and dagger nature of the previous night's conversation. Now, Pratt can be a little dramatic. The symposia at the Villa speak to that, but this was something extraordinary. Pratt led me through a small doorway from the *andron*, a kind of living room where symposia took place, to the scriptorium, where writing and, more generally, a patrician's scholarship might take place. Throughout the scriptorium, Perry had laid out folding tables covered in photographs of the pages of the Alexander Palimpsest."

Perry and I looked at each other. We had also printed out many of the pages of the palimpsest the project had made available on its website. The image of the two of us huddled over a stack of printouts in a downtown bar juxtaposed with an elite classical scholar pouring over the same documents in a recreation of a Pompeiian suburban villa 3000 miles west made us both smile.

"So," I said, "that's not unusual that he would be following the work on the website. Did he see the E-pi-mee-ka-nee-sis image before the feed went down?"

"He didn't have to, gentlemen. He had the printout in front of him. He showed it to me. And he had several other E-pi-mee-ka-nee-sis pages besides."

"Where did he get those? They aren't on the website. His student sent them to him?"

"Exactly. I think this student was consulting his old mentor for advice, a consultation Pratt believed the project was not aware of. Pratt told me that many of the E-pi-mee-ka-nee-sis pages came to him after you told me the feed was cut."

"Fascinating," I said.

"Well, yes, it is. Except, the student and Pratt had been stumped. They knew, of course, about the Antikythera inscriptions. They knew they had seen the Koine prefix before, and they knew that it usually meant 'swift.' It was my analysis," he said with the reserved pride that eventually accretes to academics, "that shed light on the E-pi-mee-ka-nee-sis prefix."

"Well," I said, "What was his conclusion? And why drop the website feed? Why stop releasing the images on the website?"

"Pratt didn't know. He only said that the prefix idea was something he hadn't put together himself and that he would communicate my interpretation to his student working on the project."

"Did they know about the Mersenne Prime?" Perry asked.

"Yes, they did, eventually. Apparently that was what seized their attention. This student – Pratt was cagey the entire time about the student's name – this student noticed it immediately and recognized the significance of eighteenth century CE knowledge written in a third century BCE manuscript.

"Well, of course, I'm completely intrigued about this whole thing, so I began trying to get some information about the student. Somewhere between the second and third bottle of wine, Pratt told me something very interesting. He had met the student at an exhibit of the works of Athanasius Kircher at Green Library at Stanford. He had been introduced to this student by the chair of the mathematics department."

I also knew about Athanasius Kircher, an intriguing figure in his own right.

"The Jesuit polymath?" I said.

"Exactly," said Perry. "It makes sense that a student of the mathematics of antiquity would be a fan of Kircher's. He's known as the Baroque era's answer to Leonardo DaVinci. He attempted a translation of Egyptian hieroglyphs 200 years before Champollion. He wrote extensively on biblical allegories and advanced a critique of a literal Noah's Ark, which he considered impossible given the number of species, their nutritional needs, the length of the voyage and the dimensions given in Genesis. He also worked on the Voynich Manuscript, an enigmatic work in an unknown language still mysterious to this day. He constructed a universal artificial language, wrote on geology, biology and medicine. In 1646 he published *Ars Magna Lucis et Umbrae* about an early device for the projection of images. He was one of a growing movement of rationalists who sought to demystify technology and create a very distinct separation between supernaturalism and the unfettered pursuit of the scientific method through the formulation of hypotheses based solely on the application of reason to the observation and analysis of natural phenomena."

"The interesting thing about Kircher," I said, "is that he was, I believe, a very devout Jesuit."

"Not that unusual, actually," said Martin, "given the early history of the Jesuit order. The Society of Jesus, as it is known formally, was originally founded by Ignatius Loyola to give a military structure to the counter-reformation then sweeping Europe. They fought against church corruption and often found themselves at odds with the hierarchy, if not the theology of the early modern Church. They found rationalism, for which they'd become renowned – or infamous – a corollary to faith, rather than its antagonist, and are considered the most significant contributors to experimental physics of the seventeenth century. And that's how I coaxed a bit more from Pratt. This student of his is a Jesuit initiate, and found his calling for god only after he had undertaken an undergraduate program in complex mathematics, where, Pratt told me, he became fascinated with prime numbers, idolizing early mathematical figures like Euclid, Archimedes and Eratosthenes, who invented the sieve method Euler probably used, at least in part, in some of his calculations of the Mersenne primes."

"So this student would have been the perfect person to have on the Alexander Palimpsest team," I said.

"Exactly," said Martin, "and when he hit a block in the road, he called on his old mentor Pratt, who might shed some light on any difficulties he encountered.

"So, Pratt and I discussed the implications for the history of mathematics if it could be shown conclusively that scholars in the third century BCE had found a way to discover high-order Mersenne primes. It wouldn't rock the world, but, as I said, in our little corner of academia, this was big news. We chatted late into the night, and I realized I would never make it back to DC for my class. Pratt invited me to stay awhile, and we spent the next day dissecting the pages he had gathered in the scriptorium. Sometime during the day he excused himself. He was going to contact his student and tell him about my prefix idea, he said. He was eager to pass on the extremely exciting prospect that the Alexander Palimpsest alluded to some sort of mechanized calculation, and the connection to the Mersenne Prime was so unusual and so breathtaking a concept that he couldn't wait to share this insight, through his student, with the Alexander Palimpsest team. He returned after a long absence during which he had presumably made the call. We continued talking into the night, and I took a flight mid-morning the next day."

Martin told us that when he returned to DC, he took the prefix idea up with several colleagues. They showed some interest, but, as is typical in academic circles, they were slow to adopt the relatively unorthodox interpretation of the Koine Greek prefix as an indication that the context of the text in which it was found was a description of the calculation of Mersenne primes. Professor Martin had some friends within the broader academic community who had also been following the work of the Alexander Palimpsest and who had expressed frustration with the lack of new information. Martin chose to keep his full analysis from all but a few of his colleagues. He asked for and received numerous theories about the interrupted work. Some said it was likely that funding was tight. Some decried the general public ignorance of math, science and history and blamed flagging public interest. Only one, he said, had been watching at the exact moment of the discovery. He too had seen the technicians congregate one by one near the large television screen but had not seen the word itself.

"I called Pratt a few days after I got back to DC. I left a message with the housekeeper, who told me he had stepped out to campus. I received no reply that night or the next day. When I called again, I reached the housekeeper once more, only to find out that Pratt hadn't been home for the last two days. I was concerned so I contacted his department. The secretary said that he hadn't seen him in weeks, not entirely unusual for an emeritus, but after some coaxing, gave me his daughter's phone number in San Francisco. I did reach her, and after a brief introduction, she said she remembered me from one of the symposia evenings she had taken part in. She was concerned as well, because, she said, her father had been missing for several days. She had been contacted by the housekeeper, and was considering filing a missing persons report. I asked if it was uncharacteristic of him to travel without notifying anyone. She said it was unusual, but she wondered if he might have flown out to meet 'a student' whom he had mentioned days earlier. Pratt was overly excited the last time he spoke with her, and mentioned that the student was making headway on a project of great importance. She said he may have told her what the project was, but as a financial analyst, her interest didn't stretch to ancient manuscripts. She wished her father well and hadn't heard from him since that conversation.

"So," I said, "he's in communication with the 'student' regularly, he gets excited about the findings, you show up and deliver the prefix insight, and he contacts the student to inform him of your discovery. He then, what, hops on a plane to meet the student first-hand, maybe to look over the unpublished pages and help dive into the mathematics angle."

"Well, if he did indeed fly out to meet the student, there's only one place he would go," said Martin. "He went to the museum, in Baltimore."

"Exactly," said Perry. "Are you gents up for a road trip?"

Regard your good name as the richest jewel you can possibly be possessed of - for credit is like fire; when once you have kindled it you may easily preserve it, but if you once extinguish it, you will find it an arduous task to rekindle it again. The way to gain a good reputation is to endeavor to be what you desire to appear.

—SOCRATES

13

Two matters now consumed the inner circles of court. A schism had taken place in the Seleucian kingdom, and dynastic infighting was rarely bloodless. The Master was true to his pharaoh's faith in his ability to continue to supply useful and timely intelligence. Of the many messages intercepted were orders to have certain provincial Seleucian governors murdered, ostensibly field executions for mismanagement but more likely instruments of creating vacancies for the new regime's supporters. One dispatch contained the impassioned pleas of a provincial guard captain that he be excused from the act of murdering the official he had sworn to protect because he would be killing his own brother. Another dispatch was intercepted that laid an accusation of disloyalty at the feet of the man if he declined. Implied in the message was a threat that his family would share the fate of traitors to the crown. A further dispatch explaining the actions of that particular soldier was never intercepted, but it was later discovered that the provincial official, a governor of a small outpost in Cappadocia, had uncharacteristically wandered into the mountains without an escort and succumbed to exposure. What lay in store for the already uneasy relations between Ptolemy and his fractured neighbor was difficult to predict.

The other great matter of secret discussion was the appropriate resolution of the treachery of Sosibius. A public execution was a difficult prospect to stage-manage. Eratosthenes had no stomach for the spectacle of capital punishment, and for his part in unmasking the plot, he was still uneasy that his device should ever be turned to destruction so closely associated with him. Had Sosibius been discovered colluding only with Seleucus, an infamous enemy of all Egypt, the pharaoh would not have hesitated to have him castrated, disemboweled and dragged through the streets of Alexandria, from the heights of Lochias past the Serapeum and into the agora and the Soma so that not even Alexander's ghost would miss the spectacle. But Sosibius had been working with native Egyptians to overthrow their own pharaoh with the support of a foreign power. The implications for the internal security of the empire were clear. Sosibius maintained his innocence, even under the duress of innovative torture practices imported from Rome.

Eratosthenes marveled at the obstinance of the man and wondered why he would not render a confession and replace the pain of torture and certain lingering death with the quick relief of a clean run through the back of the neck, as was promised should he divulgence the specifics of the plot and the names of the conspirators.

The Ptolemaia was soon approaching and the Pharaoh grew more and more nervous that the conspiracy might yet move forward without the continued supervision of its ringleader. The Master confided in me that Ptolemy had asked him for advice, which he could not render, for fear of "becoming that which I am not, a man of ambition and action, when I am simply a humble servant of science." Ptolemy closed off his court to all but a small handful of courtiers, Polymius and Procopios among them. Eventually it was agreed that, while security at the Ptolemaia would be increased to include a tremendous army presence, a substantial number of secretly armed native mercenaries paid directly from this inner circle should also be present on the day, for fear of how infected the Greek leadership had become with the conspiracy. Polymius and Procopios, the Master thought, had begun to capitalize on their elevated influence by guiding the pharaoh's every decision.

Their combined influence finally eclipsed that of Sosibius when several members of the Greek aristocracy fell ill and died under unusual circumstances. On the island of Tyre, which the great Alexander had acquired with difficulty, the governor loyal to Ptolemy fell ill after a scouting expedition, an unusual outing for the pharaoh's representative to undertake personally. In Ptolemais, one of the pharaoh's most important fortified settlements in Judea, the governor, having just returned from Alexandria where he presented to his pharaoh fifty talents of silver in honor of the Ptolemaia, dropped dead within sight of his city on the return trip. His physician declared it exhaustion, but the diagnosis was met with incredulity by Ptolemy's new chief ministers, who then duly introduced a sense of incredulity in the pharaoh himself.

It was only after a curious incident did the Master truly begin to question the intelligence he had given his pharaoh, and he later recalled that it was his experience with Archimedes in the Athens of his youth that gave him an idea that would have enormous repercussions for the court of Ptolemy III and his successors. I speak, of course, of the Master's careful recreation of the code of Archimedes to submit purposefully erroneous properties of the Parthenon so that his correspondent might reveal himself.

When new encoded dispatches arrived, they were logged into a ledger with the details of their interception, including the date and location of interception, each message's sender and its intended recipient. To this description was added a designation of which agent of the pharaoh's had intercepted the letter and, if different than the interceptor, a designation of the copyist who was in the pharaoh's employ. Polymius and Procopios held this information tightly, yet it was no great matter for the Master to produce a table of place names and event dates and cross-reference that with the codes assigned to various agents of the pharaoh. He then examined all dispatches from the 'Sosibius' message, as we began to call it, and discovered that only several other messages had exactly the same sender, point of interception, intended recipient, and copyist.

We secretly turned the device to decoding these other messages. We discovered that the nature of the messages was unusual. While written in the same polyalphabetic code as the others, they had very little information contained in them. For example, one was a report of the weather in Antioch; another was a contract for grain and wool to be delivered to a town in Bactria, far from the war preparations of either of the Seleucian kings.

The more messages the device decoded, the more damning they became by their unimportance. The Master, more sophisticated than his Egyptian ward, began to realize the implication of the Sosibius letter delivered among these trifles. It became his suspicion that the Sosibius message had been forged and planted with low-level Seleucian couriers who would have been the easiest to infiltrate. It was an easy step then to consider those agents at court who would be well-placed to recreate the code and inject it into the intelligence stream. He first thought of agents of the Seleucian king, who might wish to discredit one of the Pharaoh's chief ministers, but it would make little sense to incur suspicion about the method of delivery when they had the ability to ensure its interception with other high-level messages. Ptolemy did have a large intelligence organization, but the Master was certain that his spies and couriers, while inhabiting the channels of espionage, had no access to the structure of the code in which their dispatches were written. He deduced then, the unthinkable, that Polymius, Procopios or both of them, with their access to the Pharaoh's network of spies and the code itself, must somehow have designed the implication of Sosibius.

It was then that he put a plan into place to plant a message of his own to determine the truth of his suspicions. I still do not know how the Master entirely achieved it, but he orchestrated a remarkable series of events that exposed a plot to overthrow the dynastic integrity of one of Alexander's greatest generals.

The master had surmised that the intelligence contained in the first dispatch was real. A plan was in place, known to the Seleucian court, to promote or support defections among the pharaoh's high ranking courtiers. This defection was to be undertaken at the Ptolemaia, when troops would be massed within the city and prepared to control the population. Suspicious that Polymius and Procopios were well-placed to execute components of the plan and remembering their greater than usual secrecy, he crafted counter-intelligence to subvert their efforts. Though all of this was unknown to me at the time, I may now recount the ordeal with complete accuracy.

Knowing that several Greek aristocrats in Ptolemy's personal guard had grown disillusioned with what they saw as the erosion of Greek influence by Ptolemy's inclusion of native religion in state ceremony and what they considered his less than suitable land grants, Polymius and Procopios coerced these of Ptolemy's intimates to assassinate their pharaoh in public during the Ptolemaia. In the disorder of the accession of a young king, Ptolemy's five year old son, Seleucus would move on Coele-Syria, where, once conquered, the conspirators would meet their families where they had already been relocated. These members would be given large land grants and those who did not escape or survive the assassination would be assured of the prosperity and care of their families.

Having engineered what they considered a stronger code resistant to the device's capabilities, Polymius and Procopios corresponded regularly with their Seleucian allies. While they conducted secret face-to-face negotiations with their Alexandrian conspirators, the weakness of their plans lay in their use of a code to speak to Seleucus that Eratosthenes had deciphered and the contents of which the Master could deliver directly to his Pharaoh.

Onesimus urges me not yet to divulge the entire plan. It is better for posterity that I show rather than tell of the immensity of the attempted insurrection set against of the dazzling display of the greatest Ptolemaia Alexandria had yet seen. I yield to his expertise, he is quite an adept at Hesiod, and has a flair for his favorite poet's ambition. Let me retrace my narrative and place the coup within the context of the beating hearts and hooves, the glimmer of silver and gold, and the clanking of swords and spears that travelled like the roaring winds of Olympus from one end of Alexandria to the other.

The appointed day of the Ptolemaia finally arrived. The hulls of the ships I had labored over so diligently rose out of the harbor like long slivers carved from the royal palace itself. The largest boasted ten stories above the waterline which held gardens, temples and fountains while at regular intervals arose even larger towers on which had been secured artillery and ballistae of such complexity that Archimedes, Philo, Ctesibius and Abdaraxus had been seconded for their design. I accompanied a small contingent from the Academy that included The Master, the great engineers, and other luminaries.

As Chief Librarian and tutor to the heir apparent, young Ptolemy, the Master was given pride of place on a small dais adjacent to the Great tomb of Alexander. The gossiping ancients Callimachus and Aristarchus of Samos, then so pallid and near to death that they had been painted like catamites, were arranged far from Apollonius of Rhodes, so that Callimachus should not have to look at him. If Callimachus appeared near death, Cleanthes and Timon of Phlius, visiting from Athens, looked worse in the Egyptian heat than the decomposing body of Alexander, who died in the year Cleanthes was born. Cleanthes had embraced the invitation to attend the Ptolemaia as a demonstration of stoic fortitude. Timon had insisted that the satiric poems, the *silloi*, he had composed in honor of the occasion be presented under his own direction.

Also visiting from Athens, Chrysippus, the Stoic philosopher, busied himself with an adversarial philosophical discussion with Panthoides, the sole representative of the Megarian school. It was said their longstanding philosophical feud transcended political boundaries, and it had been decided by Sosibius, long before his indictment, that they be kept as far apart as possible. Conon of Samos, the court astronomer, was placed near his aged countryman, Aristarchus. Nicomedes was planted between the Stoics and the skeptics and Archimedes, Ctesibius and Philo of Byzantium were seasoned in where they might have the greatest ameliorating effect.

Astride these vanities loomed the Master, on this day and many others an example of composure in the midst of chaos. As his ward, I sat behind him with several other select and mostly aristocratic students. Diocles and Apollonius of Perga quoted Theocritus to each other as Aristophanes failed to engage in conversation the undeniably ingenious but rather bland Abdaraxus.

The royal dais was carved from a single block of marble. It depicted three scenes of Alexander in as many panels. The left-most relief depicted the great general liberating Egypt from its Persian overlords generations before. The panel farthest right depicted the ancient oracle at Siwa pronouncing Alexander a living god. The panel in the middle, by far the largest of the three, depicted in an uncharacteristically stylized way Alexander gazing out across the bay of Alexandria to the Mediterranean beyond. With both hands, Alexander placed a wreath of laurels upon the head of Ptolemy I, his greatest general and companion, who was oddly situated with one foot on the island of Pharos and another near the exact spot in the agora where the dais had been erected. The significance was clear. Atop this block of marble, ten cubits high and thirty cubits broad, sat Ptolemy III, natural and divinely anointed successor of Alexander and undoubted king and pharaoh of everything within and much beyond the horizon.

Next to him sat Berenice, who had recently caused a sensation of patriotism by cutting off her hair in dedication to Aphrodite for her husband's safe return from Syria. Eratosthenes, then compiling a biography of Berenice, considered the story a fairly typical expression of contemporary apocrypha. Conon of Samos, more of a romantic than the Master, was so moved that he named the constellation *Coma Berenices* after her sacrifice. Berenice's young children, Arsinoë and Ptolemy, fidgeted in their seats as their infant brother, Magas, slept in the arms of a wet-nurse. The king's younger brother Lysimachus appeared in robes designed specifically to present a conspicuous austerity in deference to his reigning relation.

As expected, the royal party was accompanied by a small contingent of palace guards in full Greek dress uniform. His retinue included Polymius and Procopios, other advisors, and several other court functionaries. The entire party sat on chaises of gold and were attended throughout the ceremony by a small army of servants and slaves hovering with wine, plates of grapes, dates, figs, fine meat, fresh fish and baked delicacies.

The procession began with the pomp of Osiris, at the head of which were the Sileni in scarlet and purple cloaks, who opened the way through the crowd. Twenty satyrs followed on each side of the road, bearing torches; and then Victories with golden wings, clothed in skins, each with a golden staff six cubits long, twined round with ivy. An altar was carried next, covered with golden ivy-leaves, with a garland of golden vine-leaves tied with white ribands; and this was followed by a hundred and twenty boys in scarlet frocks, carrying bowls of crocus, myrrh, and frankincense, which made the air fragrant with the scent. Then came forty dancing satyrs crowned with golden ivy-leaves, with their naked bodies stained with pleasing colors, each carrying a crown of vine leaves and gold; then two Sileni in scarlet cloaks and white boots, one having the hat and wand of Mercury and the other a trumpet; and between them walked a man, six feet high, in tragic dress and mask, meant for the Year, carrying a golden cornucopia. He was followed by a tall and beautiful woman, meant for the Lustrum of five years, carrying in one hand a crown and in the other a palm-branch. Then came an altar, and a troop of satyrs in gold and scarlet, carrying golden drinking-cups.

Then came Philiscus the poet, the priest of Osiris, with all the servants of the god; then the Delphic tripods, the prizes which were to be given in the wrestling matches; that for the boys was nine cubits high, and that for the men twelve cubits high. Next came a four-wheeled car, fourteen cubits long and eight wide, drawn along by one hundred and eighty men, on which was the statue of Osiris, fifteen feet high, pouring wine out of a golden vase, and having a scarlet frock down to his feet, with a yellow transparent robe over it, and over all a scarlet cloak. Before the statue was a large golden bowl, and a tripod with bowls of incense on it. Over the whole was an awning of ivy and vine leaves; and in the same chariot were the priests and priestesses of the god.

This was followed by a smaller chariot drawn by sixty men, in which was the statue of Isis in a robe of yellow and gold. Then came a chariot full of grapes, and another with a large cask of wine, which was poured out on the road, as the procession moved on, and at which the eager crowd filled their jugs and drinking-cups. Then came another band of satyrs and Sileni, and more chariots of wine; then eighty Delphic vases of silver, and Panathenaic and other vases; and sixteen hundred dancing boys in white frocks and golden crowns: then a number of beautiful pictures; and a chariot carrying a grove of trees, out of which flew pigeons and doves, so tied that they might be easily caught by the crowd.

On another chariot, drawn by an elephant, came Osiris, as he returned from his Indian conquests. He was followed by twenty-four chariots drawn by elephants, sixty drawn by goats, twelve by some kind of stags, seven by gazelles, four by wild asses, fifteen by buffaloes, eight by ostriches, and seven by stags of some other kind. Then came chariots loaded with the tributes of the conquered nations; men of Ethiopia carrying six hundred elephants' teeth; sixty huntsmen leading two thousand four hundred dogs; and one hundred and fifty men carrying trees, in the branches of which were tied parrots and other beautiful birds. Next walked the foreign animals, Ethiopian and Arabian sheep, Brahmin bulls, a white bear, leopards, panthers, bears, a camelopard, and a rhinoceros; proving to the wondering crowd the variety and strangeness of the countries that owned their monarch's sway.

In another chariot was seen Bacchus running away from Juno, and flying to the altar of Rhea. After that came the statues of Alexander, Ptolemy I Soter and Ptolemy II Philadelphus crowned with gold and ivy: by the side of Euergetes' father and grandfather stood the statues of Virtue, of the god Khnum, and of the city of Corinth; and he was followed by female statues of the conquered cities of Ionia, Greece, Asia Minor, and Persia; and the statues of other gods. Then came crowds of singers and cymbal-players, and two thousand bulls with gilt horns, crowns, and breast-plates. Then came Amon-Ra and other gods; and the statue of Alexander between Victory and the goddess Neith, in a chariot drawn by elephants: then a number of thrones of ivory and gold; on one was a golden crown, on another a golden cornucopia, and on the throne of the late Ptolemy Philadelphus was a crown worth ten thousand aurei; then three thousand two hundred golden crowns, twenty golden shields, sixty-four suits of golden armor; and the whole was closed with forty wagons of silver vessels, twenty of golden vessels, eighty of costly eastern scents, and fifty-seven thousand six hundred foot soldiers, and twenty-three thousand two hundred horse.

The procession had begun moving by torchlight before day broke in the morning. It went through the streets of Alexandria past the royal dais within the vast agora before the tomb of Alexander, where, as in the procession, everything that was costly in art, or scarce in nature, was brought together in honor of the day. As the suggestion of dusk began to fall on the great city, Ptolemy soon gave the signal to his chief admirals, who each signaled to their particular command in the great harbor beyond. Arranged in advance by the great showman Sosibius, who all courtiers knew to be languishing in a dungeon below the royal palaces, the marble dais began to lift up so that huge bronze wheels were revealed to be operating underneath. The Master's and Archimedes' gearing mechanisms had been employed so that only 3 connected *tethrippon*, large chariots drawn by four horses abreast, were needed to move the entire block. The academicians and the other students and I saw our queue, and we descended our dais in order of age and fell in line behind the pharaoh's cortege.

The entire assembly made its way from the Soma, through the agora, down the Canopic way and onto a large viewing stand, near the palaces, that had been specially constructed for the day. The pharaoh's arrival had been orchestrated to correspond with the last rays of Helios, and just as the symbols had been given to the admirals, a chorus began to sing on queue as Ptolemy again lifted his hand and pointed to a floating platform that had been situated midway between the great lighthouse and the shore. He dipped a golden staff topped with dipped naphtha into a burning cauldron and passed the flaming torch to a captain, who ceremoniously passed his fire to a battalion of torch barriers.

This small group processed out from the platform in ten lines, each heading for a point at shore which had a connection to each hull. As each rank of torchbearers reached their shore points, they dipped their torches into a cauldron, lighting and sending out into the sea a flame carried in a lead channel filled with naphtha. The fires raced each other toward their designated ship and, fire itself bending to the will of Ptolemy, a torch bearer on each hull touched the flame to another series of channels which lit each hull from vast chandeliers designed into the structure of the ship. The channels rose to each of the ballistae-bearing towers. Soon men assigned to each ballista lit a projectile already loaded into the giant devices. The effect was of ten sons of Helios rising in tandem over the harbor with hundreds of smaller bodies orbiting around them.

Ptolemy again raised his hand, and with his son and heir beside him, gave the signal to fire. Acting as one huge wave, hundreds of projectiles issued out from the ten ships toward the platform. The precision with which each ballistae had been attuned disallowed a single projectile from missing its target, which exploded with the appearance that Helios, Ptah and Osiris together had ascended from the Bay of Alexandria.

The crowd erupted in cheers and adulation. Several people fainted. The priests of Serapis shouted incantations, the ladies of Aphrodite danced naked on the shore, their every curve and hidden place revealed as if they danced at noon. A huge cheer arose from the hippodrome, where preparations for public games had been suspended so those in attendance might witness the harbor radiating like the heavens.

A contingent of aristocracy, each representing a nomarchate of Egypt, presented the royal party with fifty golden crowns for Ptolemy III, thirty for

Berenice II, and twenty to their son, the heir young Ptolemy, beside other costly gifts. It was later estimated that one thousand talents, more than had been required to feed and supply Alexander's army on its march into Egypt, were spent on the amusements of the day. Ptolemy was master of earth and sea, no dominion could withstand the might of his arms nor the allure of his wealth. The entire demonstration served to resoundingly display the divinity of Ptolemy, the majesty of his person and the largesse of his treasury. Nothing was beyond his gift, nothing was beyond his power. He could harness the fires of Helios and send them, unerringly, against any foe of Egypt.

The crowd was incoherent with joy and drink. The royal guard pressed against crowds wishing to burst forth and offer praise to their pharaoh. I looked to see what expressions of joy, gratitude or irony might sit upon my Master's face only to discover that he was no longer beside me. Archimedes too was gone, though none of the academicians or my fellow students, themselves beset by drink, seemed to notice. The rest of the evening was spent in high spirits with my contemporaries. I fell to my sleep in the gardens of the Academy that evening praising the god-king Ptolemy and spilling my last drop of wine into my mouth while uttering an homage to the Fortunes for having been there, at the Academy, in Ptolemy Euergetes' Alexandria, the navel of the world.

It is here that Onesimus now suggests I record the Master's exploits that same evening, known to me fully only years later. As I have already said, the Master, understanding the code, was able to reproduce it and fold into the conspirators' correspondence messages of his own design. With the full knowledge of Ptolemy III, he devised an ingenious test of the extent of the conspiracy. The Master intercepted the actual plans of the Seleucian forces and replaced them with his own as soon as they were received. He then allowed Polymius and Procopios the latitude to use the device as they wished, thus providing them the reassurance of having decoded what they considered actual messages from abroad. In like manner he submitted coded messages to Seleucus by invoking Theodotus of Aetolia, governor of Coele-Syria headquartered in Ptolemais, north of Jerusalem, who was made aware of the Master's plan. It was suggested in this manufactured correspondence to Seleucus that Theodotus might be easily turned to the favor of the young Seleucian king who was even more eager than his predecessor to grow his empire.

The correspondence was now entirely in the Master's hands, and he deftly spread misinformation to Polymius and Procopios as well as among the faction to the north. To the Seleucians, the Master explained that Theodotus was to arrange his patrols in such a way that the Seleucid force might pass by Ptolemais and remain unseen by the forces of Xanthippus' army in Judea. He was to lie hidden beyond Raphia and await confirmation that the assassination attempt on Ptolemy III had been successful. With news of the assassination, Theodotus was to arrange his defenses in such a way that the Seleucid force would have no trouble overrunning the fortifications, but no suspicions would be raised that Theodotus had been complicit. He would then be given false orders to return to Alexandria but would instead take a small and loyal retinue northeast, where he and his family would be granted large estates on the Euphrates.

For the Egyptian conspirators, Eratosthenes arranged a trap of such cunning it is a shame the world can never know the full extent of its genius. Writing as the young Seleucid king, the Master convinced Procopios and Polymius that an assassination at the Ptolemaia was now deemed too dangerous and would suggest complicity at such a high level as to alarm the Greek aristocracy which must be won over to the legitimacy of the child Ptolemy IV even as he served as a puppet king for Seleucus. He suggested the attempt be made at night, some days later, and be made to look like the attack of a vengeful slave.

The season of the Ptolemaia called for Ptolemy to ceremonially survey his garrisons and major cities several times throughout a fortnight of celebrations along the Nile. Those most loyal to Ptolemy would be with him, away from the capital, while enough troops would remain in Alexandria to handle any civil unrest that might meet the news of Ptolemy's assassination. The young Ptolemy IV and his retinue were scheduled to accompany his father, and it was decided that when the Pharaoh reached Naucratis, two days into his travels, he and his companion Berenice would be assassinated in their tents. In Naucratis Ptolemy IV would be proclaimed, with Polymius and Procopios as co-regents. Polymius and Procopios agreed, and made the appropriate face-to-face arrangements with the disaffected members of his bodyguard.

The second night arrived. The conspirators entered Ptolemy's tent, but Eratosthenes and other intimates of the pharaoh had substituted an Egyptian slave. As the assassins made ready for their attack, loyal members of the Pharaoh's retinue burst forth and took the conspirators into custody. I am told the slave was rewarded for his accomplished portrayal of a sleeping pharaoh and was given extra rations during the royal journey. Months later it was rumored he accidentally drowned in the river Asclepius, in Lebanon. Polymius and Procopios, when called to the pharaoh's tent, pretended to reel back at the news, making gestures to the gods that their god-king had been spared. Eratosthenes then produced the intercepts indicting the pair, and Ptolemy declared that they be beheaded along with the other conspirators that same evening.

All were put to death. In the retinue, secreted throughout the journey as during the Ptolemaia, stood loyal Sosibius, cleared of all suspicion and now securely in the Master's debt and once again in his Pharaoh's most complete trust. The Seleucian force was ambushed in Judea, as was planned, and though the army wasn't destroyed, it was pressed back with minimal losses to Ptolemy and with great losses among the forces of Seleucus. The intrigues of court thus stifled momentarily, the Master, much risen in the esteem of his pharaoh, returned to the work of mechanical decryption, and his pharaoh's loyal advisors to the business of governing the Kingdom of Egypt.

Several more months passed in happy moments at the Academy. I studied in residence, and I made great strides in acceptance with my Greek compatriots. I continued working on the device in brotherhood with my fellow students under the guidance of the Master, Archimedes, Ctesibius, Philo, Conon and Nicomedes. With the removal of the traitors Procopios and Polymius, Eratosthenes shared with Sosibius the responsibility of intelligence liaison between the Academy and the court.

The device proved invaluable in reporting the eventual, some said inevitable, retreat of the secessionist Antiochus Hierax later in the same year of the triumphal Ptolemaia. Seleucus II Callinicus, though not having killed Antiochus, nevertheless declared him of little threat, and, having consolidated his inheritance, once again set out to trouble Ptolemy in Syria. General Xanthippus, who had now fully embraced the Master's unbreakable code and instituted it – though somewhat laboriously – throughout the armies under his command, held off the Seleucian vanguard between Tyre and Damascus.

Ptolemy, with artful prescience, declared 40 days of celebration in honor of Serapis during which time he made a pilgrimage in full court procession along the Nile. He traveled from Alexandria first to Naucratis, where he celebrated a local custom now forgotten to me, then on to Heliopolis, Memphis, Oxyrhynchus, Ptolemais-on-the-Nile and ancient Thebes, where he sacrificed forty bulls to the native gods in the ruins of the temple of Luxor. Thus, he retraced the route of his father's Ptolemaia in reverse, reasserting a connection with the glory of his family and their dynastic link to Alexander.

Already in place was a longstanding tradition from the time of Euergetes' grandfather of the *syntaxis*, an annual stipend paid from the royal treasury to each Egyptian temple. It was also part of this tradition that the high-priesthood, mostly hereditary, was responsible for distributing to each priest his share of the temple's income from Alexandria. By the decrepitude of the houses of the eternal gods in Upper Egypt, Euergetes may well have wondered how the syntaxis was being spent. Choosing to overlook the discrepancy until his return from Syria, Ptolemy instructed his courtiers to distribute special funds for the restoration of the ancient temples to the glory they had known under the old dynasties with which he wished to associate himself.

Arriving in Luxor, Ptolemy found that the priesthood in the distant frontier showed a sufficient amount of deference to the Ptolemaic court on the Mediterranean, but their distance from the centers of administration had always allowed a seditious element to remain among the native population. Embedded among the relics of the Egyptian pantheon, Ptolemy began to believe himself a true descendent of this ancient culture and sought to understand the expectations of a pharaoh traveling in a mission of conquest to Asia.

There have been many princes and likely will be many others who prefer to rule first through the sword. It is a credit to Euergetes' curious mix of pragmatism and sincere Hellenic pluralism that he assembled the hereditary elders of the priestly cults that he might consult with them. Even as plans were devised for massive renovation projects along the length of the Nile, Euergetes the Hellenist sought opinion on appropriate feast days, fair labor practices for Egyptian serfs and the growth of semi-autonomous rule in local affairs. Euergetes the pragmatist, wishing to head off the usual temptations of a subdued populace in the absence of their prince, offered estates, military positions and Greek educations to the sons of high-born Egyptian officials. These were all worthy of discussion, it was decided, but most important to Upper Egypt was the return of the cult statues and religious treasures carried off by the Persian tyrant Cambyses generations before.

With the view that the restoration of religious idols was much less than he was prepared to concede to the outposts of empire, it was here that Euergetes gladly made his famous pronouncement of repatriation. He would, he declared, restore to Egypt's plundered soul, the glories and totems of the ancient dynasties. In Thebes Ptolemy encamped for several nights of feasting before leaving the natives of the deep interior to move north once again, up the wide Nile and into long-contested Coele-Syria to confront a usurper threatening the natives of Ptolemaic Judea.

We must not believe those, who today, with philosophical bearing and deliberative tone, prophesy the fall of culture and accept the *ignorabimus*. For us there is no *ignorabimus*, and in my opinion none whatever in natural science. In opposition to the foolish *ignorabimus* our slogan shall be: Wir müssen wissen — wir werden wissen! ('We must know — we will know!')

—DAVID HILBERT

14

The Wallace Art Museum is in Baltimore, Maryland's Mount Vernon neighborhood, a few blocks from the Johns Hopkins campus. An hour drive from DC, the Wallace has become a diversionary tourist spot mostly because of its earlier work on the Archimedes Palimpsest which remains on display. We arrived around 3pm and spilled in from the street into a magnificent hall in the Palazzo style. The building and collections had been gifted to the city of Baltimore in the 1930s by the Wallace family, steel and railroad magnates who made their money during reconstruction after the Civil War. The museum's brochure stated that "The collection touches masterworks of ancient Egypt, Greek sculpture and Roman sarcophagi, medieval ivories, illuminated manuscripts, Renaissance bronzes, Old Masters and 19th century paintings, Chinese ceramics and bronzes, and Art Deco jewelry."

A local attraction for decades, the acquisition of the Archimedes Palimpsest a dozen years earlier had made the Wallace a world-class research institution, an image burnished by the work now being done on the Alexander Palimpsest. The brochure mentioned the Archimedes manuscript heavily and bore on its cover a digitally enhanced spectrographic image from Archimedes' *Method of Mechanical Theorems*, in which Archimedes demonstrated his mastery of the principles of leverage and finding the center of gravity of irregular objects. Martin was the first to ask the docent where the Alexander Palimpsest exhibit was. She directed us down an exhibition hall containing Egyptian and

Greek art. At the end of the hall a small sign said: 'ALEXANDER' PALIMPSEST. An arrow indicated a small door to the left.

We walked through a long corridor that was lined on the left with a finished wall with moldings appropriate to the museum's design. The right side of the corridor was lined with construction paneling. Every few feet signs stating 'pardon our dust' alternated with images of architectural renderings of a remodeled corridor designed to house Hellenistic art. It was planned to be a collection to complement the future exhibition of a fully preserved and restored Alexander Palimpsest. At regular viewing ports visitors could observe the work on the other side of the barrier. Dozens of pedestals were distributed throughout a large space, awaiting the priceless artifacts to be redistributed from the Wallace's own collections and borrowed from similar exhibits throughout the world.

We reached the end of the corridor, where another sign pointed us to the right. The corridor then opened onto a large viewing gallery. A curved wall of glass was sunken partially into the floor before us, allowing a one hundred eighty degree view into the same clean room we had watched online. We were all surprised to notice that nothing looked particularly out of place. The large screens showed close-up high-resolution images of the palimpsest, technicians with dust-masks stared into scanning electron microscopes, and tables upon tables held individual pages meticulously detached from the palimpsest by professional conservationists. In the center of it all, the tiny palimpsest itself, the pages that hadn't yet been separated and analyzed crumpled together in the same state in which the owner had purchased the entire manuscript at auction.

Before leaving Washington, Professor Martin had called a colleague who had done some past consulting work for the museum. Though this colleague didn't work with the Alexander Palimpsest directly, he did have a friend who was associated closely with the project and to whom he would be happy to provide an introduction. As we gazed out at the clean room, Martin's eyes locked on a man carrying a page of the palimpsest in a small plastic container. A flicker of recognition passed between them. The man held up his hand, placed the container on a table and disappeared through a service door.

"Michael Hawley," said the man bounding up behind us onto the viewing platform from the corridor from which we'd come. "I heard you might be stopping by."

Martin introduced Perry and me.

"This is fantastic," I said, indicating the clean room.

"Truly," said Perry.

"Isn't it," said Michael. "It really is. I'm so fortunate to be a part of it. I've worked on hundreds of ancient manuscripts, but it's rare to work on a project that promises to increase our understanding of its contemporary provenance as significantly as the Alexander does."

"What can you tell us about its authorship?" asked Martin.

"Well, I can tell you it's incredibly exciting. We don't know who wrote it. It seems to be a dictation to a third party, the handwriting changes throughout, so it might be fragments of several authors. We've made out the names of Euclid, Eratosthenes, Apollonius, Aristophanes, Aristarchus, several of the Ptolemies, and of course, Archimedes himself. The damage is quite extensive, as you can see," he said as he indicated one of the pages on display on the large monitors. "For example, in this page alone, the one we've been imaging for the last few hours, we can make out the names Ptolemy, probably Ptolemy III, and there's mention of his Ptolemaia, a kind of state-wide inauguration the Ptolemies had at regular intervals. The book is really a mystery, because it reads like a journal, but it also chronicles ship-building, presumably in preparation for the Ptolemaia itself. It also seems to have messages in code, which our analysts ran through the computer. It's writing in a polyalphabetic shift cipher that wasn't really used until the renaissance.

"The Vigenère cipher," said Perry, proudly. I nodded to him in recognition.

"Exactly. This is exceedingly complex cryptography for the period. We can decipher a relatively small block of text in a few minutes with a brute-force attack. Essentially the computer tries every combination until it starts hitting on patterns. When it sees words start to emerge, it self-corrects until it finds the key and decodes the message. We had a cryptography consultant who cracked it in a few minutes, but he used the supercomputer at Loyola University. A code like this would have been essentially unbreakable in the third century BCE."

"Babbage only cracked it in the nineteenth century CE," Perry offered.

"Exactly," said Michael. "You know your cryptography. And Babbage almost went mad teasing out any weaknesses in the Vigenère. He even outlined processes to mechanize decryption, but it never came to fruition."

The word *mechanize* froze all three of us. We waited for Michael to continue.

"So the mystery is, first, who came up with a polyalphabetic shift cipher when the Caesar cipher," he directed an inquisitive look to Perry who returned it knowingly, "was the state of the art?"

"And," I said, what does that have to do with Euclid, the Ptolemies and the Library of Alexandria?"

"We had a cryptography expert on staff, as I said, who has a theory that some of the manuscript is a series of letters between an engineer of sorts and Ptolemy himself, asking for money to help decrypt messages. So the question is, who started writing polyalphabetic shift ciphers in the first place, what was so important that it required this level of, truly, sophisticated protection, and how could anyone in the third century BCE have ever decrypted these messages with any speed and in any serious bandwidth of information flow. I can see someone pulling a Babbage and working on a single message for months, if not years, but even in antiquity, the usefulness of the information gained from a decoded message years after its interception is questionable."

Again, the three of us looked at each other. Within a minute Michael had essentially referred to mechanized calculated and the imperative of speed or *swiftness* in effective cryptanalysis. Then something occurred to me.

"You said you *had* a cryptanalyst on your team?" I said.

"Well, I guess I shouldn't use the past tense. We had a consultant who I first met on the Archimedes palimpsest project. He had heard of it in the news and he volunteered his services. He's been working with us on the odd manuscript here and there for the better part of the decade since. You know, he seemed almost disappointed with the Archimedes project, which is surprising, because that was a huge boon for Archimedes scholarship and the study of the mathematics of antiquity, which is his particular interest. Oh, and I say *had* because he stopped coming in to work. He was a volunteer, to be honest - he wasn't an employee. He signed a non-disclosure, for sure, but we don't pay him, and we've had volunteers up and leave before. Most are academics or graduate students. Sometimes they get exhausted with the strains of volunteering and maintaining an academic schedule or working on their own projects. It's odd though, because he seemed fascinated from the start. But anyway, you don't want to hear about our staff problems –"

"You know, it's funny," said Martin, "classics is a relatively small world. I remember working with a young student who was crazy about antiquity's knowledge of advanced mathematics," he lied. "He was hard to miss, he was a Jesuit brother, and a very accomplished mathematician."

"You know Francisco?" asked Michael with an interest level significantly more heightened than before. "Francisco DiScenna, he's who I'm talking about. He's who just disappeared."

"I hardly see him anymore," said Martin, "we collaborated a few times on some unpublished journal articles. He's a brilliant guy."

"That he is, but odd. Very anti-social. Very focused. He lived and breathed this stuff. Cryptography, mathematics, prime numbers. When he found the Mersenne-" Michael stopped himself.

"What," Perry said.

"Nothing really. Non-disclosure and all that. The owner of the palimpsest is a little paranoid, if you ask me. But we can only talk about what gets cleared and put up on the website. Dr. Martin, how well do you know Francisco DiScenna?"

"Not very well, why?"

Michael gestured to the camera observing the observation platform. Then, in an unusually genial and loud voice he said, "Well, gentlemen, that's what we do here. I'm so happy you made the trip. I had hoped you'd have time to suit up and see the conservation work first hand, but I understand you have to get back to DC. Please come back anytime."

Then he leaned in to Martin quietly and whispered something under his breath. He bounded back up the corridor and disappeared around the corner into the construction area through which we'd passed.

"What was that all about," I asked.

"Let's find out," said Martin as he indicated with his hand that we should head back toward the museum's entrance.

Martin led us in frustrating silence through the Egyptian gallery, past the docent, out the door and half a block away from the museum before he said, "That was so odd."

"Yeah," I said, what was all that at the end?"

"He told me to meet him at Mount Vernon in 30 minutes."

"Mount Vernon?" I said, "As in Washington's plantation on the Potomac, that's an hour drive back to DC and another 20 into Virginia.

"He must mean Mount Vernon here. A hotel or a coffee shop or some-"

We all noticed the sign Martin was staring at. A geographical indicator matching other Johns Hopkins place indicators scattered throughout the neighborhood pointed north with the words, 'Mount Vernon Place.' We turned the corner to see a tall monument, some 500 feet north, set in the middle of a traffic circle.

"Of course," said Perry. "Mount Vernon Place, it's a neighborhood."

"We crossed the traffic and stood in a grassy area at the foot of the large column dedicated to Washington."

"What's' going on? This seems a little cloak and dagger," said Perry.

"I don't know, but a few things are odd," I said. First, the feed is cut, ok, maybe funding runs out, maybe not, but it's on the same day that a technician, who we now know is probably the Francisco guy, first sees the E-pi-mee-ka-nee-sis page. He alerts everyone's attention, and then he leaves soon after."

"And," said Martin, "I was getting the sense that he doesn't know about the E-pi-mee-ka-nee-sis prefix. I thought for sure Pratt had told the student, who, I agree, is probably this Francisco, and Francisco didn't share it with the team? I mean, maybe it's a dead-end, but Pratt told me that his student had been 'elated' with the theory. If it made sense to him, why keep it to himself? Investigate it. Prove it. Publish it."

"And then Francisco ups and leaves," said Perry. I get he's a volunteering consultant, but I don't see how an academic can maintain a reputation by agreeing to work on a project and leaving without notice in the middle of it."

"Ah," Martin said, "here he is."

Michael approached the traffic circle in near a sprint as an awkward academic could be expected to muster. He jogged across the street and stopped in front of us, sweating and panting politely.

"I'm sorry for the awkwardness back there," he said. "Listen, I need some information on Francisco. He's completely disappeared. I've known him for years, we worked together, as I said, on the Archimedes Palimpsest. He got in because a few people at Stanford vouched for him."

"Dr. Pratt?" said Martin.

"Yes!" said Michael. "Absolutely. "Pratt's worked on a few things with me over the years. I'm a conservator. I know about parchment, I know about spectography, I know schoolboy Latin and Greek. Sometimes we solicit analysis from a lot of sources. I first met Francisco through Pratt a decade ago. Pratt vouched for him up and down. He had very few references outside a very narrow field. But he did great work, he always volunteered. Some of the other consultants asked for money when the museum saw an uptick in interest with the Archimedes. Not Francisco. But I really need to know where he is. You said you talk to him occasionally?"

"I'm sorry Michael. I deceived you a bit. I don't personally know this Francisco, in fact I didn't know his name until you told me."

He quickly told Michael the story of Dr. Pratt, his flight to Stanford, and our interest in the project having seen the last day of the web feed.

"I just wanted to find out who this student of Pratt's is," Martin said, "because I firmly believe Pratt flew here several days ago to meet with him. I don't know him at all and have no idea where he's gone."

Gentlemen, I need to know everything you know. We knew Francisco was sharing images outside the organization, strictly against the non-disclosure agreement. I was planning on confronting him and asking him to leave the project. On the same day that we discovered he'd been downloading images onto a thumb drive, he claimed to make a discovery of a very unusual kind. I'm going against every non-disclosure I've signed to tell you this, but Francisco discovered something quite amazing on the last day he worked with us."

Martin looked at Perry and me. We indicated that he should be the one to disclose what we also knew.

"We know," said Martin, "they had the presence of mind to write down the word everyone was pointing at on the screens before the feed was taken down. We know Francisco found a Mersenne Prime, almost two thousand years before that specific prime was discovered."

Michael seemed pained, but he yielded to this new knowledge. "Ok, well, I must have your assurance that this goes no further."

"I don't see it a state secret that you found a Mersenne Prime," I said.

"Exactly," said Perry, "Interesting, yes, revelatory in relation to the history of mathematics, obviously. But we're not talking about espionage here. Who wouldn't want to be the first to publish such a discovery? In the same circles that have made the Archimedes palimpsest such an asset to the Wallace, the publications of a third century BCE Mersenne would have them flocking here, to your credit."

"The Mersenne is interesting, yes," said Michael. "But that's not why we cut the feed."

"What," I asked, "So why did you cut it?"

"Because, the day after Francisco realized he was looking at a Mersenne two millennia before anyone had considered such a number, I walked into the clean room as soon as I arrived at the museum, as I do every morning. Others started filtering in and we got to work. I noticed that Francisco was running late, but it didn't really seem odd to me until I heard a gasp from one of the conservators. As you know from watching the feed, we remove one page at a time from the palimpsest. That page goes through a specific process that you've witnessed. By the end of the conservation project we will have imaged every page and rebound the manuscript in its entirety. When the conservator approached the manuscript that morning, she was startled by what she had found on the table. Though from afar it looked like the Alexander, it was in fact a thirteenth century prayer book we had in our own collection.

"I immediately reviewed the security tapes. Francisco had decided to stay late to work on the Mersenne. Most of us, as excited as we were, left around 3am that morning. Francisco was the last to leave the room. I watched on the tape as he left, came back with an archivist's box, took the prayer book out, substituted it for the Alexander and placed the Alexander into the box. The Palimpsest was gone and so was Francisco. One of our own walked right out the front entrance with the most significant bibliological find of the decade, perhaps the century. He obviously didn't care to hide his tracks. And he hasn't been seen since. I'm not supposed to even talk about it. We haven't contacted the police because we don't want the publicity. We've contacted everyone in the community we could think of. I tried to reach Pratt myself, and was told that he had left Stanford and hadn't given any return date."

"You're not suggesting-" said Martin.

"I'm not suggesting anything. I'm saying that Francisco left abruptly, took the manuscript, obviously discussed it with someone else, someone in a very select group of scholars who would share his specific interest in the Alexander, and one in that group has also disappeared voluntarily. And," he said slowly, pointing at Martin, "now you tell me that *you* – his star student - were the last one other than his housekeeper to see him. You show up here to view the palimpsest days after it was stolen. I need answers, Dr. Martin, or we have a serious problem."

"Let's get back to the museum," said Martin. "We have a few things to tell you."

Michael led the three of us through the service entrance of the museum and into the upper floor where the administrative offices were located. He took us to a conference room, where he asked us to stay. The room was surrounded on three sides by glass overlooking a large warehouse space where desks were arranged at regular intervals. Stacks of paper, old books, scholarly journals and the artifacts of modern human habitation – coffee cups, DaVinci bobble-heads, Mona Lisa heads on pinup bodies – stretched out before us in this den of archivist geekdom. We could see Michael consulting with several of his colleagues who eventually looked our way. They approached as a group. Michael introduced us to all of them. A half dozen in all. The woman Michael identified as the Executive Director of the museum, Sandra Fikes, spoke first. She asked us to explain ourselves again, from the beginning. Her tone was more inquisitive than accusatory. This time we included everything.

Perry and I explained our infatuation with the video feed, our crude cocktail napkin rendering of the Mersenne Prime, our interest in finding a plotline for a thriller novel with actual consequences. The latter they took little notice of. Martin explained his interpretation of the Mersenne prefix, drawing on the white board on the single solid wall of the conference room.

"So, let's regroup," said Fikes, "we've been working with a sleeper thief for years. He chooses now to steal the remainder of the still-bound pages – about half - of a priceless manuscript after a decade of essentially free access to dozens of priceless manuscripts, including our most famous and probably most valuable, the Archimedes. He comes with few but stellar references from trusted colleagues in his field, and now one of those colleagues, his mentor – *and yours*, Dr. Martin, has gone missing."

"And he chooses to steal the manuscript only after he personally identifies the highly anachronistic Mersenne Prime," said Michael. "He wasn't moved to steal it when we became almost certain it was written by a colleague of the greatest minds at the Library of Alexandria. He doesn't steal it after we discover a lost Idyll of Theocritus, he doesn't care much about the most complete description of the topology of Hellenistic Alexandria ever recovered from antiquity.

"It hinges on the Mersenne, then," I said redundantly.

"He could sell it," said Fikes. "He could sell it for quite a bit, in a private sale."

"But," I said, "I assume that his work was satisfactory enough up to this point, up until he started sharing the photos, to ensure his continued relationship with the Wallace, correct?"

The director nodded.

"Well, then," I said, "stealing it now doesn't make any sense. Sure it's valuable to a manuscript collector, but so is the Archimedes, which you said he had more or less free access to. But more importantly, presumable the manuscript would have been photographed, digitized, translated and published. The original would be put back together as you did with the Archimedes, and it would have been displayed. Any time between the reincorporation of the manuscripts pages and its exhibition in a locked cabinet, he would have had access to it, right? I mean, even if it sits on a table for two hours before you put it on display, he would have had access to it. That's the time to take it. That's when it's complete and the most vulnerable – and the most valuable."

"So," Fikes said to herself, "He doesn't want to sell it. At the very least, its value isn't diminished significantly by the absence of the pages we still have."

"Wait," said Martin, "we're going about this the wrong way. Francisco, if he's the student Pratt was talking about, is a fanatic about this stuff. A real nut. This is personal, it's almost a religi-"

Martin wrapped his knuckles on the conference table. "Did you know Francisco is a Jesuit initiate?"

Quizzical faces stared back at him.

"Dr. Martin," said Michael, "I didn't know that, but wouldn't a devoutly religious person be less likely to steal something?"

"Yes," said Martin, "To steal *something* would be unlikely. To steal something to sell to make money seems to contradict his ideology as I'm familiar with it. But what if he were protecting something?"

"You think," said Fikes, "that he stole a priceless manuscript from one of the most sophisticated conservation efforts in the world to protect it?"

Martin, Perry and I all looked at each other. We obviously shared the same thought.

"Not *it*," I said, "not the manuscript, not the Alexander itself. He wanted to protect – or hoard – the rest of the text for himself or someone else. Think about it, the guy is involved with prime numbers, he's 'obsessed' with the mathematics of antiquity. He doesn't flinch at the Archimedes, you've done dozens of other projects and he views these with only passing interest. He's in the perfect position to-"

"How'd you get the Alexander here, Michael," asked Martin. "I mean, you're a credit to the field of conservation, and the Archimedes is a huge feather in your cap, a project executed brilliantly, but you're not the only center of conservation of ancient manuscripts, not even ancient mathematical texts. Beinecke at Yale, the British Museum, the Nag Hammadi Library in Cairo; There are a dozen other first-rate conservation facilities out there. How did you get the Alexander *here*?"

Fikes shifted her weight uncomfortably from foot to foot. "The owner of the Alexander knew what we did with the Archimedes."

"And how did you get the Archimedes a decade ago?" asked Perry.

"That was a fluke, actually," Michael said. "I emailed Sotheby's and they connected me with the owner's agent, who agreed to have us do the work."

"And who is the owner?" asked Martin.

"You know we can't tell you that. In fact, I don't know myself. Only a few members of the board know. Our contract states that any breach in anonymity means the immediate revocation of the Archimedes loan."

"And" asked Martin, "you have a similar contract with the owner of the Alexander?"

"Yes," said Fikes, "essentially the same."

"So," I said, "Francisco hears about the Archimedes, jumps at the chance to study a previously unknown work in his field, secures letters of recommendation and introduction and starts volunteering his considerable expertise on the Archimedes, works on other projects here and there, and then maybe serendipitously, maybe not, the Wallace's reputation, a reputation that Francisco helped in part to establish, lures the Alexander here. He sees the Mersenne and steals the manuscript."

"Folks," said Martin, "it's obvious to me what's going on. Francisco found an indicator in the presence of the Mersenne of whatever it is that he's looking for, and he's certain enough to ruin his reputation and risk prison that the rest of the Alexander has something he needs. I don't know why Pratt's involved here, but we do know that we have two missing scholars expert in the study of the mathematics of antiquity and a missing, half-translated manuscript that hints at its author's knowledge of prime numbers and the *mechanization* of computation. I'd say we have a mystery on our hands."

A rope stretched along the length of the diagonal produces an area which the vertical and horizontal sides make together.

—BAUDHAYANA, Baudhāyana Śulbasûtra, c. 800 BCE (400 years before Pythagoras)

15

Onesimus here reminds me to mention the Master's personal role in the conclusion of the Laodicean War. To this point, the Master had been the driving force behind the mechanization of cryptography, a force entirely new in the history of warfare. His close circle had created a means of encryption and decryption that eluded the most brilliant of Egypt's enemies, foreign and domestic. All this he had done from the relative safety of the converted storerooms of Alexandria.

One evening, while our group was working on a mundane dispatch, an exhausted rider appeared in the workshop. Eratosthenes was handed a sealed order bearing the cartouche of Ptolemy, written undeniably in the pharaoh's own hand. His pharaoh had ordered him to make preparations to meet his cortege in Pelusium on his return trip from Thebes. The Master was to assemble the minimum number of his intimates required for the journey and was, at once, to prepare two of the enormous devices for travel overland into the heart of the Seleucian front lines.

A trusted guard would escort him to Pelusium where Eratosthenes would join the campaign to press Seleucus back into the interior of the old Persian Empire. It was the pharaoh's intention that one device be left with the forces of Xanthippus, who would push northwest into Anatolia, and the other to go east with Ptolemy, where he might choose to lay claim for his dynasty to the entire inheritance of Alexander.

I volunteered immediately. Aristophanes, Abdaraxus, Diocles and Apollonius also relished the idea of an "academician's crusade," as we referred to it, and began making preparations for the journey. It was decided that

Archimedes would remain behind with Ctesibius, Conon and Nicomedes to continue the intelligence operations with Sosibius.

Before we left, Archimedes and Eratosthenes engineered carriages of hard Lebanon cedar to be fitted around each device. The machines, each the height of two men and as wide and long as the three tethrippon that had pulled Ptolemy's dais at his grand festival, were suspended within a nested series of spheres in a manner that would allow the device to remain upright, independent of the position of the carriage. The appellation given this concept was the 'gyroscope,' a design that Conon and Nicomedes had adapted from the Master's armillary sphere. At the front of each device a small enclosure was provided for the operator, who would sit suspended several feet above the ground as he worked the controls. The whole assembly was covered with a superstructure of bronze plate.

When this was presented to Sosibius he sniggered so heartily that his composure was regained only after several cups of wine. Sosibius, who had gone on campaign with Ptolemy II Philadelphus and knew well the composition of a baggage train, insisted that we fasten to the superstructure a miscellany of odd containers, satchels and layered amphorae, that the lumbering peculiarity would look as much as possible to an observer, Seleucian or otherwise, like an unusually large transport. In this way the devices could be made to be pulled over rough terrain, made impermeable to assault by projectiles, and made as inconspicuous as possible, all the while generating intelligence in service of Ptolemy.

The first day's travel from Alexandria was difficult. We were forced to stop at Canopus to make adjustments. We finally found our stride several days ride from Naucratis, where the twelve horses required to pull each device seemed finally to adjust to the load. The reception of the army as we pulled two precarious mountains of supplies through the city gates was a mixture of surprise and amusement. Eratosthenes gave a mock-bow to the huzzahs from a phalanx from Cyrene, who, of course, had no idea that a message from Seleucus was even then yielding to the great poet Callimachus' frequency analysis by means of the entrails of cogs, gears and camshafts beneath its odd exterior.

We marched for several weeks from Naucratis to Pelusium, where we were joined after some time by a Ptolemy flush with his victorious procession down the Nile. Ptolemy cloistered himself in the councils of war for several days, and, acting on ready intelligence made available by the presence of the device in his cortege, eventually made ready to march straight to Judea, where he would attend a festival put on by the priests of the Messianites in honor of his past expressions of benevolence there.

Indeed, the Jews in Judea seemed much more obliging than those in Alexandria. Perhaps it is only because, with the exception of the rather bawdy Casanios the bronzewright, I knew only Jewish academicians of dour temperament. I must make a partial exception here for Artapanus, an Alexandrian Jew of great merit, but of whose humorous intent I was often uncertain. When I first came to the Academy we once got each other drunk in the Temple of Isis, something of a trademark for him in all the houses of our pantheon. His contention that Abraham gifted Egypt with Astronomy, Joseph with bureaucracy and Moses with the mass circumcisions of the Ethiopians was to be found in the same throat as his somewhat patronizing assertion that all that was good in the world was due to the accepting monolatry of the Jews.

It has become a rather poor joke among the ranks of phalangites, those affable young Greeks of the countryside, that the gates of Jerusalem were thrown open to the Ptolemies with as much fanfare as the legs of her native daughters. Of course, as a man of the Academy I abhorred such slanders then as I abhor them now. I'm sad I said as much to these fellows one evening after too many cups of wine, for which my punishment was a jovial if instantaneous sequestration of my person to a series of experiments on the truth of the proposition. I'm afraid to say that the proposition held. To my anecdotal evidence I may also add the testimony of several guardians of the Law of Moses who attested to the most enterprising of these young women stretching a point among their kinsmen that the occasional miraculous conception was a credit to their messianism. These priests proved regular zetetikoi themselves at the same establishment of which I became so fond before the divine armies of the Pharaoh King of Egypt mobilized once again, birthed through the city gates and into the harsh hill country of Judea.

We then marched to Ptolemais, where we joined forces with Xanthippus before moving to meet Seleucus near Damascus. We were surprised to find only a small force, which surrendered with little bloodshed. The military commander opened the gates of the city. Ptolemy ordered a festival for the Damascenes during which he installed his brother, Lysimachus, as provisional governor. Placing a large order for their fine steel and cloth to be sent back to Alexandria, Ptolemy then moved east toward the Euphrates.

After several weeks we reached Babylon. Ptolemy had already received favorable replies to the emissaries he sent in advance of his army. Many of the academicians and historians in his company wondered if the same sights and sensations that had gripped immortal Alexander and propelled him farther east would have a similar effect on his greatest general's grandson. The question became irrelevant when Ptolemy saw the condition of the city.

The spectacle that greeted Alexander two generations before was gone. The city had languished after his death in the wake of the conflicting ambitions of his generals. Ptolemy himself paid homage to the site where Alexander had died in the palace of Nebuchadnezzar. He then patronized a small festival to a local deity whose name I can now no longer recall. There was a small library still remaining, the contents of which Ptolemy had copied and sent back to Alexandria. In this spirit he also sent scribes to various ancient sites in that ancient land, especially to Nineveh, from which the library now may claim copies of the entire the Library of Ashurbanipal. Indeed, the story of Gilgamesh was often cited by Artapanus years later as a Mesopotamian confirmation of his own peoples' creation myth told from an eastern perspective.

Ptolemy, acting on intelligence that Seleucus was busy with a rebellion in Anatolia, left Babylon. After only a month's stay, Ptolemy pressed his forces southeast to the ancient city of Parsa, or as Alexander's chroniclers had named it, Persepolis, the City of the Persians.

It was known widely, even then, that Persepolis had sustained heavy damage during the campaigns of Alexander. A famous story placed the root of its destruction in a drunken party, which Cleitarchus has recorded with his characteristic understanding. Thais, the (in)famous Athenian hetaera of Alexander, is said to have made a clever remark that "it would be the finest of all his feats in Asia if he joined them in triumphal procession, set fire to the palaces, and permitted women's hands in a minute to extinguish the famed accomplishments of the Persians."

Indeed, as Abdaraxus, Diocles, Apollonius and I walked in silence through the ruins of Persepolis, Aristophanes pulled an anthology from the baggage train and read aloud the words of Cleitarchus himself, among others:

> This [incitement by Thais] was said to men who were still young and giddy with wine, and so, as would be expected, someone shouted out to form up and to light torches, and urged all to take vengeance for the destruction of the Greek temples. Others took up the cry and said that this was a deed worthy of Alexander alone. When the king had caught fire at their words, all leaped up from their couches and passed the word along to form a victory procession in honor of Dionysius.

Promptly many torches were gathered. Female musicians were present at the banquet, so the king led them all out for the victory procession to the sound of voices and flutes and pipes, Thais the courtesan leading the whole performance. She was the first, after the king, to hurl her blazing torch into the palace. As the others all did the same, immediately the entire palace area was consumed, so great was the conflagration. It was most remarkable that the impious act of Xerxes, king of the Persians, against the acropolis at Athens should have been repaid in kind after many years by one woman, a citizen of the land which had suffered it, and in sport.

But Alexander's great mental endowments, that noble disposition, in which he surpassed all kings, that intrepidity in encountering dangers, his promptness in forming and carrying out plans, his good faith towards those who submitted to him, merciful treatment of his prisoners, temperance even in lawful and usual pleasures, were sullied by an excessive love of wine. At the very time when his enemy and his rival for a throne was preparing to renew the war, when those whom he had conquered were but lately subdued and were hostile to the new rule, he took part in prolonged banquets at which women were present, not indeed those whom it would be a crime to violate, but, to be sure, harlots who were accustomed to live with armed men with more license than was fitting.

One of these, Thais by name, herself also drunken, declared that the king would win most favor among all the Greeks, if he should order the palace of the Persians to be set on fire; that this was expected by those whose cities the barbarians had destroyed. When a drunken strumpet had given her opinion on a matter of such moment, one or two, themselves also loaded with wine, agreed. The king, too, more greedy for wine than able to carry it, cried: "Why do we not, then, avenge Greece and apply torches to the city?" All had become heated with wine, and so they arose when drunk to fire the city which they had spared when armed. The king was the first to throw a firebrand upon the palace, then the guests and the servants and courtesans. The palace had been built largely of cedar, which quickly took fire and spread the conflagration widely.

When the army, which was encamped not far from the city, saw the fire, thinking it accidental, they rushed to bear aid. But when they came to the vestibule of the palace, they saw the king himself piling on firebrands. Therefore, they left the water which they had brought, and they too began to throw dry wood upon the burning building. Such was the end of the capital of the entire Orient. . . .

The Macedonians were ashamed that so renowned a city had been destroyed by their king in a drunken revel; therefore the act was taken as earnest, and they forced themselves to believe that it was right that it should be wiped out in exactly that manner.

It is unlikely that Alexander's cosmopolitanism would have condoned the destruction of a city he had already occupied, but the stories of the long march and the resulting depravity of his army had even then passed into legend. It is still spoken of now, even with a Greek on the Persian throne in the wake of the conquests of Alexander, how raw the memory is of the Persian rape of Athens two centuries before. It is possible that vengeance combined with drink overcame Alexander's ecumenicism.

Whatever the reason, the destruction was evident even as we approached the shattered walls of the city, where a completely unexpected sadness overtook the army. There was no garrison to speak of. A small settlement persisted nearby. It offered no resistance and seemed so near to starvation they hardly noticed our presence. Ptolemy walked with the Master in silence as they ascended the remains of the one hundred eleven grey limestone steps of the Persepolitan Stairway.

Within the Library of Alexandria there may be found an account of one of Alexander's architects who was moved by the unusual design of these steps to make a study of the dimensions of the structure. He found each step to be as wide as four grown men laying end to end with treads of less than an Egyptian cubit and a rise a third that size. The effect was of a grandly forward procession on a gentle incline. Alexander himself is said to have ascended with his horse, the stubborn Bucephalus, but it was more likely from the evidence of the carvings there that the steps were designed for pedestrian grandees that they might maintain an elegance of stature as they rose toward the ancient throne of Persia.

The Master and his pharaoh circled the remnants of Darius' great Apadana Palace, built ten generations ago. They passed through the Hall of a Hundred Columns, only half of which still stood. They marveled at the Tripylon Hall, the Tachara Palace of Darius, the Hadish Palace of Xerxes and a smaller palace of Artaxerxes II. They stood in the imperial treasury, long emptied of the contents for which it was built. As they exited the complex through a massive portal the Persians had called the Gate of all Nations, they both wept openly, moved by the magnificence of two immense bulls with the heads of bearded men. As he had done in Babylon, Ptolemy issued orders to his surveyors to make a list of all the Egyptian statuary left at the site, that it might be hauled back, in ignominy he felt, to his thriving kingdom.

It is touching for me now to remember the esteem in which Ptolemy held his Chief Librarian and the weight he placed upon the Master's counsel. Several years Euergetes' senior, Eratosthenes, I believe, came to stand in for something of a father figure of honest intentions. The early lives of the Ptolemies, then and more so now, are overshadowed, as if by requirement, by domineering mothers, perverse sisters and absentee fathers. It is best understood in this light that a real friendship developed between Euergetes and the greatest of his academicians of Alexandria. Eratosthenes later told me, without the slightest hint of pride, that he had urged Ptolemy, on their walk through the broken city of the Persians, to consolidate his eastern march not with a vainglorious incursion into the lands that broke the spirit even of Alexander. There was plenty of purposeful glory to be had against Seleucus in Anatolia, where his pharaoh might find himself closer to Hellas and, not inconsequentially, nearer his supply train.

Had Eratosthenes had the honor of counseling Euergetes' grandfather, filled as the first Ptolemy was with the conceits of the generation of Alexander during his numerous struggles against his other diadochoi, it is possible his advice would have been brushed aside. But he was addressing an astute administrator, a pragmatist and a true believer in the emerging concept of a cooperative balance of power through a shared self-interest. Ptolemy resolved to honor his commitment to recover the Egyptian religious icons, procure as much from Asia for his own treasury as his diplomacy allowed, and send a palpable message to Seleucus that the King of Persia could be humbled at any time by the strength and wealth of Egypt.

To effect all three of these goals, Ptolemy fanned out embassies in a diplomatic arc from Parthia and Bactria in the North and Northeast, recently in rebellion against Seleucus, and east to the Mauryan court of India. In the ancient capital of Persepolis Ptolemy would sponsor a festival in honor of all the gods of the region, the gods of Egypt and the gods of Hellas. This, which was called the Festival of the Pantheon, gained its spirit from a repurposed internationalism, the Pan-Hellenic games, and the Ptolemaia.

Concerned that in the periphery of the Greek world it was unlikely that enough athletes competent in the Greek competitions of sport could be assembled and in the interest of providing substantial amusements, Ptolemy supplied his embassies with an open call for as many "spirited rogues and strongmen" as each city might muster. The Pankration, or 'all might', would be, beside the homage ceremony to Ptolemy, the penultimate event of the Festival of the Pantheon. Still popular even now, the Pankration has been a staple of the Olympic Games for four hundred years. It's mannish blend of wrestling and boxing with few rules save for the prohibition on biting and gouging of eyes, and the prizes announced in the dispatches, mobilized a small army of the virile west toward Persepolis.

Ptolemy also announced a poetry competition and the awarding of silver to the best plays by native dramatists. I saw the Master's hand in Ptolemy's declaration of a competition to solve outstanding problems of mathematics, to my knowledge the first competition of its kind.

Within weeks, spectators, competitors, poets, playwrights and academicians streamed into Persepolis in a reverse portrayal of Alexander's destruction generations before. Ptolemy ordered the construction of temporary villages to house them, divided according to their nationality and roles within the festival. The Parthian strong men encamped near the spirited Bactrian rogues; they all drank heartily and fought amongst each other in good humor. The poets and playwrights squabbled about housing conditions and jealously guarded the odes, paeans, idylls, declarations and tragedies they had brought with them from their outposts of empire. Academicians arrived with bold notions on conic sections, infinite calculations and prime numbers, the Master's particular fascination.

After some weeks of this display of genial depravity and artistic rivalries, word reached the court that Arsaces I, separatist King of Parthia, and Diodotus, once satrap and now King of Bactria, had both stalled their progress one day's march from Persepolis. Both, fearing that they would be the first to enter and so diminish their own final, triumphal arrivals, had encamped unwilling to move until the impasse had first been broken by the other, and, on principle, both determined to arrive before the presumably lesser delegation of court functionaries of Ashoka, en route from the Mauryan Empire in India.

Ptolemy rode to their encampment himself at the head of 5,000 cavalry and escorted them past the crumbling walls of Persepolis. It is a testament to Ptolemy's pragmatism that he dispensed with the courtly displays he invoked so often in Egypt. Then again, as Aristophanes opined at the time in his journal, "it is entirely possible that Ptolemy realized that there is little face to lose in a tripartite entrance into an abandoned capital filled only temporarily with the revelers at a festival of provincial importance."

The festival was, even by Aristophanes' reckoning, a fair success. The games lasted many more days than planned, such was the interest of the people of the countryside in the Pankration. The athletic prizes were duly distributed, and several plays were found to be of acceptable quality to merit the awarding of placings at all. I know from the Master that Ptolemy was so bored by his second day in the Hall of a Hundred Columns, where the plays had been staged, that he despaired of giving any award at all.

An Armenian peripatetic named Azekiah, refusing to socialize with the other dramatists for reasons unknown, nevertheless presented a rather fine piece titled the 'Poor Man of Nippur,' apparently adapted from ancient sources. At the end of the performance the Pharaoh rose with the visiting kings of Asia to salute Azekiah as an accomplished satirist. This honor Azekiah accepted with grace, though he declared drunkenly at his victory banquet that the Poor Man had been intended to induce catharsis of the gravest kind. Diocles and Apollonius breathed life into another layer of meaning suggested in The Poor Man's story that most certainly had not been intended by our new Armenian Aeschylus.

Eratosthenes had been delighted to judge the mathematical competition until it became obvious that many of the conjectures had been made and proved in Alexandria, not least by himself and his coadjutor Philo, who had also made the trip. One mathematician had traveled for three weeks to present a geometric construction for doubling the cube, to whom Philo could only comment that his eponymous solution, the Philo Line, was well known in Alexandria. Again, Philo could only be flattered when a Bactrian boy entered into the competition a crude model of a chain-driven ballista, which Philo had invented with Ctesibius years before. The Master and Philo read a discourse by a young Parthian tax collector on calculating the area under a curve, already well understood by Archimedes. Apollonius, even at his young age, strained to cast off his paternalism as he critiqued with great sensitivity several mistakes in conjectures that he himself had made in his youth. He had already begun his treatise *Conics*, which is now the definitive text in the holdings in the library on several concepts for which he provided names: 'parabola' (place beside), 'ellipse' (deficiency), and 'hyperbola' (a throw beyond) were already in use among educated Alexandrines of the day.

For Eratosthenes, the state of intellectualism as a hobby in the provinces was contrasted with the purpose-built Museum, Academy and Library of Alexandria. Still, these entrants were thinkers of great, if late, creativity, and Eratosthenes and Philo were in the process of picking a winner when a contingent of a half dozen men from India arrived, without any representatives of government, letters or sport.

The men, who made homage to Ptolemy with such deference and sincerity and who were thereby found completely honest and agreeable, were invited to dine with Euergetes and his courtiers in his tent. The nominal leader of the group, Pingala, a mathematician at the Mauryan court of Ashoka the Great, made no apology for his patron, saying only that the great king had received the emissaries from Ptolemy and considered their arrival of little event. Though his patron did not intend to send a formal delegation, Pingala and his colleagues were intrigued to learn of the presence of Eratosthenes within Ptolemy's cortege and set out to the west immediately that they might meet the man who had measured the Earth.

Onesimus reminds me that I have so far neglected to include in my narrative the triumph of the Master's geodesy. I remind Onesimus of my original purpose for writing this memoir: to chronicle for posterity the unknown achievements of Eratosthenes and the events leading up to the commencement of the Alexandrian Project. Onesimus reminds me that it is by no means certain, especially given the tenor of the decadence in which the current pharaoh, Ptolemy V Epiphanes, has shrouded the Academy, that the Master's public achievements will continue to be known in every cultured land. He has convinced me to include it here. But I also include it because it was not in honor of the Master's poetry, his calendar reforms, astronomical calculations, or music theory, (all marvels in their own right as well known to the school children of our day as the exploits of Alexander), that the mathematicians set out from India. These sons of a culture ancient even to Alexander came to hail the man who had proven, finally and beyond all doubt, that the Earth was round and had shown its circumference exactly at 252,212 stades.

Shortly after arriving in Alexandria at the behest of Euergetes, The Master had read in the great library a curious report from the southwestern border town of Syene, along the banks of the Upper Nile and situated almost exactly on the Tropic of Cancer. A priest of the triad deities Khnum, Satis and Anuket mentioned in a dispatch the position of the sun during the ceremonies of the summer solstice. It was a credit to his pharaoh, he had written, that the sun refused to cast a shadow during the celebration of the ancient gods under the protection of the house of Ptolemy. Of course, this property was well known to my race, as were many other properties of nature, long before great Alexander stepped into our eternal land. The Master realized that a similar phenomenon at exactly the same day and time was not observable in Alexandria and that it quite obviously had nothing to do with a divinity's preference for the dynasty of the moment. Indeed, during a similar celebration at the Temple of Serapis, the temple's columns cast a small, but noticeable shadow upon the congregants. He deduced from this that not only must the Earth be a sphere - an extant but by no means universal view of the time – but that it must be possible to contrive from the distance between Syene and Alexandria and the differences in angles between the shadows at midday the approximate curvature of that sphere.

It is a credit to the Master's intellectual vigor that he pursued these experiments in the few gaps between his responsibilities to the code breaking effort in those frenetic early years in his Pharaoh's service. His work on the subject, which I esteem one of the library's most prized holdings, *On the Measurement of the Earth*, was widely distributed and eagerly copied so that even in this far corner of Greek civilization word of the Master's triumph had spread to the wisest of Ashoka's courtiers.

I have already stated here that it was this familiarity with the Master's geodesy that impelled Ashoka's courtiers to undertake their journey to Persepolis, and it was in honor of their devotion to the universal pursuit of mathematics that so pleased Euergetes that they were invited to table among the inner circles of the traveling court. As the meal was cleared away and each kylix refilled Pingala begged leave to hold council with the academicians and Ptolemy alone. Ptolemy cleared his courtiers and sent word to his royal bodyguard that the assembly not be disturbed. This he made them swear under threat of an encore presentation of the 'Poor Man of Nippur.'

Pingala had brought with him into the Pharaoh's tent several scrolls which, he admitted apologetically, were scrapings of worn copies of, among other works, Callimachus' ode to Demeter and the much admired Argonautica of Apollonius of Rhodes. Many better copies remained with the court librarians, Pingala assured us; these were overwritten as a matter of economy. Ptolemy took little notice, but we, as academicians, understood the cost of writing material, and young Aristophanes nodded with irony that the great men of Alexandrian letters had been wiped clean equally in the service of mathematics.

Pingala first unrolled a scroll of the Mauryan holy texts, which they call 'Vedas,' written in the particularly beautiful Indian liturgical style, the creation of which the Mauryans attribute to a divine personality. Indeed, Pingala explained that 'Vak', the goddess associated with speech, had given Pingala's ancestors the means to converse with one another thousands of years before. From memory Pingala recited before the assembly the following from one of these Vedas then unknown to us, but of which we may now claim several copies resident among the catalog of the library:

> "When men, Brhaspati!, giving names to objects, sent out Vak's first and earliest utterances all that was excellent and spotless, treasured within them, was disclosed through their affection."

> "Where, like men cleansing corn-flour in a cribble, the wise in spirit have created language, friends see and recognize the marks of friendship: their speech retains the blessed sign imprinted."

> "With sacrifice the trace of Vak they followed, and found her harboring within the Rsis. They brought her, dealt her forth in many places: seven singers make her tones resound in concert."

> "One man hath ne'er seen Vak, and yet he seeth: one man hath hearing but hath never heard her. But to another hath she shown her beauty as a fond well-dressed woman to her husband."

Pingala bade forgiveness from his host for this necessary diversion, claiming that the Vedas were partly the reason he was called to mathematics and, subsequently, on to our small party in Persepolis. The great pharaoh waved off his apology. Still steeped in the sadness of this abandoned cultural outpost, he welcomed the erudition of eastern aesthetes. Ptolemy stirred in his seat approvingly and suggested a public reading of this epic known as the Veda be offered to the Festival as soon as might be arranged. Pingala bowed gracefully and equivocated, with some embarrassment, as the Mauryans do not consider their holy texts suitable for reading to the uninitiated.

Pingala then explained in some detail his own work with the Vedas, his *Chandahsutra*, This, he offered humbly, was not unlike in spirit though poor in comparison to the life's work of our own Callimachus, whose meta-analysis of the literature of antiquity remains an example for the world. In the *Chandahsutra*, of which its author presented a copy to Euergetes, was an analysis of the stresses, intonations and rhythms of speech. This he discussed in even greater detail for nearly twenty minutes before wise Ptolemy, Light of Ammon, son of Zeus, and, I must admit, the rest of our small group, stirred with boredom. It is remarkable to me, even now, that Aristophanes, then only sixteen and the youngest of our circle, was so easily able to understand and, later, to converse with Pingala about this specialty, which indeed later formed the basis of his own. Sensing he was losing his audience's attention, Pingala unrolled a second scroll, on which a faint Callimachian ode to Demeter could still be seen beneath the proud strokes of Sanskrit.

Of course, this sacred writing was alien to us, but at regular intervals strings of symbols had been inserted as intercalations in a treatise that bore the diagrams so familiar to our mathematical texts. Pingala explained each symbol as representative of a quantity, and that this method of representing amounts, known to Indian mathematicians for some generations, had been of little consequence until Pingala had discovered its convenience in performing mathematical calculations. Of particular interest had been Pingala's reworking of the system using positional notation. There need only be ten symbols, placed in a chain in a particular order, to represent any quantity. The party was not immediately moved, and only until Pingala explained the nature of this positional base-ten system of enumeration did the Master rise, as if prodded by the muses.

Again, Onesimus the pragmatist reminds Hesperos the dreamer that it is by no means certain which system of account will triumph within or beyond the lands of the Ptolemies, to say nothing of the Grecophone world. Even today, these 'Indian numerals' are specific to mathematics of the Academy and precious few centers of learning beyond. The cumbersome system of our ancestors is still very much in the main, and the insidious sexagesimalism of the Babylonians still rules the navigator's chart and the geometer's square.

Indeed, for some time, Diocles and Apollonius of Perga managed their household and derived their income by providing the onerous service of transliterating discoveries at the Academy into the various colloquial numbers as required by a disparate clientele. Abdaraxus, overtaken with Pingala's methods all those decades ago, submitted before his recent death a conclusive account of the history of the cooperative evolution of enumeration, and to his corpus I must not forget to add the Master's incisive monograph on the subject, both of which may be found among the library's catalog.

At the urging of Onesimus, therefore, I mention the juxtaposition of Archimedes' famous grains of sand. The text is among the most widely cited texts on large enumeration within the holdings of the library, and despite Onesimus' unhappy predictions, I refuse on principle to imagine a world in which this does not continue to be so. It is good enough for me to relate that one might reflect on the ingenuity of Archimedes in his troubles to create new numerals, myriads upon myriads, to calculate his famous grains of sand, especially because the numerals of the day were not equal to his task. It was his genius alone that transcended their limitations, until the innovations gifted by the East upon the West at the mathematics competition fifty years ago. I include here only Archimedes' dedication of that famous work, written to the king of his native Syracuse, that his own words may stand above my humble attempt to pay him the honor that is his due:

"There are some, King Gelon, who think that the number of the sand is infinite in multitude; and I mean by the sand not only that which exists about Syracuse and the rest of Sicily but also that which is found in every region whether inhabited or uninhabited. Again there are some who, without regarding it as infinite, yet think that no number has been named which is great enough to exceed its multitude. And it is clear that they who hold this view, if they imagined a mass made up of sand in other respects as large as the mass of the Earth, including in it all the seas and the hollows of the Earth filled up to a height equal to that of the highest of the mountains, would be many times further still from recognizing that any number could be expressed which exceeded the multitude of the sand so taken.

But I will try to show you by means of geometrical proofs, which you will be able to follow, that, of the numbers named by me and given in the work which I sent to Zeuxippus, some exceed not only the number of the mass of sand equal in magnitude to the Earth filled up in the way described, but also that of a mass equal in magnitude to the universe. Now you are aware that 'universe' is the name given by most astronomers to the sphere whose center is the center of the Earth and whose radius is equal to the straight line between the center of the sun and the center of the Earth. This is the common account as you have heard from astronomers. But Aristarchus of Samos brought out a book consisting of some hypotheses, in which the premises lead to the result that the universe is many times greater than that now so called.

His hypotheses are that the fixed stars and the sun remain unmoved, that the Earth revolves about the sun in the circumference of a circle, the sun lying in the middle of the orbit, and that the sphere of the fixed stars, situated about the same center as the sun, is so great that the circle in which he supposes the Earth to revolve bears such a proportion to the distance of the fixed stars as the center of the sphere bears to its surface. Now it is easy to see that this is impossible; for, since the center of the sphere has no magnitude, we cannot conceive it to bear any ratio whatever to the surface of the sphere.

We must however take Aristarchus to mean this: since we conceive the Earth to be, as it were, the center of the universe, the ratio which the Earth bears to what we describe as the 'universe' is the same as the ratio which the sphere containing the circle in which he supposes the Earth to revolve bears to the sphere of the fixed stars. For he adapts the proofs of his results to a hypothesis of this kind, and in particular he appears to suppose the magnitude of the sphere in which he represents the Earth as moving to be equal to what we call the 'universe.'"

I issue a small aside here to mention - though it is better stricken from the final draft of this memoir - the cavalier attitude of one of those students attendant upon a different Aristarchus at the Serapeum during his demonstration of epokhe. This young man made a snide remark about the dilettantism of undertaking a study of how many grains of sand might fill the universe. I am pleased to say that I and Aristarchus cracked the student gently on the side of his head, that he might regain respect for the intrepidity of Archimedes' abstractions.

Still, I shall reproduce here, briefly, the various ways large numbers had been represented in the age of Euergetes and for generations before him. Great Alexander would have had with him on his eastern campaign mathematicians and astronomers who used the acrophonic system, still taught to the stultified students in old Athens, regrettably. Many will still know it, but it is interesting to note that it involved taking the first letter of the name of each numeral as a symbol for the numeral itself, from a quantity of one to the myriads of myriads, developed especially by Archimedes in his answer to King Gelon.

Let us confront the old ways head-on. A singular unit is known as I, five as Π, ten as Δ, one hundred as H and one thousand as X, according, of course, to the first letter of the terms used for these quantities. This, as in everything of worth and value, the Romans have copied from the minds of Hellas. The system before our time had in its higher orders a symbol for multiples of five, so that the mathematician wishing to consider quantities not within normal human experience must contend with, for example, a rendering of five thousand by taking one thousand, X, multiplied five times, as indicated by a modified symbol Π:

ΓΧ

Thus, the relatively small number of stades involved in the Master' calculation of the circumference of the Earth was represented by building one upon another from several symbols to create the following additive representation:

ΓΧ ΓΧ ΓΧ ΓΧ ΓΧ **X X H H Δ I I**

The mathematics after Alexander, of course, is something of an improvement, in that the larger numerals grew not to encompass other numbers but to introduce new symbols to stand in their stead. Rather than add numerals as the barbarians do, a letter was ascribed to each place in the following way, α', β', γ', δ', ε', ς', ζ', η', θ', ι', with the relocation of the ' symbol from the right to the left to denote when one was to consider the numeral small or large. This was the ingenious method in place at the library, and to which Archimedes, the first of his countrymen to consider seriously the mathematics of the infinite, added his myriads multiplied several times by themselves, so that tens of thousands might be taken tens of thousands of times over again. In this way it was easily demonstrated that an alphabetic numeric system proved itself in every way superior to the acrophonic it had replaced, leaving the barbarians of Latium with the singular particularity of the numerals they seem to scrawl upon every monumental surface. Thus, at the moment of our interaction with Pingala our mathematical texts represented the Master's triumphal stades as:

$$\overset{\kappa\varepsilon}{M},\beta\sigma\iota\beta$$

And it was in this calculation that Archimedes, admittedly with the Master's help and collaboration, invented a system we have called exponentiation. This system allows a number to be raised to a specific multiple or, more importantly for extremely large numbers, certain powers of itself. In the example above, Archimedes then devised a method of adding exponential quantities, so that a myriad, M, might be raised to a power, A, and another myriad might be raised to a power, B, and the two might be added so that the total value was a myriad raised to a power equivalent to the sum of A and B. Among those students who understand its implications at the Academy this system is still widely used, and indeed, Aristophanes had proven his worth no less as an expositor of enumeration than as a grammarian by his work on the prosody of written and symbolic communication. I am sorry to say that Aristophanes', Archimedes' and the Master's efforts at popularization outside this small circle has been unsuccessful, so ingrained in tradition is the eternal land of Egypt and her Greek masters.

I return now to the Festival of the Pantheon, and to Euergetes' tent and the presentation of our visitors from India. The state of Greek numerals was as I have just mentioned, and the state of her mathematicians one of ingenious but laborious flights of calculation. A complete corpus of Mauryan texts were later copied and sent to the library, and it is my recollection that the following of their number which I now consult was the one Pingala placed before the pharaoh during the festival, bearing as it does the stamp of his mathematical grammar. This gives something of the flavor of the consubstantiality of Indian mathematics and Indian mysticism. Reviewing this after all these years I feel the same kinship with that ancient civilization as I did then, when I first realized the similarities in our shared sense of considering mathematics in terms of the divine.

Hail to śata	hundred	10^2
Hail to sahasra	thousand	10^3
Hail to ayuta	ten thousand	10^4
Hail to niyuta	hundred thousand	10^5
Hail to prayuta	million	10^6
Hail to arbuda	ten million	10^7
Hail to nyarbuda	hundred million	10^8
Hail to samudra	billion	10^9
Hail to madhya	ten billion, ("middle")	10^{10}
Hail to anta	hundred billion, ("end")	10^{11}
Hail to parārdha	one trillion, ("beyond parts")	10^{12}
Hail to us'as	the dawn	
Hail to vyuṣṭi	the twilight	
Hail to udeṣyat	the one which is going to rise	
Hail to udyat	the one which is rising	
Hail to udita	the one which has just risen	
Hail to svarga	the heaven	
Hail to martya	the world	
Hail to all.		

Below this passage Pingala had written three tables, each arranged in columns of ten. The first was the complex sexagesimal Babylonian system in the style characteristic of writing with a reed stylus on soft clay. This system was widely known at the time and had the benefit, the Master commented to Pingala, of having as its base what the Master considered a 'superior highly composite number.' It use of base 60 likely lay in *dactylonomy*, or finger counting, a subject the Master touched on extensively within his wider treatise on *ethnomathematics*, another field of his own creation. Pingala indicated the Babylonian table with a brush of his hand.

It was noted by the Master that 12 may be easily counted on one hand by utilizing the thumb as an indicator and all the remaining finger joints as placeholders that then might have their value transferred to one of the five fingers of the remaining hand. 60, by virtue of its composition, also allowed for easy division by 2, 3, 4, 5, 6, 10, 12, 15, 20 and 30, making its convenience for trade, measurement and timekeeping obvious. The Master's fascination with prime numbers was paramount among his interests, and he remarked to Pingala that the number 60 was further fascinating because it is the sum of a pair of twin primes 29 and 31, the sum of four consecutive primes 11, 13, 17 and 19, and it is adjacent to the primes 59 and 61. It is also the smallest number which is the sum of two odd primes in six ways.

Indeed, Archimedes, who had introduced the Master to pure geometric forms as part of the key for their early encoded correspondence, was said to count among his most favorite the icosidodecahedron, a solid with twenty triangular faces and twelve pentagonal faces, thirty identical vertices, with two triangles and two pentagons meeting at each, and 60 identical edges, each separating a triangle from a pentagon.

The next table was filled with the familiar Greek alphabetic numerals in a grid known to the sophisticates of all cultures:

α	β'	γ'	δ'	ε'	ϛ	ζ'	η'	θ'	ι'
ια'	ιβ'	ιγ'	ιδ'	ιε'	ιϛ	ιζ'	ιη'	ιθ'	κ'
κα'	κβ'	κγ'	κδ'	κε'	κϛ	κζ'	κη'	κθ'	λ'
λα'	λβ'	λγ'	λδ'	λε'	λϛ	λζ'	λη'	λθ'	μ'
μα'	μβ'	μγ'	μδ'	με'	μϛ	μζ'	μη'	μθ'	ν'
να'	νβ'	νγ'	νδ'	νε'	νϛ	νζ'	νη'	νθ'	ξ'
ξα'	ξβ'	ξγ'	ξδ'	ξε'	ξϛ	ξζ'	ξη'	ξθ'	ο'
οα'	οβ'	ογ'	οδ'	οε'	οϛ	οζ'	οη'	οθ'	π'
πα'	πβ'	πγ'	πδ'	πε'	πϛ	πζ'	πη'	πθ'	ϟ'
ϟα'	ϟβ'	ϟγ'	ϟδ'	ϟε'	ϟϛ	ϟζ'	ϟη'	ϟθ'	ρ'

The last table was filled with entirely new symbols which echoed their appearances above next to their Sanskrit names:

1	2	3	4	5	6	7	8	9	10
11	12	13	14	15	16	17	18	19	20
21	22	23	24	25	26	27	28	29	30
31	32	33	34	35	36	37	38	39	40
41	42	43	44	45	46	47	48	49	50
51	52	53	54	55	56	57	58	59	60
61	62	63	64	65	66	67	68	69	70
71	72	73	74	75	76	77	78	79	80
81	82	83	84	85	86	87	88	89	90
91	92	93	94	95	96	97	98	99	100

It was this image that moved Eratosthenes from his seat. It was as if the muses had budged him, and later all of us, from Plato's cave into the warm embrace of Helios. I am only a competent writer of prose and so I have no ability to build up momentum to such a revealing and axial moment. I have used the Indian numerals throughout this text where appropriate, in the style of the modern Academy, Library and Musaeum, and their inclusion here in a chart will not have the intended effect on modern readers. But Onesimus, who has studied more recently than I from the collections can attest to the scant use of the Indian numerals even today among works not chiefly about mathematics. It is worth comparing Archimedes' *Sand Reckoner* using the original, alphabetic notations with his revised work which employs the new symbols, aided in no small measure by the synthesis of Apollonius of Perga, who, as a young man at the time and unwedded to conformity, embraced them immediately. In Archimedes' original text he required pages upon pages to write his conclusions, brilliant as they were. Using the Indian numerals, Archimedes' and Eratosthenes' exponentiation, and Apollonius' refinements, I may make note in line with the text of the number of grains of sand which may fill the universe. The number is, simply, 10^{63}.

Several scrolls later we realized that Pingala had come to Persepolis to ask Eratosthenes to comment on a proposed solution for the conjecture that every even integer greater than 2 can be expressed as the sum of two primes. This problem was already well known to the Academy. Though at that time the problem was unsolved – Eratosthenes found an elegant proof before his death - the Master was able to show easily that Pingala had erred in his own construction of a solution, which was itself not far from the approach of which the Master later availed himself. Eratosthenes then took up another matter of geodesy of concern to Ashoka for the purposes of taxation. The numeral tables Pingala had provided were simply primers so that Eratosthenes might consult with Pingala in mathematical language most suitable to the task at hand. Looking back on our fallen sense of superiority, we could only wonder at how far the civilization of Hellas had come in spite of our childish numerical notation. That we might pride ourselves on our achievements in spite of this Eratosthenes could only say, "It's as if Greek mathematicians and Indian mathematicians have found ourselves on the same unknown shore. We both shake off the sand and look back to our vessels, ours a tired skiff and theirs a mighty quinquereme."

The Master gladly conferred with Pingala on a small matter of geography with which the latter had concerned himself, and, in gratitude, Pingala gave copies of his texts to Ptolemy that they might travel back to the Museum. Ptolemy, in kind, gifted to Pingala several of our texts, including a copy of the complete works of Aeschylus, Sophocles and Euripides that Ptolemy had 'borrowed' from Athens.

The mathematics prizes were eventually distributed, with several special citations awarded for 'acts of intellectual cooperation,' - to my knowledge the first of their kind. Apollonius and Aristophanes spent many days with Pingala and his cohort, learning all they could about the grammatical rules and symbolic language they had developed. It is worth noting that Ptolemy was so moved by our eastern visitors that he permitted their access to the devices, which had continued spinning in silence beneath their camouflage during the entirety of the campaign. I was not in attendance when Ptolemy, the Master and Pingala inspected the machine, but I can make of it only the account that afterward the Master wore an interesting mixture of pride and expectancy for the remainder of the eastern march. I was only later to discover that Eratosthenes had seized on Pingala's numerals as a natural replacement for the cumbersome manipulations then taking place within the device and could not wait for the return to Alexandria, that he might immediately institute these reforms.

On the eleventh day of Pingala's stay in Persepolis, a rider arrived with an intercept from the west. Pingala stood mesmerized as the Master and I worked the dispatch through the device. It took only minutes for the gears and camshafts to reveal that Seleucus had regained his hold on Anatolia and was moving east, once again calling into question the fate of Coele-Syria.

Ptolemy ordered the festival's conclusion and, giving the requisite propitiations at the temple, made ready to reverse course to face his great antagonist. During the last evening in Persepolis we all bid Pingala and his associates travel with us, back to Alexandria. It was not a half-hearted request. Ptolemy offered to honor all of them with positions at the Academy. Understandably, they refused, stating that they could no more leave their prince than Ptolemy's academicians could leave theirs. This was a comment in which Ptolemy took great delight, though I do not know exactly in which spirit, voluntary or obligatory, Pingala considered the nature of an academician's allegiance to a specific court. Whatever his meaning, Pingala then praised Ptolemy for his patronage of so fine a collection of academicians and, especially, for his elevation of Eratosthenes, to whom due to his breadth of knowledge and expertise in poetry, chronography, mechanics, mathematics, astronomy, music and geography, Pingala referred as 'beta;' Eratosthenes was, Pingala remarked, the second best in everything. Thus, after too brief a time in our presence, Pingala and his colleagues set out east for India as we broke camp for a journey back to the troubled West.

We marched from Persepolis to Susa, an ancient Persian capital, then north to receive homage at Ecbatana, where Ptolemy was eager to retrieve the last of the cult statuary he had promised to repatriate to the Egyptian priesthood. We then journeyed from Ecbatana southeast through Seleucia-on-the-Tigris, the first Seleucian capital before Seleucus I Nicator relocated his court to Antioch. Even then this Seleucia was a city of renowned cosmopolitanism. She, too, threw open her doors to Ptolemy, who allowed the campaign a brief respite while he gave offerings to the Temple of Demeter there and observed a rite of the Lesser Eleusinian Mysteries.

We then returned to Babylon, where we encamped long enough only to recover those Egyptian items the agents left by Ptolemy earlier had recovered from ancient Uruk and smaller sites. While pausing here, Ptolemy received foreboding notices from officials in Thebes, Ptolemais, Oxyrhynchus and Memphis that the Nile showed every indication of a poor inundation.

We then followed the Euphrates northwest to Dura-Europos, where we were amused by the vivid graffiti that adorns its walls. I pause here to say that Abdaraxus had a rather intense affair with the wife of a colonial official, on whom he tested a steam-driven device he had devised on the long, and one must say, lonely, march from Persepolis. The irony was not lost on our group that the practical natural philosophy of his mentor, Ctesibius, which was so appealing to the priests and congregants of the Serapeum, should prove so successful in more intimate supplication.   Unfortunately, his monograph on the subject has disappeared from the library and his prototype has been wiped from the registered devices of the Musaeum. Onesimus jests that Diocles must have taken it. This conjecture may have its merits.

We soon approached the plains outside Antioch and skirmished with Seleucus' army for some days while we prepared for the decisive battle. Xanthippus surrounded the city easily, and no report could be made of Seleucus' specific location. Ptolemy rode to the north and Xanthippus to the south so that the city's supply routes were blocked. In this manner our army blockaded the Seleucian capital for several months. During this period Diocles and Apollonius fought back-to-back against a Seleucian raiding party that had infiltrated our small academician's encampment mistaking it as the pharaoh's own.

Fearing an impasse, Ptolemy ordered special alterations be made to his siege engines under the Master's supervision. Abdaraxus, suffering terribly from some unknown ailment or from the treatments of mercury he had been prescribed by the court physician, nevertheless crafted the great ranging apparatuses along the lines of those of Archimedes that were so prominent at the Ptolemaia. Eventually, Antioch relented, and, with only minor resistance we were able to take the city and, with the support of Ptolemy's navy, the port city of Antioch, Seleucia Pieria.

At the same time, Ptolemy, who had earlier received word in Persepolis that his possessions in the Aegean, including the Cyclades, had been overrun by Antigonus II Gonatas of Macedon, received better news that his ally, Aratus, had retaken Corinth from Antigonus, thereby securing the remainder of his Aegean outposts. Ptolemy made ready to fortify Antioch and move on to confront Seleucus in Anatolia when the traveling court received yet another dispatch from Alexandria. Seizing upon Ptolemy's long absence in the East and spurred by native discontent at the poorest harvest in years, the Egyptian priesthood in several majority Egyptian cities south of Thebes had placed themselves in rebellion.

Ptolemy held a council of war, and it was decided that Xanthippus would continue the occupation of Antioch and project power into Asia Minor while Lysimachus would continue to consolidate Seleucian control of upper Syria from his base in Damascus. Young Theodotus would remain military governor in Gaza, and Ptolemy would march immediately to Pelusium and, if his return to Egypt was not enough to restore order, up the Nile to crush the native rebellion. We marched for several weeks, and I was glad of the haste by which we passed by Jerusalem as it had been nearly nine months since I had heard from the phalangites of the hospitality of the daughters of Israel.

As the cortege passed from the boundary of Coele-Syria, now indisputably in Ptolemy's hands, and into Egypt proper through Pelusium, the Master remarked that he had gained an even greater respect for his prince. Other men might have pressed on, as Alexander had, for the glories and riches of the East. But in refusing to neglect the security of his kingdom for the glories of conquest, Euergetes had proven himself in the eyes of the academicians in his service a dexterous diplomat and a professional sovereign. This was a boast, asserted the Master, of which those in the service of the other descendants of Alexander's diadochoi could never avail themselves.

Upon reaching Pelusium the Master was greeted by Sosibius privately. Sosibius had arranged for the importation of a year's worth of grain from abroad, en route from Syria and Cyprus even as Ptolemy had resumed his march from Antioch. Sosibius had also assembled a small contingent of mercenaries from the Sinai desert, Cyrene and Carthage who were prepared to march south in the event that Ptolemy had not returned in to time to forestall the separatists from reaching Memphis. Sosibius had entertained the thought of arming suitably

Hellenized Egyptians from Alexandria, who might leave the experience with an even greater investment in their government than before, but others in Ptolemy's service had argued against this, and the foreign mercenaries had been hired at great cost. Sosibius admitted that, while he had tried to keep the affair private, news had reached Alexandria that foreign mercenaries were marching on the capital, alarming Alexandrine Greeks almost as much as it frightened their native neighbors.

Ptolemy understood the paradox well. Through the wars of Alexander's successors, native troops had been employed to middling effect, some embracing the opportunities to gain the rewards of decent pay and land grants, others accepting professional military training with an eye to a future where their experience might be turned against an occupying prince. Ptolemy had arrived in time to avoid the issue, and the mercenaries were disbanded overnight and sent back to their respective homes with pay only for the journey to Egypt. A small band of them set fire to a temple of Isis, which, while easily put out, scandalized the Alexandrian elite and, some said, emboldened the natives of old Rhakotis, the Egyptian quarter.

Ptolemy sent a force of five thousand to Alexandria, three thousand to Naucratis, two thousand to Hermopolis and two thousand each to "escort" the mercenaries of Cyrene and the arid Sinai back to their homelands. He then marched the remainder of his force south, where news of his return to Egypt was enough to disband the separatists before he arrived. As has been mentioned, Euergetes was a pragmatist, and where others might have made examples of smaller outposts like Aphroditopolis or Dendera, Ptolemy marched through these settlements, and the larger cities of Heliopolis, Memphis and Oxyrhynchus, with magnanimity, as if rebellion and sedition were as unthinkable as the Nile changing its course from the Mediterranean to the Red Sea.

At every stop, Ptolemy distributed enormous quantities of grain to the local populations, meticulously restored the repatriated statuary and cult icons to their previous locations, ordered armies of scribes and masons to renovate native inscriptions and rebuild ancient temples and received homage and dedication from a newly infatuated priesthood. This triumph culminated at Thebes, where Ptolemy was met with such gratitude and praise that all forgot the trouble of the previous months. The temples were well on their way to revitalization, and the return of Cambyses' hostages were a matter of national pride. It was here, during the height of his popularity with the natives, that

Ptolemy was officially invested with the epithet 'Euergetes' or benefactor, a name with which he is still linked in all official reports.

Ptolemy returned to Alexandria in triumph. There he received an embassy from Seleucus that confirmed what Eratosthenes' intelligence had already told him: Seleucus was prepared to sue for peace under the assurance that all of Ptolemy's holdings captured during the Laodicean 'War' and his Syrian campaign would remain in Euergetes' hands. His grandfather's empire had reached its height, never to be regained, I imagine, in my lifetime.

Two years later, at Ptolemy's birthday celebrations held in Canopus, a large delegation of priests met in the newly built temple of Osiris and asked for and were given permission to memorialize Euergetes' favors. Ptolemy himself laid the cornerstone of the new construction during his preparations for the eastern campaign and presented, as was customary, a gold plate inscribed with his dedication that it might be closed up within the foundations.

This synod of priests voted unanimously on a commemoration of Ptolemy's victories and submitted to Sosibius the text of several decrees they wished to erect at suitable locations throughout the immortal land of their ancestors. I am afraid to say that what these priests lacked in style they more than made up for in the quantity of the paeans sung in Ptolemy's name. Sosibius altered the text according to the needs of court and it was his innovation that the decrees be displayed in the native language and Greek, that the twin audiences of Ptolemy's domestic empire and foreign visitors might equally comprehend his power. Indeed, the near-dead Callimachus and spry Apollonius of Rhodes contributed language, and Apollonius of Perga who had been so taken with Pingala's prosody, added further flourishes. The text was a triumph, and I reproduce it in some measure here, to save the flow of narrative from the inconvenience of forcing a consultation within the library of the annals of the Court Circular:

> [Ptolemy and Queen Berenice] took care of the statues of the gods, which had been robbed by the barbarians of the land Persia from temples of Egypt, since His Majesty had won them back in his campaign against the two lands of Asia, he brought them to Egypt, and placed them on their places in the temples, where they had previously stood. He has kept up peace in Egypt advantageously by warring for its weal in valleys and plain foreign parts, and marched against many peoples and their Chiefs who commanded them, they were rendering fortunate

JAMES ADDOMS | 180

those who live as his subjects, not only inhabitants of Egypt, but also of all lands subject to their Majesties. When moreover there happened a year of a deficient water of Nile during their reign, and all the inhabitants of Egypt became faint-hearted at this event, for fear, memory made them think of the dearth which once did occur in the time of the former Kings, in consequence of the deficiency of the Nile to the inhabitants of Egypt in their time.

So lavish was the pharaoh's gratitude for The Master and the Academy that had made the code-breaking possible and so aided in his campaign in the East that Ptolemy showered resources upon us. Archimedes and The Master were excused from their teaching assignments that they might pursue their passions, and several times the pharaoh and some of his more trusted intimates came to inspect the progress of the devices, to which all of us were making constant improvements.

The Master updated the devices to work with the Indian numerals, and soon turned them to calculating small sums in the fashion of Archimedes' grains of sand. And it was during this time that I realized how Archimedes had ingeniously turned the device to use in ballistics, even demonstrating for me on a small scale how he had achieved the accuracy of the ballistae at the Ptolemaia. The workings of this subsidiary device, reproduced on each of the pharaoh's ships, is admittedly beyond the scope of my undertaking here, but I am told that the late Archimedes has written a treatise on it which his circle at the Syracusian court will in due course register within the reserved holdings of the library.

Several years passed in happy abstraction, the Master with his mechanized mathematics, Archimedes with his devices of inordinate complexity, Ctesibius and Abdaraxus in support of these efforts. I must say that I added one or two refinements that were welcomed by our small group, and by this time Diocles, Apollonius and, I must say, even the reluctant Aristophanes welcomed me as an equal fellow of the Academy. It was during this flurry of activity that the Master made his most profound mathematical discovery, and with it, the beginning of the Alexandrian Project and the seeds of the antidote to the trials we had yet to endure.

METALOGUE
THE VERY NEAR FUTURE

16

INDECISION. His pulse raced with the sort of indecision that assured him that he was on the brink of discovery, for what awaits the man who has met his own God, for what would he live once God had invited him into God's mind and only in the presence of God would man ask these questions of himself? His mind steadied itself as surely as his feet made another turn. He touched the pack slung over his shoulder. *He* had found the complete sixth source, *he* was destined to complete the journey. *He* had put together the clues scattered across twenty two centuries. *He* had solved what no one else in the order had solved. *He* was the inheritor of the birthright of the initiates.

He need only follow the Map to bring light to darkness. He touched another small volume through the canvas of his pack, reciting a passage from memory, the work of a fellow brother and initiate:

> "The sciences have sworn among themselves an inviolable partnership; it is almost impossible to separate them, for they would rather suffer than be torn apart; and if anyone persists in doing so, he gets for his trouble only imperfect and confused fragments. Yet they do not arrive all together, but they hold each other by the hand so that they follow one another in a natural order which it is dangerous to change, because they refuse to enter in any other way where they are called."

-Brother, Initiate, Marin Mersenne, *Les Préludes de l'Harmonie Universelle (1634)*

"The sciences are the manifestation of human consciousness speaking through the divine inspiration," he said into the cavern. "In this act, I join all the sciences together again, and trace them back to their source. The indissoluble numbers are the foundation of everything, and I have found them here."

He had retraced his steps, his initial calculation of distance had been based on the prime numbers arrayed in an Ulam Spiral. He had overestimated the distance. The Mersenne Prime was the key, NOT the perfect number. The Mersenne Prime was mentioned purposely in the text. It was not only the first of an astonishing sequence of discoveries, it was the axial moment in which the sixth source proclaimed its supremacy and its divinity – and it had been coded into the rock-cut passages below the strange landscape. He found the spot, exactly after the following sequence from the opening of the cave:

Pass 2 junctions, turn;
Pass 1 junction, turn;
Pass 4 junctions, turn;
Pass 7 junctions, turn;
Pass 4 junctions, turn;
Pass 8 junctions, turn;
Pass 3 junctions, turn;
Pass 6 junctions, turn;
Pass 4 junctions, turn;
Pass 7 junctions, turn.

He came to a smooth shelf cut into the wall. Almost undetectably, the Mersenne itself was carved into the rock, accompanied by a dedication to the muses in familiar Koine Greek. His hands flew across the dark stone, looking for a lever or a button. Then, he remembered the words of Mersenne himself, an initiate, a brother, possessed of as much of the ancient knowledge as any of his fellows. Marin Mersenne, master of harmonics.

He began to tap a sequence on the rock wall.

» BOOK III «

THE SHORE OF ANTIKYTHERA
BENEATH THE THIGH OF THE BULL

I can offer you, I fear, no new light, for I have made no fresh discoveries in the question at issue. But I will tell you what I have heard from Sulpicius Gallus, who was a man of profound learning, as you are aware. Listening one day to the recital of a similar prodigy, in the house of Marcellus, who had been his colleague in the consulship; he asked to see a celestial globe, which Marcellus's grandfather had saved after the capture of Syracuse, from this magnificent and opulent city, without bringing home any other memorial of so great a victory. I had often heard this celestial globe or sphere mentioned on account of the great fame of Archimedes. Its appearance, however, did not seem to me particularly striking. There is another, more elegant in form, and more generally known, molded by the same Archimedes, and deposited by the same Marcellus, in the Temple of Virtue at Rome. But as soon as Gallus had begun to explain, by his sublime science, the composition of this machine, I felt that the Sicilian geometrician must have possessed a genius superior to anything we usually conceive to belong to our nature.

Who can believe that Dionysius, when after a thousand efforts he ravished from his fellow citizens their liberty, had performed a nobler work than Archimedes, when, without pretense or apparent exertion, he manufactured the planetarium we were just describing. Surely those are more solitary, who, in the midst of a crowd, find no one with whom they can converse congenially, than those, who, without witnesses, hold communion with themselves, and enter into the secret counsels of the sagest philosophers, while they delight themselves in their writings and discoveries. Who can be esteemed richer than the man who wants nothing which nature requires, or more powerful than he who attains all she desiderates; or happier than he who is free from all mental perturbation; or more secure in future than he who carries all his property in himself which is thus secured from shipwreck? And what power, what magistracy, what royalty can be preferred to a wisdom, which, looking down on all terrestrial objects as low and transitory things, incessantly directs its attention to eternal and immutable verities, and which is persuaded that though others are called men, none are really so but those who have cultivated the appropriate acts of humanity?

—MARCUS TULLIUS CICERO, De Re Publica

Many are feeding in populous Egypt,
Scribblers on papyrus,
Ceaselessly wrangling in the birdcage of the Muses.

—TIMON OF PHLIUS

17

Onesimus is more prone to linguistic clarity than I. My account of the famous lecture which I intend now to insert into this narrative has been deemed too lofty, as I had intended to include a long exposition comparing the Master's intrepidity with mathematics and the military achievements of Alexander which I used several days ago at a small ceremony in honor of Eratosthenes' life. I here add a hint of its flavor:

> As Alexander must have done while surveying previously impregnable battlements and citadels from Asia Minor to the Indus Valley, it was then I believe, when the intellectual expansionist Eratosthenes fully realized his inheritance of a sacred knowledge already ancient to our world. Alexander had redrawn the political map; Eratosthenes, on that morning 40 years ago, had begun to besiege the greatest fortresses of the natural world.

Onesimus, more Callimachian than I, recommends the following:

> The Master had spoken of a boyhood fascination with what he himself would later name the systematic study of the landscape: geography. It was in the pursuit of a fundamental, empirical understanding of the environment he inhabited that he began reading the available texts on the natural world. It was upon Democritus' theory that he built his world from the

smallest indivisible components of matter. It was from Plato
that he, passed patiently to as unworthy a pupil as Hesperos,
received the highest incorruptible Forms of nature and
metaphysics. Even from the Jews and the isolated, subatomic
toil of 72 divinely inspired scribes would he become familiar
with the singular, elemental translation of ancient Hebraic
religious texts codified in the *Septuagint*, still now in this
turbulence among the most esteemed articles in the library.

Onesimus maintains an impish fascination with the Jewish creation
myths now gaining ascendancy; like many of his generation, he never misses an
opportunity to mock the certainty of their monotonous, monolatrous self-
importance. Indeed, the Master had read widely of the work of the Jewish
scholars, many of whom he counted among his friends, but I see no connection
between some sort of prosodic atomism and prime numbers beyond the happy
circumstances of our communion with Pingala and the minds of Maurya.

Onesimus has joked that anyone wishing to critique the religious
practices of a race must first preface such a critique with a suitable list of those
of their number with whom the one offering the critique is happily acquainted.
I am too old for such sophistry, and either way, Onesimus jokes that he will
arrange the final narrative to his liking, as I am unable to read the final product
by myself and am thereby disallowed a critique. Perhaps he really means that
he shall keep me wrangled in so many diversions from the main narrative that I
shall die standing at my desk, hovering over my unfinished manuscript. I must
focus again on the Master and his famous lecture!

It is fair to say that Eratosthenes, in the years after his pharaoh's
triumph in Asia, had turned his intellect and his devices to a more complete
solution for the value of the relationship between a circle's circumference and
its diameter in which a circle was squared into a polygon of an infinitude of
indissoluble sides. Proving that this number was unending (an intuitive proof
of which now resides in the library), he then took up a statement in a minor part
of Euclid's tract, *Elements*. Euclid's proof of which the Master most often spoke
concerned the building blocks of mathematics. Of these 'prime' numbers Euclid
proved a series must be infinite. The Master devised an ingenious approach to
solving the problem of factoring large numbers into two constituent primes,
and, universally praised throughout the Academy, the Master undertook to

deliver a small lecture on his process to the pharaoh and other luminaries at court.

The lecture had been arranged by Archimedes. Eratosthenes had spent the hours before with his friend in imitation of the symposium, exchanging ideas and wine under the protection of the god Dionysus, from whom a creative spirit radiated like the heat of the Egyptian Sun. It was then, in the spring of the ninth year of the reign of Ptolemy III Euergetes that Eratosthenes addressed his fellow scholars in the marble pilaster-lined hall in the temple of the Muses - the *Musaeum* - and unveiled his recent work on calculation that would become the basis of the Alexandrian Project.

The Master entered the hall slowly from behind a row of students seated in a semi-circle. They sat on smooth sandstone benches arranged around a central raised platform on which was erected a large brazier burning incense in honor of the Muses. The students' faces betrayed origins as diverse as the reach of Ptolemaic influence. He passed his students Dionysodorus of Caunus and Archaelaus of Athens. The mischievous twins Agathocles and Agathoclea, friends of the young heir to the throne, gossiped with their mother, Oenanthe, in hushed tones. Oenanthe had married a Greek nobleman, himself named Agathocles after his own grandfather the tyrant Agathocles of Syracuse, King of Sicily. She was not a student or an academician, of course, but her presence was tolerated by the Academy as she had spent much of her late husband's estate endowing academic posts and buying her children favor at court. I sat next to the inseparable Diocles and Apollonius of Perga, though I don't think I was noticed as they were engaged in mutual adoration of the new Damascene fashions worn by Aristophanes, who entered with an air of superiority that had so put me off to him early on and which he has now seen fit to relinquish as new Chief Librarian and, in that capacity, a humble priest of the Temple of the Muses.

Indeed, Aristophanes, who had then not yet applied the epithet, *of Byzantium*, had spent the few years after the eastern campaign aspiring to lay the intellectual groundwork to eventually replace Eratosthenes as head of the library. He had already displayed a flair as a grammarian. At the age of seventeen, just one year after his return from the Academicians Crusade, Aristophanes had extended Pingala's methods by introducing a well-received scheme for an accent system to designate pronunciation in the evolving stress-based system of Greek that had all but replaced the tonal, pitched system known to Homer. He had also by then championed the interpunct, a curious marauding dot separating poetic verses indicative of the amount of breath a speaker might need to draw before plodding through a particular passage. For a short passage, a *komma*, for an intermediate passage, a *kolon*, dots were placed mid-level or level with the bottom of the text, respectively. When an orator was to bombard an assembly with stately unified assaults – *periodos* – he would stay the injunction of courtesy with a dot level with the top of the text. This somewhat pedantic system was nevertheless indicative both of the new systemization of all fields of knowledge and the triumph of the accretion to Alexandria of much linguistic authority within the expanding Grecophone world.

Beside Aristophanes and inseparable from him sat the ten year old heir of Ptolemy III, himself named Ptolemy in the tradition of Alexander's successor kingdoms. Ptolemy was instructed in the traditional privileges of kingship by an elevated place at court and had displayed an early love of learning and a yearning for wisdom that was to be subsumed during his administration by a devotion to favorites and orgiastic displays of religion. Still, at the time we had no idea that he would be anything other than a model of the learned toughness of his father. Young Ptolemy's passion as a boy lay not in the low arts of war, but in the recounting of epics of Homer, with Aristophanes as guide. Officially, he was tutored by the Master in his capacity as Head Librarian, to whom this task had devolved upon his appointment, but young Ptolemy showed less interest in the Master's geodesy or the mathematics of Euclid and Archimedes than Aristophanes' literary criticism of Homer and Hesiod and those academicians through whom boomed the voice of Calliope.

Slightly forward of the students sat the academicians in the Pharaoh's service. All were present at the lecture who were not otherwise employed presently in some business of state. Archimedes had pushed in between Ctesibius and Philo, who were having an argument about the properties of a pneumatic pump the latter had recently installed in the Serapeum against the wishes of the former, who judged it not yet ready for public display. Conon, the Court Astronomer, and Nicomedes discussed something I could not hear, but must have been of great importance, if small contention, owing to the simultaneous ovoid gesticulations they were drawing in the air. Callimachus, even closer to the appearance of death than at the Ptolemaia, made a great show of indifference to Apollonius of Rhodes by engaging himself in two simultaneous conversations with Aristarchus of Samos and a visiting scholar from Athens, the noted grammarian Euphorion of Chalcis.

Arranged in a still more intimate semi-circle and almost entirely and comically engulfed in a colonnade of willowy gray smoke from the censer were Ptolemy's courtiers – the satraps, the strategoi, other military commanders and paramount among these, Sosibius, who now enjoyed the pharaoh's every consideration. Elevated among these, of course, on a platform of Lebanon cedar clad in gold: The pharaoh-king Ptolemy III Euergetes and his consort Berenice, chief benefactors of the library and the intellectual life of the state.

The Master surmounted the dais and made the appropriate obeisance to his monarch-patron, invoked the guidance of the Muses and prevailed upon the wisdom of Serapis. Seeing this, even the proudest of the Academy ceased their conversation that they might prepare for the Master's presentation. Eratosthenes, feeding on the hush of his audience, theatrically reached above his head to unroll the foremost of several wide canvases suspended above.

On the canvas the Master had inscribed within several grids of ten by ten Pingala's familiar numerals, which, in the several years after the eastern campaign, had become widely known among the men of the Academy:

1	2	3	4	5	6	7	8	9	10
11	12	13	14	15	16	17	18	19	20
21	22	23	24	25	26	27	28	29	30
31	32	33	34	35	36	37	38	39	40
41	42	43	44	45	46	47	48	49	50
51	52	53	54	55	56	57	58	59	60
61	62	63	64	65	66	67	68	69	70
71	72	73	74	75	76	77	78	79	80
81	82	83	84	85	86	87	88	89	90
91	92	93	94	95	96	97	98	99	100

The Master raised his hand to indicate the grid and addressed Euergetes. "My lord, I have taken up the numerals again, with which, by your grace, we have plied the most abstract yet most honest of truths. My lord grant me leave to ask of the others here assembled if all are familiar with the numeral grid before you?"

All nodded their familiarity, though many of us strained to restrain a laugh as Callimachus nodded with such vigor that his wig shifted noticeably on his head. As if he did not see their recognition and wished to relive a triumph, the Master once again grasped a stylus and began making markings on the canvas.

"You know, Gracious Lord, that prime numbers are numerals indivisible by any other numeral except itself and the numeral one. Thus, with the exception of the number two, the only even prime, we may remove each even number instantly, at a stroke." He slowly shaded in every square containing an even number.

1	2	3	4	5	6	7	8	9	10
11	12	13	14	15	16	17	18	19	20
21	22	23	24	25	26	27	28	29	30
31	32	33	34	35	36	37	38	39	40
41	42	43	44	45	46	47	48	49	50
51	52	53	54	55	56	57	58	59	60
61	62	63	64	65	66	67	68	69	70
71	72	73	74	75	76	77	78	79	80
81	82	83	84	85	86	87	88	89	90
91	92	93	94	95	96	97	98	99	100

"The next prime is the numeral three. By your wisdom you already know we may remove multiples of three." He quickly shaded all grids which contained multiples of three except three itself. "And the Center of Truth, My Lord Euergetes, knows we may do this for the next primes, five and seven." Again his small stylus scratched across the canvas:

1	2	3	4	5	6	7	8	9	10
11	12	13	14	15	16	17	18	19	20
21	22	23	24	25	26	27	28	29	30
31	32	33	34	35	36	37	38	39	40
41	42	43	44	45	46	47	48	49	50
51	52	53	54	55	56	57	58	59	60
61	62	63	64	65	66	67	68	69	70
71	72	73	74	75	76	77	78	79	80
81	82	83	84	85	86	87	88	89	90
91	92	93	94	95	96	97	98	99	100

"Because 11 x 11 is greater than our representation here, My Lord, you know that we must discard that operation, but that is the next step and so on, throughout the prime number sequence." He stepped back from the first canvas and pulled down the second of the canvases above him.

1	2	3		5		7			
11		13				17		19	
		23						29	
31						37			
41		43				47			
		53						59	
61						67			
71		73						79	
		83						89	
						97			

The Master then began to scratch out the primes from 1 to 97 in his rehearsed technique no doubt honed in imitation of the ridiculous posturing in the Stoa:

$$1 \cdot 2 \cdot 3 \cdot 5 \cdot 7 \cdot 11 \cdot 13 \cdot 17 \cdot 19 \cdot 23 \cdot 29 \cdot 31 \cdot 37 \cdot 41 \cdot$$
$$43 \cdot 47 \cdot 53 \cdot 59 \cdot 61 \cdot 67 \cdot 71 \cdot 73 \cdot 79 \cdot 83 \cdot 89 \cdot 97$$

In a grave stentorian mirroring the heavily scratched interpuncts, he said, "My Lord has recognized by his own wisdom and the Light of Ammon, father of King Ptolemy and Light of the World that we see only the primes from one to ninety-seven." The room nodded their familiarity with his famous 'sieve' method for producing primes. He had developed this method in Athens years earlier, and reveled again in a youthful triumph.

"It is true that the final representation, removed of the shaded boxes, looks haphazard and random. You have, Wise Lord, of course, already recognized the patterns in those grid squares which were removed; you see patterns in the negative spaces between the primes." He pointed to the halving of the chart along what would be infinite perpendicular lines when the even numbers were removed and the creation of curious repeating patterns, presumably infinite, during the process of removing multiples of three, five and seven.

"Should we continue in this way, we should find a method of detecting and isolating all the primes, a series we know from Euclid must be infinite."

He again reached above him and unrolled a third canvas identical in style to the first and now displaying a much larger grid of one hundred by one hundred small squares. The sieve had been applied and the patterns repeated as expected.

"This grid demonstrates the continuation of the sieve. As My Lord recognizes, the calculation of this pattern, while simple, is increasingly time consuming as we increase the order of magnitude of the sample. One man may scratch off a grid of ten by ten while he is dressed. He may delight in a grid of one hundred by one hundred in an afternoon. What of a grid of one thousand by one thousand, a thousand thousand by a thousand thousand? As we leave the familiar area of the lower primes for myriads of myriads of numeral fields each multiple must be sifted throughout the series. The task is exponentially more difficult the larger the series we wish to sift. What if there were a way to map these primes," he waved a hand at Archimedes, "or easily test for its 'primality' a large number with as many digits as the esteemed gentleman's grains of sand?"

Archimedes smiled genuinely, in a manner foreign to many in attendance, counter as it was to his reputation as partial to the Stoics; the proposition before him apparently forcing him to consider a bemused solidarity with his friend's very real fear of a nebulous infinity of the abstract, an order in the universe that was or was made systematically incomprehensible to the human mind. Archimedes knew that his old friend Eratosthenes had an element of the showmanship of the priests of Serapis, and that nothing short of an impressive performance equal to the wind and smoke and miraculous floating spheres and suspended chariots of the temples would impress the most cynical members of the Academy.

"I have considered the problem for some time. We may imagine the complexity of the problem visually as if we are looking at the dome of the sky. We know from dear Aristarchus of Samos that we are not in the center of a perfect sphere." The Master nodded to ancient Aristarchus, the father of the school of geocentrism. "But," continued the Master, "let us imagine it so, that we exist on a point that extends out from us equally in all directions, and let us assume that on the interior of this larger sphere is painted a distribution of stars by which the meanest of navigators may always fix their location."

I digress here again, a crag of the hill upon which the Master – in the form of Sisyphus it would much later seem – propelled his audience. Even then, students and academicians argued about the shape of the world. Eratosthenes had proven Aristarchus of Samos correct that the Earth's shape was a sphere and had long since shown its exact circumference. Yet followers of Thales of Miletus still contended against this evidence with notions that all things were comprised of water and the Earth was merely a slip of land floating in an infinite sea. Anaximenes, a follower of old Thales' student Anaximander, removed his Earth from an infinite sea to an infinite sky. Still others argued for Leucippus's student Democritus's view that the world was made of indivisible particles. The Master shared this view, but did not share Democritus's passion for an Earth whose surface was a taught membrane stretched across an immense drum. Such was the spirit in Alexandria in those untroubled days, many ideas contending with each other and given full throat in the Academy.

"And we know that quite truthfully," The Master continued, gesticulating into the air, "if an abstraction, each point that may pass through this center does in fact pass through it and that an infinity of points may pass from the dome above, through the center of the Earth and right on to the point opposite inside the terrestrial sphere. Let us now pretend that the whole of the possible minute points inside that sphere represent every numeral that is possible, that has ever been possible and that ever will. We may then treat the stars as the primes, those numbers whose universal primality in past present and future, shine out as beacons among travelers of mathematics."

Archimedes smiled again. He knew from his own discussions with Euclid that another more bizarre truth rested upon the analog of the sphere as an infinitude of points equidistant from a central focus, that lines originating in the focus and extending from those points must pass beyond the arbitrary limit of the sphere, that those points must then immediately diverge, opening up space filled with other lines that were there all along, greater than the infinity of lines confined by the original and extending with the others out to another arbitrarily larger sphere surrounding a necessarily larger volume than the infinite sphere it enclosed. The question of infinities larger than infinities was, like the Western ocean and Eastern Asia pulled taught on Democritus's drum, a topic still on the fringes of debate at the Academy.

Eratosthenes walked over to a small wooden table near the billowing brazier. He placed his hand dramatically on a piece of cloth draped over a boxy shape. "Wise Lord, gentlemen of the Academy, have we not mechanized randomness before? Have we not made advances against the infinite? Have we not forged in metal the routine processes of the mind and can we not do it again, with repetition upon repetition to mechanize the tedium of calculation?" He referred here only askance at earlier undertakings.

He grandly removed the cloth from the object on the table and unveiled an ungainly bronze device about the size of two arm's lengths on either side. A large wooden crank on one side was connected through a camshaft to the first row of one hundred towers of gear wheels, arranged in lines of ten stacked ten gears deep. On each dial was printed a numeral from one to ten. He majestically turned the handle. The small audience leaned forward as if to hear the expected clanking or grinding of metal on metal sometimes heard in the quiet mornings before the temples filled with supplicants and the machinery of the gods hissed and whirled clandestinely beneath the congregants' feet, unheard among the incantations of the attendants of Serapis. To everyone's surprise, the machine ran silently, a testament to an auditory differentiation between cantankerous religious spectacle and the well-oiled application of practical mathematics.

Eratosthenes paused after several revolutions of the handle and asked young Ptolemy to read the gears, a request with which he gleefully complied. The result had no immediate significance to the gathering until Eratosthenes explained that they were looking at the product of a famous assertion. A method of discovering primes based on powers of two minus one had given some hope that greater primes than those available generated with the sieve method might be detected. The first four of these were easily done with one of Eratosthenes' tables. The primes 3, 7, 31, and 127 were well known.

"Let 'I' represent an indissoluble, prime number," said the Master, "let us represent as 'n' the number's place in the series and let us also say that 'n' is itself a prime or composite number. Let us then perform the following procedure in it." The Master wrote the now-familiar exponentiation notation on the canvas:

$$I_n = 2^n - 1$$

"In words we may say that the designating number 'n' of an indissoluble number is equal to the numeral 2 multiplied by itself 'n' times and that total reduced by one. Now, we can easily demonstrate the primality of the solution for 'n' from one to seven."

$I_{(2)} = 2^{(2)} - 1 = (4) - 1 = 3$
The number 3 is a prime number

$I_{(3)} = 2^{(3)} - 1 = (8) - 1 = 7$
The number 7 is a prime number

$I_{(4)} = 2^{(4)} - 1 = (16) - 1 = 15$
The number 15 is not a prime number

$I_{(5)} = 2^{(5)} - 1 = (32) - 1 = 31$
The number 31 is a prime number

$I_{(6)} = 2^{(6)} - 1 = (64) - 1 = 63$
The number 63 is not a prime number

$I_{(7)} = 2^{(7)} - 1 = (128) - 1 = 127$
The number 127 is a prime number

Eratosthenes now induced Ptolemy to turn the handle a specified number of times. After several revolutions, the second bank of gear towers clicked into motion. After every click each of the secondary banks and one column of the first would revolve a set number of times. After another series of revolutions the handle froze, forcing young Ptolemy to stop the device.

The first bank now read:

$$8 \cdot 1 \cdot 9 \cdot 1$$

"Eight Thousand One Hundred and Ninety-One. My King, my Pharaoh, as you no doubt recognize, before you sits a model, a taste and sampling of a mechanized version of carrying out routine mathematical functions at a rate and precision never before possible.

"I have written a formal proof, following Euclid, that 'n' must *always* be prime to generate a prime number using this process. Should 'n' be composite, it will always yield another composite, which is not our interest here. As 'n' grows in value, manual calculation becomes complex. That is, its computational complexity increases at a rate rendering it unfeasible by traditional means. Let us examine the device's function; it is demonstrating a solution to the following process:

$$I_{(11)} = 2^{(11)} - 1 = (2048) - 1 = 2047$$
The number 2047 is not a prime number

"The device is programmed to halt only when a number has passed a 'primality' test encoded within the device itself and therefore, the device's continuing on represents a 'solution' as to each successive numeral as a power of two less one. In this way, any number may be entered into the device to test its 'primality', using an adaptation of the sieve. Let us now examine the displayed result:

$$I_{(13)} = 2^{(13)} - 1 = (8192) - 1 = 8191$$
The number 8191 is a prime number

"The first four primes of these series were discovered by Euclid, with greater difficulty as the power to which the 2 is raised is made larger through each successive multiplication. It was compounding hardship then, that one must, by trial and error, attempt raising 2 to greater and greater powers. He knew of the third and fourth such numbers, 2 raised by 5 less 1 is 31 and 2 raised by 7 less 1 is 127, the largest prime discovered by this method so far.

"And he knew also that the number to which two is raised must be prime but that simply raising 2 by a number that was itself prime was not a guarantee of producing a prime with this method. For example, as I have shown, when 2 is raised by 11, itself a prime number, less 1 the result is 2,047. This can, with some work or by applying the sieve method, be shown to be the product of 23 and 89 and thus not a prime number, as Euclid was aware.

"As you have all no doubt observed, this seems an inefficient and incomplete method of generating primes, since we have the sieve to aid us up to 10,000, but what of numbers larger than a myriad? It is my belief that the mechanization of calculation will help us unlock the primes and determine the pattern that surely must be hidden within what you see on these dials in the next number in that sequence. The initial dials quite quickly run through raising 2 to a particular power and then, while stored within these wheels, the second battery determines if the number itself is prime using a sieve method I have adjusted specifically for the device. I had started the device at the beginning, with 2 raised only to 1. The device must be cranked as many times around equivalent to the power to which two is raised and then it must be cranked once again to transfer those numbers to the secondary batteries, which continue utilizing the sieve method as the first battery continues to resume calculation of the next power. Should the sieve method detect that the product of one of these operations is prime, the lever will be locked and the device will be stopped for observation. Let me demonstrate."

Eratosthenes took the handle himself and cranked four more times. He pushed the handle in and again the second battery raised and clicked over the settings from the first battery. He pulled the lever out and now powered the clicking of the second battery which was determining the primality of 2 raised by 17. He continued much longer than before and various coughs and sighs could be heard from the royal contingent. After nearly five minutes, an eternity in royal demonstrations, the handle froze and the gears snapped into their final positions.

"What?" said Euergetes finally, hesitating for another to indicate success. "It is broken?"

JAMES ADDOMS | 198

"My lord, the device has displayed the next number in the sequence. It indicates by the number of revolutions of the first battery that 2 has been raised by 17 reduced by 1 and has resulted in a number, displayed in the first battery's dials. You will read the number:

$$1 \cdot 3 \cdot 1 \cdot 0 \cdot 7 \cdot 1$$

"One Hundred and Thirty-one Thousand and Seventy-One. Because the machine has stopped itself, we know that this is prime. You may all record the number and attempt a solution yourselves. I promise you this number is prime. I have continued this way through the series and I can tell you that this device will continue until I reach a prime number that has a number of numerals greater than this model can provide."

He recited from proud memory, "The next numbers are five-hundred-twenty-four-thousand two-hundred-eighty-seven." This he scratched on the canvas:

$$524,287$$

"And," he took a deep breath, "two billion one-hundred-forty-seventy million four-hundred-eighty-three thousand six-hundred-forty-seven." Again he scratched the number on the canvas as he spoke:

$$2,147,483,647$$

"The accuracy of the mechanized calculation of 2,147,483,647 as a prime number is confirmed - particularly the latter - by the labor of myriads of divisions."

Diocles and Apollonius nodded in agreement, as they had volunteered for a calculation that had seemed so innocuous and become so time-consuming they had nearly gone off mathematics entirely.

"Now, you will all no doubt realize, as our Glorious Pharaoh, Lord of Upper and Lower Egypt has already done, that we must have missed a great deal of the primes in between. But these numbers –"

"Sir, you amaze us yet again," said Ptolemy, thoughtfully.

"You honor me sir," The Master said, bowing elegantly.

Aristophanes rose. "Eratosthenes, it is remarkable, and it is an ingenious mechanization of known operations, but I believe if I follow your discussion, to begin to touch the higher limits of infinity of this set, you would need to increase the batteries at a sharply increasing rate."

"The rate would increase, that is true-"

"And the cost!" Euergetes loosed a devilish laugh, his handsome smile the pampered inheritance of his harsh-featured grandfather's austere march with Alexander in his conquest of Asia.

"Yes, my Lord."

"Surely," said Euphorion of Chalcis, rising from his seat, "the number of numerals in the solution will be roughly equivalent to the number of dial batteries the device requires, and as the numbers get larger, I believe the number of calculating batteries required will begin to get larger by factors upon factors of the number of numerals."

"Yes, Euphorion, some compensation may be required with larger batteries, so that as batteries increase in number, so must their heights increase-"

Euergetes waved a nimble hand toward the dais. "How many 'batteries' of gear-works will a device require to reach infinity?"

Archimedes addressed his Pharaoh thoughtlessly, as if making a joke, "a greater infinity of batteries, Ptolemy."

Euergetes was chastened; his demeanor soured. It was one thing to maintain familiarity behind he private walls of the palace, it was quite another to accept its display in a room of courtiers and academicians, however distinguished the speaker. He rose, gathered his long purple chlamys in his hands and stepped away from his seat toward the machine. He placed his hand upon its handle.

"An infinitude of resources from a finite, if distinguished treasury is a bold request, Director, even for you. If you will prepare a more modest appropriation I will support your undertaking. It will be a charming display at the festival of Dionysus. It will be made of silver and we will repose it in the temple of Serapis, with winged Nike who is of like design." Euergetes moved to exit the chamber.

Eratosthenes sensed his hold on the audience had slipped. He called out boldly, "My lord."

Euergetes stopped, his pages nearly toppling into him. He was not accustomed to the beckoning calls of academicians in public.

He turned to face the head Librarian. "Director?"

"My Lord, this is but one application of such a method. It will display these few unique prime numbers only. There is much beside that it may yet be made to do. The primes of this form are but one composition of the primes, one tiny portion of an infinite whole.

Euergetes shifted his weight from one lithe leg to the other. He stared impatiently at the Master, who, temporarily losing his mastery of the skills of the temple showman had been consumed within the potential of the device and could not speak with the circumspection his office required of him.

"My Lord," said Archimedes after a long silence in which not even my fellow natives dared waft their palm fronds, "Eratosthenes and I have discussed the application of the device on the calculation of munitions tables, for the rapid and accurate determination of an enemy ship's location from a specific point on shore and the exact angle and speed a projectile would need to be thrown for maximum impact. We may also see its application on astronomical observations for navigation at sea."

Archimedes, involved in the design of the device since the earliest conversations his friend had had with him - Archimedes, the reflecting pool and occasional synthesizer for each of his friend's grand ideas - spoke cautiously, as if far removed from the enterprise and only now considering its potential: "I believe it has merit and promise, my lord."

Eratosthenes regained the reality of the Musaeum. "Yes, my pharaoh, the light of the Academy. It does have great promise to serve you, my Lord, should your wisdom find it so."

Euergetes was inveigled instantly as if suddenly propelled to the command of a siege tower. Maintaining his commitment to the enlightened pursuit of science above the barbarism and sad necessities of – always defensive – war, he said calmly, "As I have already agreed, director, you may pursue it, in a more modest fashion. I will ask you this, your demonstration here has taken a table top, if you square your device it would take up the dais you're standing on. Should you proceed you would require a room as tall and as wide as this hall itself. I do not wish to arise one morning to find the entire city has been entombed in a device for calculating the prime numbers. Might we pursue a less ambitious course, Director?"

The Master replied, "Your wisdom prevails, as always, my Lord."

Euergetes signaled to his coterie that he was prepared to leave. Incense wafted, royal standards rose and the assembly bowed slightly as the entourage glided past the students and academicians. As soon as Ptolemy had quit the hall, the room erupted in laughter and applause. Eratosthenes had secured a future for his project, and some academicians with larger ambitions had delighted, if only slightly, at seeing their master lose his composure in the service of his intellect.

To see a world in a grain of sand
And a heaven in a wild flower,
Hold infinity in the palm of your hand,
And eternity in an hour.

—WILLIAM BLAKE, Auguries of Innocence

18

Martin, Perry and I remained in the conference room while the museum staff met in an enclosed office across the hall.

"What do you make of all this?" I asked Professor Martin.

"It's a riddle, for sure," he said. "I see why they don't want negative publicity, I mean, the public profile of the Wallace would go up if every television in America was tuned to new broadcasts of a 'theft at the museum,' but the Wallace's stock-in-trade is their conservation program, and I bet future manuscript owners would think twice about lending their property to a team who had allowed a ten year volunteer to walk out the door with a priceless manuscript."

"And how is Pratt involved in all of this?" asked the infinitely analytical Perry. "There are four options. One, he knew about the planned theft and flew here to stop it. If he knew about it and wanted to stop it, it's a mystery why he didn't just call the museum staff to alert them. Two, he knew about the theft and flew here to meet with Francisco at some predetermined location to assist with the recovery of the rest of the work. Three, he didn't know about the theft, and had arranged to meet Francisco to talk about something that couldn't be discussed over the phone or understood from the continued supply of images. Four, his disappearance is a coincidence and his trip had nothing to do with Francisco or the manuscript."

"You forgot about a fifth option. The timing is right," said Martin, "for them both to have coordinated a trip somewhere else. Think about it, Francisco steals the manuscript, and arranges to meet Pratt somewhere else."

"Ok," I said, "but look, either way, it's not just like he's got pages filled with Koine Greek that he and Pratt can translate at a Starbucks somewhere. Michael said Francisco took the remaining unseparated pages. Those pages were scheduled for the same process that the others went through - a fairly complicated and specialized process at that. The pages have to be delicately unbound, they have to be photographed and exposed to all sorts of imaging conditions to isolate the palimpsest text from the text on top of the Alexander writing. Let's assume that he doesn't care about the physical object, so he doesn't need a clean room, he doesn't need preservationists, he doesn't need archivists, and he obviously doesn't need to worry about scanning and cleaning the images for distribution, as was done with the first pages and the entire Archimedes. So what does he really need, at minimum?"

"Well," said Martin, "he needs to be familiar with or have access to someone who is familiar with the technical details of palimpsest recovery methods. Pratt would know how to do that. He was one of the few crossovers, a technical specialist, a mathematician and a classics scholar."

"Right," said Perry, "but, he needs access to the equipment to do it. He can't just have multispectral imaging equipment set up in a storage locker somewhere. He needs access to an institutional set-up and he needs a great deal of time to do it. Meaning, even if he breaks into another museum or an academic department, he's going to need days, probably weeks to perform the imaging alone, even if he doesn't care about preservation."

"Assuming he wants access to the rest of the text itself and doesn't value the Alexander as a physical object, where would he go to do it?" said Martin.

Before I or Perry could form an answer, the museum staff walked back into the room.

"Look," said Fikes, "as we've said, we don't want to involve the police. This is a delicate situation for the Wallace. I've been talking to my colleagues. After we discovered the theft of the Alexander, I approached the board for more experts to help identify clues in the pages we do have as to the value of the manuscript from an informational standpoint. They contacted the owner, who was adamant that no other staff be brought in. The terms of the loan, as you know-"

"I know," said Martin, "non-disclosure."

"Exactly. My position here is difficult. The people in this room are the only people other than Francisco, the board and the owner who know the Alexander is missing. We've got imagining specialists, translators, classical historians" she said, indicating the others in the room.

"You've got a mathematician, too," said Martin, indicating Perry.

"What?" asked Fikes.

"It's true," said Perry, "my father was nuts about my becoming a financial analyst. I hold a bachelors in finance, but the math always intrigued me more than the financial markets, and I'm pursuing a Ph.D. in classical exegesis and discreet mathematics at–" Fikes waved him off with her hand.

"Dr. Martin," she said, "we're serious people here. This isn't the place for dilettantes and amateurs. We need serious people–"

"Dr. Fikes," said Martin, "may I ask what you have your doctorate in?"

After a hesitation and a cowering look from Michael, Fikes answered, "museum curatorship, from Johns Hopkins University."

"A stunning achievement, no doubt, Dr. Fikes, but not exactly the kind of granular expertise we're looking for."

Fikes again hesitated, then softened her demeanor. Addressing me, she asked, "and I suppose you're a Koine Greek expert with a background in digital spectography and number theory?"

"No," I said, "undergrad in Archaeology at George Washington." Fikes rolled her eyes and began to form a smile. "And an MFA in creative writing from Georgetown."

"Jesus," said Fikes, tapping her knuckles on the conference table. "Listen Hemingway–"

"Actually," said Perry, I'd call him a polymath. What was your Mensa score?"

"I can't remember," I said, "not bad." I turned to Fikes. "A polymath is a person who has a broad range of interests and knowledge in–"

"I know what a goddamn polymath is."

After a long pause, she addressed all three of us. "Ok, Dr. Martin, there's not much I can do with the non-disclosure regarding the three of you. You arrived knowing everything except that the book was stolen. And it seems you've added something to our understanding of the Mersenne, though we were aware, generally, of the Alexander's mention of mechanized calculation. We disclosed that information in hopes that you would have information about Francisco which you did not have. I feel we haven't violated the spirit of non-disclosure. I want that book back and I want to know what the hell is in it."

"Folks," said Martin. "I think we can help each other. You want the Alexander back with as little publicity as possible, I want to know what's in the book as much as you do. You can keep us in the dark, we'll go back to DC and keep all this secret, and your team can struggle on hoping to figure out what's in the missing pages. Or, you can screw the non-disclosure, and we can take a stab at making sense of all of this."

Fikes thought for a moment, and then said, "Ok, gentlemen. I'm going way out on a limb here. Follow me."

"Where," I asked. "Just bring up the translation you had been posting on the website and we'll take a look at it."

Michael loosed a small laugh. Fikes allowed herself a knowing smile.

"You don't think we put the good stuff on the website, do you? We control the disclosure timetable and the publication rights." Fikes started for the conference room door. "You want to be in the club, Hemingway, then let's get into the club." She turned to Michael as she left the room. "I have a few calls to make, Michael, show these three down to the vault."

The 'vault' was a plain basement storage area directly below the glass-walled conservation room we had viewed on the web feed. One floor above our heads, tourists gaped at the conservation work, unaware that the team inside was displaying the same few pages it had displayed for days. In the center of it all, the decoy and much younger prayer book, to the untrained eye a reasonable physical manifestation of what a visitor might expect an ancient codex to look like.

The room was an unromantic mixture of filing cabinets, utilitarian desks and low-hanging fluorescent lights. It smelled vaguely musty. Martin, Perry and I congregated around a table, where high-resolution images of pages were spread out haphazardly. Michael logged into a computer on the table, typed a bit and rolled his chair to the corner of the room where a printer had started whirring. He returned with three copies of a text in English.

The text started with what looked like a section of a poem from Theocritus, an ancient Greek poet who flourished in the third century BCE. It then had a second poem from *Platonicus* by Theon of Smyrna. Both quotations, explained Martin, were part of a traditional ancient practice of rendering homage through poetry to the Muses.

"The next section," said Michael, "is where we believe the actual text starts." He read the first sentence aloud as we read the block letters on the page:

THE WORLD IS FILLED WITH THE DEAD.
I HAVE COME FROM THE AGORA WITH ONESIMUS.

Perry, Martin and I spent several hours reading the translation in front of us. It was a remarkable first-hand account of a native-Egyptian academician at the Academy of Alexandria at the time when Archimedes, Eratosthenes, Apollonius of Rhodes, Aristarchus of Byzantium and Aristophanes served a succession of Ptolemaic Pharaoh-Kings. This was antiquity's precursor to the Institute of Advanced Study at Princeton or a modern think tank. When I encountered the section about the creation of a calculating device, I called Perry and Martin's attention to the passage, only to find they were re-reading the passages themselves to make sure they had a full comprehension of the immensity of what they were reading. Twenty-two hundred years ago, an ancient Manhattan Project had taxed the resources of the wealthiest nation in the world and had consumed the greatest minds of antiquity.

It explained in detail the friendship between Eratosthenes and Archimedes, political intrigues, the ambitions of courtiers and a first-hand account of the construction of the immense Ptolemaic ships that would become legendary. The manuscript had repeated original letters between Eratosthenes and Ptolemy III Euergetes. It spoke of Eratosthenes' recruiting academicians across political boundaries under the aegis and secrecy of a repurposed cult of the Eleusinian Mysteries, known from the pre-Greek culture of Mycenae. It's most interesting section included an account of a demonstration Eratosthenes had given the court of Ptolemy III, a demonstration of a device to easily calculate and display the Mersenne primes.

"This is the first mention of the Mersenne form in the manuscript. The page we were viewing when Francisco alerted us to their mention was one of the last we had separated from the manuscript. As you can see, it ends here, with a discussion of the preparations for what History has called the Battle of Raphia, sometimes referred to as the Battle of Gaza."

"The pages seem slightly out of order," I said.

"Exactly," said Michael. "That's not unusual."

"Because the manuscript's content was of little value to whomever wrote over it," said Martin, "it's likely the pages were separated and cleaned and rebound without precise regard to the original order. It would be like arranging a deck of cards in order, then deciding you wanted to wipe them clean to use as note cards. You're not intentionally shuffling the deck, but you might get something out of place here and there."

"Ok, so this is all we know," I said, "we know that Eratosthenes developed mechanized calculation in the third century BCE, we know Archimedes was involved, we know that Ptolemy funded the project, and we know several prototypes were built, including at least one device capable of decrypting very complex codes."

"But," said Michael, "I still don't get the personal value here."

We all agreed the manuscript was a priceless first-hand account and breathtaking new insight into the genius of Hellenistic mathematics and mechanization. But the deeper interest of a Jesuit initiate eluded us. Fikes had an assistant send out for sandwiches and coffee. We read for several more hours until we had finished the portion left with the Museum.

Fikes asked us for our interpretations, and from the pages we had access to we could only guess that the remainder contained some specific explanation of ancient mathematics and technology to which the vague references in the first part referred. The manuscript ended with a cryptic reference to a network of informants - unknown history of no small value to students of the period. It was not, however, a piece of information inherently valuable in the hands of a single person or a threat to be guarded against public dissemination. The manuscript also mentioned an unbreakable code, no doubt sophisticated in its time, but which, by modern standards, was likely to be little more secure than the Vigenère when attacked by a modern computer. Fikes asked us to sign non-disclosure agreements, which we did with the requests that we be kept up to date with any developments and retain the copies of the palimpsest we had been given. The three of us returned to Washington where the puzzle remained a constant preoccupation for all of us.

It was with this bristling frustration that Perry and I met for our most recent writer's group meeting. With disparate chunks of knowledge of an ancient machine for manipulating primes, Perry's felicity for the mathematics of Public Key Cryptography and his tirade rail against ATM fees, Martin's connection to an obsessive classicist, and a Jesuit's theft of half of an ancient memoir that I took out my credit card to buy another round of drinks. It was then that everything clicked into place.

Shepherd.
A song from Daphnis! Open he the lay,
He open: and Menalcas follow next:
While the calves suck, and with the barren kine
The young bulls graze, or roam knee-deep in leaves, And
ne'er play truant. But a song from thee, Daphnis – anon
Menalcas will reply

Daphnis.
Sweet is the Chorus of the calves and kine,
And Sweet is the herdsman's pipe. But none may vie with
Daphnis; and a rush-strown bed is mine
Near a cool rill, where capeted I lie
On fair white goatskins. From a hill-top high
The westwind swept me down the hard entire,
Cropping the strawberries; whence it comes that I
No more heed summer, with his breath of fire,
Then lovers heed the words of mother and of sire.

—THEOCRITUS, Idyll IX

19

To dispel an occasional malaise, made deeper by the day's events, the Master, the sun setting before him, chased the fiery orb west along the Canopic Way. I walked at his side. As we strolled among the settling dust of living bodies plodding around us each of my senses writhed and reacted to the serpentine rhythms of our adopted city. The docklands, so real and so unlettered, smelled of the cheapest perfumes doused liberally to cover the stench of human and animal waste, of decomposing food, of rot, of poverty. The teeming center of the city, equidistant from the sweet shelter of infamy from which we had come and the promise and pomp of the palace complex and the library, contained a curious mix of a fainter sensation of decay and the hope of advancement signified by furious trading in spices like cinnamon and coriander and the freshly chopped cedars imported from far Lebanon.

I had by now taken many walks with the Master pacing alongside in silence. I knew by a curious intonation is his declaration that 'he was taking the air of Alexandria' that I was expected to join him. When the intonation was not there, I set upon the scrolls The Master selected from the library for me, and when the intonation was present, I was filled with promise that the sum of Callimachus' catalogue was mine in the silence between us. I still do not know how he had come to find me of any value at all. He later had uses for me, and set me to various tasks in service of the project. I still do not know, in those first years before I proved my mettle with forging the mechanics of the infinite, why he chose me. He would talk to me kindly of the barbarity manifested in the way the Greeks regarded non-Greeks, a barbarity eschewed by Alexander himself against the natural inclinations of his commanders in the Asian Campaigns. Alexander took as his wives a Persian and an Aryan, and beside his Macedonian-Greek lover Hephaestion, whose funeral pyre Alexander raised to the sky, had many other foreign conquests beyond the battlefield.

I am reminded now of a brief passage in the Master's treatise on geography in which he described in detail the peoples of disparate lands which only Alexander could hold together as one. Onesimus has located the exact scroll. The passage admirably lays out the Master's view on the matter:

> I must withhold praise for those who divide the whole multitude of mankind into two groups, namely, Greeks and Barbarians, and also from those who advised Alexander to treat the Greeks as friends but the barbarians as enemies – It would be better to make such divisions according to good qualities; for not only are many of the Greeks bad, but many of the Barbarians are refined – Indians and Arians, for example, and, further, Romans and Carthaginians, *who carry on their governments so admirably*.

I, Hesperos, add the emphasis, for such a calamity never befell the leisurely pursuit of science or promoted its military tack so much as the confluence of mismanagement by the governments of the these empires. Another digression, old man! The Master continued:

And this is the reason why Alexander, disregarding his advisors, welcomed as many as he could of the men of fair repute and did them favors – just as if those who have made such a division, placing some people in the category of censure, others in that of praise, did so for any other reason than that in some people there prevail the law-abiding and the political instinct, and the qualities associated with education and powers of speech, whereas in other people the opposite characteristics prevail. And so Alexander, not disregarding his advisors, but rather accepting their opinion did what was consistent with, not contrary to, their advice; for he had regard to the real intent of those who gave him counsel.

In light of these sentiments it is possible that he felt kindly toward me because of my race. And, in truth I did begin to understand those things that are virtuous to a Greek and, seeing them echoed in the characteristics of the noblest of my countrymen, I understood that there was no true division, as the Master had long known, between the races. I aspired to these virtues, and discovered that the Master's coming to the Light was indeed a product of his civic instinct and his love of education. I copied him in these and all ways and in imitation was led to the Light.

I remind Onesimus how curious a thing it is that, as one knows the death of one's father is imminent, as he was father to me, one summons less and less courage to ask why one should be so honored with such unequal consideration. The courage had drained from me that I could no longer stare directly at him in his last days, for fear I might burst upon his sickbed and demand a reckoning, a bill of account a slave could never repay.

The Master walked idly, ambling along the docks and through the narrow side streets. He talked kindly but openly of his students, fellow academicians and the pharaoh himself – I seem to remember a joke that I did not fully understand about Theocritus writing so floridly because he had never left cities like Alexandria and Syene to spend one fortnight in the bucolic pastures that so inspired his imagination. It is sacred myth now that the Master hired an insolvent fellow of the Academy to pace out the distance for his famous calculation, but the Master would never have left the gathering of so important a point of information to the wiles of a student on leave. He, himself, walked at the van of a contingent pulling his wheeled hodometer along the route, meticulously correcting for any usual passes or necessary diversions. The imaginary student, he said, should have been left to ghost-write the idylls of Theocritus and Theocritus to the prosaic mapping of the plains; How large a world Eratosthenes would have created for us had not the true figure ticked revolution by revolution of his hodometer but the whole of the distances between Alexandria and every public house, lodging post and brothel en route to Syene!

Of course, the brothels in Alexandria were more notorious and far superior to those of the border towns. Our walk that day took us into old Rhakotis, the district where such houses were a large portion of the registered enterprises. If one were not the pharaoh or a priest or could not support a young mistress and a dutiful wife, one was given to lingering after the markets closed, embracing the streets near Lake Mareotis. Here the night took on its intoxicating anonymity from the caustic smoke billowing from cheap oil lamps hanging just along the rooflines. Perhaps this is the memory of an old man distorted by a pining for the bloom of youth, but one had the distinct feeling then that we were truly one race, among the docklands, and that each of our brothers in Alexandria and in Antioch, in Athens, in Babylon, in Carthage and in Rome, were all living the same lives separately beneath the canopy of brown-grey oil-smoke that seemed to stretch around the middle sea into the farthest reaches of humanity.

Eratosthenes had little interest in the streets near Lake Mareotis as a participant, but always as an anthropologist. The species of men in the Academy, in the palace, in the temples, in the fields and in the brothels interested him equally. In this as in all things he was committed to the atomism of Leucippus and Democritus; the unseen, undirected, toiling parts made the whole. Beneath the earthly shroud, academicians could gossip with prostitutes; priests with their *erômenoi* could recline together and toast the guile of Dionysus. The cabinet rooms of a sexual shadow government bustled with the intensity of a dusky chancery on the periphery of the city far from the Academy and the palaces, another focus of power around which orbited the satellites of the Ptolemaic state.

Onesimus groans - again, an old man's imagery - I am worthy of Theocritus!

The public spaces adjacent to the palace complex to which the Musaeum was annexed gave way to clarity of breathing and a vague sense that one had purchased one's intellectual and olfactory freedom at a premium, somewhat ignobly. Still, to look back now if only in contemplation if not in stance, as the Jews wrote in their myths, might be as to become a pillar of salt staring longingly at some dangerous but familiar place unable to fully commit to the next chapter to which one was commended by providence. Lake Mareotis was behind us as we returned to the Academy. We rushed past the dormitory complex of the slaves and then that of the students.

Again the *geography* was all around us. The geography of nature which the Master labored so long to overcome and quantify descriptively was reproduced proscriptively here in architectural form. The students were given the smallest and most modest accommodations. They slept four to a room not much larger than the space required to hold the cots on which they slept. Here students self-segregated themselves by nationality and then even by familial status. An Athenian with an Athenian, a Macedonian with a Macedonian. As his predecessors at the Academy had made arrangements for the occasional promising pupil to gain entry on merit alone, the Master now inherited the unusual situation of the self-segregation of students at every time outside the Academy into conditional groups. The Master remarked that assigned sleeping arrangements by lot or even by forced integration of wealthy and humble students would be taken up at the next meeting of his colleagues.

Still, his mind raced back to the frustrations of his presentation, of the commercial value expected of his ideas in an empire constantly under a real or imagined threat of war and therefore under the threat of losing the vast peacetime surpluses which have been required in all ages for true emancipation of the mind.

As if from nowhere, the Master said, "When men are hungry, when they are afraid, when they fear their neighbors as much as they fear the distant rumblings of a foreign army, there can be no time for expressions of wonder at the workings of the universe, there must be always a slip back to burnt offerings, back to the temples! In times such as these the academicians slip away and favor is sought of the general, the priest and the benefactor. The academician must append his work to the ordinary or be forgotten, designing and maintaining the automata in the temples like the groaning statues of Serapis and his levitating chariots. In a time of crisis all the Academy is pressed for survival into the service of the military needs of the state and the creation of miracles for the stupefied and afraid."

As we left the grounds of the Academy, his mind must have momentarily released these concerns. His humor returned, he again amused me with jokes of which I could only feign appreciation as we exited the palace complex and began the winding trail up to the Lochias promontory, where Archimedes held court at the easternmost triple-focus of Alexandria. Here the wealthier members of the Musaeum live quite literally in the shadow of the Pharos, the great lighthouse still beaming the call to Egypt. The Master had been offered an immodest accommodation in one of the most prominent villas in this exclusive academic village. He had declined it in favor of living, as custom dictated and as Socrates had done, among his students. Above the grid of the city he must have felt a kind of geographical freedom from the palace and the patronage of the state. I now live in Lochias and keep only a houseman, a cook, a gardener and a groom, in imitation of the Master's asceticism.

I remind Onesimus that, in those days, there was not such an ostentatious display of depravation as is the current Alexandrian fashion after the style introduced by Ptolemy IV and made positively infamous by Ptolemy V. Then: A sheepish girl leaving here, a delicate boy scurrying there, and somehow the wine merchant and the tailor omnipresent everywhere among the villas. Today the rays of Helios meets streets filled with broken potsherds and torn cloaks from the revelries of the night before. The Academy, in all times, enjoys its luxury.

Eratosthenes was let into Archimedes' home by his houseman. I was induced to use an entrance in the alley behind the villa. I found the Master and Archimedes recumbent on recliners in the andron. The Master settled on a couch opposite him as the servant brought each of them a kylix of wine. A glance from Archimedes indicated that I too should be served. The knave thrust a wooden bowl into my hand, filled it, taking care to spill several drops of wine on my cloak, and disappeared martially through a false door. I forgave his natural response to what he could only interpret as my impudence in appearing as a guest of one of the greatest minds of the present epoch. After some time spent in silence, Archimedes addressed the Master.

"You did well enough today, old man."

"You do even better –" he softened his body posture slightly and eased back onto the cushions behind him, "you look even better in Euergetes' eyes. It is a time of men of invention, Archimedes. It is a time when a man may profit who benefits the empire of the earth and not of the mind."

Archimedes hesitated and then let out a forced laugh. "What is it with you, always this intention that you should be unhappy, that you are aggrieved? Are you not an esteemed man here, the director of the library, the champion of the whole of the Musaeum, the tutor to the pharaoh himself?"

"The pharaoh," said Eratosthenes, "must keep the interior happy, unresentful and productive. He is, of course, a shrewd pragmatist, one might even say he possesses great intelligence, but he has little interest in the pursuit of the abstract. He cannot afford another uprising. I understand his position, Archimedes, I am no fool. But why fight if we cannot reap the fruits of the dominance of our culture where it matters, the systematic cataloguing of the natural world, of men, of letters, of the poets, and of mathematics?"

"He is a hegemon of deep passions and broad interests; you are too hasty in your judgment of him. You expect Periclean laurels. Of course, he is tasked with maintenance of this kingdom." Archimedes smiled as he beckoned for his wine to be refilled. "So, we shall have a toast to Euergetes, shall we?" The servant appeared again, staring at me as he refilled our cups.

"How are we to mix the wine, Archimedes, shall we continue to have it full, and run afoul of our daimons, or shall we discuss the affair candidly?" Eratosthenes was playfully alluding to their time in Athens spent in imitation of the raucous gatherings in which the King of the Symposium elected from its members would indicate the tone of the evening by his choice of the ratio of water to wine. Wine without water was indicative that the king planned an evening of entertainment; The addition of water to the mix indicated by degrees how serious the evening's discussion was expected to remain.

"You are the guest, Eratosthenes, and since we have not a full symposium-"

Eratosthenes immediately began to drink earnestly from his undiluted kylix.

"Wait! I now remember that I had some moments of disorientation after you fled from the lecture hall, nearly as hastily as our pharaoh. Like an observer at Marathon but in much graver spirits, as if I were a Persian sympathizer, I sought commiseration among comrades."

Eratosthenes waved his empty kylix to the attentive and much put upon houseman. "What is this," he said mockingly, "you must have an audience at all times Archimedes?"

"The flower of our countrymen, Eratosthenes, your colleagues – they wish to talk you out of your poor mood, and since talking you out of anything is as foolish an undertaking as has ever tasked the Academy, I suggest we have no water with our wine, as Dionysus would entreat us. Why trouble yourself so? Give the pharaoh what he needs and he will give you what you want. Why, my exploits in engineering at Syracuse-"

"Spare me your mechanical lectures friend and have this man fill our cups again. We salute Dionysus!"
The three of us each consumed another vessel of wine before the houseman announced the arrival of Diocles and Apollonius of Perga.

"Young Diocles, young Apollonius," said Archimedes.

They each sat down on a chaise in anticipation of the houseman's attention.

"Master, it was indeed a display today. Diocles is much taken with the mathematics, and I too. But the device, Master, can it in fact do as you say, and map the primes?"

"My dear Apollonius, what the Master says it can do it can do," said Archimedes. "The principle is simple –"

"The principle is not simple at all," I said. "It is of immense complexity."

Diocles spoke. "Master, I believe I understand the concept."

Eratosthenes had been less of a disciplinarian than his predecessors. He had had enough of posturing in the Stoa and favored the dialectic, the discussion among equals, as a conduit for scientific and moral instruction. The result was that his students often felt equal to him, or felt that such a posture was expected of them. Eratosthenes however, could confound that expectation when necessary.

"Perhaps, Diocles, you will give us your account of its additive powers, the simplest of its functions."

Diocles stared at the floor.

The Master pulled back kindly. "It is complex, but not beyond you. I will hold a small discussion on it soon. I value your reflections, and yours too, Apollonius. You were taken with the device itself?"

"Yes Master, quite taken."

"The truth is, Aristophanes was correct in his approximation of the size of a device required to map even the lower primes. The device employs the sieve, but there are limitations by resorting to that method alone. I am even now working on a method to augment the sieve in such a way that the accuracy of repetition by mechanization may be used more efficiently."

"And what of the military implementations," said Diocles. "They are most intriguing."

Poking Diocles in the side, Apollonius said, "He has been playing at soldiering again, like when we were boys. Swordplay with wheat sacks for armor and Silphion stalks for spears."

The houseman appeared from nowhere and announced the arrival of Aristophanes. The others and I arose from our recliners.

"Friend, you honor us," said our host.

Aristophanes bowed slightly to Archimedes as the servant filled a kylix near to overflowing with wine. He drank a sip and smiled widely, the dimples set in his face casting shadows the Master should have found worth measuring.

"No water. So – you took it as harshly as I thought you would. Master, no man could have introduced such a concept to a Ptolemy-" Aristophanes raised a kylix and said quickly by rote afterthought, "Benefactor, benevolent ruler and patriarch, son of the sky." He nestled into a chaise. We all took our places again on the recliners around him.

"No, it was quite a success," I said.

"Indeed it must have seemed so, Aristophanes," said Archimedes, gesturing to his kylix. "You were drunk throughout the entire presentation."

The men laughed. The young people stared through the wall.

"So, the device shall calculate, how did you phrase it Archimedes, the Master's chief propagandist, munitions tables for the rapid determination of an enemy ship's location and the angle of projectiles? And a device with applications for navigation at sea!"

The men smiled again, and the nimble houseman was prepared to deliver yet another full kylix into the hands of Aristophanes.

"Don't worry, friend," said the Master, "the device will never be able to unravel Hesiod before you've gutted him entire."

"Well then," said Aristophanes, "my position is secure. Thank Dionysus. I was worried." Again the men laughed. We joined them.

"And, Aristophanes, how is your young amanuensis, Ptolemy the younger?" asked the Master.

"He delights in me. He cannot immerse himself enough in the sophistication of my rhetoric or our joint recensions of Homer."

"There is real power there, Aristophanes," said Archimedes. "Hold tight to him as you would an unbroken yearling. He will be pharaoh soon enough, and by then Eratosthenes will have been banished to some damned place with his machine – and I with him."

The thought of the Master, his great intellect entwined with crankshafts and papyrus rolls, staring up at the Goat Fish, the Dolphin, the Great Fish and the Thigh of the Bull and calculating their movements in a hovel on the shores of Antikythera made us all smile again, and each of us in turn made motions for the servant.

The conversation continued in this way for several more hours. I fell asleep on the chaise and woke to find only the houseman glowering at me, the rest going about their business at the Academy. In the years to come I often thought back on that evening among that jovial company. Like all irony, sewn from seeds of truth, it still amazes me how prescient a humorous remark can be.

The actual infinite arises in three contexts: first when it is realized in the most complete form, in a fully independent otherworldly being, *in Deo*, where I call it the Absolute Infinite or simply Absolute; second when it occurs in the contingent, created world; third when the mind grasps it *in abstracto* as a mathematical magnitude, number or order type.

—GEORG CANTOR

20

I phoned Martin immediately. Perry and I met him at his office and rushed headlong into a spirited exegesis of everything we'd come to understand about the Alexander Palimpsest. Perry and I explained why a Jesuit might be interested in the prime factorization problem, that it is the core mathematical problem at the heart of Public Key Cryptography, that he might have any number of reasons for valuing such information and for wanting to keep it a secret, that he may have wanted to ensure the security of modern communication or that he may have wanted to expose weaknesses in Public Key Cryptography to bring about a change in the dominance of consumerism-entrenched-in-technology over faith. We even questioned whether the attainment of the solution of this problem might be a spiritual object to him, like a piece of the true cross or the crown of thorns.

We knew the rest of the history of Eratosthenes' tenure at the library well enough. Polybius was required reading of all classicists, and the records of Ptolemaic Egypt left in inscriptions like the Rosetta stone and in papyrus hoards discovered at Oxyrhynchus told of the increasingly decadent political life of Ptolemaic Egypt. It is known that upon the succession of the infant Ptolemy V Epiphanes, his mother Arsinoë was put to death, probably by Sosibius, acting to secure his position against shifting alliances at court. Sosibius later lost control of his government and was put to death by Agathocles, though the method of death has not survived. We know that Agathocles continued his ruinous form of government and was confronted by numerous uprisings and that finally a large contingent of Greeks and native Egyptians rose up against him and his sister.

Under the command of Tlepolemus, military governor of Pelusium and a member of a distinguished Persian family who had migrated to Egypt in the late third century BCE, these forces of insurrection surrounded the palace at night and forced their way into a forecourt, where they met little resistance from disenchanted palace guards. Polymius records that Agathocles was killed by his friends so he might avoid a more terrible punishment from the mob. Agathoclea and her mother, it is said, were dragged from their rooms or perhaps from a temple where they hid as priestesses. The mob, robbed of the prize of making a spectacle of the death of Agathocles, "literally tore them limb from limb," as recorded by Polybius in the Histories. The rest of Ptolemaic history and the succession of Pharaohs up until Cleopatra VII's death and the absorption of Egypt by Rome in 30 BCE is common knowledge for every history undergraduate.

We had put all the pieces together except one: if Francisco had really discovered proof of the device in those pages, proof that it physically existed somewhere, and that he might learn from it how to render the division of incredibly large numbers into their two constituent prime factors, where might such a device have remained hidden from twenty-two centuries of exploration, construction and sprawl. We naturally considered Alexandria. But after hundreds of archaeological projects had been undertaken, nothing suggested the existence of an underground cavern or enormous storerooms.

The fate of the library is unknown, although it was mentioned as a center of learning well into the Roman Imperial period. Marc Antony is said to have given the bulk of the library of Pergamon to Cleopatra as a replacement for the books lost when Julius Caesar's forces accidentally set fire to the library, though this may be later propaganda intended to tie Antony even more strongly to Egypt and against his native country. Ammianus Marcellinus cites the attack of the Roman Emperor Aurelian as the end of the library. Still another account has whatever is left of the library being systematically dismantled by Christians under the leadership of Bishop Theophilus of Alexandria, acting under orders of Theodosius, who outlawed Paganism. Several Arab historians claim that the library was destroyed in 642 AD during Muslim occupation of the city. It is suggested that this too may be propaganda to demonstrate Islamic dedication to rooting out heretical texts, as all writings not recognizing the prophet

Mohammed would have been considered at the time. The exact location of the main library is unknown, and may lie under several layers of the modern city. The Serapeum's storerooms still exist, and it is thought that this "daughter library" may have contained several thousand scrolls, since relocated, destroyed or disintegrated. It seemed unlikely that a space large enough to conceal Eratosthenes' device would have survived undetected amid the growth of one of the busiest cities on the Mediterranean.

We continued to meet almost daily, pouring over archaeological journals, re-reading what we had of the Alexander palimpsest, trying to interpret Polybius and other contemporary sources for clues. This continued for several weeks. When we arrived for another of our sessions, Martin, usually excited to engage in several hours of speculation, greeted us this day in a solemn mood. He had had a call from Pratt's daughter that morning. Fighting off tears, she told them that a couple picnicking at Fort Howard Park in Maryland not far from Baltimore reported to the police that they had found a body along the shore of Chesapeake Bay.

Several days later, Martin received another call from a colleague at Loyola University. He had seen the story on the news and had called the police and then Martin to tell them that he had seen Pratt only weeks earlier on campus after dark, walking with a man he didn't recognize. They seemed to be having an argument, he had told the police.

The story unraveled quickly from there. "Yes, indeed," a graduate student had told Martin's colleague after being told of his Pratt's death, "I let a man matching Pratt's description and another man into the university's science building." She recognized him from his photograph in his CV that was linked to from online journal articles she'd cited for her dissertation.

"Pratt and Francisco," Martin explained, "had told the graduate student and several custodians who interrupted their work at night that they were working on an extracurricular project they had said was sanctioned by the department chair. No one thought anything of it. Pratt's fingerprints, taken from his home, were matched with prints on several pieces of equipment including a small synchrotron accelerator. It is a device also used by the Wallace staff to bombard palimpsests with synchrotron light that then bends around unreadable text, highlighting the text against the paper on which it is written."

"They probably only needed a few nights," said Martin. "If they didn't care about conserving the pages, they could have ripped them out and run them through whatever process worked best. They really just needed the images of the writing. They then need only destroy the manuscript so no one else could read it."

"I can't understand what happened to Pratt," said Perry.

"Neither can I," I said. "It sounds like they were collaborating."

"From what I understand, the police are checking into Francisco DiScenna. I'm sure we'll have more answers soon."

"He seems very calculating," said Perry. "He may have needed Pratt as cover to get into the lab. Maybe they were collaborators initially and a disagreement broke out as they learned more about what they were dealing with. Ethical differences?"

"I'm interested in what happened," I said, "but not as interested as I am in where Francisco is now. Did the manuscript mention a location, did it have this impossible equation? Could a device like that really have the capacity to work on composite numbers so large our own supercomputers can't find their prime factors?"

We continued in this vein for another hour or so before Martin finally started to show the wear of grief over the loss of a friend. Perry and I left, deciding to give him several days before we contacted him again. When we next arranged to see him, he had heard again from Pratt's daughter who told Martin how her father had died. He had been strangled and dumped into the river shortly after. Martin was making preparations to fly out to California to attend Pratt's funeral.

No leads on Francisco DiScenna had been uncovered. His disappearance was as mysterious as his life. The police had trouble finding anyone outside a very small community of academics at Stanford who had known him personally. A search into his records revealed that he had been raised in a Jesuit boarding school, without any contact with his parents, something even his late graduate advisor either did not know or had never shared with others. DiScenna had started the process of taking holy orders. His small group of colleagues said he was brilliant but distant. The police had interviewed neighbors, they had looked into his finances, had taken his apartment down to the studs looking for anything that could explain why he would do something like this. They found an apartment completely devoid of personal effects, save some toiletries, academic texts consistent with his field and a heavily worn bible.

Pratt's daughter, learning that the police might find some answers in DiScenna's work, sent a copy of DiScenna's ten-year-old unfinished doctoral thesis and asked that Martin analyze it. It was titled:

"Non-Traditional Methods of Representing the
Real and Imagined Distribution of Prime Numbers:
Beyond the Riemann Zeta Function."

Martin had understood some of it, and enlisted others in the university to help him with a fuller understanding of the paper's almost 400 pages. One colleague had declared it gibberish. Another found several ideas creative, but said DiScenna had failed to provide any rigorous proof, presumably the reason the immense paper remained unfinished. Martin himself found the introduction unusual for a technical paper. It began with two quotes from the Bhagavad Gita that Martin recognized as having been used by J. Robert Oppenheimer during his work on the Manhattan Project. The first was the now-famous quote, "I am become death, the destroyer of worlds," used by Oppenheimer when he realized the full destructive power of the atomic bomb. The second was a lesser known quote:

In battle, in the forest, at the precipice in the mountains,
On the dark great sea, in the midst of javelins and arrows,
In sleep, in confusion, in the depths of shame,
The good deeds a man has done before defend him.

The use of the passage by Oppenheimer was attributed to two days before the Trinity Test, the first artificial nuclear explosion, on July 14th 1945. The rest of the paper was a very complex mathematical analysis of number theory. The paper's eponymous zeta function was particularly opaque to us, but in general, Martin explained, it was part of a hypothesis by mathematician Bernhard Riemann in 1859.

"While the mathematics seemed daunting," Martin said, "Its premise is quite simple: while it is currently and potentially systematically impossible to develop an algorithm for 'mapping' the prime numbers, it is possible to know something about their distribution. Riemann counted the primes up to ten, to a hundred, to a thousand and so on." Perry had already Googled 'prime distribution,' which produced the following chart to the billions:

x	Count of the number of primes
10	4
100	25
1,000	168
10,000	1,229
100,000	9,592
1,000,000	78,498
10,000,000	664,579
100,000,000	5,761,455
1,000,000,000	50,847,534

"Riemann had theorized that an algorithm might approximate an order in this progression, and while still a hypothesis, much mathematics assumes Riemann's particular algorithm is true. So it looks like Francisco DiScenna had claimed in the abstract of the paper that he had found a way to move beyond approximations with very large numbers of digits, closing in on larger intervals the greater the computer resources at the disposal of his algorithm."

"Well," I said, "that makes sense."

"Yeah," said Perry. "I think this guy was obsessed with finding order in what others perceive as chaos. He was uncomfortable with doubt or approximation. That seems to me to be spirituality in another guise."

"He found transcendence through mathematics," said Martin. "He obviously thought he was very close to something."

"Unnervingly close," I said. "Frustratingly close. I wonder if this guy started to go crazy. If that's why he's been convinced there's some mathematical clue in the writings of Hellenistic mathematicians."

"The Alexander Palimpsest," said Perry, "makes it seem as if Eratosthenes and Archimedes did indeed mechanize calculation, but it's unfathomable that ancient technology and comparatively primitive, if ingenious, number theory could solve a problem that the world's fastest supercomputers cannot."

"Also," I said, "Let's think about the relevance of this project to the ancients for a moment. They had no way of knowing that this mathematics would be employed in Public Key Cryptography. They were still debating the existence of atomic structure. They knew nothing about the electron. How could they imagine a world of electronic commerce and communication?"

"They knew about the primes," said Martin, "and we now have proof that they wished to map them. It possible Francisco guessed that someone had made greater progress than we traditionally accept for the period, but–"

"I know," said Perry. "It's an intriguing mystery. How did he know to even look for something like the Alexander? The Archimedes only proved that math had made it further in antiquity - a little further - than we assumed, but it didn't contribute any new knowledge to modernity. Everything lost had long been rediscovered by the time the Archimedes was found."

"I don't see someone obsessing about Hellenistic mathematics unless he had some idea of what he'd find. Is it possible he was aware of some other text that mentioned it? Is there something we're missing?"

"If there's a copy of the Alexander out there, we would have heard of it, and if there was a copy extant, DiScenna wouldn't have needed to steal this one."

"Except," said Martin, "there is a copy, *of sorts.*"

Perry and I both gave him a look of incredulity. Then I remembered our first meeting with Martin.

"The Antikythera Mechanism," I said.

"Exactly," said Martin. "He would have been intrigued by any mathematical device from antiquity, perhaps he detected an additional significance, or had just enough evidence of such a device that he sought out a more complete explanation of it."

"That's pretty thin, gentlemen," said Perry. "Very thin."

"Well," Martin said, "maybe there's something else floating out there. If we take this Hesperos account as genuine, there were several people involved in the project in Alexandria – all men of letters eager to preserve knowledge. Is it shocking to imagine one of these others wanting to immortalize their accomplishments by passing it down to posterity?"

"And none of these men included the location of the device in any of these accounts?"

"Maybe they were incomplete," said Perry, "maybe there are other copies of this narrative that have been found that give just enough information to tantalize without complete information."

"We may never know," I said. "Do you really think it's possible that he found a solution to the prime factorization problem? I mean, isn't that problem orders of magnitude more complex than number sieves and Archimedean pneumatics?"

"We have proof of the Mersenne," said Perry.

"Indeed we do," said Marin. "Unequivocally."

"We do," I said, "but you've got to look at this rationally. There can be no question that antiquity's minds and the minds of modernity shared much in common, but we've seen a rapid expansion of the quantity of exceptional talent as a function of a growing percentage of a given population. We've also seen rapid specialization in the modern period. Let's forget for a moment the possibility of the existence of what we might call a computer."

"Might," said Perry, "it's a programmable computer in every way, by definition."

"Ok, Ok," I said, throwing up my hands in agreement. "But, we're talking about the 'computing' power of a calculator here, maybe a little less. We're talking about the computers that worked on the Apollo mission. I'll grant you that a computer doesn't have to be electronic, *per se*, to solve complex operations, but–"

"You're talking about Moore's Law," said Perry, "the doubling of computing power every 18-24 months."

"Well, almost," I said. "Moore's Law is the tendency under market forces of the doubling every 2 years of the *density of transistors on integrated circuits*. Similar concept to the 'doubling of computing power,' but more about the upper limits of the capacity of these circuits."

"What's your point?" asked Martin.

"My point is that we're not even talking about integrated circuits. An integrated circuit is tiny in the human scale, it's near-microscopic. The Alexander Palimpsest is talking about a computer the size of the storerooms of a Hellenistic palace. Look, this 'Hesperos' records it here, in the exchange between Ptolemy and Eratosthenes." I pulled out my copy of the Alexander Palimpsest.

"Aristophanes says, and I quote, 'Eratosthenes, it is remarkable, and it is an ingenious mechanization of known operations, but I believe if I follow your discussion, to begin to touch the higher limits of infinity of this set, you would need to increase the batteries at a sharply increasing rate.' And Eratosthenes says, 'The rate would increase, that is true.' And then the king, Ptolemy, who seems fairly astute but not a math genius, understandably makes a quip about the cost of such a project, to which a certain Euphorion of Chalcis agrees: 'Surely, the number of numerals in the solution will be roughly equivalent to the number of dial batteries the device requires, and as the numbers get larger, I believe the number of calculating batteries required will begin to get larger by factors upon factors of the number of numerals.' Then Hesperos quotes Ptolemy as quite understandably curious about the cost, saying, 'How many 'batteries' of gear-works will a device require to reach infinity?' setting up a pretty good joke by Eratosthenes that the device will require, 'a greater infinity of batteries, Ptolemy.'

"It's actually remarkably similar to a modern congressional hearing, in a way. A team of scientists proposes an ambitious project and the legislature, or chief executive in this case, asks legitimate questions about funding. It's a risk versus reward conversation, and it continues to this day. So, these guys aren't stupid. They know what the device can do and what it can't do, and it ends up being the size of a bank vault, and they can't hope to keep looking up Mersenne primes unless the space available to them increases exponentially."

"You're talking about the increasing *space* required," said Perry, "but what about the increase in *sophistication* required? Technology builds upon itself exponentially, not logarithmically. I'm not a computer expert - but consider this." He walked over to a small whiteboard and spent a few moments drawing a diagram:

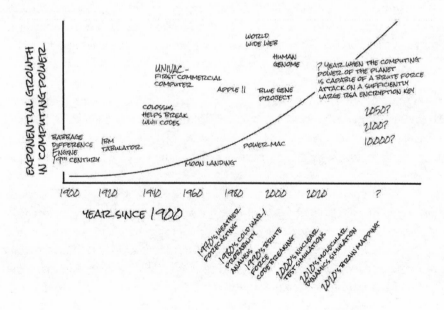

"Now, notice Babbage is an outlier, he's in the mid-nineteenth century, and his ideas weren't realized in his lifetime, but it sounds like Eratosthenes' device, if it actually existed, is something like Babbage's Analytical Engine. In fact, I'll grant that the Antikythera Mechanism might be a much earlier 'computer' in the sense that it takes input in the form of cranking of gears; performs a function on it; in this case explicit in the physical arrangement of the gears; and produces an output: the phases of the moon, the Olympic games, the Metonic cycle, etc. But it doesn't have the capacity to *store* information and then perform a function on that data.

"To perform a calculation on a number's primality, I can't imagine the sophistication required of a mechanical device, but, it has to have some capacity to store information, which Babbage called, unsurprisingly, the "store" in his Analytical Engine. The user threw punch cards in, reminiscent of the 'programs' of fabric patterns in looms used since the eighteenth century. These cards were essentially instructions, and so Babbage could tell his computer to do various things that a single-purpose device like the Antikythera Mechanism could not do. In other words, it was programmable. He called the unit responsible for performing calculations on stored data the "mill," and it was able to multiple, divide, add, subtract and do square roots. Babbage was given a huge parliamentary grant, £17,000, about $1 to $2 million in today's money, and he still couldn't make his earlier Difference Engine work exactly as he'd envisioned it, to say nothing of the exceedingly more complex Analytical Engine.

"Then, let's jump from Babbage to early tabulators. These were card-reading devices that would pick up on binary states, in this case a punched hole or the absence of a punched hole. This technology started with looms for pattern reproduction and was used a bit in the late nineteenth century to help census workers. The tabulators were used until the Second World War, when these devices were fully electrified. Colossus was probably the world's first 'true' computer as we'd envision it now. Electro-mechanical relays would be used to do calculations, replaced eventually by vacuum tubes, and then, of course, transistors.

"Now, transistors are key. They're absolutely key. Now we start to see computing power take a sharp uptick, because you don't need the same space to perform greater and great numbers of calculations. Miniaturization continued, following more or less Moore's Law. Integrated circuits become predominant, packed with hundreds and thousands of transistors. That's what we see in the Apollo Program, a huge advance over Babbage and tabulators, but still about the power of a scientific calculator.

"Fast forward to the PC revolution, Apple, the software explosion, the World Wide Web. This all in a few-decades. We've cracked the human genome a second ago, in the timeframe of recorded history, and the Prime Factoring Problem, absolutely central to Public Key cryptography, is decades or centuries ahead of us. That's taking into consideration exponential growth in computing power. So, today, to crack an incredibly large composite number, one with a huge key length, it would take all the computers in the world the age of the universe to attempt a brute-force attack. My point is pretty obvious-"

"You don't think it could have been done in antiquity?" I asked.

"Well, my point is that we have seen an incredible increase in capability in a relatively short amount of time," said Perry. "Impressive in *our* time, and, I suppose, not impossible in another."

"So, you're suggesting," said Martin, "that in the space of one or two lifetimes, the Academy of Alexandria went from Euclid to complex prime factorization?"

"It's not *im*possible," said Perry.

"These were smart guys," Martin said.

"Without a doubt, for their time as well as ours," said Perry. "But mathematics, and science in general, builds upon itself. Their developing a sophisticated algorithm for factoring incredibly large composite numbers would be impressive, for sure, but we know they were impressive."

"It's possible," said Martin, "that there are many pathways to prime factorization in particular and many modern problems in general."

"I would say," said Perry, "that it *is* a universal constant that science and discovery occur in response to now well-understood societal stimuli."

"Though, don't forget," said Martin, "there's great debate now about the beginnings of the earliest technologies, the switches from one epoch to another, the so-called gaps in our technological evolution. It was widely believed that language is critical for developing the social behaviors that would allow for the dissemination of the knowledge of tool-making, for example, within a population. Now some anthropologists and linguists are suggesting that language may have evolved *after* tool-making, as the improvement of axes, say, from spears may have been required to first secure safety and a stable food source before allowing for a social unit in which language could evolve.

"My point is that, while it may well be a maxim *that* technology evolves in response to stimuli, it may by no means be constant *what* those stimuli are. There may be many paths to valuing prime factorization; one path obviously follows the advent of electronics and electronic commerce and communication, as was the case in the modern period; another may simply be the difficulty of exchanging cryptographic keys over vast distances. In fact, one might argue that the key exchange problem was greater in antiquity than it is in the modern period. In other words, we imagine that technology like ours must resemble a culture like ours and must follow the same self-propelling technology milestones that our society points to in understanding the current epoch. This is, quite obviously, not the only way of viewing the classic 'march of progress.'"

"We do know," I said, "that Eratosthenes and his group cracked the frequency analysis problem. Until now we thought only Al-Kindi had done it eleven-hundred years ago."

"And we know," said Perry, "that they developed a variable-shift cypher, like the Vigenère, two millennia before Vigenère did."

"We don't know," I said, "at least without the second part of the Alexander Palimpsest, if they figured out an encryption system based on prime factorization. We know they thought about it. We know it was an idea, but we have absolutely no proof that they knew how to implement it, that they knew about one-way functions, or that they could have created a device to factor large problems."

"Well," said Perry, "devil's advocate. We're talking about modern key-lengths because we have modern computing capacity. We talk about key lengths in binary bits, we don't know what base they used, but either way, let's take a look at this."

Perry again took to the whiteboard. "Now, he said, consider this line no longer exponential, as in the growth of computing power, but logarithmic. That is, the rate at which the computing power needed to attempt a brute-force attack a certain key length is a function of the acceptable time period required for an attack. Again, we also have to consider the 'computing' power of the time period. I don't have specifics, but I get the general idea. Forget supercomputers. Imagine you're dealing with Babbage's analytical engine and your potential brute-force 'attacker' is dealing with a pen and paper."

"Stylus and Papyrus," said Martin.

"Either way," said Perry, "the key length doesn't have to be huge. RSA encryption works because it uses these *e-nor-mous* key lengths. Here, check this out."

Perry pulled up an article on his laptop. "The RSA Factoring Challenge was a competition to allow hobbyist simulate attacks by would-be attackers to help test the strength of these keys. Let's consider a key length of one hundred decimal digits." He wrote '100' on his logarithmic scale on the bottom left. On his laptop, we saw the composite number with its solution.

RSA-100 = 1522605027922533360535618378132637429718068114961380688657908494580122963258952897654000350692006139

Constituent Primes:

RSA-100 = 37975227936943673922808872755445627854565536638199 × 40094690950920881030683735292761468389214899724061

"According to this, it took 'a few days' in 1991 to compute on a then sophisticated but now antique computer. It says the same factorization can be repeated today in four hours on your average 64-bit laptop computer. $500 at any consumer electronics store. Obviously this key length is out. Let's fast forward, the next few numbers, RSA-110, cracked in '92, RSA-120, '93, RSA-130, '96, RSA-140, '99. Now keep in mind also, these are published numbers that have been distributed to the world in a highly promoted challenge. Somebody's credit card number or an encoded funds transfer from Bank of America to the Federal Reserve Bank of New York have these key strengths, maybe, but different keys, for each different transmission.

"So, if someone, hypothetically transferred funds in RSA-100, it would take an elite computer several days to attack it with brute-force. Now, keep in mind, these were just intellectual exercises. The key-strength of important communications, since these encryption methods came out, was at least 40, 56, or 112 bits, not bad protection in the late '70s or early '80s when only huge institutions could hope to factor these numbers. RSA itself currently recommends a 512 bit key length for day-to-day stuff. When that number was solved by the RSA challenge, it took the team 8,000 MIPS years to do it. MIPS is a useful benchmark. It stands for Million Instructions Per Second. A MIPS year is equivalent to 31.5 trillion instructions. So it took this computer approximately 25.2×10^{12} instructions to crack."

Both Martin and I started at Perry, waiting for the nebulous MIPS and bits to form into a comprehensible whole.

"Look at it this way," Perry said. "Only in the early 1980s could a processor, Intel's I think, perform more than 1 MIPS. That means that a 512 bit key attempted on that computer would take 25.2 x 10^6 seconds to crack, divided by 60 seconds a minute, 60 minutes an hour, 24 hours a day, 365 days a year. That's about 8 years of constant effort to crack a message for a payoff of information that's now 8 years old. You get the idea. As the keys get bigger, the computing power required gets logarithmically more complex. Now, a key the size of really secure communications these days, say a key length of 768 bits, or 232 decimal digits, so large the English language does not have a name for the number of placeholders, was cracked in 2009:

RSA-768 =
12301866845301177551304949583849627207728535695953347921973224521517264005072636575187452021997864693899564749427740638459251925573263034537315482685079170261221429134616704292143116022212404792747377940806653514195974598569021434l3

Constituent Primes:

RSA-768 =
334780716989568987860441698482126908177047949837137685689124313889828883793878002287614711652531743087737814467
999489
×
36746043666799590428244633799627952632279158164343087642676032283815739666511279233373417143396810270092798736308917

"This article says that more than 10^{20} instructions were required, a conceivable task in months with networks of supercomputers, but the equivalent of two thousand years using a single standard desktop computer has some pretty obvious computing obstacles implicit in it. Now, digital certificates for e-commerce websites that take credit card numbers use 2,048 bit encryption. You've already seen that these problems are logarithmic; the challenge estimates that such a key would take longer than the age of the universe to crack with all the computing power known on Earth.

"So, these keys are essentially secure, but more to our point, it would take vast orders of magnitudes larger than the available space of the entire universe and vast orders of magnitude more time than the age of the universe to construct and operate Eratosthenes' device. It's a cool concept, it's brilliant mathematics from antiquity, but I think he got to the Mersenne given in the Alexander, truly an amazing feat, maybe a few higher Mersennes besides, and was happy enough with that extraordinary accomplishment that his apprentice write about it in this journal."

"If he was using considerably smaller key lengths," said Martin, "and anyone intercepting the device had only the use of written mathematics, this machine might have been highly secure."

"Exactly. For the purposes of third century BCE cryptography, someone trying to read messages encoded by two of Eratosthenes' machines on either end of a secure network of communication would be like Babbage working out solutions to keys created by the computers that ran the Apollo mission."

"So," I said, "the Alexandrian computer as a code-making and code-breaking device is plausible."

"Very plausible," said Perry.

"What it seems you're saying isn't very plausible," I said, "is relevance to modern cryptographic techniques. This is a very interesting technique, but not a game changer. Plenty for the scholars of ancient mathematics to feast on, not so much for modern cryptographers."

"You're forgetting your own 'epochism'," said Martin. "An intellectual virus poor old Pratt never suffered from." Perry and I both looked at each other with fleeting, grave smiles. "Another of the 'isms' up there with sexism, racism, ageism, ethnocentrism, and exceptionalism – the belief, tacit or explicit, that some other group is less worthy, less capable or less likely to succeed based on some perceived characteristic of weakness. Epochism is no different. You assume that another 'epoch,' another age was less sophisticated. You've just spent 15 minutes explaining and weeks considering the impossibility of the device because it would be too slow, too big, and frankly, too irrelevant, to be of interest to modern mathematicians."

"I've outlined physical boundaries-"

"Boundaries as you expect them, Perry, boundaries the modern world confronts."

"Not if you change the dynamic. Not if you change the zeitgeist," Martin said with a paternalistic smile on his face.

"These are boundaries every world confronts," I said.

"Perhaps, but is it so impossible," said Martin, dropping into his time-worn chair amid books containing knowledge collected throughout four and a half thousand years of oscillating heights and depressions of human history, "that Eratosthenes found a short-cut."

The so-called Pythagoreans, who were the first to take up mathematics, not only advanced this subject, but saturated with it, they fancied that the principles of mathematics were the principles of all things.

It is not once nor twice but times without number that the same ideas make their appearance in the world.

—ARISTOTLE

21

It has been a month since I last spoke of the Master outside our small circle at the Academy. I tremble even to write of him now, as I have done so freely in this narrative. But Onesimus and I, and our brethren of the Academy, have these last weeks been pressed into such an unusual service that recollections of the Master's stewardship of the Library and Musaeum now wash over me like the fast-flowing waters of the great Nile herself.

Aristophanes, only recently made Chief Librarian, has been called to offer testimony by Ptolemy V Epiphanes of the expenditures of the Academy. Aristophanes, it seems, has been accused of giving too little value for the monies granted by the crown to the library and Musaeum in light of the troubles in Upper Egypt and the expectation that the Academy should, above all else, aid in the development of weapons of war. It was our duty to provide evidence before the council of Alexandria, and it has been made obvious to us what our "evidence" should indicate. We tried our best to remain true to the spirit of the Academy. I was asked few questions, which I believe were answered in such a way as to remain consistent to my feelings of loyalty to Aristophanes and the late master's memory. Sadly, other academicians, acting on an impulse for self-preservation or jealousy, gave accounts less fulsome in their praise of the new

Chief Librarian. Not among these, I must say, is young Aristarchus, who gave a middling account, offering both praise of the current administration of Aristophanes and a public plea to his fellow academicians that they spend less time in abstractions and more on the application of their wisdom to the defense of the realm.

History will no doubt record in detail the troubled times in which the empire of the mind now finds itself. The composition of this recent tribunal will bear this out. Aristomenes, that old codger of an Acarnian and friend of Agathocles, looms over everything and means, I believe, to remain an informal regent and embedded advisor now that Ptolemy V has attained the age of majority. The fussing priests of the Ptolemaic cults were there to plead the case for a renewed vigor of opposition to the secessionists in the south, who even now control Abydos and the portals of heaven.

No fewer than fifteen emissaries from Rome were in attendance, poised in the shadows with their painted faces and gilded armor waiting, no doubt, to make their unofficial patrimony of the dilettante Ptolemy IV an official annexation of his son's, the current pharaoh's, kingdom. Paramount among this delegation is a certain perennial visitor from Rome, Marcus Aemilius Lepidus, who delights in his belief that Ptolemy IV left in his will the very real impression that Rome, now triumphant against Carthage, should act as a natural guardian of the Egyptian homeland. How I despise Rome! She has copied all that is good and virtuous of the people of Hellas but none of our restraint. She has no native philosophy to speak of, her gods are direct transcriptions of our pantheon. Even now her armies march into distant lands seeking the booty of conquest with none of the beneficence or cosmopolitanism of Alexander.

But Onesimus urges me now to return to my narrative in a chronological fashion, as is best. I return to the years after the eastern campaign and the great lecture, when the Master's influence at the court of Ptolemy III Euergetes was at its height, when men of letters were more esteemed than men-at-arms. Let us hope this narrative – and our library - will survive the tumult of the degradation of our culture. I will return to that time after the eastern campaign, but strongest in my memory in light of the current inquisition aimed at the Academy are my memories of the growing, odd behavior at this time of the heir presumptive, young Ptolemy, or Ptolemy IV, as he would become.

Educated from a young age with the full resources of the entire Academy, his interests had turned to poetry and philosophy, but most predominantly to the syncretic Greco-Egyptian religion. So engrossed was he in the cult of his own family's apotheosis that he often soured the discussions on comparative religion that were, until his influenced waxed upon his tutors, a hallmark of the ecumenical spirit of the Academy.

It is remarkable that the recent trial of Aristophanes should be the event to remind me, because, though he was older than the young heir presumptive, they were, as I have mentioned, quite inseparable. After the great Decree of Canopus, which made known externally and internally the close association between the native priesthood and the Ptolemies, domestic resistance nearly subsided in all but the most renegade strongholds. All of these strongholds, save one, existed far away from the center of Ptolemaic control. All Pelusium paraded effigies of the Ptolemies, all Memphis delighted in their patronage, all Naucratis wept with fear that evil should befall even one strand of Euergetes' coiffured mane. Yet deep in old Rhakotis, the Egyptian quarter, resentment continued to build among the middling natives.

I recall now finding Amasis in the agora one evening, drunk as I had ever seen a man, protesting at the 'foolishness' of the Canopic Decree. The natives had sold their history, he said, for a few statues and one season's tribute of grain. The Ptolemies were an occupying power to him, and recognizing me, seized upon my robes and begged me to use my privileged place at court to effect a deed of regicide. Before I could protest, he was seized by the pharaoh's bodyguard and taken away. I imagined I would never see him again, but I realized that he was not the only native disaffected in the new union between the old priestly class and, as Amasis saw them, the Macedonian occupiers. The behavior of Euergetes' son was a matter of concern for those of us who realized a small but stalwart local contingent needed little excuse to make known their discontent.

It was generally agreed among the Master's circle that, while some suspected the young Ptolemy may have, even then, harbored notions of an attempted coup, he was hardly rapacious enough to navigate beyond the sensual and religious activities within his own courtiers. Young Ptolemy's own personal retinue, full of nearly a thousand of his own hand-selected attendants, had been at drink permanently since shortly after the Decree was handed down at Canopus. One such incident may suffice to speak to young Ptolemy's character.

I can vividly remember having attended the Master, himself attendant on the cortege of Euergetes during a tour of the progress of the construction along the Upper Nile. In his own village of tents within his father's encampment, the future Ptolemy IV had fallen prey to several straight days and nights of drink and wild amusements. One afternoon – I believe we were encamped two or three days north of Thebes - Ptolemy awoke late in the day in the middle of a flailing pile of limbs that writhed around him. Pleased to find the party ongoing, the future king of Egypt bellowed once more for his kylix and seeing that his sobriety threatened to stop the festivities, donned a mask of Osiris and commanded them to continue as he once again descended into drunkenness. It was reported by the pharaoh's spies within his son's retinue that young Ptolemy demanded that he officiate at marriages he arranged on the spot, and that he commanded six couples to be wed before him. Two couples were to be comprised of men and women, two of men and men, and two of women and women. This would not have scandalized the attendant Greeks as much as news of his actions positively outraged the native population.

He compelled each couple to separate into one each of six tents he had specially prepared with the finest incense and stocked with the finest wine and, in turn, consummated with each couple the 'dignity' of their marriage. This whole time he remained in the dress of Osiris. At the end of this intercourse, when all couples were spent and a Silphion salve was applied as necessary, he brought his contemporaries and favorites, the siblings Agathocles and Agathoclea, into his private tent.

The agent reported that at the instigation of these favorites and full of drink, the future pharaoh castrated by his own hand a male servant who had spilled a drop of wine on young Ptolemy's robe. After the servant limped away and in a rage at what he had been induced to do, Ptolemy commanded the siblings to violate each other in the manner of Egyptian pharaohs, perhaps foreshadowing his eventual union with his own sister, as is the pharaonic way. The siblings complied with what the agent shockingly reported as only half-hearted remonstrations. Seeing their unmasked comfort, Ptolemy fled the tent. The Pharaoh's agent pursued young Ptolemy, lingering only long enough to observe that the absence of the young royal did not stop brother and sister from their lovemaking.

So fulsome was his dedication to the cult and its trappings that even his apologists argued that his dilettantism left little time for subversive politics, and even fewer hours to machinate in dark recesses of palace corridors. The inner circles of government acquitted him of political maneuverings, and accused him, silently of course, of simply making himself an attractive puppet for any who might seek to control him. We could never have known then how dangerous and how malleable the young Ptolemy would become.

The Master's work was still, at this time, encouraged by his king and, might I even say, friend, Ptolemy III Euergetes. I have on my writing desk one of the few copies made of the Master's *On the Method of Secret Writing*, dedicated to his noble prince. It is possible that the specialist reader my wish to consult the entire text, restricted as it is to those academicians who have written approval from the pharaoh himself. I include the Master's incipit here, somewhat in the Homeric style, that his ingenuity with ciphers and the prime numbers might be appreciated by a wider audience than the cryptanalysts in Ptolemy's circle.

> Oh odes of Hellas! What anabases thine enemies have undertaken to thwart your graces; from the valleys of Attica to the steppes of Asia, your virtue is assaulted on every front. Yet you have achieved a subversion of your own. You have made known to your enemies the method of your impervious prose, and you, in turn, have made known to yourselves alone the methods with which that opacity may be made clear, as the skies of Olympus open and the clouds part above the house of Ptolemy!

I note also the use by the Master of poor Aristophanes' marks of exclamation and his judicious use of the komma. What an age were we living in then! – when the indissoluble numbers protected our secrets and made all other confidences as plain as the words of a crier in the agora. Onesimus is well-versed in the Master's method, but he is curious about the manner of its development. I have proposed a small game of code-making that Onesimus has now accepted.

I have just sent Onesimus to the storerooms to fetch a lockbox with two latches and two locks attached to its face. It is my intention to repeat the same demonstration the Master gave to his pharaoh and then to the fellows of the Academy.

First, I have removed a lock and its key from one of the latches on the box and these I have given to Onesimus. The other lock and key I have taken for myself. Next, I have written a small note on a piece of papyrus and I have enclosed it in the box, affixing my lock and, turning my key. I have locked the box and I have retained my key on my person. I now place the box on a long table between us. The table is to act as a representative of any stretch of territory that necessitates long-distance communication between sender and recipient.

Now, in traditional dispatches, the sender and the recipient must have exchanged copies of keys beforehand. We Egyptians, who invented locks, were the first to use this method to transact in gold along the Nile. Normally, the recipient, in this case Onesimus, would receive the box and simply apply the same key that was used to lock it to unlock it. But, as the Master was fond of pointing out, it is conceivable that a rider might be intercepted when delivering a key. When we imagine the key not as a physical object but as a password or the incipit keys employed by Seleucus, we can see how easily a key may be compromised. Now, let us imagine in this arrangement that a courier has carried the locked box safely to Onesimus. Whether on the other side of the world or the other side of the table, it is of little difference.

Now let us presume that we have not wished to risk an exchange of keys, and that Onesimus is not in possession of the same key that I used to secure the box. In this novel arrangement, Onesimus receives the box but does not try to open it. Onesimus merely places his lock on the second latch, turns his key to lock it, and returns the box to me, now secured with two locks of different configurations. Upon receiving the box again, I use my key to remove my lock. I do not worry myself with Onesimus' lock, as I do not have the ability to open it. The box, now removed of my lock, is still locked during its transition from me back to Onesimus, who, receiving it, needs only apply his key to open the box and acquire its contents. Thus, the box at all time is locked from intruders by at least one lock, and this novel approach has the added benefit that I need never have possession of Onesimus' key nor he of mine.

This system was known to the Master, though, for obvious reasons, it was hardly used. For practical purposes, the use of a rider from Ptolemy in Alexandria, for example, to a stronghold in Syria some weeks march away, then a return to Ptolemy for the removal of a key and another several weeks back to Syria effectively doubles the time needed for secure communications. In answer to this problem, the Master devised an ingenious method for making keys in the abstract.

The Master first imagined a plaintext message as the scroll in the box, and a key as the method used to generate a lock, or in this case, a coded message. The Master's genius lay in the ability for sender and recipient to communicate in code without ever having to share their private keys. During the Master's decoding of the Seleucian dispatches, his device aided him greatly in analyzing the frequency of letters to divulge the message and its key. Once discovered, the Master could assume that a great majority of messages composed at the same time were likely to be encoded with the same key. What if, the Master asked his sovereign in the presence of the Academy, one might undertake to send a message with a completely random key each time, and what if the key might be the same size as the message, so that frequency analysis would be useless in an attack against it?

Euergetes, an intelligent man, proclaimed the enterprise impossible. Eratosthenes, undeterred, gave each academician and Ptolemy a random key, and told them to await delivery of a shared message. These keys would remain public, in a table of keys that anyone might consult. He then devised a method in which each recipient would generate a private key, unknown even to the Master, with which they might maintain, in a manner analogous to the boxes, their own unbreakable lock.

Another demonstration was given, and Euergetes was so delighted with the result that he dismissed half of his couriers. The Master's solution lay in his other work with prime numbers, and a peculiar property of semi-prime numbers, that is, those numbers like 4, 6, 9, 10, 14, 15, 21, 22, 25, and 26 which are not prime themselves but are divisible by two and only two prime numbers. In the case of 4, its constituent primes are 2 and 2, 6 is comprised of 2 and 3. In this manner one might continue factoring these semi-primes into constituent primes of great length. The length of the number Eratosthenes used in his example, as attested in his notebook, is exactly 442 digits, a calculation with which his new device was easily tasked.

The example given his pharaoh was the brief passage Eratosthenes had used to explain the workings of his early code-breaking device:

```
OI CI UI F BYNI YYNB HZ XNOHY HNI T
B XABRY DZ MJ FI TBUZFL HI RLMI OF
KZRKBOYHJ EYOI CI MFI OLYNI YJ B
ORGZ RADUI RLBF BF HMF Z CZ RBKOY
DYZI RZYNBFI RLNI TORGRBTBFNI
L NI J OYI Y OZ RHZ MYNB OF Z URYNBD
CI DMI OAORYNB OF KZ RKBXYOZ RZM
XNOAZ HZ XNBF HI RLHYI YBHCBRI R
L CI DRZYQRZUUNI YYNBDLZI RLHI
DORYOCBZMUI FUNBRYNBDI FBMOG
NYORGZ FNZAL ORGXI FABDUOYNYN
B OF BRBCOBHI RLYNEHXBZ XABZ MD
ZEFKAI HHI FBYNBZRADZRBHFBCI
ORORGUNZI FBMOYYBLJ DRI YEFBI
RLBLEKI YOZRYZYI QBXI FYI YZRK
BJ ZYNORXZAOYOKHI RLXNOAZ HZX
ND XAIYZ LOI AZGEBZMYOCI BEH
```

As Euergetes had guessed and as Onesimus had solved, both of them with the aid of frequency analysis, the passage is shown to be:

I am aware that the Sophists have plenty of brave words and fair conceits, but I am afraid that being only wanderers from one city to another, and having never had habitations of their own, they may fail in their conception of philosophers and statesmen, and may not know what they do or say in time of war, when they are fighting or holding parley with their enemies. And thus people of your class are the only ones remaining who are fitted by nature and education to take part at once both in politics and philosophy.
—PLATO, Dialogue of Timaeus

While yielding easily to frequency analysis, this might be made slightly more difficult by employing a variable shift cipher, as the Master indicated years earlier. In that instance, he had used a key based on Euergetes' own name. Knowing this key, repeated here from the Master's earlier letters, it is the work of a child to begin to notice patterns in the encoded text:

P T O L E M Y U R G S A B C D F H I J K N Q V W X Z
x y z a b c d e f g h i j k l mn o p q r s t u v w

Onesimus now interjects to note that the Master was even at that early date referring to his prince with the epithet, 'Euergetes,' or 'benefactor,' several years before the assembly of the synod at Canopus. 'Euergetes' was an epithet of the Master's own creation, a kind of aspirational epithet, as if to say that the Master was so assured of Ptolemy's favorable disposition toward his efforts that his benefaction should be noted before the fact. This line of thinking is ancient, and employed to great effect, for one example, in the messianism of the Jews. One sets forth the hope of the coming of a benefactor. It is the better part of wisdom for someone so inclined to act in satisfaction of such an aspiration. Ptolemy the Benefactor provides a handy example; so enamored was he of a self-image as benevolent patron of the arts of mathematics and religion that it would have been remarkable had Sosibius *not* placed the epithet in the throats of the thankful Egyptian priestly class. These digressions soil the mind!

Now, the Master proposed to encode the same message using a word-for-letter transposition of a large semi-prime number of exactly the same number of characters as the message itself. This would render frequency analysis impossible, because, unlike in the example above where one letter always stands for another uniformly throughout the entire message and, likely, throughout many messages composed at the same time and place, a one-time encipherment used a distinct key *each time* a message was composed. Let us now imagine the text encoded using the Master's new semi-prime as key. First, the sender chooses a large prime number, their key made public and distributed by Eratosthenes. They then multiply this by their private key, another prime number known only to themselves. This yields a fairly large semi-prime, let us say something like the following:

```
2 6 0  1 4 2 8 2  1 1 9 5 5 6 0 2 5 9 0 0 7 0 7 8 8 4
8 7 3 7  1 3 2 0 5 5 0 5 3 9 8  1 0 8 0 4 5 9 5 2 3 5
2 8 9 4 2 3 5 0 8 5 8 9 6 6 3 3 9  1 2 7 0 8 3 7 4 3
1 0 2 5 2 6 7 4 8 0 0 5 9 2 4 2 6 7 4 6 3  1 9 0 0 7
9 7 8 8 9 0 0 6 5 3 3 7 5 7 3  1 6 0 5 4  1 9 4 2 8 6
8  1 1 4 0 6 5 6 4 3 8 5 3 3 2 7 2 2 9 4 8 4 5 0 2 9
9 4 2 3 3 2 2 2 6  1 7  1 1 2 3 9 2 6 6 0 6 3 5 7 5 2
3 2 5 7 7 3 6 8 9 3 6 6 7 4 5 2 3 4  1 1 9 2 2 4 7 9
0 5  1 6 8 3 8 7 8 9 3 6 8 4 5 2 4 8  1 8 0 3 0 7 7 2
9 4 9 7 3 0 4 9 5 9 7  1 0 8 4 7 3 3 7 9 7 3 8 0 5 1
4 5 6 7 3 2 6 3  1 1 9 9  1 6 4 8 3 5 2 9 7 0 3 6 0 7
4 0 5 4 3 2 7 5 2 9 6 6 6 3 0 7 8  1 2 2 3 4 5 9 7 7
6 6 3 9 0 7 5 0 4 4  1 4 4 5 3  1 4 4 0 8  1 7  1 8 0 2
0 7 0 9 0 4 0 7 2 7 3 9 2 7 5 9 3 0 4  1 0 2 9 9 3 5
9 0 0 6 0 5 9 6  1 9 3 0 5 5 9 0 7 0  1 9 3 9 6 2 7 7
2 5 2 9 6  1 1 6 2 9 9 9 4 6 0 5 9 8 9 8 4 4 2  1 0 3
9 5 9 4  1 2 2 2  1 5  1 8 2  1 3 4 0 7 3 7 0 4 9 1
```

This number was used by the Master in one of his early examples. An infinite field of numbers, we know from Euclid, is available from which to choose. One might imagine this as an encoded dispatch, and anyone intercepting a rider bearing this formulation would find the interception fruitless. Yet it would be quite easy for the recipient to apply the known public key of the sender and their own private key, to determine the suitable arrangements for letter-for-number substitution. The Master's complete text on the matter is quite advanced, as has been mentioned, as it contains several other unique properties adapted from the modular arithmetic of the Babylonians. It resides within the holdings of the library as a closely guarded secret of the

Ptolemaic state. The copy in my keeping was a gift from the Master and remains among my most prized – and most clandestine – possessions. I have yet to decide whether to include it among the appendices attached to this account.

Ptolemy's delight, however, was short lived. Because the code was impenetrable, Ptolemy feared that its weakness lay not in an interceptor's ability to read a message, but in the capture of one of Ptolemy's agents familiar with the process itself. It might happen, Euergetes realized immediately, that the Seleucian court could adopt this method so that, while our messages themselves would remain impenetrable to Seleucus, so too would his messages become impenetrable to us. It would be as if, Euergetes said, the secrets of Archimedes' great siege towers were given to the world, so that all nations were so well matched as to assure mutual destruction in the event of a simultaneous incursion by all parties.

The Master agreed. The security of the system rested on the ease of multiplying two prime numbers and the impossibility of reversing that multiplication. In other words, the Master cautioned Ptolemy, to decode a message without the key would require the factoring of a semi-prime number into its constituent primes. This multiplication the Master called a one-way-function, and it was quite impossible to reverse it by trial-and-error alone.

Ptolemy could not resist implementing the system, and it was in appreciation of the dangers of its distribution that he summoned his top commanders, including his brother, Lysimachus, and the generals Xanthippus and Theodotus, to Alexandria, that they might appear before him personally. Under pain of death for themselves and their families, they must promise to be the only members of their garrisons who would have knowledge of the method. This they were made to swear and were made to give an oath that the method not be divulged in the unlikely event of their capture.

Thus it became the policy of the Ptolemaic state to coordinate sensitive intelligence only at the highest levels, using the Master's ingenious method rooted in Babylonian arithmetic and the prime numbers.

Several more years passed. Ptolemy continued his campaigns in the south as benefactor of the native religion. He sustained his project of improvements to the temples there and endowed Canopus, Naucratis, Heliopolis, Oxyrhynchus, Pelusium and Cyrene with vast public works projects in the syncretic Greco-Egyptian style. In Alexandria, itself teeming with workmen, artisans, merchants, priests, academician and courtiers, Ptolemy received embassies of every major power. Many came in peace, some to gather intelligence on the stability and wealth of Ptolemy's interior and overland possessions. All left laden with gifts for foreign princes and the goodwill of a benefactor secure in his kingdom.

In the same year as the great assembly at Canopus, we received an embassy from Carthage. Their great national hero, Hamilcar Barca, had defeated a vast army of mercenaries and had forty thousand of their number executed, a fact that shocked Euergetes. Quite uncomfortably, an embassy of Rome was in attendance in Alexandria at the same time. Rome had maintained designs on Sardinia, upon which the war weary Carthaginians were prepared to relinquish any claims.

In the next years Hamilcar Barca's exploits became legend in Alexandria, as he flounced the authority of the aristocratic Carthaginians, led by Hanno, by pursuing a campaign in Iberia. In a tribute of friendship, though some said as a mission of reconnaissance, the Roman consul, Titus Manlius Torquatus, sent a delegation with a silver effigy of himself and Ptolemy standing in friendship. Ptolemy was depicted rather heavier than he was in reality. Titus was depicted, triumphant, closing the gates of the temple of Janus, as is their rare custom of denying access to the temple in times of peace. The gates of the two-faced god did not stay closed for long, and they have not been closed again by the two-faced Romans in my lifetime.

Eratosthenes gave Ptolemy foreknowledge of the resurrection of the ambitions of Antiochus Hierax, who, having defeated Seleucus at Ancyra, claimed all of Anatolia, save Pergamum, for himself. An embassy sent by Hierax arrived in Alexandria, which Ptolemy received coolly and with little fanfare. Attalus I of Pergamum also sent an embassy, to which Ptolemy responded with much kindness.

Again the Romans troubled us, as we were forced to countenance a visit from the poet Gnaeus Naevius who insisted on staging his *Bellum Punicum*, a recitation of the labors of the legendary Aeneas. The Master had the misfortune of attending a symposium in the poet's honor held by the worthy Apollonius of Rhodes. Callimachus made his way through the villas of Lochias in time to denounce the entire party. It was said the whole affair was a contributing factor to his death only two years later.

We also received intelligence, followed in the usual fashion by an official visit from the victorious party, that Leonidas II, apparently on advice from the gods, abdicated the Spartan throne in favor of his son-in-law, Cleomenes III, a noted reformer.

Several years later, though no delegation was present, the Master also received correspondence from Pingala that Ashoka had died. Pingala, worried about the disintegration of the Chinese states east of his late king's empire and the deaths of several influential Chinese philosophers of his acquaintance, wrote of the ambitions of a warlord hoping to unite by force all the unhappy Asiatics of that region.

Chrysippus, visiting from Athens, was called back to Greece in the wake of the death of his mentor Cleanthes. He was to assume leadership of the school of the Stoics there. Before Chrysippus' departure, the Master hosted a symposium in honor of the great Athenian which I was fortunate to attend. Ptolemy too, attended, disguised in the robes of an academician. Toward the end of the evening, the conversation turned to honoring Cleanthes for his work, but also for his longevity, having been the last tangible link between Alexander and the present epoch. That symposium was unhappily the last such gathering to include the estimable Aristarchus of Samos, who died some few days later.

Ptolemy issued edicts that two remembrance ceremonies be held throughout Alexandria. The first, in honor of 99 year-old Cleanthes, the dreaming pragmatist and former boxer, was concluded with the Master's eulogy in which he said of the old man that when asked if he would break the fast he had been compelled to make due to a mortal ulcer, he replied, "as I am already half-way on the road to death, I will not trouble to retrace my steps."

The festival in honor of Aristarchus of Samos was held at the royal observatory in the palace quarter. To this intimate gathering of academicians Ptolemy extolled the virtues of the novel heliocentrism of this adopted son of Alexandria and praised in particular the innovations he had made in fixing the length of the months to the accuracy of a fraction of a second. This calendar, developed in consultation with Eratosthenes and still resisted by the native priesthood, has nevertheless replaced the measurements of Meton and Callippus and has been imported as the definitive standard by the courts of the East and West.

Conflicting intelligence, delivered with the security of the Master's new code, indicated that Seleucus had surely marched on Parthia where he received a minor defeat. It was not clear whether Seleucus had pulled back to the interior of Persia or whether his person had been captured by Arsaces. Euergetes laughed in reflecting that his once great adversary who threatened the whole of his eastern possessions was now the captive of the rather trivial leader of an aggrandized cadet branch of the Dahae Scythians.

The Roman embassy, now permanently established in Alexandria, attempted to gauge Ptolemy's reaction to a mission of Roman envoys sent to Massilia to negotiate with Hamilcar Barca, who was encamped there. Ptolemy gave no indication of support or condemnation, much to the frustration of the short-tempered Romans. The Romans, hoping to gain favor with Ptolemy, shared intelligence that further fascinations were taking place in Western Anatolia. The Galatians, having grown accustomed to tribute from Attalus, attacked Pergamum when Attalus neglected to make his annual payment. Twenty thousand of these wild Celts went to Pergamum to enquire as to whether the tribute had been overlooked, only to find themselves soundly defeated outside the city's walls by an Attalus so emboldened by the victory that he granted himself the epithet Soter, savior of the Pergamene people.

The Romans also declared open hostility to the ascendancy in Illyria of a new king, Pinnes, after the death of his father, Agron. Agron's second wife, Queen Teuta, effectively in control of the government, instituted a campaign to drive the Greeks out of Illyria and sanction the activity of Illyrian pirates who had begun preying on Roman shipping in the Ionian and Adriatic seas. Ptolemy offered a gesture of support by mobilizing a token fleet from Cyprus. The Master later told me that Ptolemy also sent a secret envoy of friendship to the Illyrian court. These men returned to Alexandria so flush with refutations of the accepted image of the reputed harridan and approbations for the political acumen of Queen Teuta that Ptolemy considered seriously a policy of providing support to Illyria as a check against Roman expansion.

Of course, these activities in Anatolia and Greece were already known to Ptolemy before the Romans gleefully made a show of their generous sharing of intelligence. Ptolemy had tasked his strategoi with a plan for the Egyptian response to the victor in the perpetual skirmishes between Rome and Carthage, and it is likely the Master had told Ptolemy of the envoy to Massilia before the Romans did. As it happened, Ptolemy's support could not prevent the murder of the Roman ambassador, Lucius Coruncanius, and the subsequent Roman occupation of an island whose eponymy Apollonius of Rhodes had explained in his Argonautica by recounting the story of Poseidon's abduction of the nymph Corcyra to a previously unnamed place. Rome pressed on into the Illyrian garrisons at Epidamnus, Apollonis and Pharos, establishing protectorates there.

It was during this time that the King of Macedonia, Demetrius II, died, succeeded by his nephew, Antigonus III acting as regent for the future King Philip V, then only ten years of age. Antigonus then, like Ptolemy later, gradually began to express concerns about Roman ambitions everywhere, and commenced a policy of toleration toward Queen Teuta's sanction of piracy that strained his relationship with the Aetolian League and the Achaean League who were likewise under threat of piracy in the Ionian and Adriatic and who favored friendly relations with Rome.

The grievously permanent Roman embassy grew less obeisant when word reached Alexandria that Hamilcar Barca had fallen to their army in Hispania, ending his campaign to conquer by arms and diplomacy the Iberian Peninsula. Greek colonies there were forced to acquiesce to Roman rule, and Hamilcar's successor and son-in-law, Hasdrubal was forced to concentrate on a domestic policy that redirected resources from a march on Rome to the founding of Cartago Nova as his capital city.

In the same year that Hamilcar fell, an embassy arrived from Attalus proclaiming his victory over Antiochus Hierax and his annexation to Pergamum of the vast majority of Anatolia. This embassy was welcomed warmly by Ptolemy. Several weeks of feasting were proclaimed in honor of the victory of Attalus along the banks of the Harpasus in Caria. I was quite surprised at this, as I had expected Ptolemy to prefer the split attentions of Seleucus, recently campaigning again in Persia. It was Eratosthenes' belief that the noble prince Ptolemy had come to find within himself a kind of respect for the relentless Seleucus. Having no further ambitions beyond what he had already gained in Syria, Ptolemy was glad to see the humbling of a man like Hierax, given this epithet, 'the hawk,' in honor of his grasping and ambitious character. Ptolemy, thought the Master, could not respect someone so willing to move against his own brother in pursuit of personal glory.

The hawk had, the Master said, violated a sense of fair play that Eratosthenes' believed Euergetes held in his analysis of international affairs. Though Euergetes eventually gave asylum to Antiochus, he forced him to live in well-advertised ignominy so that even a dispatch from Seleucus himself did all but thank Ptolemy for his regal solidarity. Hierax met his end in the Egyptian quarter where, stumbling drunkenly from a house of prostitution, he was set upon by robbers. It can never be known whether they recognized him as the infamous usurper of Asia or merely saw an opportunity for thievish gain. It is unlikely, the Master joked, that the identity of the robbers' prey was known to them, as the Hawk's poverty was so well known that no self-respecting gang would deign to waste their time. Indeed, so humiliating was his true end that a story was later invented by his few remaining supporters that he had fled not to Egypt but to the land of his former allies, the Galatians, who had aided him at the battle of Ancyra. It was there, not in a brothel in Egypt, they said, that Hierax was betrayed by the monstrous barbarians. Even today this story continues to circulate as something of a call to martyrdom among the dozen or so Anatolians who remember that the hawk ever lived at all.

A young student – I cannot now remember his name – sailed from Sparta for the Academy in that year or the next. Onesimus can consult the records at the Musaeum and strengthen my memory here, in the manner of the slogan of the Romans, *ex post facto*, or as it is said in Alexandria, the reinvention of history. This student achieved distinction for two things while in attendance at the Academy: his laugh, the sound of a low, trill bleating, and his ex post facto stories of Cleomenes III, whom he claimed as a relation, and the success of the reforms in Sparta. Real history is less kind to Cleomenes' reforms, as indeed it was to Cleomenes himself.

It was this student's contention that it was due to their curious dual throne that Sparta had witnessed her decline. For generations, their peculiar institution of diarchy had been maintained long after the model of the Greek polis grew to eschew, at least in name, the position and honors of kingship. According to their traditions, the two royal houses, the Agiads and the Eurypontids, were descended, respectively, from the twins Eurysthenes and Procles, the descendants of Heracles who supposedly conquered Sparta two generations after the Trojan War. This student claimed kinship, through Cleomenes with the famous Agiad kings, Leonidas I, whose bravery at Thermopylae is universally known, and Pleistarchus and Pleistonax, who sullied the memory of their more famous relation by undertaking to destroy Athens and contribute to her decline. It is ready history how, in the aftermath of the wars between these cities, the Greek mainland was so exhausted as to make easy work of the conquest of Phillip II of Macedon, who left his son Alexander the inheritance of all Hellas.

Cleomenes III, recently succeeding to the Agiad throne of Sparta, immediately found himself tested by the Achaean League, then in the ascendancy on the Peloponnesus and working for its unification under Aratus of Sicyon. The *ephorate*, five elected magistrates who, with the King, form the main executive body of the state, voted to send Cleomenes on campaign to undertake an occupation of Athenaeum, a town claimed by Sparta and Megalopolis. Cleomenes successfully occupied Athenaeum, and Aratus maneuvered the member-cities of the Achaean League to declare against Sparta.

Cleomenes seized on the situation, advancing far into Arcadia before being recalled by the ephors. When news of the fall of Caphyae reached Sparta, Cleomenes was once again ordered into the field. He caused much havoc near Argos and was forced into a battle with his five thousand troops against an

Achaean force of twenty thousand men near Pallantium. So fierce was the reputation of Sparta's fighting tradition that Aratus withdrew to Elis, a Spartan ally, where Cleomenes forced a decisive battle near Mount Lycaeum.

Cleomenes was undermined at home, where the ephors worked against him. Cleomenes co-ruler Eudamidas III died and Cleomenes installed his uncle on the Eurypontid throne, only to find his uncle assassinated upon Cleomenes' return. Strongly suspecting the ephors and remembering their wavering support for his campaigns, Cleomenes abolished the ephorate, executing all but one who managed to find sanctuary in a temple. Furthermore, he curtailed the powers of the *gerousia*, an oligarchic council of elders, replacing them with a hand-picked *patronomoi*, a board of six elders sympathetic to his agenda. He also consigned nearly eighty opponents of these reforms to exile.

It was these reforms and the redistribution of land to the citizens of Sparta of which the student spoke so highly, with particular praise reserved for the enfranchisement of Sparta's free but non-citizen class of *perioikoi*. Cleomenes completed this coup by installing his brother, Eucleidas, on the Eurypontid throne. These stories energized some in the native separatist movement. Ptolemy, more reluctant than any other prince in recent memory to prohibit the free speech of his subjects, rejected the urge to prohibit Cleomenes' mention in Alexandria. Nevertheless, he maintained a policy of mild character assassination by encouraging stories, probably unsubstantiated, of Cleomenes' unnatural religious appetites. It is my memory that this student became a friend of the young Ptolemy, the crown prince, whose obvious religious dilettantism gave great credence to a presumption of natural depravities in the Spartan race.

As the Peloponnesus, North Africa, Hispania and Illyria seemed on an inexorable path to war, the perennially self-serving Roman embassy in Alexandria continued to inveigle the entire Ptolemaic court in ceremonious distractions. Initially, Ptolemy met these displays with bemusement and on one or two occasions the pharaoh explicitly sanctioned the intrusions with the presence of the royal family, as they almost always heralded Euergetes, Berenice and young Ptolemy as the triple foci of their celebrations. Of these ceremonies, including feasting in the agora and embarrassing offerings at the temple of Serapis, the Master opined that they were surely designed to keep Ptolemy concentrated on domestic affairs as Roman armies marched with near-impunity throughout Iberia and Illyria while the infamous Roman Senate simultaneously and opportunistically explored the weaknesses of Seleucus and the humbled Carthaginian outposts in the Mediterranean.

JAMES ADDOMS | 250

Soon the opportunistic Romans contracted with the temple of Serapis and the temple of Demeter to provide monthly demonstrations of the friendship between Egypt and Latium so that all Alexandria might be made to rejoice in a treaty that did not exist. The Romans offered to restore a small caryatid porch, a copy of an original attached to the Erechtheion, in Athens, in honor of their victories against Carthage in their first war against that unhappy land. Discovering these trespasses into the religious affairs of his kingdom, Ptolemy raged in his palace apartments. Eratosthenes, attending his pharaoh, made the following suggestion. It was obvious, the Master said, that the Roman envoys wished to undermine Ptolemy in a subtle way within his own kingdom, imply an alliance where none existed, and demonstrate the wealth of their state by their ostentatious spending as authorized by their senate in Rome. For Eratosthenes, the opportunity to catch the Romans at their own game was irresistible.

He urged his pharaoh to wait until the Romans made some further suggestion of sponsoring public displays. The pharaoh would then except, and have prepared his own spectacle that showcased not only the religious or cultural life of Egypt, but her immense intellectual and natural resources. Indeed, Eratosthenes urged his prince, this was a blessing in disguise. The Romans would offer a sum to cover some minor public amusement of middling propaganda value, and Ptolemy would turn it to a demonstration of Egyptian cunning, wealth and the comparative paucity of the donations from the legislature in Rome.

As expected, the Roman delegation soon approached the court flush with plans for Roman sponsorship of the upcoming festival of the lesser Eleusinian Mysteries. Ptolemy, prepared for this, agreed in so uncharacteristically enthusiastic a way as to set the Roman delegation on edge, a sight enjoyed by all at the Academy. Ptolemy asked what the legation was prepared to spend, to which they responded that, for such an important ceremony, Rome had granted no less than five hundred talents of silver in honor of the power, prestige and - dare they say, friendship - of the House of Ptolemy. Ptolemy agreed and suggested that, in light of all the arrangements they had undertaken themselves, he might relieve them of the burden of planning such a spectacular event. Ptolemy made arrangements to have the treasury take possession of the silver at the Romans' earliest convenience, assuring them that they would be kept informed of the progress of the preparations. The Romans had little choice but to obey and fall at the feet of Euergetes out of thanks for his thoughtful hospitality. It was said later that such screaming and oaths emanated from their rented rooms on the Lochias Peninsula that academicians in residence there had trouble sleeping for several nights.

Ptolemy was so delighted that he forgot himself and appeared the same evening at Archimedes' home, where he knew the academicians were likely to be assembled. Dressed in a simple robe, he had traveled inconspicuously with only two bodyguards. Finding Archimedes, the Master, Ctesibius, Abdaraxus, Aristophanes and me considering a response, he bid Archimedes' leave to send a runner for the whole of the party who had been engaged in the Alexandrian project, as he considered this fellowship the core of the intellectual life of his empire. I had never before sat in the presence of the pharaoh, and on this occasion, I did just that, indeed, I shared a drink with him. He seemed happy to be among the closest things he might consider to friends in Archimedes and Eratosthenes, and we had all consumed our first and then second kylix when the exhausted runner appeared with an incredulous Philo of Byzantium, Diocles, Apollonius of Perga, Apollonius of Rhodes, Conon, the court astronomer and Nicomedes. All thirteen of us, comprising too large a party for the andron, burst into the inner courtyard as genially and collegially as if we were all first year students at the Academy. Euergetes was eager to hear of the masterful preparations this team might contrive, making explicit his position that money was no object.

The pharaoh's own suggestion was that we invite, under guarantee of safe passage, Hasdrubal, Cleomenes and Queen Teuta to Egypt to sit as tripartite grand-marshalls of a parade through the streets that would begin at the Soma with divine sanction of Alexander and end with a reception at the Roman embassy. We knew this was in jest, or at least we took it so, and we, all of us, raised our glasses in laughter. Soon the conversations turned to serious feats of engineering. The young people congregated in a group that enthusiastically put forward a proposal, against my advice, that Lake Mareotis be dammed and drained temporarily, and the festivities be held there. Knowing the lake well, I did not see this as a particularly workable prospect.

Philo and Conon favored the construction of a dam at one of the cataracts of the Nile, and a procession from Alexandria to end at an especially constructed temple atop its earthworks. Diocles and Apollonius of Perga suggested, desirous of a repeat of the Festival of the Pantheon in Persepolis, that a similar competition be staged either in the city's existing hippodrome or, as Abdaraxus added, perhaps in an entirely new structure specially built for the occasion. Ptolemy agreed instantly, and delighted in the idea of having another opportunity to display the supremacy of Alexandrian sport, letters and mathematics.

In a private conversation with the Master and Archimedes, I suggested that the great hulls left from the Ptolemaia, while still in good repair, were nevertheless languishing in disuse in the Great Harbor. Might they not be turned to better use as a seat of spectacle? Euergetes, overhearing this, slapped me on the back and congratulated me for wide thinking. It might work, he suggested, but yet, he favored each of these ideas. The dam seemed implausible at present, and too far from the center of power. But what of harnessing nature in another way? What of defying the Mediterranean that ran from the mouth of the Tiber at Ostia to Alexandria's Great Harbor? What, he said in a hushed voice, of defying Poseidon himself? The assembly refined their plans, and my last memory of that evening before drink entirely overtook me was of the Master shaking his pharaoh's hand as Euergetes was helped out the door by his companions and into the bright Alexandrian night.

Preparations were commenced immediately. The Festival of the Mysteries was only several weeks away, and Ptolemy issued a proclamation that this reprise of the Festival of the Pantheon should run simultaneously with it. Again he summoned athletes, poets, grammarians, historians, mathematicians, dramatists and the like. Again he announced prizes, and again he added his imprimatur to an exodus out of their homelands and into Egypt of the greatest minds of the world.

The Romans greeted the news with feigned excitement as they began to wonder at an increase of activity throughout Alexandria. A week after they suggested their sponsorship of the Festival, the Romans watched as a workforce of five thousand men descended on the Great Harbor. The ten hulls were first cleaned thoroughly and then repainted in bright colors. Enormous beams of Lebanon cedar were seconded from the boat works on Lake Mareotis and ported through the streets of Alexandria with some fanfare.

The ten hulls were drawn together so that there was only a boat-width between them. The two largest ships were rowed to central positions and the planks were then laid across each vessel to create the infrastructure for an enormous platform that would spread 8 ship widths in either direction from a towering central structure made from the hulls on which Amasis had labored so carefully years before. Soon even more lumber filled in the decking so that a continuous platform reached across all ten hulls. This decking was fitted around the existing temples, gardens and private apartments so that these disparate ships were made to resemble an enormous coherent whole. The size and scale of the effort began to resemble, floating effortlessly in the Mediterranean, the palace complex on land.

The Romans were astonished, and we know from intercepting each of their dispatches to Rome that they both marveled at and feared the rapid deployment of the resources of Egypt on such an immense scale. Only two weeks after construction began, the entire structure was made larger than the agora of Athens and the Circus Maximus of Rome taken together. On the deck Ptolemy ordered the construction of a hippodrome, two theaters and temples to various Roman gods, which were, of course, copies of our own. Ctesibius, Abdaraxus and Archimedes, papyrus diagrams in hand, barked orders to dozens of foremen, who in turned dictated to an army of carpenters, tile layers, plumbers, horticulturalists, painters and sculptors. These craftsmen created such a wonder that, where only ten large hulls had existed weeks before, an entire floating city larger than many border towns now gleamed in the Alexandrian sun. In a ceremony of consecration Ptolemy gave this structure the name of *Ptolemais Berenicia*, after himself and his consort.

The appointed day of the festival arrived. The attendees marveled at a sight unimaginable anywhere else in the world. Games and chariot races were held onboard the vessel. The theaters were filled with performances of new works interposed with stagings of the old standards of Aeschylus, Sophocles and Euripides. The Mysteries, held mostly on shore, were reworked to include a triumphant evening of feasting on board the *Ptolemais Berenicia*.

Visitors from all courts attended in the manner of the Olympic Games, where a truce was declared in all lands for the duration to ensure safe passage to and from the festival. Euphorion of Chalcis, again making the fabled philosopher's run from Athens to soak in the glory of Alexandria, was fêted throughout the festival no less by the Seleucian delegation than by Ptolemy, as they had designs on him themselves. An abridgement of his epic of mythology, *Thrax*, was well-received; his satirical poem, *Arae*, was so like to the style of Callimachus that he was awarded the second prize in the poetry competition, some said on those grounds alone. So taken with Euphorion was the Master that he begged leave, and received it, to give a demonstration of the device and the method of his rendering of the prime numbers.

Panthoides and Chrysippus, arriving separately from Athens, each wasted little time before inquiring of the lodgings of the other, so that they were never without each other's antagonism or deep in conversation about the philosophical weaknesses of the other. Panthoides reworked his well-known paper, *On Ambiguities*, in which he argued that something might be shown to be possible which can never be true. Chrysippus, who may have misunderstood the subtlety of Panthoides' arguments, took issue with what he considered a misuse of language. Aristotle's 'logic' had been concerned with relationships between what can be known, what can be shown and what can be inferred from these relationships. Chrysippus moved beyond Aristotle to illuminate how imprecisely human language grasped these relationships, and undertook in a new treatise, *On Propositional Logic*, to outline a system of formal rules for formulating and proving conditional deductions.

They both entered these new treatises into the philosophy competition, which were found to be, however incisive, merely regurgitations of earlier stances. These were awarded honorary prizes, based solely on the immensity of their authors' reputations. A certain Menippus, even then gaining a reputation as a scholar and a satirist, arrived near the same time and composed, on the spot, an answer to Panthoides and Chrysippus. Ptolemy received Menippus' work with delight, entertaining him among a private group of courtiers at the palace. This, earnest jester, or *spoudogeloios*, as Ptolemy called him, was gifted at piercing the veil of sophistry while papering over his jabs and cuts with serious scholarship on the nature of existence. This ad hoc construction, *Letters Artificially Composed as if by the Gods*, won the top prizes in both the philosophy and the new satire competitions, a creation for which we may thank the stalwart Armenian, Azekiah, and his *Poor Man of Nippur*.

At the closing ceremonies of the Festival of the Pantheon, Ptolemy awarded these honors in person, and the entire ceremony was crowned with the fanfare now common at the Ptolemaic court. Again torchbearers sent a uniform stream of fire throughout the city, again Archimedes' catapults and ballistae sent the arms of Helios across the evening sky. The Romans, completely overwhelmed with the spectacle, could only stare in awe of the entire proceeding from their dais on the *Ptolemais Berenicia*, specially constructed in their honor.

Several days after the conclusion of the festivities, Ptolemy summoned the Roman delegation to the palace. In the presence of the entire court, the Academy and delegations from Carthage, Illyria, Sparta, Rhodes, Syracuse, the Achaean League, the Pergamenes and the court of Seleucus, Ptolemy thanked the Romans for their patronage, and made a public declaration that the friendship of Rome and Egypt should be secured for all time. In honor of this new relationship, Ptolemy noted that the festival had taken place at the expense of one thousand talents of silver and that, for their part, the Roman's should be honored with a gift of a Serapeum in Ptolemy's own honor to be constructed at their convenience near the forum in Rome. To this end, Ptolemy donated two thousand talents of silver – four times the Romans' budget for the celebration of the Mysteries – to accompany the "understandably homesick" delegation back to Rome, conveyed across the Mediterranean at Ptolemy's expense.

Unfortunately, the Roman delegation did not make it back to Rome without incident. On their journey across the Mediterranean a great wave overtook the poor Roman vessel in the waters southwest of Rhodes. We later heard that most of their party drowned, only two of their number having survived long enough for rescue by a Cilician merchant ship. Soon reports came in from all of Ptolemy's Aegean possessions that much of his shipping had been imperiled under similar circumstances. The priests of Poseidon claimed that their god had been displeased by the impudence displayed in the construction of the *Ptolemais Berenicia*. The evidence for this was clear, they said, by a wave that did not break enough against the moles of Pharos Island to stop it from causing the separation from the main superstructure of two of the hulls supporting the great platform.

Delegations from Syracuse, Crete and even a small outpost on the remote island of Antikythera arrived with stories of the destruction of their sea walls and the loss of great parts of their merchant vessels – though, it seems Antikythera's solid bedrock lessened the potential destruction on land. Ptolemy dispatched relief forces to his possessions and many friendly courts as well. The saddest news came from Rhodes, where the great Colossus, an Olympic-sized statue of Helios, was toppled into the bay. This statue had been erected by the Rhodians in honor of their victory against the marauding Antigonus Monopthalmus, one of many unworthy successors of Alexander. In this victory they had been assisted by Ptolemy I, a history that his grandson, Euergetes, was particularly proud of.

I have laid out an account of Ptolemy's mission of assistance to Rhodes, but Onesimus has deemed the passage an ink stain too far; in his words it is, "merely corroborative detail, intended to give artistic verisimilitude to an otherwise bald and unconvincing narrative." This passage he uses to great effect to critique the students and pompasts of his day, and it has been widely copied and circulated among the effete. It is of special importance to his Latin colleagues, who have already begun exporting our phrases back to Latium, where they will appropriate anything and call it their own. At the urging of Onesimus – or perhaps to placate him – I have removed my "bald and unconvincing narrative" and instead have turned to the words of young

Polybius, who, with the following passage on the earthquake at Rhodes, can hardly be indicted on either account.

(An) earthquake occurred at Rhodes, which overthrew the great Colossus and the larger part of the walls and dockyards. But the adroit policy of the Rhodians converted this misfortune into an opportunity; and under their skilful management, instead of adding to their embarrassments, it became the means of restoring their prosperity. So decisive in human affairs, public or private, is the difference between incapacity and good sense, between idle indifference and a close attention to business. Good fortune only damages the one, while disaster is but a means of recovery to the other. This was illustrated by the manner in which the Rhodians turned the misfortune that befell them to account. They enhanced its magnitude and importance by the prominence which they gave it, and the serious tone in which they spoke of it, as well by the mouth of their ambassadors as in the intercourse of private life; and they created thus such an effect upon other states, and especially upon the feelings of the kings, that they were not only overwhelmed with presents, but made the donors feel actually obliged for their acceptance of them.

Hiero and Gelon [of Syracuse], for instance, presented them with seventy-five talents of silver, part at once, and the rest at a very short interval, as a contribution towards the expenses of the gymnasium; gave them for religious purposes some silver cauldrons and their stands, and some water vessels; and in addition to this ten talents for their sacrifices, and ten more to attract new citizens: their intention being that the whole present should amount to a hundred talents. Not only so, but they gave immunity from customs to Rhodian merchants coming to their ports; and presented them besides with fifty catapults of three cubits length. In spite too of these large gifts, they regarded themselves as under an obligation to the Rhodians; and accordingly erected statues in the Deigma or Mart of Rhodes, representing the community of Rhodes crowned by that of Syracuse.

Then too Ptolemy offered them three hundred talents of silver; a million medimni of corn; ship timber for ten quinqueremes and ten triremes, consisting of forty thousand cubits of squared pine planking; a thousand talents of bronze coinage; three thousand talents of tow; three thousand pieces of sail cloth; three thousand talents for the repair of the Colossus; a hundred master builders with three hundred and fifty workmen, and fourteen talents yearly to pay their wages. Besides this he gave twelve thousand medimni of corn for their public games and sacrifices, and twenty thousand medimni for victualling ten triremes. The greater part of these goods was delivered at once, as well as a third of the whole of the money named.

In a similar spirit Antigonus offered ten thousand timbers, varying from sixteen to eight cubits in length, to be used as purlins; five thousand rafters seven cubits long; three thousand talents of iron; a thousand talents of pitch; a thousand amphorae of the same unboiled; and a hundred talents of silver besides. His queen, Chryseis, also gave a hundred thousand medimni of corn, and three thousand talents of lead. Again Seleucus, father of Antiochus, besides granting freedom from imports to Rhodians sailing to his dominions, and besides giving ten quinqueremes fully equipped, and two hundred thousand medimni of corn; gave also ten thousand cubits of timber, and a thousand talents of resin and hair.

Polybius, of course, was not there, and keeping true to his own aphorism that history is best received in truth only by those who had occasion to record it first hand, I must offer an addendum that the figures attributed to Ptolemy here are quite low. His magnanimity was unmatched in the response to the crisis at Rhodes, and indeed, it was his lead that was followed by the other princes about the Aegean.

It is also possible that the Seleucian contribution here is understated. Despite the formal frigidity between our two courts, the Master and Ptolemy rather liked Seleucus. He had been betrayed by his own brother and several satraps besides, and yet he had maintained his throne against harsher odds than other men had contended against and lost. Seleucus was, finally, well-conditioned to begin to attend to domestic affairs in his kingdom. In the interests of fostering peace and therefore commerce between the two kingdoms, Ptolemy sent an embassy to determine Seleucus' interest in a dynastic match between the young Seleucian prince, himself named Seleucus, and Euergetes' daughter Arsinoë. Unfortunately, this embassy arrived in Antioch to find a city in mourning.

Sometime during the progress of Ptolemy's ambassadors through Syria, Seleucus had fallen from his horse and died while hunting on the outskirts of Antioch. His son, Seleucus III had been declared after a brief flurry of intrigue at the Seleucian court, and it was Seleucus III who formally welcomed the Ptolemaic embassy. In Alexandria, Ptolemy sent instructions that the offer of dynastic joining, perhaps already known in Antioch, nevertheless be delayed in the interests of waiting to see how Persia would be managed by its new king.

After only two years, we learned from a dispatch that young Seleucus III Soter had been assassinated in Anatolia by members of his army while on a pyrrhic campaign against Attalus I of Pergamon. The court was in turmoil as many made claim on the throne. Once again, Persia was thrown into chaos.

And thus, the great threat posed first by Seleucus II Callinicus, his brother, the hawk, and potentially, by his eldest son Seleucus III seemed, at present, to have abated in the interests of the empire's struggle to reorganize a state shattered by the loss of three rulers within several years of each other.

Antiochus III, a younger brother of the slain king, emerged as inheritor of the Seleucid dynasty and was proclaimed in Babylon, in the heart of the ancient Persian Empire. The state he inherited was in such disarray that Ptolemy considered an offensive against Egypt unlikely. The young prince Ptolemy, in eager agreement and now more and more sharing in the duties of the government at his father's side, urged that more resources be placed at the disposal of court extravagance than the maintenance of northern strongholds.

The pharaoh, thus satisfied with the needs of the state, continued to indulge his Chief Librarian in the pursuit of loftier abstractions, and this approval was manifest in an unlimited budget for making real the dream of a device to help him map the primes.

It was in this happy pursuit that we spent several more years occupied at the Academy until one evening we were summoned from the workshop by a courier of the pharaoh's physician. We arrived at the royal apartments to see Ptolemy, only fifty years old, sickly and reclining on his bed, surrounded by friends and sycophants. His wife, Berenice, held his hands as a priest of Serapis rubbed oil on his forehead. At the foot of his bed, his children Ptolemy and Arsinoë chanted half-hearted incantations in time with a hierophant of the cult of the Eleusinian Mysteries. The king was, inexplicably, near death. He called for Eratosthenes and Archimedes, who both leaned in to have final words with their pharaoh and to kiss his ring in the style of Alexander. Just as unexpectedly as we were summoned to our pharaoh, Ptolemy III was summoned by Ptah, Ammon, Helios and Serapis to the land of the gods, and the kingdom now devolved upon the son, proclaimed before his father was removed from his bedchamber as Ptolemy IV, Pharaoh and King of Egypt, blessed of Ptah, light of life, true successor of Alexander.

METALOGUE
THE VERY NEAR FUTURE

22

ECSTASY. The rock wall swung silently away from him, the only sounds his own breathing and air flowing from the room before him into the passageway in which he was standing. He entered the small chamber and inhaled deeply the air made of atomic pieces of sulfur and remote stale antiquity. His flashlight puttered in the damp until several knocks against his palm brought it back to life. A dull beam illuminated before him a wall of patinated bronze. He saw one gear and then another. An entire wall was covered in interlocking cams and crankshafts. He realized he was standing before an even more intricate door, its outline faint but distinguishable beneath millennia of decay.

This door had a small panel set into its middle with the Indian numerals printed on 19 dials. He intuited that this next code would be the next Mersenne Prime. He knew it by heart, and entered it into the panel. With every turn of each successive dial he saw camshafts grudgingly moving around the door, like tumblers in a lock. He knew that only with the correct sequence in place would the door open. He was humbled by the advanced mathematics in front of him. If the code was indeed the next Mersenne Prime, it demonstrated knowledge of a number that was not known to history until 1883, and then only arrived at after months of calculation. He began to believe that the caverns and doors were laid out so that only someone seeking the truth of the primes, someone who knew them as he did - as the fundamental building blocks of mathematics – would be invited to pass through.

He remembered when he first discovered the magic of the primes. He had been at study in Father's library. Always solitary, he had trouble making friends with the other boys, more interested as they were in sports and girls than bookish pursuits. Knowing of his interest in codes, Father had given him a copy in English of the great Arab Polymath Al-Kindi's eighth century CE *A Manuscript on Deciphering Cryptographic Messages*. Even then, Father taught the simulacrum of religions in light of the true and complete perfection of mathematics. Al Kindi, a Muslim, Father, a Christian, labels of superstition and arbitrary division grafted on to and purposefully obscuring the One Truth known to all initiates since the ancients. He remembered a passage from the Muslim that has always stayed with him:

> One way to solve an encrypted message, if we know its language, is to find a different plaintext of the same language long enough to fill one sheet or so, and then we count the occurrences of each letter. We call the most frequently occurring letter the 'first', the next most occurring letter the 'second' the following most occurring letter the 'third', and so on, until we account for all the different letters in the plaintext sample. Then we look at the cipher text we want to solve and we also classify its symbols. We find the most occurring symbol and change it to the form of the 'first' letter of the plaintext sample, the next most common symbol is changed to the form of the 'second' letter, and the following most common symbol is changed to the form of the 'third' letter, and so on, until we account for all symbols of the cryptogram we want to solve.

It was then that Father began creating single–shift alphabetic ciphers for him to solve. Once, shortly before he left the Academy, he was given a code that he could not break. It would not yield to frequency analysis. Father promised him that if he could solve the problem he would be given a recommendation that would secure his initiation into the Society. He worked for days on the problem, and realizing the code must incorporate some other type of cipher, appealed to Father for help. Father gave no answer, save for a list of books on cryptography from Vigenère to Charles Babbage and from the Enigma code to Public Key Cryptography. The last of these, the work of several academicians in the 1970s, piqued his interest wholly.

Once he understood the encryption system Father had used, he decoded the brief message in several days, trying every key until the message yielded. Father had used a relatively small key, which allowed for brief factoring time. He still remembered delivering the plaintext to Father, ensuring his initiation. The message was, simply:

> An encryption method is presented with the novel property that publicly revealing an encryption key does not thereby reveal the corresponding decryption key.

He knew this passage from the important work on Public Key Cryptography done by Professors Rivest, Shamir and Adleman in the 1970s. Their paper had opened his eyes to the realization that mathematics was not only the pursuit of the purest of subjects, devoid entirely of the subjectivity which eluded him, but that a world culture entirely composed of worshipping the false idols of consumerism, nationalism and secrecy had been built upon a foundation bound up in the properties of these numbers.

He finished the sequence and checked it once more for errors. He had entered the ninth Mersenne Prime:

$$2\ 3\ 0\ 5\ 8\ 4\ 3\ 0\ 0\ 9\ 2\ 1\ 3\ 6\ 9\ 3\ 9\ 5\ 1$$

Pushing a small lever to the right of the bank of dials, he anticipated the same rush of air from the next cavern as he had experienced from the opening of the first door.

Nothing. He checked the dials again, making sure of their perfect alignment. He again pushed the small lever, this time with more force.

Nothing.

Again he pushed the lever, this time banging his fist against the small bronze object repeatedly.

This doesn't make sense. The Mersenne primes are the keys.

He stood in silence for several moments, again the only sound his quick breaths in the small space before him. Nineteen dials, the same as the number of digits in the next Mersenne Prime. No other number made sense.

What would the academicians of Alexandria, at the height of their power, use instead of a nineteen digit Mersenne? Perhaps a nineteen digit prime that wasn't in the Mersenne format? There had to be billions of nineteen digit primes. What special characteristics would the ancients find important enough in a nineteen digit prime to encode into a security system designed to allow only the enlightened to pass? He stared at the door, culling his mind for quotations, anything from the Chronicle and the sixth source.

Then, a curious thought entered his mind: the ancient maxim at the root of dozens of ancient fraternities of esotericism, indeed the teachings of The Mysteries themselves: "as above, so below." In this case, because the dials were horizontal, he concluded a horizontal not vertical mirror image might be the key. The answer might lie in a palindrome, a string of characters which read the same right to left as they do left to right. He knew from a study he had conducted long ago that there are probably millions of nineteen digit palindromic primes in base ten. He thought of two and entered the first in the bank of dials:

$$9\ 9\ 9\ 9\ 9\ 9\ 9\ 9\ 9\ 2\ 9\ 9\ 9\ 9\ 9\ 9\ 9\ 9\ 9$$

The lever remained unmoved. He tried the second:

$$1\ 0\ 0\ 0\ 0\ 0\ 0\ 0\ 0\ 8\ 0\ 0\ 0\ 0\ 0\ 0\ 0\ 0\ 1$$

Again, the lever would not yield. If the dials needed a specific palindromic prime, he hadn't come across any clues that might suggest which of the millions of nineteen digit palindromic primes it might be. In desperation he set the dial again, back to the original Mersenne:

$$2\ 3\ 0\ 5\ 8\ 4\ 3\ 0\ 0\ 9\ 2\ 1\ 3\ 6\ 9\ 3\ 9\ 5\ 1$$

Again he thought to himself, *what nineteen digit number would the academicians at Alexandria use? With the device spinning out numbers that would not be known for two millennia in the future, what nineteen digit number would the academicians at the Musaeum—*

He smiled at his mistake. He moved the two farthest right dials several places and pushed the lever again. This time he had remembered to honor the nine Muses for which the Musaeum of Alexandria, *the Temple of the Muses,* had been named. With slight pressure applied to the lever, the door swung effortlessly away from him, his torch throwing the first rays of light into a cavern that stretched into darkness. His was the first light the room had seen in more than two thousand years.

» Book IV «

KNOW YE NOT
THAT YE ARE GODS

Philo was a parasite of Agathocles, the son of Oenanthe, and the friend of
king Philopator. Many statues of Cleino, the girl who acted as cupbearer to
Ptolemy Philadelphus, were set up at Alexandria, draped in a single tunic and
holding a cup in the hands. And are not the most splendid houses there those
which go by the names of Murtium, Mnesis, and Pothine? And yet Mnesis
was a flute-girl, as was Pothine, and Murtium was a public prostitute. And
was not Agathoclea, the mistress of King Ptolemy Philopator, an influential
personage—she who was the ruin of the whole kingdom?

The question may be asked, perhaps, why I have chosen to give a sketch of
Egyptian history here, going back a considerable period; whereas, in the case
of the rest of my history, I have recorded the events of each year in the several
countries side by side? I have done so for the following reasons: Ptolemy
Philopator, of whom I am now speaking, after the conclusion of the war for
the possession of Coele-Syria, abandoned all noble pursuits and gave himself
up to the life of debauchery which I have just described. But late in life he was
compelled by circumstances to engage in the war I have mentioned, which,
over and above the mutual cruelty and lawlessness with which it was
conducted, witnessed neither pitched battle, sea fight, siege, or anything else
worth recording. I thought, therefore, that it would be easier for me as a
writer, and more intelligible to my readers, if I did not touch upon everything
year by year as it occurred, or give a full account of transactions which were
insignificant and undeserving of serious attention; but should once and for all
sum up and describe the character and policy of this king.

—POLYBIUS, Histories

Everything is more beautiful because we're doomed.
You will never be lovelier than you are now.
We will never be here again.

—HOMER, The Iliad

23

The singular god of the Hebrews has rather an insidious way of creating within his sayings the promise of deliverance from a particular pestilence, period of civil unrest or despised overlordship in the person of a messiah. It is said that Cyrus the Great of Persia was one such messiah, and that Alexander himself was also foretold in the books of their covenant. I find this propensity to tip one's hand to another who would claim messianic status quite unbecoming. That is why the gods of Hellas and of ancient Egypt fit so well together. They leave no crack in the façade of belief that might be exploited, no toehold for the demagogue in the veneer of popular religion. If one wants to subvert the religious order for one's own gain, one must be proclaimed a god at Siwa, or else rule in infamy at the head of one hundred thousand men. Onesimus asks what such ruminations have to do with the years before our great clash with Antiochus III, and I have no answer except to claim an oblique association: I do believe a question of literary exegesis gave us a small head start in our preparations for the invasion of the Seleucian King.

I remember back to our days after the death of Ptolemy III Euergetes, spent in deep discussion and experimentation at the Academy. The library's collections were at their height, and much of Ptolemy III's bequests remained for disbursement amongst the scholars. The Master was then only in his mid-fifties and I was not yet twenty-six. The new Pharaoh Ptolemy IV was a capricious youth of twenty-three.

Inquiry at the Academy took on many topics. Archimedes worked out more and more mathematical proofs for planes, circles and vivisections of space. Eratosthenes further refined his geographic measurements and continued work on the device's power to illuminate the mysteries of the indissoluble numbers. Aristophanes continued his literary achievements. Academicians who were followers of the Canaanite religions continued to discuss among themselves and openly and happily with followers of the Hellenic ways their translation of their holy books. On this last topic there was great debate. The content of the translation was of little interest to any but the Jews, their predecessor translators having returned to Jerusalem or died. The process of divine writing, however, was spiritedly contested and debate raged at the Academy about the manner in which the Hebrew scholars had been given divine guidance to translate their scriptures into Greek.

Some believed the spirit of their god moved their pens or touched their minds, so that they wrote and thought in unison. This was my least favorite interpretation. A true god does not force the pen or subvert the mind. He does not have to. I favored another, minority opinion that happened also to be the Master's, though it appealed to me upon hearing it before I knew of the Master's opinion. It was believed by some of us that the Jews, having shared a common experience, common mysticism, common practices, that these would create a force within them; that all the false translations and alternative translations would be filtered through this force and meet their free will, so that only the correct interpretations rose to revelation by the legitimacy of their inherent confluence with those of shared communion. Onesimus again rolls his eyes at this mysticism, but I find this infinitely more satisfying than that an actual divine presence authored the books, for this circumvents the will and reason of man.

Nevertheless, it was this debate which sparked our interest in messianism, foreign as the idea of an intermediary is to the Hellenic way of appealing directly to the divine, which drew the attention of the Master when the serendipitous arrival of such an intermediary was mentioned in one of the Seleucian dispatches. Antiochus, gathering together the fragments of his empire, was not yet prepared to move on Coele-Syria. He instead concentrated his forces on securing the old borders of his father's kingdom. In the while, he endeavored to create a messiah for the Jews that would cause an uprising favorable to Seleucian influence.

The dispatch mentioned by name a certain Mattathias, who Antiochus believed would greet a messiah most credulously. Mattathias' history is well known to the Academy now, and in his own hand (Onesimus has located the document) he describes his lineage:

267 | E P O C H

"Arising from a rural priestly family from Modi'in, like all fit priests, I served in the Temple in Jerusalem. I am the son of Yohannan, grandson of Simeon, the Hasmonean, and great-grandson of Asmon or Hasmonaeus, a Levite of the lineage of Joarib for being the 5th grandson of Idaiah, son of Joarib and grandson of Jachin, in turn a descendant of Phinehas, 3rd High Priest of Israel."

This rural yet impressive lineage must have appealed to Antiochus. As a lineal descendant of Phinehas, the high priest of Israel during the Jewish festival of Exodus, Mattathias was ceremoniously placed to remind the inhabitants of Coele-Syria of the mythical oppression meted out by the pharaohs of Egypt. Even the Jews of Alexandria, of their own volition and who have studied all extant texts on the subject, understand that this mass migration could not have happened, though the relations between their ancestors and the native pharaohs was not ideal. Yet, the symbolism proved irresistible, and Antiochus cleverly outfitted a Seleucian Jew with all the knowledge a messiah would need and sent him, in the night, into Jerusalem.

This caused a minor sensation as this false-messiah did gain several followers. When shown to Mattathias, he was decried a fraud. Though the Jews have a splendid history and a talent for mythmaking that rivals in some passages even Homer, the Jews seem not able to help themselves creating opportunities for charlatanry. The messiah, expertly schooled in the books of law, was able to justly argue that it was written that the true messiah would be denied, thus affirming his messianic mission.

The messiah was eventually put to death by Jewish law and on the orders of Theodotus. The execution had some effect when a small legion of formerly content subjects of Ptolemy attempted a move on the governor's house, that the murder of their messiah might be avenged. This small insurrection was easily put down, but a new spirit of resentment began to rise among the population.

With this mention of native dissatisfaction and complementary Greek disquietude, Onesimus has reminded me to finalize my appraisal of Amasis, and this is as good a time as any to finish my narrative of his unhappy life.

A year before Euergetes died, he had invited Cleomenes the reformer to seek asylum in Alexandria. Cleomenes had pressed his hand with the Achaean

League, and found himself, after several victories and reversals, at a disadvantage near Sellasia, north of Sparta. There, Antigonus III, the Achaean league and the Illyrians all made a show of the destruction of Cleomenes, so that his only recourse was to retreat and leave Sparta to the forces of occupation.

Other commanders may have regrouped, but it is a peculiarity of that race that the occupation of their city completely dejected them, in a manner unlike the Athenians, who had abandoned their city during the second Persian invasion two hundred years earlier. Indeed, Themistocles, whom history has recorded as a man of daring élan, was persuaded in this course not least because he wished to show his then-allies, the Spartans, that Athens would do all that was required for the defense of Attica, including surrendering their own homeland in a temporary measure to forestall permanent disaster. Whether Cleomenes considered this irony I cannot say. He fled with a small party south, into the Aegean and into the waiting arms of Ptolemy, who wished to show that Egypt was above such squabbles in his decision to offer asylum.

Cleomenes was only two years in Alexandria when he realized that the new sovereign, Ptolemy IV had no interest in helping him regain the Spartan throne. His speeches in the agora and the Soma turned so seditious that he was soon placed under house arrest. A man of cunning, he evaded his guards and ran to old Rhakotis, where he believed he might find comrades willing to upset the court of the young king. I was there, with the Master, when news reached the palace of this uprising. When it was reported by a page that Cleomenes had barricaded himself in the Egyptian quarter with about a dozen malcontents, I feared the worst, and rushed to the docks to confirm what I knew in my heart to be true.

There I found nearly one hundred of Ptolemy IV's household guard butchering this small group. Through the melee I could make out the figure of brave Cleomenes, falling on his sword – though some later claimed that he had poisoned himself, I know what I saw – and beside him, Amasis, whose gaze I met as a spear passed through his neck. I begged permission to pay honor to his body, and this I was granted as a privilege of my position at the Academy. Thus ended my friendship with Amasis, who died, as perhaps he knew he always would, at the hand of a Ptolemy defending, as might be a surprise to him in his youth, the misplaced ideals of a deposed Spartan king.

My hand trembles as I remember Amasis, who was both friend and foe and always a countryman. But what does it mean to call an Egyptian a countryman when I am now a Greek? These ambiguities are perhaps left to the philosophers, like old Panthoides. Like him, I find myself now hoping that something might be shown to be possible which can never be true.

Dear Onesimus reminds me to continue the narrative of the march to war with Antiochus, as if he feels that the point of my entire memoir is to record the military exploits of the Ptolemaic state. As I have made clear throughout my dictation, my remembrances are of the Master and the way of life that pervaded the Academy, and it is against that backdrop that I have endeavored to explain those forces within the government that helped or hindered the cause of the Alexandrian Project. I have explained how it was that the Master came to know Archimedes and how both of them, while called to serve the machinery of state, forged a lasting intellectual partnership among the brightest lights of our age. I have explained how the Master was first taken with mechanization as an aid to military intelligence, yet how that mechanization was turned to the use of the mind for probing vast numerical abstractions. Intellectual life and statecraft are, sadly, intertwined, and it is with sadness that I admit their interconnectedness, but as I now remind Onesimus, the story of one would suffer without the telling of the other.

Doubtless gifted historians with the candor of Thucydides and the wit of Callixinus will record the time of the Ptolemies up to now, but what will they record? The gleaming armor and courageous deeds in a thousand clashes between Alexander's successors? Will they record the vast temples to Serapis and Poseidon? Will they record the effects (if not the causes) of the miraculous moving statuary? The talking goddesses? The flying chariots? Inventions all of them born of the genius of the Academy! No, those narratives of virtue and sacrifice will echo through the ages as we have received Homer, and no one will be alive who knew how far the mind had triumphed over the force of arms, how mere thoughts created a Pan-Hellenic kingdom in the ether, anchored in far corners between all men of careful inquiry in every nation. That is the purpose of this memoir, and to record it faithfully, I must revisit the conditions of the court of Ptolemy IV, in the dark days before the battle of Raphia changed everything forever.

I was in attendance on the new Pharaoh many times with the Master, but two occasions speak well enough to Ptolemy IV's character. One was a brief matter. In the course of an infamous evening of drink and wanton self-indulgence, the young pharaoh watched as a slave set a vessel of wine too near the edge of a table. Chastising the slave with foul words, the slave made the impertinent gesture of speaking back, attempting an explanation that he had yet to have occasion to rest after attending to the pharaoh's twenty-four hour orgy and binging. Many a slave had been executed for less in barbarous states, but at the center of the world, in enlightened Alexandria, it was shocking even to the palace courtiers to witness the method of punishment ordered by Ptolemy IV. The pharaoh gave orders that the slave be bound with long ropes to the masts of four of his ships. Barely surviving being hoisted above the bay of Alexandria, the slave writhed in the air until the pharaoh could muster all of his household retinue that day in attendance in the great city. Golden chaises were set out for the pharaoh and his favorites Agathocles and Agathoclea, and all in the palace grounds were ordered to bear witness to the slave's impudence. Because we had already been in attendance at a poetry reading in the gardens, The Master and I had little choice but to comply with the summons of the Blessed of Ptah and Osiris.

Once his retinue had been assembled, Ptolemy IV Philopator, in Alexandrine wig and painted face, asked his favorites Agathocles and Agathoclea to flip a coin. If it came up one way then the man's life would be spared and a great bacchanal would be held during which the pharaoh would serve wine to twelve favorites of the condemned slave's and the slave himself. The slaves would be fitted with golden robes and at the end of the bacchanal the thirteen would be set free. If, on the other hand, the coin came up another way, Agathocles and his sister were each to choose six slaves, three men and three women, the most handsome and beautiful they could find. This dozen would be sent to the lowest order of army barracks so that the soldiers might have their way with them. Afterward, the twelve would be subject to an infamous arranged 'marriage' and the slave now dangling above the waters off the coast of Alexandria would be drowned in the waters beneath him.

The coin was flipped. Gleefully, Philopator gave the order that the ships should be rowed to opposite points in the bay. The ships weren't long in motion before the ropes drew taught and the man's joints gave way. His body fell into one of the trireme's masts as the other three ropes crashed, bloodied and with limbs attached, onto the other decks. Twelve slaves of great beauty were paraded before the pharaoh and his retinue and were accepted greedily by the captain of the guard who marched them, naked and to roaring applause, toward the palace barracks. It was said later than Agathoclea had the coin drilled and a chain and pivot put through it so she might wear it as a charm around her neck, so enamored of the face of her lover the pharaoh that she might see it on either side.

Another such example of the new king's excesses showcased not only the depravity of his character but caused political ramifications throughout the empire. The intelligence foretold of a massing of Antiochus' supplies north of Coele-Syria. It was decided by Sosibius, the Master and the late Euergetes' queen, Berenice, that Antiochus meant to strike the northern strongholds within the next two years. This intelligence was passed to the young pharaoh that he might order the appropriate military preparations. Philopator held the view that to support such an undertaking would require the dismissal of nearly half of his palace staff and the curtailing of his nightly entertainments. The young Ptolemy ordered that no preparations should be made that might provoke Antiochus, and instead ordered a mission to shower his northern adversary with gifts so that he might be met as a "brother" of Egypt rather than her rival.

When this mission, which included war elephants, chests heavy with hundreds of talents of silver and original scrolls from the library, stopped for respite in Judea, Theodotus ordered that the cortege remain under his supervision as he could not guarantee the safety of its travel through hostile territory. The mission was not yet two days north of Raphia when a small advance force under the command of one of Antiochus' generals moved on that arid plain. Theodotus successfully put down the incursion and a subsequent small riot that occurred while the governor was out on campaign. The riot was later thought to be planned by Antiochus himself. When Theodotus sent word back to Alexandria that he had saved the lives of those in the mission and protected the fortifications near Raphia, Ptolemy IV demanded an instant audience with him.

The Master having become, reluctantly, a fixture at court, he and I were there during that spectacularly unusual audience. Theodotus, having left the vicinity of Raphia in the care of a trusted lieutenant, arrived with small splendor and great dignity at the gates of the palace. He left most of his small retinue outside and appeared before the pharaoh in modest uniform with only two attendants. Ptolemy appeared through his customary column of incense attended by no less than 72 boys and 72 girls, painted all of them in the most horrifically gaudy of the old Greek ways. Ptolemy had outfitted his reception chamber with statuary of himself and his father, all clothed in the accoutrement of Greek warrior-gods, with budding lips, chiseled features and the flowing hair of Alexander.

Theodotus contemplated one of these idols with disgust as the Pharaoh ascended several steps to a throne set upon a dais made of cedar covered in gold.

Several moments of silence passed between them before Theodotus stepped forward and dipped to one knee. Staring the pharaoh in the eye, he said nonchalantly, "the enemy is repulsed, for now, great lord."

"And who is the enemy, governor?" said Ptolemy.

"Antiochus, great king."

"Did you not receive, shelter and detain a peace mission to Antiochus? Did you not refuse to allow my duly appointed representatives to journey with gifts to Antiochus?"

"I sheltered them sir, and I protected them. The area to the north is not safe. It has not been safe. Even as far south as Jerusalem, instability is rampant throughout the countryside. Factions within the city grumble with insurrection. As quickly as they are discovered, they are punished, severely. Still-"

"So, Theodotus, you decided on a whim what the will of your pharaoh might be? You allowed yourself the luxury of interpreting my wishes?"

"Pharaoh, I did only what was in your interests and what was right for the security of your kingdom."

The conversation went on for some time, until Ptolemy relented: "Well, your heart was true, but I do wish you would have consulted me first. I would like to honor my great general at a feast this evening in your honor."

Theodotus nodded his agreement and offered another, longer platitude, I believe invoking Osiris and Dionysus.

Onesimus suggests that I wandered beyond the original point that I had set out to describe another of Ptolemy's excesses. He asks now if a few slaves, a relatively small retinue and a few chests full of silver are really the threads of excess from which to weave a tapestry of depravity for a pharaoh of the Great Nile. I ask him to be patient, as that was only a minor point to the story. The pharaoh did indeed send a delegation to negotiate peace and amity between himself and Antiochus. Theodotus did repel a small force and quell a minor uprising. He did travel to Alexandria to receive not approbation, as he had expected, but resentment from his prince. These are undoubted facts, attested to numerous times in other sources with which I will fill appendices in this narrative's final form. The great excess was to come, during a week of feasting in which not even the gods on Olympus would have been comfortable taking part.

In the course of one of these evenings, seeing that Theodotus was unmoved by the spectacle, Ptolemy devised an infamous torture of a slave who had been drunk while in attendance on the governor. Too terrible to relate in its entirety, it is enough to say that a stake was driven into an orifice of the body so as not to cause immediate death, but to ensure a lingering, painful existence for several days, in this instance on public display.

I have already spoken of Ptolemy's thirst for sexual humiliation. His 'marriage' rituals were notorious. His keeping of boys in the retinue was not unusual in the Greek tradition, though it is little known among the natives, as we must content ourselves with the creation of more natives in the stead of our sexual appetites, whatever they may be. It is said that the Jews have injunctions against the use of boys by priests, and this also seems consistent with the interests of a minority population. Having by then taken a vow of celibacy, as was the custom among many at the Academy, I haven't much thought of it either way since my experience with the native daughters of Jerusalem.

The pharaoh was very fond of his arranged 'marriages' and never more so than when he might arrange the marriage of siblings, probably because he resented having recently taken his grizzly-faced and plump sister Arsinoë as his consort in the Egyptian way. In honor of the general's stay in Alexandria, he put on lavish entertainments after feasting which Theodotus often found excuses to avoid. It seems the pharaoh became more and more frustrated with the piety of his guest and insisted that he enjoy all the entertainments planned for the eve of Theodotus' return to his post in Judea. Theodotus, then a handsome man not yet fifty, caught the eye of Agathoclea, who later contrived with the pharaoh to form a plot of seduction. The pharaoh arranged some pretext that Theodotus attend him privately in a receiving chamber. When Theodotus arrived he found Agathoclea in the midst of ecstasy with her brother while the pharaoh presided in a ceremony of his own design. Theodotus, taking steps to leave the chamber, was commanded by Ptolemy to join them. Refusing, Theodotus could only standby while the Pharaoh made love both to Agathocles and Agathoclea and then the two with each other.

The next morning, hearing of the ordeal, Sosibius and the Master begged an audience with Theodotus in which they explained that the pharaoh was still young, and that they would take his religious instruction upon themselves, that he yet might not sway from the true gods into excesses of hedonism and barbarism. Theodotus was not to worry, they said. The government of the kingdom was in capable hands. It was this impression of the decadence and disharmony of court that Theodotus would take back with him to his command in Raphia.

Onesimus now asks me why Theodotus should have had such a strong reaction. I cannot say for sure. His personal philosophy was never made widely known, though it was rumored that he was an Epicurean and had taken a vow of chastity. I believe it may have been this predilection for moderation coupled with the admiration he had had for Ptolemy III and the spirit of the warrior Alexander that he felt had been corrupted in the decadence of the pharaoh's court. Whatever the cause, the incident would have consequences unimaginable during the festivities of his stay in Alexandria.

With Theodotus now secured again in Coele-Syria and ordered to send the peace mission north, Ptolemy continued his lavish lifestyle. It was during this period, I believe, when he perfected his method of executing slaves who had displeased him. He was not the first Ptolemy to torture enemies, and indeed the Master bore witness to a terrible execution ordered by Ptolemy III. A slave had stolen from the royal kitchens and so that he should be made an example of, Ptolemy had his stomach torn from him and hung above the doorway to the pantries until it had been entirely carried away by birds. Still these were brutal necessities of state, and the Master never presented evidence that Ptolemy III personally enjoyed these cruelties.

The actual circumstances of the victims' offenses escape me, though most likely the insults were unintended and slight. Ptolemy ordered the arrest of three men who had displeased him and had three small tubs constructed that completely enclosed the body while making allowance for the head of the condemned to protrude through an opening in the top. The box was fitted with a device that would squeeze the neck of the condemned if he refused to comply with an order. Onto the faces of each victim were placed rancid milk and honey so that eventually flies began to circle and overwhelm them. The victim would then be commanded to eat. If the victim refused, the screw was tightened against his neck until he relented. After several days, the victim would begin to swim in his own excrement, which attracted flies and then maggots at an increasing rate. It was said that one victim broke, by several hours, the record of 15 days before being literally eaten alive in a tub of maggots swimming through his own filth. The message was clear to anyone who would disobey Ptolemy that he wished to rule through fear rather than love, and this attitude of fear pervaded the court.

Onesimus now asks why the Master did not intervene. In truth, he did pray to the gods for deliverance, and redoubled his efforts at the Academy that he might finish the great Alexandrian Project before Ptolemy's rapacious eye turned to the generous stipend gifted the Academy by his father. I can only say that the Master began his own preparations for the security of the fruits of the Academy cloistered among his fellows, initiates all in the Mysteries with which even Ptolemy was not acquainted.

Another incident highlights the Master's strong commitment to the Academy in the teeth of whatever ministerial pressure was applied upon it. The Master, shortly after the accession of Ptolemy IV and at the instigation of Archimedes and Aristophanes, who still remained close to young Ptolemy, arranged a demonstration of the ballistic devices so proudly displayed at his father's Ptolemaia. Again, a floating target was positioned in the sea, and once an initial sighting had been taken by Archimedes, Eratosthenes encoded a small series of gears and camshafts in a particular arrangement to account for the angle and distance between each ballista and its target. The young pharaoh was invited to give the order to fire personally, which he did on all three devices. All hit the target squarely.

Amazing for any age, the effect of the device was, however, diminished slightly by Ptolemy's previous viewing of it so that its effect was more matter-of-fact than it would otherwise have been to a fresh audience. Anticipating this, Eratosthenes gave orders that the ballistae should be moved anywhere the pharaoh wished. The pharaoh ordered two moved a half stadia in both direction, and one he ordered ported up the sheer face of the Lochias promontory. Assembled again for the demonstration, and convinced by their continual attendance on him that Archimedes and Eratosthenes had not re-calibrated the devices, the pharaoh once again gave orders for the devices to launch at their target. Again, all three hit their intended mark perfectly. Delighted, Ptolemy ordered that all of his artillery be retrofitted with such devices and that such resources as the Master required by placed at his disposal for that purpose alone.

The intelligence continued to flow from the pharaoh's couriers to the Master's chamber, where his device unlocked the secrets of the agents of Antiochus. The Master reported to Sosibius and the pharaoh that it was all but certain that an invasion from the north would take place within the year. The Master pleaded with Sosibius, who maneuvered with Agathocles and Agathoclea to try, out of self-preservation, to convince the pharaoh to mount a defense. The treasury was so depleted since the time of Ptolemy III that Sosibius could not raise a sufficient force of Greeks, and so devised a plan whereby he would raise an army of Egyptian mercenaries.

It may be of value to note that the Master was personally committed to this policy. His belief, as I have mentioned, was that divisions between the races were arbitrary, and this he shared with Alexander - that merit might be the sole basis for distinction and elevation within the apparatus of the state. It was his hope that such inclusion of a majority subclass in the defense of their homeland would not only bind them together as a class with acknowledged rights, but that this action would raise the esteem with which they were held by cultivated civilization everywhere while imbuing these men with a sense of ownership in the affairs of their state. Eratosthenes admitted that such a strategy might fail to meet these goals by emboldening the underclass to establish more regional strengths, but it remained his hope that service in the pharaoh's army might recommend to the natives a more sympathetic view of the pharaoh's realm and serve as a bulwark against bad government.

Agathoclea and Agathocles were soundly against the idea, recommending instead the hiring of Carthaginian mercenaries, who were natural allies in their distrust of Rome, and Nabatean nomadic warriors, who would have no ambition to threaten the administration of a permanent state. Though more expensive than arming natives, it was a less costly option than raising several units of Greek cavalry and phalanx, and once successful in the repulsion of Antiochus, could be dismissed with ease without displacing the Greek gentry. Berenice, still a minor force on the young pharaoh, advised against any action. Speaking in private of her son's unfitness to command, she lamented the day he might take the field under any configuration of troops.

The Master continued to work on Sosibius, and Sosibius, along with the incestuous favorites, on the pharaoh until a consensus emerged that a native force must be raised, led by experienced Greek aristocrats. It was also decided that Eratosthenes and Archimedes, the two greatest mechanical minds in the kingdom, would join the force on a march north to confront Antiochus.

The deliberations continued for some time, all the while the Pharaoh continued his orgiastic religious practices. In fact, one might marvel that a force was mustered at all if it weren't for ghastly intelligence that came not from the Master's device but through the front door of the palace itself. A gift had been sent from Theodotus for the eyes of the Pharaoh only. Having received the courier, Ptolemy, without dismissing his retinue, sat on his dais as the nervous courier placed his large parcel on a table before him. Ptolemy commanded that it be opened and was delivered the horror of seeing the heads of the garrison commanders of Ptolemais and Tyre, his northern-most strongholds south of Antiochus's control. An included note said simply that these towns were now in the hands of Antiochus, and that he, Theodotus, had been given nothing for his change of loyalty except the dignity of serving a worthy prince.

It took only weeks for the Pharaoh to summon a force of seventy thousand infantry made up almost exclusively of native Egyptians, five thousand cavalry of Greek and educated Egyptian composition, and seventy-three war elephants procured from Nubia.

Onesimus laughs at the mention of the elephants, and, to be fair, they made an awkward sight. One cannot fully appreciate the complexity of native responses to their Greek overlords if one does not understand the bemusement with which the people of the ancient Nile regard the wild schemes of their masters. To see the smiles on the faces of the people as immense Nubian elephants floated up-river, teetering in tiny fishing boats, is to see a glimpse of the perpetual native astonishment that the land of the Old Dynasties should have fallen to such a race.

With these numbers Ptolemy left Alexandria for the hard road to Coele Syria, attended to personally by a retinue of thousands including academicians, map makers, musicians, sorcerers and delegations of priests from all the important cults, including a very harried delegation from the cult of Horus in Syene, where the Master had once secured an important measurement for the size of the sphere on which two armies now marched to lay claim to a small fraction of its surface. The Pharaoh was protected by a force of five hundred Hypaspists acting as royal bodyguards, which he broke up into squadrons captained by his favorites. Unconventionally, Agathoclea was given the uniform of a man and commanded one of these squadrons herself. The Queen and the pharaoh's sister, the unattractive but hardy Arsinoë, was given a regiment of cavalry for her own command, and rode and tented with her men.

It was known only after the contingent had left Alexandria for Naucratis on the long march to Coele-Syria that Sosibius had gained the support of the king's favorites by agreeing to several accommodations. The first of these accommodations was made plain in the first overnight encampment at Naucratis on the Nile. A courier reached the royal cortege with news that the King's mother, Berenice, tiresome in her resistance to the military action and so left behind in Alexandria, was found dead in her royal apartments.

Eratosthenes came to understand that a condition of the support of Agathocles and Agathoclea for raising an army was the removal by Sosibius of the influence of the dowager on the new administration. With the full knowledge of Sosibius, the pair had contracted for Berenice to be poisoned at the first opportunity, access to her person made all the easier by the absence of her usual guard now secunded to the force at Naucratis. Ptolemy, who seemed curiously unaffected, issued a lukewarm and maladroit statement of public mourning. He further invited curiosity when he ordered that the day of his mother's funerary procession be held in abeyance until his glorious return to Alexandria from the field of battle.

The Master, Archimedes and others from the Academy within the retinue realized just how uneasy a peace they had achieved with Sosibius and the pharaoh's favorites. They were unavoidably allied with a king, who had demonstrated only martial appreciation of the Academy, and his chief minister, who had shown himself capable of putting to death the dowager queen of Egypt. They had argued for inclusion of native Egyptians so that they might take pride in their polity, only to be shown the example of a trusted Greek aristocrat in Theodotus who so despised his own king he delivered an entire region in bloodless tribute to the sworn enemy of his prince.

The Master was particularly moved to anxiety, for he feared that his life's work, not least of which his processes for mechanized calculation of the primes, would be forever stalled in the face of mounting demands on his ingenuity for the production of weapons for the Ptolemaic state. It was then that the Master began in earnest his revivification of the cult of the Mysteries. He sent for adherents from all over Alexander's former empire and many lands besides, and these applicants he began to catalog as potential initiates in a more clandestine ritual, where knowledge and sacrament would join into a mystic whole that was impenetrable from the outside save for an outward appearance of pious devotion to the ancient Eleusinian order.

The academicians, with no knowledge of the other secret concessions made in the highest ranks of government, sullenly reassured themselves of their own necessity, content with their part in the presence within the armaments of the cortege of weapons of unprecedented accuracy and destructive power. It was only after the glorious battle of Raphia, in which weapons of genius created by princes of the mind waged war against an enemy rooted to the already antiquated world of Alexander, would the Academy discover the other of the compromises leading to the mobilization in Coele-Syria.

At the time, in the third year of the reign of Ptolemy IV, we knew nothing of what was to befall Egypt and the center of learning the great Alexander had established, its once supreme authority over the hearts of men or its former love of unfettered discovery. We set out with a force of nearly one hundred thousand warriors, cooks, auxiliaries, priests, whores, guides, tailors, weavers, musicians and academicians, all of us in blissful ignorance of what this most unusual, disparate force would portend for life after the engagement. At the head of it all, on an elevated chaise drawn by forty native Egyptian slaves, young Ptolemy IV Philopator, Pharaoh of Egypt and Light of The Nile, Blessed of Horus, Ptah, Osiris and Serapis, drunkenly amused himself with his incestuous favorites.

METALOGUE
THE VERY NEAR FUTURE

24

The more universal the work, the more divine it becomes. Francisco DiScenna sat beneath a portrait of St. Ignatius in Father's office. He had been at the Jesuit-affiliated St. Mary's School for Boys since he was nine years old. He was commended to the school by a conscientious social worker who had noticed in him a mature intellect that slowly resurrected then quickly submerged beneath the trauma of a cycle of some decent, most sub-par transitory families. His mother died of a heroin overdose shortly after he was born. He had never known his father.

Now a young man of sixteen, Francisco had shown great promise as a mathematician. He had worked through all the texts the older boys hated. He had surpassed his teachers and had won several regional mathematics competitions. He manipulated numbers in his head as easily as his fellow students navigated the social situations he was so keen to avoid. He saw numbers in architecture, in the weather, in news reports, in geography, in music, and most distressingly, in human interactions, which seemed routine enough for analysis, but which, like Heisenberg's Uncertainty Principle, returned wildly unexpected results when he himself became a variable.

Father had nurtured Francisco's intellect and his peculiar gift for numbers by setting him upon the most popular unsolved problem in Mathematics, a problem that remained unsolved for three and a half centuries since it was stated as a conjecture by a seventeenth century French mathematician. The eponymous Last Theorem of Pierre de Fermat became an obsession for the young Francisco. Fermat, like other mathematicians of the enlightenment, had become fascinated with the equations of antiquity. Every grade school student soon becomes acquainted with the famous theorem of Pythagoras that states that the square of the hypotenuse is equal to the sum of the squares of the other two sides. Diophantus of Alexandria, writing seven centuries after Pythagoras, placed theorems of this type into a special category and developed symbols, precursors to modern arithmetical notation, to represent them. While reading Diophantus' *Arithmetica*, Fermat is said to have pondered a conjecture that no three positive integers a, b, and c can satisfy the equation $a^n + b^n = c^n$ for any integer value of n greater than 2. Fermat cryptically claimed to have found an elegant proof, writing in his copy of the *Arithmetica* that the margin was too small to contain it. Fermat's proof, if it existed, was never found, and three hundred years had passed before Francisco took up the problem.

His passion for its solution consumed him. He had written a paper widely circulated in the mathematics community as a child prodigy's attempt at outlining a possible method for a proof, only to be devastated when it was shown to have an obvious flaw. Francisco sank into a serious depression when, later that year, another of his approaches was returned to him from a mathematics journal with a form-letter response. Though Francisco's proof was lacking, his talent was conspicuous. Two years before his eighteenth birthday, he had already received offers of full scholarships to several university mathematics departments. He awaited Father's guidance, and as a minor, a sequence of formal permissions.

"I have never wrestled more with those words of St. Ignatius," said Father. "'The more universal the work, the more divine it becomes.' Francisco, you have a great gift, a rare genius. Everyone sees it. You know it yourself. Is it your wish to leave us and enter the world?"

Francisco nodded and mumbled that it was his wish to pursue mathematics, to learn all that was known about the perfection he saw as the infallible laws governing the universe. *The more universal the work, the more divine it becomes.*

"Francisco, most here will go on to live secular lives. I believe you have a solid foundation as a Christian. God walks with you in whatever you do. But I also see potential in you for great things in the service of Christ."

Francisco again nodded agreement. He honored his mentor and shared his passion for mathematics but not his instinct for parochialism.

"Father, I walk with Christ, but I feel a calling to study. When I am with my numbers, I am with the Lord."

Father smiled. Mathematics was a driving force in his own life. He had tried to share his passion with Francisco, shared books, shared problems, treated Francisco as an adult, as his equal. He stood up to look out the window into the street below. After some time he said, "Then Francisco, let His will be done. The choice is yours, but I will make a recommendation. I have made inquiries. There is a good man, a good Christian man, who can be a help to you. I have contacted him. He was already aware of your Fermat paper. I told him how distressed you were that your proof was found to have an error. He sees your talent, and he agrees with me that it should be nurtured. There is much more to learn, and he will teach you. He is chairman of a leading mathematics department. If you're ready, I'll tell him you're interested."

"I am very interested, Father," said Francisco DiScenna as he shook father's hand and walked out of the office, his back to a searching St. Ignatius.

❖

The Stanford Campus was like nothing he had ever seen. The warm climate, the carefree students playing football on manicured lawns, the freedom and worldliness a stark contrast to the relative discipline and structure of St. Mary's. His advisor was a generous man, his colleagues were a welcome oasis of reserved rationality in a socially unpredictable world. He acquainted himself with several of them. One in particular he became fond of and they spent all their time together outside the classroom talking about the unsolved problems of mathematics.

Where other students had posters of sports stars and naked women in their rooms, this friend had a poster of Hilbert's twenty three unsolved problems of mathematics. Francisco had known of the famous German mathematician's call to arms. In a speech at the 1900 Paris Conference of the International Congress of Mathematicians, David Hilbert had outlined ten of the eventual twenty three problems, published widely later throughout the mathematics world, which set the tone for mathematical inquiry in the twentieth century. Though some unsolved problems of Diophantine equations were included, Fermat's specific conjecture was not. Sincerely appalled, Francisco had taken a black marker and written in bold letters:

#24 – FERMAT'S LAST THEOREM - Prove that no three positive integers a, b, and c can satisfy the equation $a^n + b^n = c^n$ for any integer value of n greater than 2.

Here in Hilbert's/DiScenna's table of unsolved problems was a complete tangible list of curiosities, an empirical catalog of unknowns. He felt a satisfaction he hadn't been aware of longing for.

Francisco's advisor was as Father had promised, brilliant and pious, with an amazing capacity to intertwine faith in God with a faith that all problems conceivable by man could, would and should be solved by man. Professor Reyes was a mathematician, a gifted and creative mind, and a devout Jesuit, a Professed Priest of the Society of Jesus. Both God and his Universal Language, mathematics, were knowable to humanity, Reyes insisted. This he counseled to the Jesuit scholastics under his guidance, those preparing for a life of theology *and* a specialty in the humanities, philosophy or science, as passionately as he counseled non-Jesuit students of mathematics.

Francisco excelled academically, growing closer and closer in intellectual accord with Reyes' view that mathematics was the language of God; the language of sacred texts was a mere simulacrum for the perfection of the *universal* rules of mathematics. Reyes sympathized with Francisco's frustrations too. He struggled with his own work, the work of God and man. Francisco found another mentor in Reyes, a Jesuit like Father, who yearned for understanding on a level unconsidered by most people, the driving desire to understand, to reach, to fall and work to rise up again. Politics, history, geography, mechanics, culture, relationships – these were things of this world, things accessible only through the lens of his perception. Mathematics was perfect on Earth, perfect in the distant stars. Universal. Heavenly.

It was during these meetings that Francisco's love of God and love of numbers began their transmutation, and he was shortly admitted to the order as a scholastic. The tradition priestly vows of poverty and chastity had been with him his whole life, in spirit if not yet by declaration. The vow of obedience was easy enough, for in his heart he knew he had long ago avowed obedience to the incorruptible nature of numbers themselves, an obedience innate to him since his earliest memories.

Francisco spent these several years in complete bliss. Though he had yet to give voice to Fermat's proof, he had found brothers among the Jesuit scholastics, and he had found two Fathers through the auspices of the Order.

Fermat gave him purpose, and he thought of little else. To work on Fermat was to reach dead ends and new insights. This was the journey of every pilgrim in Christendom. Reyes showed him that he was as much in the company of St. Ignatius as he was in the company of the innovators of mathematics.

He walked after Father Christopher Clavius, who, in the sixteenth century laid the framework for Leibniz and Descartes. He succeeded Father André Tacquet, a Flemish mathematician whose work prepared the ground for the eventual discovery of calculus. He stood in awe of Father Athanasius Kircher, a German who, in his *Scrutinium Pestis* of 1658, noted the presence of "little worms" or "animalcules" in the blood, and concluded that the disease was caused by micro-organisms. Father Kircher was described universally as a polymath, a word Francisco had begun to use to describe Father Reyes, a man of broad learning and even broader interests. Kircher had shocked seventeenth century intellectuals with his work on Hieroglyphics, Chinese culture, cartography, geology, and his detailed, if fanciful rendering of the continent of Atlantis. A devout man of God, Kircher advanced medicine and biology, timekeeping and nascent game theory. Francisco DiScenna marveled too at the work of Fathers Giovanni Girolamo Saccheri, among the first to tackle Non-Euclidean geometry and Father Antoine de Laloubère, who unraveled the mathematical properties of the helix.

Above them all, in Francisco's imagination, stood Marin Mersenne, who by a trick of fate was not an initiate in the Society of Jesus, per se, but who, after a lengthy enrollment at the Jesuit College of La Flèche, at which the great Descartes himself studied, took holy orders and embarked on a life of Mathematics and God. Mersenne was born, like Francisco, of lowly origins. He refused the destiny of a child of peasant parents, instead rising to become what a contemporary called, 'the center of the world of science and mathematics during the first half of the seventeenth century.' Mersenne was a prolific correspondent. He maintained a network of mathematicians and natural scientists, both professional and amateur, serving as the world's agora at the intersection of learned inquiry of his day.

Clavius, Tacquet, Kircher, Saccheri, Laloubère and, in spirit and in education, Mersenne - Jesuits all. Like these other pilgrims he undertook his journey with a full heart, knowing the journey could only lead him to a universal understanding: the truth of the One, the Perfect, the True Mind of the Universe.

Reyes and DiScenna spent much time in study of the mathematics of antiquity, from which these most simple and impenetrable equations sprang, until Francisco's intense interest in the ancient minds of antiquity prompted

285 | E P O C H

Reyes to suggest that Francisco seek the additional guidance of a colleague. An amateur mathematician, to be sure, and a man of different gods, still, Reyes suggested, Professor Pratt might be of use where an understanding of the tradition of ancient Pythagoras, Euclid, Eratosthenes, Diophantus and the equations and proofs they engendered might stoke the fires of creativity.

Francisco DiScenna met Professor Pratt during office hours after his weekly lecture on the 'History of the Mathematics of Antiquity.' Like most professors, Pratt found his time chiefly occupied after midterms and finals, when students came to stretch a point or plead a case. The rest of the first semester of his acquaintanceship with the mathematically pious and philosophically pure young Francisco DiScenna was spent in long monologues of exposition. Did Francisco know about the automata of Heron of Alexandria? Had he studied antiquity's obsession with the primes? How had he not known about the virus of 'epochism' invading campuses since the enlightenment, obscuring extant theorems, halting progress, slowing advance?

Dr. Pratt was famous for an addition to his home, a copy of the Pompeiian Villa of the Mysteries. In this he took great pride, inviting students and colleagues to attend symposia as equals. Before students were to leave for winter break, Pratt held a small symposium for his intimates. Francisco was delighted when both he and Reyes were invited. They reclined on chaises, admired the half-finished paintings in the Roman style. The queerness of the mock-rituals – Pratt insisted on calling the furniture and the cups by their original, borrowed Greek names – was a source of bemusement for Father Reyes and scholastic Francisco. They enjoyed a kylix in the andron, toasted a kykeon which some students requested be filled with Vodka and tonic rather than wine and grated cheese. The evening was full of stories from the pantheon, of new work on Homeric Scholarship, of points of Koine Greek pronunciation, and most of all, the society and friendship of intellectuals and polymaths Francisco DiScenna had craved since he was a child.

Mostly Francisco listened. He enjoyed hearing Father Reyes chatting with Professor Pratt about comparative religion. The religion of antiquity was a curiosity, a non-threatening literature of demigods and heroic folklore. Greek mythology and the Mysteries of which Pratt often spoke were legends, as threatening to faith in the true God as a book club discussion of Tolkien or Lewis Carroll. Francisco's faith in a God of mathematics secure, he continued his work on Fermat, noting the relation of the problem to Elliptical curves, Reyes' area of expertise in which DiScenna obediently and joyfully immersed himself.

DiScenna tested out of most of his undergraduate requirements and was given a special dispensation to complete his undergraduate work in 3 years, with an immediate transition to a PhD program in mathematics to follow, under the continued guidance of Father Reyes. So taken was he with his new life, he rarely wandered beyond the corridors of the mathematics department or the straight path between it and his dormitory. Reyes, thinking Francisco might benefit from a break from his studies and Stanford, had invited Francisco to accompany him to a series of lectures in Cambridge, England, at the newly opened Isaac Newton Institute for Mathematical Sciences. One of the lectures piqued Francisco's interests entirely. A certain Professor Andrew Wiles was to speak on a topic that had begun to gather shades of intrigue among the conferees. It was said that he had worked in secret for six years, had made a major advance, and that one of Mathematics' longest standing mysteries would be revealed. Francisco thought of Hilbert's 23, and wondered which of them might have been pried open by Professor Wiles. The placard outside the lecture room read:

Programme for Workshop
L-FUNCTIONS AND ARITHMETIC

Wednesday, June 23 1993
ANDREW WILES

Elliptic Curves and Galois Representations

A thin, blond Andrew Wiles discussed, as advertised, elliptical curves and Galois representations. He worked an Olympian ode in mathematical notation spanning centuries of advances in algebraic geometry, concepts that Francisco had not yet fully grappled with as an undergraduate. The audience members gradually realized the significance of the arc upon which Wiles was taking them. Halfway through, Father Reyes let out a very audible exhalation that startled Francisco seated beside him. Toward the end, Wiles wrote the famous formulation, as familiar to Francisco DiScenna as his own name: *No three positive integers a, b, and c can satisfy the equation $a^n + b^n = c^n$ for any integer value of n greater than 2.* Beneath it Wiles wrote, simply, 'Q.E.D.,' *Quod erat demonstrandum*, a form of intellectual punctuation as ancient as the mathematics of early antiquity.

287 | E P O C H

The crowd erupted in cheers, a mathematics lecture momentarily transformed into the varsity passions of a football pitch. DiScenna sat motionless. Before his eyes his God had been proven, *demonstrandum,* and, in an instant, it had been taken away. Wiles had met *his* God before DiScenna had had a chance to make him his own. He spoke rarely on the flight back, evading Reyes' questions and resenting his mentor's triumphalism. How could Reyes not know his star student's life was at an end?

Arriving back at Stanford, he felt a need to give form to his despair. He visited his old acquaintance, still displaying Hilbert's/DiScenna's table of unsolved problems. Bursting into the room of the friend to who he had only ever spoken of mathematics, he cried uncontrollably as he scratched several times through #24. Inconsolable, he wrote after the stricken line, simply: Q.E.D. and its popularization, *thus it is proved.*

Francisco DiScenna closed himself off entirely. Both Pratt and Reyes could see that his entire personality had changed. His passion for mathematics was gone. His passion for God was gone. They worried his passion for living had gone. He stopped attending lectures. He didn't return emails or phone calls. He was detained by campus security one evening after screaming in front of the mathematics building. They demanded he see a university counselor, who prescribed antidepressants. When they contacted the counselor, after another bout of screaming, her advice had been only that he continue to take the medication, and find something – anything – on which to refocus his energy.

Reyes and Pratt showed up together one evening at Francisco's room. Knocking loudly, Francisco eventually let them in. They were startled to find his room torn apart and his walls full of newspaper clippings trumpeting Wiles' achievement. He screamed, he pleaded with Reyes to tell him why God had taken his life's purpose from him. Reyes told him that it was natural to question one's faith. It was expected, even from the most devout. Reyes assured Francisco that he understood that God and mathematics were of the same substance, as much for Francisco, he knew, as for himself. Reyes pleaded with Francisco to consider other problems. Francisco told him about having drawn a line through #24, to which Reyes responded that there were many other problems left to solve, that there would always be problems, beyond Hilbert's list, beyond problems known to the age, there might be an infinity of problems, and only after answering them all, would man come to know God. We might only approximate God, he said. Like Archimedes, we might try to square the circle, getting closer and closer. That was a noble effort. That was enough for one lifetime.

Eventually Francisco returned to classes, took up his studies. Pratt knew an intellect like Francisco's needed a difficult problem to solve. He suggested several unfinished mathematical problems, hesitant to set the bar so high that he would create the potential for catastrophic failure. Francisco had talked about Riemann's Hypothesis. Reyes placated but cautioned him, knowing that generations of mathematicians had tried before him, generations that did not link so closely the aim of their professional research with their personal notions of the divine.

One evening, Francisco told Reyes that he had read a biography of Georg Cantor, a passionate mathematician, like them, who had gone mad contemplating infinity. Cantor had claimed to hear a voice, a daimon, pulling him forward toward the study of mathematics. He often quoted Corinthians: *That which has been hidden to you will eventually be brought into the light.* Cantor, by many accounts, was the most gifted mathematician of the nineteenth century. He had considered the problem the ancient mathematicians agreed to set aside, so unfathomable did it seem that one set of infinity might be larger than another. Indeed, said the ancients, there are infinitely many numbers between integers. A ready example of this is the number π. π resides between 3 and 4, yet it itself is infinite. For every irrational number like π there are infinitely more infinitely long rational numbers between each integer, and any unbounded set of integers were, themselves, infinite. Another example, one that set Cantor on his quest to contain infinity, was the problem known since Archimedes of the infinity contained within a circle. Since Archimedes and likely before, all motion was considered in relation to a curve. Mathematicians knew that within a circle, an infinite number of points resided. Archimedes was content to set aside a fuller understanding, noting only that this most fundamental and impenetrable mathematics worked, if it might not otherwise be fully known. Cantor understood the infinity of motion as the driving force that made up divine creation.

He felt, as Francisco felt, that his personal religion was not one of grace or redemption; only in knowing the underlying mathematics of the universe was to truly understand it and, in the understating, know the mind of God. Cantor's great breakthrough, his Continuum Hypothesis, had upended mathematics for a century; the shockwaves of his challenge to the notion of arriving at any mathematical proof with complete certainty would continue to highlight the contradictions of infinity to the present day. Though Cantor's place in mathematics was secured – the Continuum Hypothesis took pride of place among Hilbert's 23 – his obsession with contradictions within the perfect language of God had cost him his sanity. He died in an asylum, to the end filling notebooks with an epic of disjointed formulae, incoherent prayers that he might yet be the recipient of the promise in Corinthians: *That which has been hidden to you will eventually be brought into the light.*

Francisco admitted to Reyes that he saw something of himself in Cantor and his devotion. He wrote to Father that he had found a new interest, that he might try to redeem Cantor's faith, if not his mathematics. This Francisco would do on his own terms, and thereby save Cantor and himself. Father counseled moderation, to which Francisco agreed, replying that he was well aware of the dangers of enveloping his mind in problems without likely solutions. But Francisco knew that he was different. He had seen patterns all his life. He knew no other experience of the world. When his colleagues played games on the lawn outside the mathematics department, the air filled for him with nothing but numbers plotting trajectories. When he attended a concert, he heard nothing, saw only the calculations of harmonics. Everything was predictable. Everything was knowable. He could yet know the methods of God.

Cantor's infinities within infinities were just a starting point. Francisco sought a unified theory of mathematics. He wanted to solve every unknown problem in a single, elegant equation. He knew the only peace he could find within his mind was a general proof for nothing less than a sentiment spoken often enough at Pratt's symposia: *The Lord said, Know ye not that ye are gods?* Man could be one with God, if only he had the courage to navigate through the uncertainty that Francisco knew lay between himself and a certain, provable, knowable, complete understanding of the universe.

Cantor soon slipped beyond his interest. The notion that infinites within infinities existed was a matter of mathematical fact. It did not affect the solidity of his sense of purpose. The universe could not be designed that way. That was only a perception, a misunderstanding of a larger truth. He began with a complete study of the Riemann Hypothesis. Riemann had become obsessed with prime numbers. Francisco began to feel that prime numbers were the unassailable building blocks of mathematical truth. He devoted an entire month to Goldbach's conjecture, a cousin of Riemann's hypothesis, which suggests but does not prove that every even integer greater than 2 can be expressed as the sum of two primes. Riemann studied the distribution of primes, Goldbach studied their relationship as the raw materials of number theory.

This work calmed Francisco. He again attended Pratt's symposia, where he soon began to dominate the conversation on the mathematics of antiquity. In particular, he became an admirer of Eratosthenes and Archimedes, who he knew were colleagues and contemporaries millennia ago. Eratosthenes, everyone knew, was the first to seriously consider a method for producing a 'map' of all the primes, so that one might envision asking the value of the nth prime, to which, Eratosthenes dreamed, one might someday have a ready answer. Eratosthenes' famous 'sieve' method for isolating primes was grade school mathematics, but he felt a kinship across centuries with a mind so attuned to the elegance of numbers. As his city burned away around him, Archimedes had been discovered lost in thought, so absorbed had he been in his circles of infinity. Archimedes, too, was a kindred soul, the higher plane of mathematics so engrossing as to blot out the petty political realities of the moment.

So engrossed had Francisco become that summer after the devastation in Cambridge that he was oblivious to a rumor circulating that a minor flaw had been found in Andrew Wiles' Fermat proof. Reyes and Pratt were so concerned that he would hear of it and drop all his progress to return to Fermat that they censored as much as possible the conversation of their students. An email was issued, the first of its kind in the history of Stanford, Pratt thought, that under no circumstances were mathematics students to discuss Fermat with Francisco DiScenna. It took less than a day for a student to corner Francisco on the quad, and less than half that time for Francisco to appear, rapturous, in Reyes' office, his marked-up copy of Wiles' proof in hand.

With Reyes' grudging approval, Francisco took a leave of absence from the fall semester. He sat alone in his apartment, breaking only to eat and sleep. Reyes knew that the concepts in Wiles' proof were beyond an undergraduate student, even a magnificently gifted student like Francisco. But there was nothing to do but humor him. Reyes allowed the semester break, demanding only that a progress paper be submitted by Christmas, and if it didn't show legitimate promise, DiScenna was to resume his work on Goldbach, on Riemann, on anything, and leave a potentially insoluble problem alone. DiScenna agreed, and presented his paper to Pratt on the last day of the fall term.

Upon resuming in the spring, Reyes and DiScenna anxiously went through his paper point by point. There were numerous flaws in DiScenna's argument, and Reyes, despairing of ever helping to guide DiScenna to a constructive career, as a measure of tough love, threatened to expel him from the mathematics department if he did not resume classes and take on a project more suited to the skills of even this most talented of undergraduates. DiScenna relented and resumed his coursework. It was an open secret that he continued with Fermat through the spring and into the summer, only occasionally venturing out to Pratt's symposia, which he genuinely enjoyed, steering away from the kylix and kykeon so they would not interfere with his antidepressants.

Francisco achieved again a measure of happiness and stability that he began to fear could only come from pursuing Fermat, however clandestinely. In early September, it was Reyes' unhappy duty to tell Francisco that a colleague from Cambridge had confirmed a rumor that Andrew Wiles had 'circumvented' the one shortfall in his proof. The paper, Reyes told Francisco, had already been submitted for peer review. Both Pratt and Reyes were surprised at how well Francisco took the news. He agreed Wiles' claim to the proof was a fait accompli, and that a career working on the primes so dear to Riemann and Goldbach was not an insignificant consolation.

He attended every one of Pratt's symposia that semester and the next, and almost two years after meeting Wiles in Cambridge, he read with a void passivity the May issue of *Annals of Mathematics*, comprised entirely of Wiles' 'Modular Elliptic Curves and Fermat's Last Theorem,' and 'Ring Theoretic Properties of Certain Hecke Algebras,' a supporting paper on the correction of the original flaw that Wiles had coauthored with a former student. Three hundred and fifty-eight years after Fermat made his famous conjecture in the margins of the work of an ancient Alexandrian, Francisco DiScenna visited his other mentor, Professor Pratt, and toasted with every kylix he drank each of the Muses that had been so kind to Andrew Wiles, the only mortal currently alive and one of only a select few since antiquity who have glimpsed the face of God.

That same month, Francisco DiScenna graduated a full year ahead of his class. He prepared himself to enter a PhD program in mathematics under the guidance of Father Reyes and declared himself ready to take the final vow on the path to becoming an initiated member of the Society of Jesus. Though he had different notions of the divine - Francisco's God was not the anthropomorphic God of the Society - he outwardly used the same language as the other initiates. His piety and devotion to God were beyond question in the eyes of the several panels of interlocutors, and Francisco saw little distinction between the Truth in scripture and any number of other Truths longed for by Hilbert and generations of mathematicians since antiquity. Truth was as much in the God of Abraham as it was in Goldbach's Conjecture, Riemann's Hypothesis, even the frenetic apparent contradictions of Cantor. God, as indeed Cantor himself had proved, was the Absolute Infinite.

Father, who had recently retired from St. Mary's School, flew to California to stand as Francisco' only family present at his graduation. Pratt invited Francisco, Father and Reyes to a special symposium, deliberately light, for their guest's sake, on the Jesuit-Pagan syncretism of their usual meetings. Reyes and Pratt were delighted to discover that Francisco's Father, the learned Jesuit, was as interested in the mathematics of antiquity as they were. The conversation stretched into the night, and after a suitable prayer, Father himself indulged his host with a kind kylix in dedication of all Mysteries, ancient and modern. Then, as if the words were his own, Father quoted St. Ignatius as Reyes closed his eyes approvingly:

> "Altogether, I must not desire to belong to myself, but to my creator and to his representative. I must let myself be led and moved as a lump of wax lets itself be kneaded. I must be as a dead man's corpse without will or judgment; as a little crucifix which lets itself be moved without difficulty from one place to another; as a staff in the hand of an old man, to be placed where he wishes and where he can best make use of me. Thus, I must always be ready to hand, so that the Order may use me and apply me in the way that to him seems good..."

This was the true spirit of a religious life, Father said, and all three of Francisco's mentors agreed that he should look not to the momentary disappointment of Fermat, but to greater mathematics still, and to the Divine, which were, in Francisco's mind, one and the same. That same week Father watched with pride as young Francisco DiScenna, only nineteen, became a proper Jesuit scholastic, in the tradition of Ignatius, Clavius, Tacquet, Kircher, Saccheri, Laloubère and Marin Mersenne.

For several years Francisco continued with Riemann, outlining methods of attack that were suitably modest for a university thesis. He had learned by now that success, or simply survival, in academia required a subtlety of outward intent not dissimilar in appearance to the presumably genuine professions of humility he observed in his Jesuit brothers. But, to Francisco, it was one thing to declare one's unworthiness to enter into the service of the Lord. It was quite another to set one's private academic ambitions so high that not even Euclid, Eratosthenes, Cantor or Riemann could hope to achieve them.

To demonstrate progress, he had been forced to divide his ambition into discrete patches of mathematics. To prove Riemann correct, he would need to embrace emerging approaches and new methodologies, he might even have to invent some novel approaches to algebraic geometry, and he would need to master all previous work with prime numbers.

One evening, reclining with a kylix, he listened as Pratt spoke nonstop of a book that had just sold at auction. The relatively small world of the mathematics of antiquity had been sent into an orgasm of excitement: A palimpsest had resurfaced that had been recognized in the early twentieth century to be a lost work of Archimedes overwritten by a thirteenth century prayer book. The book had sold for $2 million to an anonymous buyer. Noting Francisco's interest, Pratt found a copy of a magazine article that explained that the manuscript had found a home at the Wallace Art Museum in Baltimore and would undergo a lengthy period of retrieving from under the later text the words of Archimedes. There was even an open call within Pratt's small academic circle for volunteers to help with the restoration effort.

Francisco was immediately interested. Though Francisco did not know Greek, the language of the Archimedes Palimpsest, Pratt assured Francisco he could give him some basic lessons. Surely Francisco's expertise on algebraic geometry might be useful during the translation work. And, Pratt argued, a break from pure theory to work with students of mathematics-as-artifact might give Francisco's mind a chance to refocus, to examine new perspectives. Pratt and Reyes sent letters of recommendation to the Wallace, soon followed by other recommendations from colleagues and fellow students who agreed with Reyes and Pratt that Francisco would benefit from a diversion.

Francisco agreed, and to his surprise he nearly forgot Fermat, Cantor and Riemann during a happy summer spent in residence with the Wallace conservation team. He absorbed every step of the process. He was fascinated with the use of successive passes of ultraviolet and infrared light. Francisco was delighted to have Pratt with him when several stubborn pages had been flown to Stanford's Linear Accelerator, where they were bombarded with highly focused x-rays, revealing even more of the text. As Francisco became aware that advanced mathematics played a larger and larger role in uncovering this ancient text, he began to feel a sense of destiny, that he had been chosen to be a part of – literally – illuminating that which had been lost or forgotten. The words of Corinthians, those favored by Cantor, came to him like the x-rays and fluorescence passing through the palimpsest itself: *That which has been hidden to you will eventually be brought into the light.*

After several more months in Baltimore, Francisco appeared unexpectedly at The Villa of The Mysteries. He spoke so quickly that Pratt could not understand everything Francisco was saying. Was anyone else here? No.

JAMES ADDOMS | 294

Amazing discovery. Digital spectography. Advanced spectography techniques. Principle component analysis. Francisco laid a manila folder on a reproduction Attic table. To Pratt's simultaneous horror and excitement as an antiquarian, Francisco fanned across the table top three meticulously unbound sheets, each one at least a thousand years old. Two appeared consecutive, distinct from the order of the third. Francisco's own Greek was imperfect. He needed Pratt to confirm what he thought he had read on the first two pages: a fragment of a letter, or a testimony, or a memoir promising to "discuss 'The Master's' selection of ... network covered over by his wisdom ... order of the Mysteries of Eleusis; and on the third: *There is a solution to the problem of the primes.*

His Greek had been close enough, Pratt admitted. But this was a stolen piece of a million dollar manuscript now laying in an unprotected space in his own home. Francisco couched his apology in a justification. Pratt knew about the Mysteries, he had spoken at length about them. And Francisco knew about prime numbers – to what else could the manuscript be referring? Prime numbers were infinite. Archimedes knew that as much as Francisco did. Infinity was *his*. He had been denied Fermat so that he could do *this*. There *is* a solution to the primes. God had sent him this message. There were no coincidences. *That which has been hidden to you will eventually be brought into the light.*

Pratt protested. He agreed not to call the Wallace immediately, a call that would ruin Francisco's career and probably send him to jail, if Francisco promised, absolutely promised to return these pages the next day, exactly where and in exactly the condition he had found them. Francisco agreed. But *what* do the Mysteries of Eleusis have to do with prime numbers? The Mysteries were an ancient cult. Fun to think about, like the neo-pagans who chanted on the quad during the solstice before marching toward the pub. The rituals of Eleusis were fascinating, Pratt's passion, in fact. But even he couldn't make a connection between the rights of Demeter and the changing of the seasons and Archimedes, to say nothing of prime numbers.

Well, there might be a connection. Alexandria, Egypt. Eratosthenes developed the first sieve method for generating primes, hadn't he? Hadn't he been a close colleague of Archimedes? Hadn't Euclid worked and written in Alexandria? Hadn't Archimedes written the very manuscript Francisco was helping to uncover? Hadn't Archimedes been among the greatest mathematical minds of antiquity? Why would he talk of a network 'covered over'? Covered? By whom? From whom? Who would want to hide knowledge of prime numbers in antiquity? Why would a cult of Demeter care about prime numbers?

Pratt had no ready answers. It didn't make sense, even to him, the preeminent scholar on the Alexandrian Golden Age. Of course, the Christians had persecuted the pagans, but that wouldn't happen until centuries after Archimedes and Eratosthenes were dead. The Ptolemies were generally supportive of the Academy of Alexandria. Any mathematical, literary or scientific advances only served to glorify the Ptolemaic state. Of course, Ptolemy IV had turned away from his father's scholastic bent, and his son, Ptolemy V, had been absolutely an enemy of rigorous scholarship. And then, of course, there were several native rebellions. Ptolemy V had lost Upper Egypt for twenty years to a resurgence of Egyptian identity under native Pharaohs. But this fragment was an anachronism. It was out of place. It was either much later writing, or it was a puzzle he'd be happy to ponder – write a paper on even – if Francisco would only get these pages out of his house, return them to the Wallace. He could wait for the published translation.

Francisco returned the pages to the Wallace, where they eventually evinced minor vexation among the conservation team. In light of the isolated passages, a resident scholar suggested that they must be much earlier writing from an Athenian, perhaps the fourth century BCE Hypereides. Palimpsests were notorious in the conservation community because, unlike a traditional manuscript that need be only restored and translated in its original intended order, a palimpsest was likely as not a grab-bag of pages ripped out of books, wiped clean and rebound haphazardly, with no fidelity to the provenance of the work from which the pages were taken.

The problem of the primes could easily refer to Euclid's proof of the infinity of primes, and of course, Hypereides, like many Athenians, would have been at least familiar with if not participants in the Mysteries of the cult of Demeter and Persephone that were celebrated regularly at the temple at Eleusis. This interpretation was eventually adopted by the Wallace. Considered relatively inconsequential in light of the larger Archimedes text, these stray lines were enshrined as marginalia in the first printed translation released several years later.

Pratt agreed not to give Francisco away, but he reminded Francisco that he needed to have a care for the perceptions of others. He must try to see how it would look if he had been found to have taken the pages. No amount of explanation along the lines of academic curiosity would protect him. Francisco agreed. Pratt was right. But now that they knew there was a connection between prime numbers and an ancient agrarian cult, how might they find where to look for the solution to the problem of the primes?

They discussed it often among themselves, but eventually their conversation returned to more conventional topics; the political climate of Alexandria, the relationship of the Academy to the state. After the translation had been published, Francisco brought up the "curious" Hypereides text in the company of Reyes at a symposia. Reyes found it interesting enough to approve of Francisco's healthy interest in the metadata of the long history of mathematics that had given the world of ideas men like Kepler, Descartes, Newton, Leibniz – he avoided any mention of Fermat – Euler and Lagrange, Gauss and Boole, Galois, Riemann, Whitehead, Russell and Hilbert. If only, Reyes groaned, Francisco could focus his energy on something useful, future lists – yes he was that talented – might include Francisco DiScenna.

Francisco could not stop thinking about the riddle of the 'Hypereides' passages. Through Pratt, he had gained an appreciation of the minds of antiquity. Reyes often started undergraduate mathematics courses with a lecture on the history of mathematics. In an hour and a half, he breezily flew across an intellectual landscape that included, briefly, Hellenistic mathematicians, the great Jesuit polymaths, and Newton, Descartes, Leibniz, Euler, Cantor, Hilbert, and Gödel – all populating a small island unto themselves – before landing on the vast continent of achievement on which Einstein, Bohr, Hawking and Feynman were the main attractions.

This, Francisco had come to understand, was neither a useful picture nor a complete one. In terms of creative genius, he imagined the Hellenistic mathematicians as men who illuminated great swaths of the natural world with the language of mathematics. There must be a favorable comparison between the intellectual achievements of antiquity and the prevailing orthodoxy of the ascendancy of the achievements of the twentieth century.

Francisco believed, as Pratt did, that intellectual work existed on an historical continuum. For Pratt, that continuum measured only the debt moderns owed to ancients through a great conversation that had been unbroken for more than four thousand years. Pratt had no concept of a march of progress toward some specified end point. Far from living in an enlightened age, Pratt considered the very real possibility that mathematicians a millennia from now might rightly consider the twenty-first century, despite its intellectual miracles, firmly rooted in the dark ages of mathematics. For Francisco, this continuum had a goal. Mathematicians *were* marching toward progress, and they marched in the same direction as the ancients, toward Cantor's Absolute Infinite: The mind of God.

This is what extremely grieves us,
that a man who never fought

Should contrive our fees to pilfer,
on who for his native land

Never to this day had oar, or lance,
or blister in his hand.

—ARISTOPHANES, Wasps

25

The army marched for several weeks, finally encamping at Pelusium, half way from Alexandria to Coele-Syria. Here we awaited reinforcements sent from Cyprus, Rhodes and as far in the interior as Syene. The pharaoh and much of his contingent stayed within the city walls in the governor's villa. We were accorded accommodations with Pamphilos, a notable politician and merchant whose two sons were enrolled at the Academy and had remained behind in Alexandria.

Our first evening was such a release from the exhaustion of the road that we spent it in sleep immediately upon being shown to our beds. On the second night, Pamphilos and his wife, Althaia, invited those of us from the Academy in the cortege to dine with him. His home was handsomely appointed, though not so much so to draw attention and the ire of his neighbors. He had but few servants, and yet I felt uncomfortable as they attended upon me, unknown to them as it must have been that I had been conceived in the reed thrushes along the Nile and not in a villa similar to the one in which they served.

After a fine meal all of us retired to the andron, where Archimedes was first to reach for the kylix.

After several moments of quiet, Eratosthenes spoke: "I know, friends, that you are uncomfortable with the modifications to the ballistae. I know that you feel that the purity of knowledge is reviled with application to warfare."

"I don't feel reviled, sir," said Archimedes, "I'm concerned with the one-sidedness of it."

"Consider this, friends," said The Master. "How many have died in all wars? How many have died in the sieging and the defending? There is no doubt Ptolemy will retake Ptolemais and Tyre with a minimum loss of life of either side. He would attempt their recapture whatever the weapons at his disposal. Perhaps our ingenuity will force concessions from the forces of Theodotus. Though his head will likely be taken, perhaps there's no need for Ptolemy to conduct a lengthy and destructive campaign."

"As a politician, Pamphilos," said Archimedes, refilling his kylix, "what are your thoughts on the matter?"

"As a businessman, trade between Alexandria and Seleucia makes me rich. As a politician, I have no thoughts, sir," he said carefully. He then waved to his attendant that the party should be left alone. The attendant propped a large amphora of wine against the wall and left the room.

"Now, if you ask me as a man who has served other men and seen men die under the late pharaoh, I say this, you may well be correct about the sieges of these two towns, and whatever small garrisons you encounter. I'm not as intimately familiar with your devices as you and your fellows are, but I saw the demonstration at the Ptolemaia. Nothing like it has been known in warfare before and I'm heartily glad you gentlemen are on our side. But, once Ptolemy seizes these two towns as easily as you claim, I have a tendency to believe that his ambitions will not be sated. Knowing that he can take back two of his possessions so easily, what would a prince do with towns to the north? Do you think he'll stop at Coele Syria?"

"Why not," said Archimedes.

"Why not indeed," said the Master. "Perhaps he'll move on Antioch, on Babylon itself, as his father did. Why not pursue Antiochus into the farthest reaches of Persia? Ptolemy Euergetes reached Babylon at the expense of few lives during the entire campaign. Why should his son stop at Jerusalem, Tyre and Ptolemais? Once master of Coele-Syria again, why not march to Ecbatana, to the Far East? Why not resurrect the triumphs of Alexander? Why not reach Rome and, subduing it, march all the way to the Western Sea beyond the Pillars of Hercules? Why send his great quinquereme to the edges of the earth with weapons of such ferocity even the Asiatic hordes must bow before him?"

"Imagine that," said Pamphilos with a laugh, "Ptolemy IV, pharaoh of the world."

"They'll never do with a pharaoh in Rome," said Archimedes, "not when they'll be forced to marry their sisters."

"Especially Scipio's sister," said Pamphilos, "what ugly children they would make together!"

The men laughed and the subject was changed to less political topics.

Onesimus asks why I should choose to record this particular conversation. I have explained to him that this is my earliest memory of a defining pan-humanitarian design the Master would implement many years later. This was in response to a threat to the existence of the Academy itself as an institution of independent inquiry, and was itself a threat, so severe would the retaliation against the Academy be should the Master's plan come to light. Of these future troubles I knew nothing, and on that night I knew only drunkenness and sound sleep, even as the Master's mind began to turn to the protection of the fruits of his and his fellows' inquiry and the inheritance of the multiculturalism of Alexander himself. But I have urged Onesimus to trust that all will be told in due course, that my foremost goal in committing memory to paper is to record the reasons that impelled the Master to take the course he did, that I will make known in this narrative how close the spirit of Alexander and the early Academy came to annihilation at many different hands. And always for want of the axial moment, Onesimus must now indulge the happenings at Raphia, for that truly was the beginning of the end.

The forces from the far colonies arrived and the army was once again on the march to Coele Syria, which we reached by June of that year. I have in my possession a recent addition to the library only recently received from sources I will explain at length in a later passage. The young Polybius has just completed a history of these days, from which I have already quoted, and I include his eloquent words here, as I am wanting as a faithful expositor of military tactics. This is the history of the campaign at Raphia in the words of that gifted historian:

> Having marched to Pelusium, Ptolemy made his first halt in that town: and having been there joined by the stragglers, and having given out their rations of corn to his men, he got the army in motion, and led them by a line of march which goes through the waterless region skirting Mount

Casius and the Marshes. On the fifth day's march he reached his destination, and pitched his camp a distance of fifty stades from Raphia, which is the first city of Coele-Syria toward Egypt.

While Ptolemy was effecting this movement Antiochus arrived with his army at Gaza, where he was joined by some reinforcements, and once more commenced his advance, proceeding at a leisurely pace. He passed Raphia and encamped about ten stades from the enemy. For a while the two armies preserved this distance, and remained encamped opposite each other. But after some few days, wishing to remove to more advantageous ground and to inspire confidence in his troops, Antiochus pushed forward his camp so much nearer Ptolemy, that the palisades of the two camps were not more than five stades from each other; and while in this position, there were frequent struggles at the watering-places and on forays, as well as infantry and cavalry skirmishes in the space between the camps.

In the course of these proceedings Theodotus conceived and put into execution an enterprise, very characteristic of an Aetolian, but undoubtedly requiring great personal courage. Having formerly lived at Ptolemy's court he knew the king's tastes and habits. Accordingly, accompanied by two others, he entered the enemy's camp just before daybreak; where, owing to the dim light, he could not be recognized by his face, while his dress and other accoutrements did not render him noticeable, owing to the variety of costume prevailing among themselves. He had marked the position of the king's tent during the preceding days, for the skirmishes took place quite close; and he now walked boldly up to it, and passed through all the outer ring of attendants without being observed: but when he came to the tent in which the king was accustomed to transact business and dine, though he searched it in every conceivable way, he failed to find the king; for Ptolemy slept in another tent, separate from the public and official tent. He however wounded two men who were sleeping there, and killed Andreas, the king's physician; and then returned safely to his own camp, without meeting with any molestation, except just as he was passing over the vallum of the enemy's camp. As far as daring went, he had fulfilled his purpose: but he had failed in prudence by not taking the precaution to ascertain where Ptolemy was accustomed to sleep.

After being encamped opposite each other for five days, the two kings resolved to bring matters to the decision of battle. And upon Ptolemy beginning to move his army outside its camp, Antiochus hastened to do the same. Both formed their front of their phalanx and men armed in the Macedonian manner. But Ptolemy's two wings were formed as follows:— Polycrates, with the cavalry under his command, occupied the left, and between him and the phalanx were Cretans standing close by the horsemen; next them came the royal guard;1 then the peltasts under Socrates, adjoining the Libyans armed in Macedonian fashion.

On the right wing was Echecrates of Thessaly, with his division of cavalry; on his left were stationed Gauls and Thracians; next them Phoxidas and the Greek mercenaries, extending to the Egyptian phalanx. Of the elephants forty were on the left wing, where Ptolemy was to be in person during the battle; the other thirty-three had been stationed in front of the right wing opposite the mercenary cavalry.

Antiochus also placed sixty of his elephants commanded by his foster-brother Philip in front of his right wing, on which he was to be present personally, to fight opposite Ptolemy. Behind these he stationed the two thousand cavalry commanded by Antipater, and two thousand more at right angles to them. In line with the cavalry he placed the Cretans, and next them the Greek mercenaries; with the latter he mixed two thousand of these armed in the Macedonian fashion under the command of the Macedonian Byttacus. At the extreme point of the left wing he placed two thousand cavalry under the command of Themison; by their side Cardacian and Lydian javelin-men; next them the light-armed division of three thousand, commanded by Menedemus; then the Cissians, Medes, and Carmanians; and by their side the Arabians and neighboring peoples who continued the line up to the phalanx. The remainder of the elephants he placed in front of his left wing under the command of Myiscus, one of the boys about the court.

The two armies having been drawn up in the order I have described; the kings went along their respective lines, and addressed words of encouragement and exhortation to their officers and friends. But as they both rested their strongest hopes on their phalanx, they showed their greatest earnestness and addressed their strongest exhortations to them; which were re-echoed in Ptolemy's case by Andromachus and Sosibius and the king's sister Arsinoë; in the case of Antiochus by Theodotus and Nicarchus: these officers being the commanders of the phalanx in the two armies respectively. The substance of what was said on both sides was the same: for neither monarch had any glorious or famous achievement of his own to quote to those whom he was addressing, seeing that they had but recently succeeded to their crowns; but they endeavored to inspire the men of the phalanx with spirit and boldness, by reminding them of the glory of their ancestors, and the great deeds performed by them. But they chiefly dwelt upon the hopes of advancement which the men might expect at their hands in the future; and they called upon and exhorted the leaders and the whole body of men, who were about to be engaged, to maintain the fight with a manly and courageous spirit. So with these or similar words, delivered by their own lips or by interpreters, they rode along their lines.

Ptolemy, accompanied by his sister, having arrived at the left wing of his army, and Antiochus with the royal guard at the right: they gave the signal for the battle, and opened the fight by a charge of elephants. Only some few of Ptolemy's elephants came to close quarters with the foe: seated on these the soldiers in the howdahs maintained a brilliant fight, lunging at and striking each other with crossed pikes. But the elephants themselves fought still more brilliantly, using all their strength in the encounter, and pushing against each other, forehead to forehead.

The way in which elephants fight is this: they get their tusks entangled and jammed, and then push against one another with all their might, trying to make each other yield ground until one of them proving superior in strength has pushed aside the other's trunk; and when once he can get a side blow at his enemy, he pierces him with his tusks as a bull would with his horns. Now, most of Ptolemy's animals, as is the way with Libyan elephants, were afraid to face the fight: for they cannot stand the smell or the trumpeting of the Indian elephants, but are frightened at their size and strength, I suppose, and run away from them at once without waiting to come near them.

This is exactly what happened on this occasion: and upon their being thrown into confusion and being driven back upon their own lines, Ptolemy's guard gave way before the rush of the animals; while Antiochus, wheeling his men so as to avoid the elephants, charged the division of cavalry under Polycrates. At the same time the Greek mercenaries stationed near the phalanx, and behind the elephants, charged Ptolemy's peltasts and made them give ground, the elephants having already thrown their ranks also into confusion. Thus Ptolemy's whole left wing began to give way before the enemy.

Echecrates the commander of the right wing waited at first to see the result of the struggle between the other wings of the two armies: but when he saw the dust coming his way, and that the elephants opposite his division were afraid even to approach the hostile elephants at all, he ordered Phoxidas to charge the part of the enemy opposite him with his Greek mercenaries; while he made a flank movement with the cavalry and the division behind the elephants; and so getting out of the line of the hostile elephants' attack, charged the enemy's cavalry on the rear or the flank and quickly drove them from their ground. Phoxidas and his men were similarly successful: for they charged the Arabians and Medes and forced them into precipitate flight. Thus Antiochus's right wing gained a victory, while his left was defeated.

The phalanxes, left without the support of either wing, remained intact in the center of the plain, in a state of alternate hope and fear for the result. Meanwhile Antiochus was assisting in gaining the victory on his right wing; while Ptolemy, who had retired behind his phalanx, now came forward in the center, and showing himself in the view of both armies struck terror in the hearts of the enemy, but inspired great spirit and enthusiasm in his own men; and Andromachus and Sosibius at once ordered them to lower their sarissae and charge. The picked Syrian troops stood their ground only for a short time, and the division of Nicarchus quickly broke and fled. Antiochus presuming, in his youthful inexperience, from the success of his own division, that he would be equally victorious all along the line, was pressing on the pursuit; but upon one of the older officers at length giving him warning, and pointing out that the cloud of dust raised by the phalanx was moving toward their own camp, he understood too late what was happening; and endeavored to gallop back with the squadron of royal cavalry on to the field.

But finding his whole line in full retreat he was forced to retire to Raphia: comforting himself with the belief that, as far as he was personally concerned, he had won a victory, but had been defeated in the whole battle by the want of spirit and courage shown by the rest.

I remind the young Onesimus of two considerations when reading history from one who was not there. No doubt young Polybius researched his sources well. He was once in residence at the Academy in Alexandria, where he made use of official and other sources. He was also welcomed at the court of Antiochus, whose ministers provided their own account of the proceedings. Most academicians agree that his account is a workable analysis of the action, though he perhaps gives more credence to the boldness and bravery of the Ptolemaic faction, of which he benefited the most in his later academic pursuits.

It is also well known that the tide of battle was turned by several of the Master's devices positioned strategically on the battlefield to shower a target with large and small projectiles even as their targets advanced and moved around the battlefield. So important was the secrecy of the devices that Polybius was granted access to official accounts and attendant courtiers only under the condition that the existence of this technology not be revealed. In Antioch, he was also asked to omit the devices for fear of revealing those that had been built by Antiochus from plans supplied by a network of informants by a process I have not yet included in this history. So, I urge dear Onesimus to take the battle account as having a legitimacy somewhere between an event witnessed by one's own eyes and the eternal triumphalism of Homer. In this case at least, Polybius does write indeed in favor of the victor, not of the Battle itself, but of the ultimate possession of the Master's and Archimedes vastly superior technology.

In the aftermath of the battle Antiochus returned to Antioch with his remaining troops. Once there he opened negotiations for a yearlong truce, to which Ptolemy agreed. The eventual peace acknowledged Seleucid control of the port of Antioch, Seleucia in Pieria, while Ptolemy claimed all of Coele-Syria. After spending four months restoring order in that area, Ptolemy returned to Egypt, while Antiochus turned his attention to dealing with a rebellion in Asia Minor.

The reason for Ptolemy's return was bound up in a curious incident in Southern Egypt on the Upper Nile. Emboldened by the absence of the court, as they had been during the administration of his father, several native priests rose up along the banks of the Nile, armed the local Egyptian population and declared several centers of autonomy from the court of Ptolemy IV. Rushing back from Coele-Syria, the pharaoh crushed these rebellions and instituted measures worthy of the old Athenian Draco for their brutality.

An edict was passed that any word spoken against any Greek by a native was punishable on the first instance by the cutting out of the tongue. Should a native so penalized continue in their subversion, presumably by physical rather than verbal means, the penalty would be death without recourse to a presentation of evidence against him. While the Master and many other academicians understood the need for strong governance among men, this curious edict had a freezing effect at the Academy. The law stipulated this punishment for natives only, yet such was the change in leadership within the court, such was their disposition against all things non-Greek, that the great histories of other peoples, the great translations, the great compilations of all human knowledge that had so marked Alexander's first three Egyptian successors were eroded within a decade after Raphia.

The Pharaoh returned to his lavish existence, honored the death of his mother as a martyr of a plot of native Egyptians to murder her, which everyone knew to be false but didn't dare question. He staged a public execution for which he borrowed an Asian custom. Sixty natives suspected of having played a part in the murder of the dowager were rounded up in the agora and, in front of the tomb of Alexander, were slowly trampled to death by elephants. Though the Master and I mercifully found excuses not to attend, it was reported that, the deaths of the first victims having occurred too quickly, Ptolemy himself mounted the howdah atop the largest of the beasts and carefully manipulated it throughout the dozen or so remaining victims until he had crushed their extremities so that they might bleed out rather than sustain an instant death.

In the midst of this barbarism and spectacle, Ptolemy IV was content to leave the major questions of state to the uneasy confederation of courtiers led by the Agathoclean siblings and Sosibius. While Ptolemy erected temples to his favorites and courted the most orgiastic of religious practitioners, Sosibius and Agathocles continued to work to amass as much influence to themselves as possible. The government of the kingdom quickly became the laughing-stock of the rest of the world, Egypt's remoteness and her geography providing the only serious impediment to the designs of foreign powers. The Master and Archimedes trembled at the thought of the rise of such a tyrannical and anti-intellectual sovereign. They began making plans to secure the legacy of the Academy.

It was in those years after the Battle of Raphia that the Master fully realized to what humanitarian service his device might be devoted. He began a series of correspondences with foreign academicians in friendly and antagonistic courts alike. He wrote to Euphorion of Chalcis, recently installed as Chief Librarian of Antioch, and ancient Pingala, both apprised of the new code. He utilized a series of courtiers to send enciphered messages to trusted allies of the Academy. His network reached not only to Antioch, but Babylon, Ephesus, the Far East, the cities along the North African coast, and into far Iberia. He sent courtiers to the finest minds of Greece and Rome, and established a web of informants committed to sharing information in the fear that the implosion of his own state might rob humanity of the genius of Alexandria should the world's knowledge remain concentrated there. How he endeavored to secure these transmissions was his most ingenious plan yet, for it was decided among his trusted circle, in those days after the decadence of Ptolemy IV became apparent, that Eratosthenes would distribute copies of his devices to sympathetic warriors for the institutions of the mind in every corner of the world. The story of how the Master achieved this feat and what obstacles he had to overcome has now become my life's work, and I record it now so that it may never be forgotten.

I will divide the remainder of the narrative into two parts. First I will record the continual degradation of the Ptolemaic state until the present administration of Ptolemy V, now only fifteen, who displays even more the ruthless character of human nature than his father. Historians will no doubt record his excesses, his ten years as pharaoh and the influence of the Agathocleans so far marking the degradation of the legacy of mighty Alexander beyond all recognition. He was many times confronted with uprisings which were dealt with in the cruelest ways accessible to him. I will mention only those horrors which further impelled the Master to the dissemination of his 'computational device' and the unbreakable code, and in so doing, discuss the Master's reasoning behind his selection of each location in a vast network pulsing with his wisdom under the aegis of the secrecy of the order of the Mysteries of Eleusis.

Second, I will endeavor to include, in necessarily partial detail, The Master's method of breaking his own code of using prime numbers of spectacular length multiplied together, with a cipher of substitution of ingenious complexity. He supplied all his correspondents with the ability to reverse the function of the large numbers, so that they might be secure in transmissions against them. In this way, nothing except his device, worked by a skilled initiate, might unravel their meaning by easily factoring into constituent primes the immense composite number which shielded the Light of Alexandria. I dedicate, with Plato's words of Socrates, this final portion to the Muses, and above all to the Master, Eratosthenes, who became the Light in the darkness.

Beholding beauty with the eye of the mind, he will be enabled to bring forth, not images of beauty, but realities (for he has hold not of an image but of a reality), and bringing forth and nourishing true virtue to become the friend of God and be immortal, if mortal man may.

METALOGUE
THE VERY NEAR FUTURE

26

At every symposiem, and the increasingly frequent meetings he insisted upon with Pratt, Francisco bombarded the classicist with questions about the Eleusinian Mysteries. If such a connection existed between an ancient pagan cult and prime numbers, particularly a mystic solution for the 'problem of the primes,' he was intent on finding it. The trappings of Catholicism and Jesuitism were only simulacra. He knew Christians had no special claim on truth. In principle, his vows taken as part of his initiation were universal. Chastity and poverty were innate byproducts of eschewing ephemeral pleasures and consumerism in favor of truth. Obedience, too, came easily. With or without swearing an oath, his life's work would be in service of the One and the True.

Francisco had taken great satisfaction in his initiation into the Society of Jesus. The Spiritual Exercises of St. Ignatius, the bedrock of Ignatian Spirituality, had taught him first and foremost to find God in all things, and as all things were comprised of the elemental Truths of mathematics, he knew this to be true. What of the Mysteries of Eleusis, Francisco asked Pratt? Were they not compatible, even similar? Pratt had for years conducted an 'initiation' into the Mysteries with his graduate students as a hands-on exercise of antiquarian immersion. Might Francisco too be initiated, become one with the True through the Mysteries as he had been through the Society of Jesus? An amused Pratt agreed, and invited Francisco to the upcoming initiation ceremony.

Pratt conducted an 'initiation' every year in Boedromion, the third month of the Attic calendar, falling in late Summer. Though the original initiations were divided into the Lesser and Great Mysteries, Pratt of necessity condensed the ceremony into two days and two nights. On 15th Boedromion, called *Agyrmos* (the gathering), Pratt and a Classics PhD student, acting as hierophants, declared *prorrhesis*, the start of the rites, and carried out the "hither the victims" sacrifice, *hiereía deúro*. The Seawards Initiates, *halade mystai*, traditionally begun in Athens on 16th Boedromion, was accomplished with a ritual ablution in the Villa of the Mysteries as the students ate from catered cheese trays and drank unendingly from the kylix. On the same day, but traditionally on 17th Boedromion, Pratt invited the participants to begin the *Epidauria*, a festival for Asclepius, the God of medicine and healing, named after his main sanctuary at Epidauros and celebrating his arrival at Athens with his daughter Hygieia, during which the students engaged in an all-night feast, known as the *pannykhis*, for which Pratt supplied sandwiches.

Traditionally begun on 19 Boedromion, a ritual procession to Eleusis began at Kerameikos, the Athenian cemetery, from which the people walked to Eleusis, along what was called the Sacred Way, swinging branches called *bacchoi*. Pratt's version commenced immediately after the feast in a short shuffle of initiates, one after another, laughing and singing the old odes as they filled the andron. Along the way, the student-initiates shouted obscenities in commemoration of Iambe, an old woman who, by cracking dirty jokes, had made Demeter smile as she mourned the loss of her daughter, Persephone. The students, once assembled in the andron, were given more drink, and Pratt and his colleagues recited a reading that the initiates were to spend the next day contemplating on their own. This included a passage from Plato's *Symposium*, though most were already familiar with it, as well as various selected works of Aeschylus, Euripides' Theban plays, and some Aristotle. The reading concluded, the conversation turned to discussion of the classics. One student made a great joke about Hesiod, which Francisco did not understand. Stumbling off into the night, the initiates were to spend the next day observing a fast as they reflected on the events of the previous evening.

The party resumed on the second night, and kylix in hand, Francisco and his fellow initiates processed from an outer courtyard once again into the andron which had, for the night's purposes and in honor of tradition, been temporarily transformed into a *telesterion*, an initiation hall important to the geography of the Mysteries in Eleusis. In the center of the telesterion stood a high table bearing a large cedar box inlaid with carvings of various stages of the Mysteries. This Pratt called the *anaktoron*, the palace, originally a distinct room within the telesterion. The roof of the 'palace' was a dome, carved in alternating quarters with two motifs: triune sheaves of wheat representing Demeter and

Persephone, and a torch used by Demeter to look for Persephone after she had been abducted and taken to the underworld by Hades. Around the dome repeated a phrase in Greek: *As above, so below.*

The anaktoron, Pratt explained to the initiates, was the holy of holies, an obvious template for similar geographies of temples throughout the ancient world, still copied in the architecture of the strongholds of Abrahamic faiths. The anaktoron could only be 'entered' by Hierophants, its contents only knowable to initiates. Pratt indicated a large punch bowl to one side of the telesterion, from which several graduate students were ladling its contents into each participant's kylix. This, he explained Villa newcomers, was a mixture known as a kykeon, once comprised of hallucinogenic herbs that he was not disposed to reproduce. He had, instead, substituted a mixture of wine and strong brandy to achieve a similar effect. Kykeon in hand, each participant was invited to swear the oath of the Mysteries:

"I have fasted, I have drunk the kykeon, I have taken from the kiste, and after working it have put it back in the kalathos.

The kiste and kalathos were allegorical. The kiste represented the store of all human knowledge available to the initiate at that moment. The kalathos represented a return of new knowledge back to the company of initiates who might benefit from it. The 'working' was accomplished in the synthesis of knowledge and creativity, the integral part of change and enlightenment. Archaeologists, Pratt explained, had been fixated on finding the objects of the kiste and the kalathos. These were never physical items, they were an early manifestation of the scientific process, enshrined in allegory and hidden in secrecy throughout epochs that did not tolerate the exploration of the mind.

The rites inside the telesterion involved three elements: *dromena* ("things done"), a reenactment of the Demeter/Persephone narrative; *deiknumena* ("things shown"), the display of sacred objects by the hierophant; and *legomena* ("things said"), stories that accompanied each sacred object. These were open to interpretation, and in honor of Pratt's love of literature and science, he included among these three elements equations, works of literature and brief biographies of 'saints' of learning. During this initiation he encouraged the recitation and discussion of the texts presented the previous evening. Combined, these three elements were known as the *apporheta* ("unrepeatables"). It was thought, Pratt said, that in antiquity the penalty for divulging them was death. His meditation on the secrecy was benign: the

Mysteries cloaked within a celebration of the seasons a society that might talk freely without suspicions of heresy. Where once they existed in a society that really did worship anthropomorphic nature-gods, the Mysteries continued as a quaint anachronism, outwardly honoring classicism while inwardly satisfying the same need for a safe space for inquiry, well into the enlightenment.

A week after the ceremony, Pratt met at Francisco's insistence. Francisco had been enamored of the process, much more intellectually satisfying than his vows of Jesuitism. The ceremony had been, Pratt reminded him, an exercise in the classics. If Francisco was having doubts about his religious path, he might well take that up with Reyes. Though Pratt himself was a humanist and an agnostic, the Mysteries of Eleusis were meant as a very collegial metaphor, and they should be construed as complementary to and not in competition with Francisco's journey as a Christian. Francisco explained his personal philosophy, that all systems for arriving at truth were equivalent, and that he had liked the focus on building on the intellect of others and giving back something of his own intellect to those who were like-minded.

Still, if that was the entirety of the Mysteries, how still might he make a connection between prime numbers and the rites of Eleusis? The Mysteries might be used as an opportunity for any initiates to talk about anything, on any topic. The Mysteries would only be useful for discussion of forbidden topics. How could prime numbers be associated with secrecy in antiquity?

This question he directed, without mention of the Mysteries to a perplexed Reyes, who didn't fully understand the question. How might prime numbers relate to secrecy? Well, not number theory generally. That, Reyes thought, must be the most inoffensive branch of mathematics. But, hadn't Cantor been driven insane by infinity? Hadn't Gödel's Incompleteness Theorems proved – through mathematics – a point of philosophy, that some conjectures we *knew* to be true might never yield to a rigorous proof? Some had said that mathematics had declared God dead. Francisco could not accept that. He did not accept that God might be malignant, that God might create a universe that was systematically inaccessible to humanity. This was heresy, and it was his life's work to prove it wrong.

Francisco asked Pratt for a listing of known members of the Mysteries. What mathematicians had been among its ranks? Surely, if it existed in a small way into the enlightenment, it must have had illustrious members. Pratt could say only that secret societies had existed forever, probably, and their pedigrees and provenances were as much filled with the stuff of thriller novels than actual historiography. There were some manuscripts said to have been written by figures associated with societies like the Mysteries. Roger Bacon, even Newton, had written extensively on esoteric topics. Both alchemists, these two towering figures of mathematics and science were as at home in the scientific method as they were in trying to change lead into gold. Of course, some serious historians of science believed that these men were trying to forge a less occult link between alchemy and rationalism, yet it was the falsifiable, the testable, the provable achievements that distinguished them as founding fathers of modern science.

Francisco began a study of all manuscripts and unsolved riddles connected with men of science and men interested in the occult. There was no dark and light for Francisco. There were no 'dark arts,' only unprovable axioms of mathematics. An unsubstantiated metaphysical claim was no less evil than Goldbach's conjecture. The former was much less likely to be correct than the latter, but he made no relativistic value judgments about either hypothesis.

He exposed himself, with the reluctant collusion of Pratt's curiosity, to various unsolved literary mysteries and curious unknowns in the history of science. With Reyes' blessing, he learned Latin, Greek and Hebrew. He devoured ancient manuscripts that had any suggestion of containing mathematical knowledge, and insisted on referring to them by their bibliographic designations. He worked on the famous Voynich Manuscript, (Yale's MS 408), a reputed scientific/alchemical notebook of Roger Bacon. This appealed to him because Bacon, as well as being a Franciscan Friar, was a noted polymath of his day. Bacon was an avowed alchemist, a standard pursuit for intellectuals of the day; Even Newton had pursued the fabled Philosopher's Stone in experiments in his rooms in Cambridge. Bacon had written the groundbreaking work, *Epistola de Secretis Operibus Artis et Naturae, et de Nullitate Magiae*, (Letter on the Secret Workings of Art and Nature, and on the Vanity of Magic), condemning frivolous magic in favor of empiricism as it was understood in Bacon's time.

Bacon himself cited another text somewhat outside the mainstream of Pratt's antiquarian scholarship, the *Secretum Secretorum*, an appealingly clandestine Latin text said to be a translation from a tenth century Arabic text translated from a lost Greek original. This 'Secrets of Secrets' was written in the form of a letter supposedly between Aristotle to his former pupil, Alexander the Great, during his campaigns in Persia. In the letter, Aristotle counsels the young Alexander on topics as diverse as medicinal herbs, astrology, gems, politics and a "strange account of a unified science, of which only a person with the proper moral and intellectual background could discover."

His work with the Archimedes concluded, Francisco, having taught himself Arabic, poured over every extant text from the House of Wisdom in Baghdad, a center of learning and translation of Greek thinkers and the hub of the ninth century Islamic Golden Age. He worked closely with Pratt, throwing himself into every undeciphered and esoteric text – Egyptian, Greek, Latin, Arabic – that had connected to it the slightest rumor or intimation of a mathematical subtext. He devoured The Book of Soyga, (Bodley MS. 908), a text recently discovered and deposited in the Bodleian Library and known to have been owned by the Elizabethan polymath John Dee. He brought his new felicity for languages to bear on Magyar Codex 12° 1, colloquially known as the Rohonc Codex, an undeciphered manuscript now in Hungary, photographs of which, in the early days of the internet, he went to considerable pains to obtain.

He studied the enigmatic Phaistos Disk. He puzzled over the tiny fragments of the Jiahu, Vinča and Banpo symbols. He spent a week in the Villa scrutinizing the Dispilio Tablet. He labored with Linear A and Cretan hieroglyphs, the Byblos syllabary, Proto-Elamite and the famously impenetrable Indus Script. All of these were examples of writing from cultures much earlier than the epoch of scholarship in Alexandria, where someone had known how to solve the problem of the primes. Still, he agreed with Pratt that all knowledge was a continuum, and what seemed complex to modern eyes might have come naturally to an exceptional thinker millennia ago.

After years of study in addition to his work on the Riemann Hypothesis, he began to despair of finding any concrete connection between ancient mysteries and mathematics. He had found tantalizing hints, in Voynich, perhaps, depending on certain linguistic assumptions, and in the Rohonc Codex, again accepting an overly credulous interpretation of selective groupings of digremes. These texts mention ancient societies and hidden knowledge, still he had not seen in these passages the fruition of the standard he voluntary took up from Cantor and repurposed in his new role as antiquarian exegetician: *That which has been hidden to you will eventually be brought into the light.*

Reyes, having extended unusual courtesy in Francisco's always expanding graduation timeline, urged his most gifted student to return his full attentions to Riemann, and to God. The Eleusinian mysteries were a fine academic dalliance, and, indeed, the classics had been a traditional subject of Jesuit Scholarship, but they were hardly to be taken *literally*. Riemann, mathematics was the work of God. Reyes gently reminded Francisco of his oath of obedience, which Francisco had believed he had upheld in spirit even before he had declared it in the presence of his spiritual directors. Obedience to his search for truth was innate, he reminded Reyes. Hadn't his mathematics been in pursuit of truth? Hadn't he sought truth in the Classics? Even the Mysteries of Eleusis, with their slightly anachronistic – and pagan – overtones, had been ordained in a spirit of Truth, had they not? He did not know, he could not know, any other allegiance and obedience.

Reyes reminded him of the essence of spirituality set down by the humble Íñigo López de Loyola in his *Spiritual Exercises*. Particularly helpful to Francisco might be the saint's Letter on Obedience, in which he describes the joy of 'true obedience' to God. Well known to Francisco, he had had no problem with this vow of obedience, yet Reyes wondered if he might do well to read it again. There were, Reyes reminded him, three types of obedience; Francisco, by showing reluctance to follow his mentor's guidance, was in danger of betraying his vow. Inconceivable, thought Francisco, there were none more dedicated to truth. He had no worldly possessions other than a portrait of St. Ignatius gifted to him, along with a worn copy of Euclid's Elements, in Father's will, several mathematics textbooks and copies of ancient texts he happened to be working on at the time. Each of them, most of all the mathematics texts, were merely tools of his devotion. He had no friends outside the Order and several acquaintances who were fellow 'initiates' in the Mysteries. He had no worldly attachments, no sexual encounters; he donated all of his surplus stipend to a charity that provided after school mathematics programs in poor school districts. He owned nothing, wanted nothing other than to serve Truth.

Yet this was hubris, Reyes said. If Francisco, an initiate, a scholastic, would not return to his mathematics on the suggestion of his superiors, he would violate his vows to the Society of Jesus and to God. Obedience was composed of threefold degrees, as Ignatius had written in his Letter on Obedience: Every superior was to be obeyed as the representative of Christ. Obeying this representative, one was obeying Christ – one was doing the will of Christ. It was not, Reyes said, Francisco's place to determine the will of Christ. The purview was Reyes' alone, as he was responsible to his superior in a chain ending with the Pope himself, the sole representative of Christ on Earth.

The lowest grade of obedience is "*external* execution of the command." This implied that while an initiate might obey, they did so unwillingly. The initiate might believe his superior's logic faulty or his motivations suspect, yet he might obey out of respect for his superior or the Society. This sort of obedience was shallow and, in the words of the humble Íñigo, was "very imperfect."

The second grade of obedience Ignatius calls the *internal* conformity of *will* with superior. It is possible to demonstrate obedience, while still disagreeing with one's superior, because one's love of Christ is capable of transforming unwilling obedience to willing obedience. Ignatius says of this stage that, "there is already joy in obedience."

The third and highest grade of obedience Ignatius styles the *internal* conformity of *mind* with superior. This, he says, is obedience not merely because one is told to obey; it is possible, writes Ignatius, "because the will can command the intellect." Now one agrees mentally with one's superior on the grounds of obedience alone. One must seek to attain obedience of the intellect, Reyes reminded Francisco. Reyes had been too lax in his guidance, he feared. He had indulged Francisco without regard for his spiritual needs. The other initiates have trained themselves to practice what Ignatius calls "blind obedience... the voluntary renunciation of private judgment." It was this ability, said Reyes, that allowed others under his charge to pursue rigorously their chosen fields while staying entirely within the spirit of Christ.

It was now Reyes' will, in coordination with the judgment of his own superior, that Francisco return to Riemann with his full attention. He expected of Francisco the third and most perfect of obedience, to Reyes and, in the role of superior, to the will of Christ. He asked for no less than a joyful heart and *the voluntary renunciation of private judgment.*

Yet, what of Ignatius' other commandment: The more universal the work, the more divine it becomes? Surely his work had attempted to incorporate universal scholarship, the finest minds working in the great intellectual capitals of antiquity. But work on Riemann was his calling now. He was to abandon esotericism and textual criticism, he was not a classicist, and his talents could best serve God by returning to mathematics.

Pratt was sympathetic both to Reyes and to Francisco. Pratt felt himself a mentor to Francisco, and wanted him to achieve some level of satisfaction of accomplishment. He also understood the fire burning within the quest to understand humanity and to uncover the genius that is so easily buried by the unguided, accidental march of time.

Francisco found himself in the grip of a crisis of faith. He wanted nothing more than to solve Riemann's Hypothesis, perhaps the most complex of Hilbert's problems left unsolved, but he had also felt that part of his calling, his reason for existing, was to rescue the great intellects from obscurity. He could prove that antiquity knew more than it was credited with. Was that not a truth that must be brought forth into the light? And, as academic as it may have been, was he not also a brother of the Mysteries in spirit if not by an unbroken line of initiation? He had sworn to God and the ancients that he would take up great problems and in the taking up, return elegant proofs back to humanity. Corinthians, Ignatius and the Mysteries were in complete agreement. He must disobey, even if it meant rejecting his vows in all three categories of obedience. He could *pretend* to stop his search for solution to the problem of the primes, but he would only be pretending, it would be external conformity. His intellect could never blindly submit, no matter how well-meaning a command his superiors gave him.

This struggle continued for months, until he discovered, in one of the manuscripts he had been working on, another cryptic mention of both a society of 'Mysteries' and prime numbers. He worked on the undeciphered language for some time until he became certain that this document was referring to the same Mysteries and the same solution to the primes. He was convinced a formula or process for mapping and manipulating primes had been discovered in antiquity, and his convictions became truth when several other manuscripts yielded supporting hints. He had yet to find the formula itself, unlikely in any event, he concluded, as formulas as he knew them were relatively modern inventions. Still, he expected to find the solution in the form of a word problem. Sophisticated mathematics had been copied down in this way since early Egyptian dynasties. As a constant reminder, he had pinned to a bulletin board a transliteration of a mathematical problem in the Moscow Papyrus, from Egypt's Middle Kingdom, almost 4,000 years old:

> If you are told: A truncated pyramid of 6 for the vertical height
> by 4 on the base by 2 on the top. You are to square this 4, result
> 16. You are to double 4, result 8. You are to square 2, result 4.
> You are to add the 16, the 8, and the 4, result 28. You are to take
> one third of 6, result 2. You are to take 28 twice, result 56. See,
> it is 56. You will find it right.

This was the format he knew his proof would take, a simple algorithm for generating the nth prime, written in words or diagrams in a fragment of a lost work, miraculously illuminated for Francisco by providence. Like Gödel had anticipated, though he knew such a formula existed, it was possible he might never be able to prove it. It was during consideration of these texts and in *internal* violation of his vow of obedience that he discovered, in one of these manuscripts, what he considered a cryptic reference again to a network or brotherhood of academics protecting some sort of secret that involved the prime numbers. But, maddeningly, only fragments survived, and these interpretations depended on suppositions of missing words or letters.

He had taken on invitations to present papers at obscure foreign mathematics conferences only to have academic cover to visit antiquarian book stores in Prague, Istanbul and Athens. He had volunteered his services to the United States Department of State to consult on the security of incunabula and manuscripts throughout Iraq, home to the ancient House of Wisdom, and Afghanistan, the 'graveyard of empires.' He continued to find only glimpses of a forgotten whole. But among the fragments he formed a vision of a once thriving network of academicians, scientists, geographers, astronomers, and mathematicians all working together on common problems, from the purely practical to the purely abstract. It was on one of these trips, in Kabul, embedded with a small State Department cultural mission advising the Afghan government on the protection of national treasures, when he received an email from Pratt. He should return as soon as possible, Pratt wrote, he had just learned from a colleague that a new palimpsest had been found, nearly twice as long as the Archimedes. The barely visible under-text identified it as a history written in Koine Greek, possibly in Alexandria, sometime between the third century BCE and the first century CE.

Francisco immediately contacted his former colleagues at the Wallace, who were as eager as Francisco to be given the opportunity to reprise the restoration effort they had applied so successfully to the Archimedes palimpsest. The owner of the 'Alexander Palimpsest,' as the academic community was now calling it, was eventually located by the Wallace. Following a brief flurry of secret negotiations, the Wallace was once again chosen to embark on what everyone assumed would be a decade-long process of restoration and translation.

Francisco became the team's most devoted member. Despite the usual non-disclosure agreements, he shared the work with Pratt, whose professional hesitation was eventually suborned by his private curiosity. The document, Pratt agreed, was an utterly fascinating account of the lives of academicians in Alexandria in the third century BCE. Francisco delighted in each new revelation: It was an historical account by someone named Hesperos who had been close to Eratosthenes during the latter's tenure as the Chief Librarian of the famous Library of Alexandria; It contained many references to prime numbers; It laid out detailed correspondence between Eratosthenes to the Greek Pharaoh Ptolemy III, the last of the Ptolemies to truly patronize science and mathematics in the spirit of Alexander; It seemed to repeat fragments of a lecture *given by Eratosthenes* on his famous sieve method for finding primes. Then, several days of silence later, Francisco showed up unexpectedly at the Villa of the Mysteries with photographs and a compelling theory about the nature of 'The Project' alluded to throughout the manuscript.

Francisco knew this was what he had been pursuing for fifteen years. He had led the team from insight to insight, and – to his horror and disgust – the Wallace insisted on publicizing each revelation as Francisco discovered it. Worse, they had set up a live subscription video feed of the entire conservation effort. The Wallace was more interested in prestige, exhibit attendance and website revenue than protecting the mathematics of the divine from the uninitiated.

In his heart he felt the shudder of anxiety all over again, the same he had felt growing with the climax of Wiles' lecture all those years ago at Cambridge. Wiles, in a room full of competitors, had thrown Fermat to the world while throwing Francisco's dream back in his own face. He would not let that disappointment come to him again. His faith had been tested once. He would not let it happen again. This time, the solution to the problem of the primes would be his, and his alone. It was too important to publicize. Humanity was not yet ready to know the mind of God.

Several weeks passed in which Francisco became so absorbed in the translation and imaging work that he slowed his collaboration with his Stanford mentor. They were getting close. Other volunteers and museum staff were now talking about very anachronistic concepts hinted at throughout the manuscript. Advanced number theory, swift calculation of problems thought impossible by the standards of the day. The daimon within would not stop: *That which has been hidden to you will eventually be brought into the light.* Hidden to *you*, Francisco thought. The daimon promised illumination to him alone – not spectography specialists, not Koine Greek experts, not historians, no others of his fellow conservators. The illumination was not for the board of the Wallace, nor its visitors, nor even the owner of the manuscript, and certainly not for an apathetic public deifying idols of detached, anti-intellectual consumerism.

After several days without communication from Francisco, Pratt received a phone call from a leader of the conservation team. Sorry to disturb, Michael Hawley said, he was contacting everyone who had given Francisco DiScenna a letter of reference to the Wallace. They were doing 'routine' background checks, all very pro forma, a request of the insurance underwriters. If Pratt did hear from Francisco, might he give Michael a call? The sudden website errors? Funding problems – all academics decried the apathy of the public to the preservations of their classical heritage. They hoped to have the site up soon, Michael said, and again, any contact with Francisco would be of utmost importance to the Wallace team.

Then, Pratt who had been all along receiving a lot of calls and emails from interested colleagues – was he following the work? What did he think of the potential scholarship that might come from an author so embedded in the intellectual fabric of Hellenistic science? – Pratt, the amateur mathematician, professional classicist and genial hierophant of the Mysteries of Eleusis, received a phone call from Francisco. He was fine, nothing to worry about, just busy. What about the call from Michael Hawley? Pro forma, all standard procedure, just as he had said. Francisco had several new images he was sending to Pratt. He needed his expertise on several passages. Francisco would be in touch soon.

Then, a call from Professor Martin. Proof that someone outside the conservation team knew about ancient Mersenne primes and the swiftness of calculation. The next day, in the Villa of the Mysteries, Pratt told Martin everything he knew without implicating Francisco. Pratt could not know for sure that anything was out of order. He could only sense a growing disquiet within as Pratt discussed the Alexander with his old student.

Pratt couldn't help overlaying the memory of another, younger student more recently in his charge who too sat across from him in the Villa of the Mysteries all those years ago – several stolen pages from the Archimedes Palimpsest on a table between them. The dichotomy between this former student, Martin, refulgent in cultivated appreciation for the struggling youth of civilization and another, Francisco, obsessed with his own place in its ascendency, gave truth to an intuition that now overwhelmed him. He knew what had happened, what was happening again.

Pratt excused himself from the conversation with Martin, calling Francisco several times before his call was answered. The message: A colleague in Washington had caught on to the significance of the same pages that, for Francisco, indicated that he was about to find in the Alexander a map to the mind of the Divine.

Francisco thought quickly. It was best, he said, if Pratt kept all that they had discovered to themselves. The Mersenne, if others on the conservation team hadn't yet realized it, the mention of calculation, all of this was Francisco's alone. He had earned it. Francisco needed Pratt's help on the final stage of his journey. He needed an accomplished classicist. He needed Pratt's influence to access the tools to bring that which was hidden, quite literally into the light. He needed his fellow initiate in the rights of Eleusis. Francisco had turned away from the false intellectualism of his Jesuit brothers. The Greater Mysteries, the true and the One awaited Pratt in Baltimore.

Pratt arrived to stop Francisco from ruining, as he had warned his student before, his reputation and his life. He found Francisco at the appointed meeting place, and, as expected, a thin and ancient volume occupying pride of place on a center table. Most of the remaining Alexander Palimpsest had already been pulled apart. Pages were strewn across the table. Francisco stood crooked over a scanner, examining a page with a faint but recognizable diagram of the sieve of Eratosthenes.

Pratt pleaded, Francisco waved him off with a hand. Francisco had done all he could without access to a synchrotron accelerator, a common enough piece of equipment at a major university. Hadn't Pratt spoken of a friend and colleague at Loyola? Ironic that they should use the property of the old order to usher in the work of the new?

There was no brotherhood, cried Pratt, no real Mysteries of Eleusis. Not anymore. The initiation had been an extra-curricular, like a cocktail party or an interdepartmental team-building retreat. The God of mathematics did exist, protested Pratt, Francisco need not find faith in antiquity to gain it in himself.

Francisco was unmoved. He removed the sheet from the scanner, replacing it with another freshly torn from the shrinking palimpsest. It has to be here: *That which has been hidden to you will eventually be brought into the light.* He viewed the page carefully, applied various imagining filters to it, and pointed at and translated the relevant Koine Greek as it became intelligible: *Mob. Ptolemy Epiphanes* - God Manifest, Francisco, smiling, said to Pratt. *Alexandria, Museum. Project. Hidden.*

The daimon within would not stop and now what had been repeating internally became a chant that Francisco said out loud. That which has been hidden to you will eventually be brought into the light.

Another page: *Mysteries. Hidden. Ciphertext. Passage. Travel. Pelusium.*

Another: *God manifest. Problem of the primes. Sieve. Pergamum. Ship. Hidden.*

Pratt, terrified at Francisco's obsessive behavior, pleaded with him to stop. Francisco ripped another page from the Palimpsest and centered it on the scanner.

That which has been hidden to you will eventually be brought into the light.

That which has been hidden to you will eventually be brought into the light.

That which has been hidden to you will eventually be brought into the light.

More adjustments. Eratosthenes. Archimedes. Onesimus. Hesperos. They're all here, they're *speaking* to me.

Pratt looked frantically around the room. He could not stand the destruction of the greatest artifact of the history of mathematics he would see in his lifetime. His eye caught a glimmer of bronze at the far edge of the table. Francisco met his eyes and followed Pratt's field of vision. A half-consumed kylix sat next to an empty twin and a large vessel between them. Francisco reached for the kylix and emptied it into his mouth, savoring it.

Ah, of course. He extended a kylix to his mentor. Pratt refused. Francisco looked chastened, then: Of course, how could Pratt, the hierophant, the chief Priest of the Mysteries, not attain the Greater Mysteries without enacting the ritual? Without acknowledging Pratt's continued protestations, Francisco filled both vessels. He reached into a leather pouch and retrieved a small quantity of powder, dropped it into a kylix, offered it to Pratt.

Pratt backed up against the wall as Francisco drank from one cup while the kylix with the substance remained in his outstretched hand. Francisco cornered Pratt against two shelves. The academic who had not known violence since a lunchtime fistfight in grammar school lurched forward, knocking the kylix away from Francisco. Pratt thought he saw a look of wounded pride in Francisco; he saw a flicker of the young man who had told Pratt how devastating his experience with Fermat had been. Just for a moment, Pratt thought he had recovered the real Francisco. The moment proved to be axial, and fleeting. Pratt pleaded in that moment. There were no mysteries. There was only appreciation, for history, for mathematics, for the Absolute Infinite, for goodness, for friendship. There is no place for violence in the pursuit of truth.

Francisco knew in that moment that Pratt had lost his faith. Francisco believed in friendship. He believed in helping is friends into the light. Without speaking, Francisco returned shortly with another kylix, prepared with a larger amount of the substance from the leather pouch. Pratt resisted. Francisco reached around Pratt's neck and forced him against the table, Pratt's hands pinned behind him.

Pratt begged. Francisco was hurting him. All this, a ruined career, theft of very valuable property and now, assault. Pratt knew, he said, that Francisco was not like other people. He knew that Francisco had trouble making friends, that he was special, that he had been singled out for great achievements of the intellect. Though mostly lived in solitude, his life until now had stood for reason, logic, mathematics. These characteristics were the antithesis of force. They were the pursuits of elegant minds, today as much as in antiquity.

Pratt reiterated what he had said many times, that maybe these cryptic references to a solution to the problem of the primes were made in the same spirit as Fermat's last theorem. Suppose Fermat had had no proof. Suppose that what he had written in the margins of Diophantus' *Arithmetica,* that he had found a proof but the margin was too small to contain it, was a sort of an intellectual call to arms. Suppose Hesperos had hoped to do the same generations before for the mathematics of antiquity. Consider, he pleaded with Francisco, that the Alexander was an enigma, purposefully vague so that future generations might search for the proof of Eratosthenes and, in the search, elevate minds throughout the world in an age where the old Alexandrian kingdoms had devolved into tribal squabbles and institutional oppression. *Suppose* – Francisco brutally clasped his hand over Pratt's mouth.

"I have fasted, I have drunk the kykeon, I have taken from the
kiste, and after working it have put it back in the kalathos."

He recited the old oath as he forced the mixture down Pratt's throat until the kylix was empty. Pratt reeled away from the table, falling on his back next to a bookshelf. Almost immediately his vision started to fog. Before falling into a deep sleep he saw Francisco pick up his own kylix, drink it, and return to the scanner. Pratt awoke on his back with his hands tied beneath him. The scene was exactly as before. Francisco was stooped over the scanner, mumbling Koine Greek. Pratt tried to force out words. He would help. He would help. What did Francisco want?

As Pratt lurched himself off his back, the room spun around him. He noticed that what had been left of the palimpsest was gone, the table now overflowing with torn pieces of centuries-old manuscript parchment. It was maddening, Francisco explained, but perhaps fitting, one final test. He was so close to the location of the device. Only a few pages would not yield to the scanning techniques. He needed Pratt's cooperation, or Pratt would have to continue to undertake the initiation rituals. Francisco had, he said, undertaken it himself dozens of times since starting his work on the Alexander. He was not worthy to pursue the mind of God without constant reminders of the ritual –

and the responsibilities – of his initiation. Francisco would untie Pratt and help him to a chair and some water. In exchange: Pratt would call in a favor.

The first evening at the University was cumbersome. Pratt, terrified, had made the call, but in Francisco's eyes Pratt's devotion was being tested. He was given another ritual before they left. Another kykeon made the trip easier, and Pratt could only make out blurred forms as the two made their way through the science building. Francisco ran Pratt's hand along the spectrometer. The product of the new Order, he said, would help reveal the truth of the old.

The trips became easier. Their presence became less conspicuous, even at such a late hour, if the kykeon was made just strong enough to effect a mild feeling in Pratt of intoxication. Once inside, Pratt would then be given a booster kykeon so that he was to find himself unable to move out of a chair. Pratt watched as Francisco ran his pages through the appropriate equipment. For several days, the two made trips back and forth in this way. Francisco in complete control. Pratt most of the time unable to speak coherently.

Finally, among the constant muttering of Koine Greek, Pratt could make out the chanting Francisco had so far refrained from during their nights in the science building: *That which has been hidden to you will eventually be brought into the light.* Again and again and again. It bore into Pratt's brain like a stonemason's chisel. Francisco had found it. In the entire Alexander there was no simple algorithm for prime factorization. He had expected that it might not be here. The author of the Alexander was not Eratosthenes, after all. He was merely a glorified shop assistant. It was unlikely that Hesperos fully understood the mathematics itself, but he had known the location of the device, and Francisco, on that last evening, bathed in the light emanating from a small monitor attached to the synchrotron, had read aloud the location of the device. It did exist. He had known all along. *He* had had faith, a faith that his mentor seemed to lack. Francisco chided Pratt, was it not the hierophant's own epochism holding back the realization of the purpose of the Mysteries?

Francisco stuffed these last, ancient sheets into his pocket and escorted Pratt through the grounds. Pratt began to gain a sense of where he was. In the interest of maintaining Pratt as upright and apparently unhindered as possible should they be encountered, as they had been several times, Francisco had been administering gradually diminishing doses in the kykeon. Usually placing most of his weight on Francisco's arm, Pratt was able to walk this time mostly unaided as the two headed across the grounds toward the car. Pratt could make out a group of students walking toward them on a perpendicular path. Pratt considered shouting but could only force a small amount of air out of his mouth.

He hadn't spoken in days. Francisco gripped Pratt's arm and smiled at the group, commenting that he, too, was working late. Pratt loosed a small shout causing one of the group to look over her shoulder. They were almost to the car. Pratt felt his strength starting to return.

He pretended drowsiness as Francisco pushed him into the car. Francisco tied Pratt's hands sloppily in his excitement. Didn't Pratt understand what Francisco had found? Francisco started the car and pulled away from the campus. Didn't Pratt understand what existed encoded in Eratosthenes' great project? It was the answer to the greatest problem in mathematics. The consequences for a dozen fields would be immense, he told Pratt. Eratosthenes had discovered a simple formula for generating primes, for factoring primes, for solving the Riemann Hypothesis two millennia before Riemann had been born. Francisco knew the exact location of Eratosthenes' device.

The implications in its discovery for every field of pure mathematics were unfathomable. This was a universal proof. Francisco smiled as he remembered father, all those years ago: *The more universal the work, the more divine it becomes.* Didn't Pratt understand what had been accomplished that night? Didn't Pratt understand that Francisco's trials with Fermat, with Riemann, with God – *with everything* – led up to this discovery? He could simultaneously reveal the perfect workings of the building blocks of mathematics, and at the same time, he could change society itself. The implications for cryptography alone were beyond the most crippling attack anyone could make on physical infrastructure. Of course he knew what his discovery would mean for the mathematics underlying security everywhere. Every bank transaction, every oppressive government agency, every secret told to stultify entire populations, to keep them in the dark, in the shadows – all this would be brought into the Light.

And Pratt? Pratt could come with him. But he had to come willingly. Francisco's arms waved across the dash pointing out to the sky in front of them. They'd have to fly where they were going, and Pratt spending the next several days on the hallucinogens at the center of the ancient Mysteries would not serve their singular purpose. Francisco grasped Pratt's hand gently. Would Pratt come willingly? If only he could see what Francisco saw, a future for the unfettered pursuit of the expansion of the mind. To know God. To become God. If only Pratt –

Pratt gripped Francisco's arm and thrust him into the dashboard. The car swerved across the road. Pratt threw his weight against the door trying to swing it open. Francisco still had a firm hold on Pratt's wrist. The car swerved back and forth, again and again. Francisco tried to steer while Pratt got his feet up and kicked Francisco over and over in his side. With his right hand firmly on the door handle, Pratt reached his left hand up to his face as Francisco hit him repeatedly with the rope that had landed on Francisco's lap. Francisco flailed the rope again, this time falling around Pratt's shoulders. Pratt's back up against the passenger window, he continued to kick Francisco, who could barely keep the car from flying off the road. Francisco grabbed the other end of the rope and pulled. In the confusion he had not realized that he had more slack than he had when the rope was around Pratt's shoulders.

Francisco stared ahead, his thoughts floated through the window. He could not hear his own breathing, the car's screeching tires, Pratt's screaming. He felt only occasional pangs of pain in his ribs. Again and again and again, he felt it far off in the distance. A blow landed on his cheek. He saw only the stars before him. He was the only keeper of faith left in the world. The fellow scholastics in the order avoided him whenever he was forced to attend mass. The other initiates in the Mysteries had laughed behind his back when he spoke earnestly of an upcoming symposium. Father had left him. Reyes had long since stopped meeting with Francisco regularly. He felt betrayed by all of them. The only true believers had died over two thousand years ago.

Thinking of them, of Eratosthenes, Archimedes, Hesperos and, perhaps this young initiate, Onesimus, the impacts to his side seemed ephemeral. In his mind, his spirit descended on Alexandria, its marble columns glistening in the sun, the festival of Ptolemy glorifying a state steeped in honoring the intellectual achievements of an entire epoch. With each step along the Canopic way the blows to his ribs seemed to decrease in frequency, almost to a standstill. He could not feel pain. He reached the Library of Alexandria. He entered the lecture hall. Before him all the keepers of the faith stood waiting for him. The Master stood in the center of the room, cranking out Mersenne primes on his device for calculating the indissoluble numbers. Above, hanging from the ceiling, he saw the formula scratched on a large canvas. He could make out only a suggestion of it. He felt a tiny tremor of pain as he passed Ptolemy, Archimedes, Aristophanes. The room swelled to encompass an entire army of soldiers, all willing to defend the library to the end. As their ranks parted, several figures approached in single file. He could make out faces. He saw Marin Mersenne, Athanasius Kircher, Saccheri, Tacquet, Clavius, each forming a procession toward the device. Euler and Riemann followed next. Behind them an angelic Georg Cantor reached out toward a destiny only Francisco had made possible.

He felt the smallest pang of pain yet as he pulled the car off the road into a park. He drove for several more minutes. Mersenne's harmonics were everywhere. He got out of the car and walked toward the canvas. He stared at the formula but could not make it out. It eluded him still. A hand touched him forcefully on his back. He whipped his body around to find himself face to face with Pierre de Fermat, from head to toe clad in collegial robes. The pain was dull now. Some far off attack had ceased. He was alone with the greatest minds of antiquity. He knew what he must do. He must make offerings under the light of the Goat Fish, the Dolphin, the Great Fish and the Thigh of the Bull. As above, so below, under the earth, at the Temple of the Mysteries.

EPILOGUE
THE VERY NEAR FUTURE

ENLIGHTENMENT. Francisco DiScenna removed the final source from his pack and held it up to the light, revealing the copies of false color images from the Alexander Palimpsest. He read it again slowly, repeating the words out loud that he had read for the first time in the presence of his mentor only days before:

> The Master, Eratosthenes, the last true Librarian of the Library of Alexandria, conceived of a way to disseminate the vast knowledge of the library before the decadent Ptolemaic state might turn passive neglect into willful ignorance of all but what was of political or military value. He devised to make many copies of the device and distribute them to friendly factions throughout the world. One was to go to Pergamon, and to that end he contracted with a private merchant to secret the vast quantity of parts in amphorae of wine. This he calculated to take two years. Another he sent in like manner to the elders of Ephesus and still another to far Hattusa, where a small remnant of the Hittite civilization might reap the benefits of Hellenism. Still more ambitious was a plan to develop the few underground academicians in Babylon into a center of scholarship. This was arranged by the way of Euromius, the slave runner, who was eager to bolster his profits by carrying merchandise that could not be repatriated or succumb to plague.

He and his brethren had previously only found mere fragments of the manuscript throughout the ages. The famous MS 408, now in the care of Yale's

Beinecke Rare Book and Manuscript Library, the odd curiosity of Magyar Codex 12° 1, now in Hungary, portions of Bodley MS. 908, in the United Kingdom, and many less complete works. Each, the brother knew too well, only hinted at the riches in the complete text.

Generations ago, the order had found half the Mersenne encoded in MS 408, and the rest of it in Bodley, MS. 908, among its enciphered blocks of letters. British and American cryptographers who had broken the unbreakable WWII Enigma code and, in crafting a mechanical code-breaking machine, laid the foundations for modern computers – these men too did not possess the determination of the order and failed at discovering the secret in MS 408. They tried for decades - *as a hobby!* – to break open the plain truth that sat on archivists' countertops from Bletchley Park to Langley, Virginia. The entire time, in front of their faces, a detailed explanation of an ancient courier-internet hybrid that distributed the works of antiquity throughout the world, disguised as meaningless gibberish to any cleric who might stumble across them. He wondered now how many palimpsests existed in the world, how many were thought of little more importance than scratch pads.

How many Gospels were written over the encoded plays of Aeschylus?

How many of Eratosthenes' detailed proofs for instantaneously factoring vast composite numbers into their constituent primes had been scraped away, now were resting, in code, on reused parchment just below absurd remonstrances from Bithynia and prosaic grain contracts from Baghdad?

Using this network, Eratosthenes then dreamed of a constant flow of scholarship, so that the empire of the mind, unmoored and beyond the reach of ephemeral kings and officious courtiers, might continue until humanity had lost the appetite for war and removed the political boundaries of empires. The project was undertaken that each scroll of the library, nearly a half a million then, would be transcribed using the device and encoded by it. The dispatches would then be sent by courier, overwritten or disguised within contracts, wills, inventories and whatever form was most unassuming to the censors of the terrain through which they might pass.

But somehow the Muse of History, Clio with her parchment roll, failed to preserve *locations, geographic identifiers, specifics*. The order searched the bibliosphere for generations, hoping to find some clue as to where one of these devices might lay dormant, able to decipher those texts within the Order's collection that were closed to them. Hermetic texts, mathematics, wisdom from the priests of Serapis, in short, the bulk of the Great Library's collection could not speak to them. Eratosthenes' code was too complex, founded in the perceived indissolubility of a complex one-way function of his own design.

At the other end, the devices whirring in their massive hidden chambers as they began to decode the dispatches. The Master envisioned an entire world of cranks, camshafts and cogwheels that bore down upon the indissoluble numbers until, one by one, each letter fell into place. The genius of all civilizations, made into the product of two vast prime numbers in Alexandria, became useless to an interceptor, but, once recovered by the reverse function performed by a sister machine, might enlighten entire communities and avoid the councils of war.

Generations came and went, sometimes discovering a new source and painstakingly decoding it across centuries, sometimes grasping for decipherment without the required tools, like peeling an apple with the boulder of Sisyphus. The full knowledge of antiquity, the knowledge of the True and the One remained just beyond the order's reach. It began to lose its way, subsumed finally under the aegis of the Christian Pope. A small core remained faithful to the ancient quest, and quite easily coated their zeal for the perfect with the not incompatible ascendancy of the Way, the Truth and the Light. And soon only but a handful of each generation, maintaining the veneer of piety, sought a higher truth in prime numbers. Father was of this circle, and yet apart from it, standing between the worlds of pure mathematics and human constructions of truth. It was he who brought the penultimate source to the attention to the order. A new kind of source, as modern as it was practical, the penultimate source sought to bridge the gap between the temporality of man and the perfection of the indissoluble numbers.

As I write this narrative, I have no way of knowing how many survive, or even if any were fully reassembled. The Master anticipated interception en route, and devised with Archimedes ingenious disguises. Many individual gears were to be packaged together in crates in which were placed an instruction panel identifying the individual pieces of the device as orreries for mapping the diurnal motions of the Sun, Moon, and the five planets. One of the missions to Euboea succumbed to a raid and the cargo was lost. A fleet en route to Ephesus was blown into the shoals near Cyprus. Most recently I have received news that the very last ship bound for the Aegean foundered off the coast of its destination. So it may be that The Master's network of scholarship can never be realized. And so it is the duty of the last of his circle to record how The Master built the device and where I have hidden the last of its kind so that future minds might comprehend the glory of Hellenism and understand what it was at its core - a religion of science and inquiry that may never rise again.

The penultimate source, now a foundational document of a modern world obsessed with consumerism, materialism and false-intellectualism, the small mathematics paper written by three professors in Massachusetts only decades ago, the new cryptography that lulled modernity into a sense of security that laid the foundation for the concealment of every closed and open circuit, every 1 and 0, every bank account, every conspiracy, every scandal, every opposition to authority and every machination of authorities all over the world:

A message is encrypted by representing it as a number M, raising M to a publicly specified power e, and then taking the remainder when the result is divided by the publicly specified product, n, of *two large secret prime numbers* p and q. Decryption is similar; only a different, secret, power d is used, where $e \cdot d \equiv 1 \pmod{(p - 1) \cdot (q - 1)}$. The security of the system rests in part on the difficulty of factoring the published divisor, n.

There was but one true authority, and that was the perfection of the prime numbers, they could no longer be denied their rightful place in the universal pantheon, and they now had the power to destroy all the inequality, the blind allegiance and the confusion of arbitrary pursuits.

The Jesuit pushed aside the second door, his heart racing with the same anticipation that Howard Carter must have felt at having been the first human in 3300 years to set eyes upon the treasures of Tutankhamun. The cavern, roughhewn from the surrounding bedrock, stretched out before him at odd angles; a serpentine infrastructure of undulating gear-works filled nearly every available space. The device was large enough to cover ten square city blocks. The whole assembly was covered in the dust and patina of over two millennia of isolation and disrepair. He walked toward what he instantly recognized as the device's control mechanism. Finding writing in familiar Koine Greek, he began searching for the proof that he had found the object of his searching.

Slowly, he brushed away the tarnish until the Koine formed the inscription he had been looking for all of his adult life. The ancient Greek, the Greek of Alexander the Great, spelled out the expected incipit, but he couldn't make out the cartouche that followed. His thumb scratched across the bronze surface until he had uncovered the entire hieroglyphic inscription.

Instinctively he stumbled back, unable to believe that he had finally found the solution to the greatest unsolved intellectual problem in history. In that moment he realized he had surpassed the sponge divers in the waters below Antikythera and the intrepidity of Howard Carter, for they had only discovered "things." He had discovered an idea, had re-discovered it. He walked in the footsteps of Euclid the mathematician, Eratosthenes who first measured the Earth and Archimedes who first mechanized the human mind. He pointed his flashlight toward the inscription and savored the moment as he read it aloud:

By the hand of Eratosthenes, Chief Librarian of the Musaeum of Alexandria, by the wise Lord Ptolemy III Euergetes, late Pharaoh of Upper and Lower Egypt, son of divine Alexander, of Ptah and Amun, Lord of the bountiful harvest of the Nile, in the eternal year of his reign. Glory be to Serapis, we dedicate the mechanization of a solution for mapping the infinitude of the prime, indissoluble numbers.

Beneath the inscription, accompanied by illustrations as crisp as the day they were carved, lay a concise mathematical proof, the first of its kind in the history of the world.

"Now," he said aloud, deep within the navel of the ancient island, "*The world is filled with the dead.*"

Q. E. D.

INCUNABULUM

This small clipping is included for the interested reader. Perry alerted me to this curiosity – found buried in a small foreign newspaper – shortly before this manuscript was sent to the press. Both the publisher and I regret its hasty inclusion at the end of the narrative; I have not yet had time to analyze its relation, if any, to the topics discussed in 'Epoch.' I hope readers will not find it an intrusion.

ATTACK ON DIGITAL CATALOG OF THE ISTANBUL ARCHAEOLOGY MUSEUMS.

EMINÖNÜ DISTRICT, ISTANBUL - An unknown cyber-attacker was able to bypass the computer security systems of the Museum of Islamic Art, a constituent branch of the Istanbul Museum housed in the famous Topkapi Palace. Museum security officials claim that the intruder was able to "quite easily" access encrypted images of the ongoing conservation of what is believed to be a 'lost' manuscript of Al-Khwarizmi, a 9th century scholar of the House of Wisdom in Baghdad. The manuscript was bought at auction for an undisclosed amount. In need of considerable restoration, the manuscript was loaned under condition of anonymity to the museum for conservation.

Rumored to be a previously unknown chapter of Al-Khwarizmi's famous, *The Compendious Book on Calculation by Completion and Balancing*, much of the text is unreadable to the naked eye. It is a palimpsest, a manuscript from which text has been scraped or washed away for reuse but of which traces remain. Initially thought to be a 12th century prayer book, the underlying Al-Khwarizmi text was discovered prior to the auction. The museum has yet to release any images or transcripts from the project. Museum administrators plan to increase digital security at the museum, but insist that the palimpsest is physically secure.

In the words of one museum curator, "The Al-Khwarizmi Palimpsest has been given extra security while we continue the conservation of this important historical manuscript. The building is a fortress."

A PARTIAL BIBLIOGRAPHY

Arrian. (1976). Anabasis of Alexander, Books I-IV. Loeb Classical Library.

Arrian. (1976). The Campaigns of Alexander. Penguin Classics.

Canfora, L. (1989). The Vanished Library. Los Angeles: University of California Press.

Cantor, N. F. (2003). Antiquity. New York: HarperCollins.

Collier, B. (1999). Charles Babbage: And the Engines of Perfection. Oxford University Press.

Crandall, R., & Pomerance, C. (2005). Prime Numbers: A Computational Perspective .

Derbyshire, J. (2003). Prime Obsession. Washington, DC: Joseph Henry Press.

Durant, W. (1935). The Story of Civilization: Our Oriental Heritage. New York: Simon & Schuster.

Durant, W. (1939). The Story of Civilization: The Life of Greece. New York: Simon & Schuster.

Freely, J. (2009). Aladdin's Lamp: How Greek Science Came to Europe Through the Islamic World. New York: Alfred A. Knopf.

Freeman, C. (1999). The Greek Achievement: The Foundation of the Western World. New York: Penguin Putnam.

Gibbon, E. (n.d.). The Decline and Fall of the Roman Empire.

Green, P. (1991). Alexander of Macedon, 356-323 B.C.: A Historical Biography. Los Angeles: University of California Press.

Hofstadter, D. R. (1979). Gödel, Escher, Bach: An Eternal Golden Braid . New York: Basic Books.

Ifrah, G. (1999). The Universal History of Numbers : From Prehistory to the Invention of the Computer. Wiley.

Lyons, J. (2010). The House of Wisdom: How the Arabs Transformed Western Civilization. Bloomsbury Press.

Marchant, J. (2010). Decoding the Heavens: A 2,000-Year-Old Computer and the Century-long Search to Discover Its Secrets. Da Capo Press.

Martin, M. (1987). The Jesuits. New York: Simon & Schuster.

Morgan, M. H. (2008). Lost History: The Enduring Legacy of Muslim Scientists, Thinkers, and Artists. National Geographic.

Needham, J., Wang, L., & Price, D. J. (2008). Heavenly Clockwork: The Great Astronomical Clocks of Medieval China (2nd Edition ed.). Cambridge University Press.

Netz, R., & Noel, W. (2007). The Archimedes Codex: How a Medieval Prayer Book Is Revealing the True Genius of Antiquity's Greatest Scientist. Da Capo Press.

Nicastro, N. (2008). Circumference: Eratosthenes and the Ancient Quest to Measure the Globe. New Yok: St. Martins's Press.

Plutarch. (1973). The Age of Alexander: Nine Greek Lives. Penguin Classics.

Polybius. (1889). Histories. (E. S. Shuckburgh, Trans.) London, New York: Macmillan.

Price, D. d. (1974). Gears from the Greeks: The Antikythera Mechanism, a Calendar Computer from Ca 80 B.c. (Transactions of the American Philosophical Society). Transactions of the American Philosophical Society.

Price, D. d. (1986). Little Science, Big Science.and Beyond. New York: Columbia University Press.

Rivest, R., Shamir, A., & Adleman, L. (1978). A Method for Obtaining Digital Signatures and Public-Key Cryptosystems. Communications of the Association for Computing Machinery.

Rufus, Q. C. (1984). The History of Alexander. Penguin Classics.

Sautoy, M. d. (2003). The Music of the Primes: Searching to Solve the Greatest Mystery in Mathematics. HarperCollins.

Schmandt-Besserat, D. (1992). How Writing Came About. University of Texas Press.

Singh, S. (1999). The Code Book. New York: Anchor Books.

Swade, D. (2000). The Cogwheel Brain. Little, Brown & Company.

Swade, D. (2001). The Difference Engine: Charles Babbage and the Quest to Build the First Computer. Viking Adult.

Vermes, G. (1997). The Complete Dead Sea Scrolls in English. New York: Penguin Putnam.

Zaslavsky, C. (1999). Africa Counts: Number and Pattern in African Cultures. Lawrence Hill Books.

39691317R00203

Made in the USA
Lexington, KY
07 March 2015